PRAISE

MW01487402

Her Three Lives

"The stuff of which blockbuster movies are made."
—*Midwest Book Review*

"Cate Holahan is a hidden gem in the thriller world, and her new suspense novel *Her Three Lives* delivers all the entertainment value and clever plotting I've come to rely on in her books. It's twisty, page-turning, and deliciously sinister."
—CrimeByTheBook.com

"Holahan shapes characters easy to care about in *Her Three Lives*."
—*South Florida Sun Sentinel*

"*Her Three Lives* is a page-turner filled with betrayal and surprises. Cate Holahan just keeps getting better and better. Read her."
—Harlan Coben, *New York Times* bestselling author

"Holahan's propensity toward melodrama at high pitch is quite entertaining."
—*New York Times Book Review*

"Slick and twisty. A high-tech spin on the domestic thriller that's packed with secrets, lies, and suspicion."
—Riley Sager, *New York Times* bestselling author of *Home Before Dark*

"*Her Three Lives* will not let you go until the final, shocking twist is expertly revealed. A terrible crime launches this dark and wonderfully complex thriller that pushes each character to the very edge. Another perfectly plotted and unputdownable read by Cate Holahan."

—Vanessa Lillie, author of *Little Voices* and
For the Best

The Darkness of Others

"*The Darkness of Others* is a deftly plotted, smartly observed page-turner that manages to thrill at the same time as capture the emotional chaos of the early pandemic years."

—Attica Locke, Edgar Award–winning author

"A novel for our mid/post pandemic times, far enough removed from the initial panic to be less painful than it would have been a year ago, but recent enough to manifest the gut-wrenching anxiety of a world that no longer makes sense. Fans of tense, psychological dramas will not be disappointed."

—NYJournalOfBooks.com

"Fans of soapy domestic suspense will be well satisfied."

—*Publishers Weekly*

One Little Secret

"A psychological thriller that will keep you up all night . . . Get ready."
—*Good Morning America*

"A domestic thriller that's actually filled with lots of secrets, some of them pretty big."

—*Kirkus Reviews*

"Engrossing . . . Holahan keeps the suspense high."

—*Publishers Weekly*

"Well-drawn characters . . . [an] absorbing page-turner."

—*Booklist*

"A great beach read for those with a penchant for scandalous secrets and gossipy, suspenseful mysteries."

—*Library Journal*

Lies She Told

"A suffocating double nightmare . . . 'To be a writer is to be a life thief.'"

—*Kirkus* (starred review)

"Recommended for anyone who enjoys Paula Hawkins or Gillian Flynn, primarily because it's better."

—*Library Journal*

"Engrossing . . . Holahan keeps the suspense high . . . until the surprising denouement."

—*Publishers Weekly*

"Holahan's gripping, commercial storytelling slips this self-reflective examination into what is first and foremost a compelling thriller, allowing *Lies She Told* to be both indicative of a genre and outstanding in its field."

—*Shelf Awareness*

"An eerie and chilling read . . . Unexpected and explosive."

—*NYJournalOfBooks.com*

"A swift and intriguing psychological thriller heavy with surprises."
—*Foreword Reviews* (starred review)

"If you can only pick one psychological thriller to read this fall, it needs to be Holahan's *Lies She Told*."
—*RT Book Reviews*

"Pure, binge-worthy entertainment—the kind of effortlessly engaging read that can only come from the author's intelligent plotting and careful construction . . . An instant hit for . . . readers looking for an addictive, layered suspense novel."
—CrimeByTheBook.com

"*Lies She Told* had me questioning my own sanity . . . The best kind of suspense . . . An excellent and compelling psychological read!"
—Susan Crawford, bestselling author of *The Pocket Wife* and *The Other Widow*

"Intricate, intense, and completely sinister—the talented Cate Holahan keeps you guessing until the final disturbing page."
—Hank Phillippi Ryan, Agatha, Anthony, and Mary Higgins Clark Award–winning author of *Say No More*

"Brilliantly conceived, chillingly conveyed, *Lies She Told* is a mind-bender of a novel within a novel, with a story that is both gut-wrenching and compulsively readable. Cate Holahan is one of the best psychological suspense writers out there, and she's only getting better. Read her."
—Brad Parks, Shamus, Nero, and Lefty Award–winning author of *The Boundaries We Cross*

"This was a thriller I couldn't put down . . . Bravo!"
—Rena Olsen, author of *The Girl Before*

"A page-turner of the top order, cleverly conceived, brilliantly executed and impossible to put down. Cate Holahan has proven herself a master of psychological suspense . . . This mind-bending tale of jealousy, love, and revenge should be at the top of everyone's summer reading list."
—Allison Leotta, author of *The Last Good Girl*

"Intelligently written . . . A gripping and highly suspenseful story that features amazing female characters caught in difficult situations they never asked for."
—Bookreporter.com

"Riveting."
—*Mystery Scene*

"A wonderful psychological suspense story."
—*Manhattan Book Review*

"*Lies She Told* masterfully weaves together the parallel tales of two troubled young wives . . . This is a fast-paced read that will keep readers riveted as the surprise endings of both story lines blossom into a crescendo of compassion and conflict resolution."
—*BookPage*

"Wow. Just wow. As soon as you think you've figured it out, Cate Holahan hits you with a twist you did. Not. See. Coming . . . A taut story."
—Alexia Gordon, award-winning author of *Murder in G Major* and *Death in D Minor*

"[A] masterpiece . . . *Lies She Told* is guaranteed to make Cate Holahan a household name."
—Joe Clifford, author of the Jay Porter thriller series

"A chilling story . . . Cate Holahan keeps you guessing—and turning the pages—right to the end."
—Patrick Lee, *New York Times* bestselling author of the Sam Dryden and Travis Chase trilogies

The Widower's Wife

"One of those rare thrillers that really will keep you reading all night."
—*Kirkus* (starred review)

"Holahan once again creates a compelling heroine who can tap into bottomless reserves of strength when push comes to shove. A fast read for domestic-suspense fans."
—*Booklist*

"In this chilling cat-and-mouse tale . . . Holahan keeps the action going."
—*Publishers Weekly*

"Ryan Monahan is so intriguing that readers will be anxious to read about his further adventures."
—*RT Book Reviews*

"Impressive, exceptional, original, *The Widower's Wife* is a compelling page-turner of a novel from beginning to end—and clearly established author Cate Holahan as an especially skilled novelist of the first order."
—*Midwest Book Review*

"A terrific mystery."
—Bookreporter.com

"Cate Holahan did a great job of weaving together a tale of how far desperate people will go . . . I can't wait to read her next book."

—*San Francisco Book Review*

"Ingenious and engrossing. *The Widower's Wife* is a twisting, *Gone Girl*–esque thriller full of lies and secrets that kept me delightfully off balance right to the end. Cate Holahan is a star on the rise."

—Brad Parks, Shamus, Nero, and Lefty Award–winning author of *The Boundaries We Cross*

Dark Turns

"Journalist Holahan's debut will appeal to fans of precocious teen conspiracies like Sara Shepard's Pretty Little Liars series, as well as to fans of grown-up, plucky-heroine-must-fight-for-herself thrillers."

—*Booklist*

"Holahan nails the preppy ambience, the cliques, the conspicuous consumption, and the coltish beauties such as golden girl Aubrey Byrne . . . [in] this *Black Swan* pas de deux with Tartt's *The Secret History*."

—*Publishers Weekly*

"A simply riveting read from beginning to end, *Dark Turns* aptly demonstrates the impressive storytelling talents of author Cate Holahan."

—*Midwest Book Review*

"In this twisting danse macabre of jealousy, obsession, vanity, and revenge, Cate Holahan gives more than a superb debut performance. *Dark Turns* provides a master class in murder."

—Jan Coffey, *USA Today* bestselling author of *Trust Me Once*

"Cate Holahan's debut novel, *Dark Turns*, reads like a mash-up of *Black Swan* and a particularly juicy episode of *Gossip Girl*."
—Charles Dubow, *IndieBound* bestselling author of *Indiscretion*

THE KIDNAPPING OF ALICE INGOLD

ALSO BY CATE HOLAHAN

THE KIDNAPPING OF ALICE INGOLD

CATE HOLAHAN

THOMAS & MERCER

Text copyright © 2025 by Catherine Holahan
All rights reserved.

Published by Thomas & Mercer, Seattle

www.apub.com

Amazon, the Amazon logo, and Thomas & Mercer are trademarks of Amazon.com, Inc., or its affiliates.

EU product safety contact:
Amazon Media EU S. à r.l.
38, avenue John F. Kennedy, L-1855 Luxembourg
amazonpublishing-gpsr@amazon.com

ISBN-13: 9781662529764 (paperback)
ISBN-13: 9781662529757 (digital)

Cover design by Olga Grlic
Cover image: © Igor Ustynskyy / Getty

Printed in the United States of America

For my daughters

. . . In the next five years, all that will be needed is a small class of button pushers. Tell the people, Dad, that the removal of expendable excess, the removal of unneeded people, has already started.

—*Patricia Hearst, communiqué to her parents, fifty-nine days into captivity*

PART I

LIZA RING

THE DAY BEFORE

The ransom note promised to be the easy part. We agreed to keep it simple: a frank recap of what happened, followed by a single demand. This is what we did. This is what must be done to undo it. Period. No need to belabor the *why*. Any discussion of motive will have the press labeling our letter a manifesto, and manifestos are contrivances of incels and mass shooters, embittered idiots lacking ideas.

Not us.

We're thinkers. Plotters. Opposites of the easily amused, screen-addicted stereotype slapped on our generation like an expiration date. That cohort may have accepted the GoFundMe future our elders intend to leave behind. But our parents forgot sticking us in extra math classes and SAT prep courses. If nothing else, we've learned the dire need to outthink the competition.

Is it any wonder, then, that I'm unsatisfied with our plan?

I sit at the table, staring at blue lines segmenting yellow paper, my thoughts flitting from outcome to outcome, an Adderall-starved brain unable to adhere to a course of action. Surely more planning is required to guarantee success. Myriad decisions must be reexamined. Stress tested.

The writing, for one.

"We should type this. The cops can match my chicken scratch."

He exhales. My boyfriend isn't performing exasperation so much as playing for time. He suggested handwriting for aesthetics rather than any concrete reason. The idea of going analog appeals to him.

"Print servers keep records," he says, alighting on an argument. "Cops can trace it faster than handwriting, especially if you use your left like we discussed."

Showing is better than telling. I pick up a pen with my nondominant hand and scrawl the first letter of a sentence. It's a *D*, though it looks more like a toddler's attempt at a triangle; Shel Silverstein's Missing Piece before hard knocks whittled it into the Big O.

I tap the sad rendering. "They'll get an expert to say the spikes are signs of sociopathy."

He smirks at me. "That's the least of what they'll say."

He's not wrong. Still, I rip the paper from the pad and crumple it in my fist, a meager show of power. I'm stronger than a sheet of loose leaf, despite my knees shaking beneath the table. "We can't have the media sidetracked," I say, picking up my case. "Typing makes it generic. And if we print off a library machine, they'll never tie it to us. This'll be a proverbial needle in a haystack."

He grins. "That's an odd expression, isn't it? Needles in hay?"

"Sorry. A decent job in this market."

His mouth shrinks as he pulls a backpack off a neighboring chair. A flash of metal accompanies the zip of the fastener's teeth unlocking. For a nanosecond, I expect a gun.

My laptop appears instead: a MacBook Pro with a quirky sticker in the corner to make it identifiable and less obnoxiously sleek.

He opens the computer. "Say we did type this thing. You don't think it's hypocritical?"

"No one's advocating a return to the Stone Age."

He ruffles the front of his dark hair. The desk light catches on red streaks, highlighting the green in his eyes. Those eyes! They impress me too much. Opalescent. Piercing. Valuing beauty is like fawning over inherited wealth. It bestows unearned credit on an accident of birth or, worse, the vain use of disposable income. Even so, the sight of him transforms my blood into champagne, fizzy, headed straight to my brain.

His long fingers rest atop the keyboard. "Ready?"

My legs continue to bounce. Until today, everything's been hypothetical. Writing makes this real.

I stand to steady my limbs, then lean over the back of his chair. He smells like my shampoo. When he emerged from the bathroom this morning, my towel wrapped around his torso, I briefly considered calling the whole thing off. Would it be so immoral to shack up together? Two bohemians unbothered by the outside world with no greater purpose than reveling in nature and each other?

I knew the answer, and so did he.

"Like we discussed?" He stares at me, unwavering. Cowardice is a luxury he's never been able to afford.

I gulp down a breath. The blank document shines on screen. Its image blurs, replaced by a face. I see her pale cheeks. Her tears.

"You alright?" His brow furrows. Empathy. The better reason I fell for him.

"Yeah."

"Because if you have doubts, I'd understand. She's—"

"A spoiled trust fund baby without a clue."

"Still."

I stiffen my spine. Dwelling on her doesn't make this easier. This isn't about her, anyway. It's far more about him.

"The more abrupt, the more they'll understand we're not open to negotiation." I take another breath and point at the computer.

He repositions his hands over the keys. "We should start with the date."

"Tomorrow's?" The word comes out like a question.

His typing answers it. I watch the month, day, and year materialize in the screen's right-hand corner: September 9, 2025. Tomorrow, then.

"Dear Mr. and Mrs. Ingold," I begin. "We took your daughter."

CATHERINE NEWHOUSE INGOLD

THE DAY OF

My daughter and I don't speak the same language. We use the same words, as neither of us is fluent in any tongue other than English, but the thirty years between us have drastically changed the meaning of common parlance. Her tomato is not my *toe-mah-to*, so to speak. It's an emoji at the ends of messages intended to convey . . . what?

Embarrassment, perhaps. Exasperation, more likely. A mere glance at my face as I take in Alice's "up-and-coming" neighborhood would elicit an annoyed sigh on her part, as if I'm already overreacting. As if her comment about the new locale being on the rise should have prepared me for such living conditions.

Up-and-coming. I'd interpreted the term as a mild warning: Don't expect a block lined with painted ladies. Imagine older brownstones, their single front doors hiding foyers with multiple mailboxes.

But this?

I stand in the shadow of a squat building on a garbage-strewn street. Plastic bags drift down the sidewalk like postapocalyptic tumbleweeds. Stolen shopping carts litter a nearby alley. There's wet cardboard—rejected scraps from the tent city bordering Alice's address.

Again, I check my GPS. Perhaps there's an east and west version of this avenue? My daughter might have made an honest mistake when sending me the location. Alice has access to dorms. Opting to live in squalor is a deliberate message.

Zooming out on my map doesn't suggest alternatives. I pocket my cell, ascend her building's steps, and pull back the door, hoping against all odds to be greeted by a doorman. And . . .

. . . No.

The vestibule's barely large enough for a single person to stand inside, albeit too small for anyone to sleep in, which I suppose is a good thing. A solid interior door blocks visitors from waltzing right through. I try the handle, and it doesn't budge. Score one for the hellhole.

The wall's sole decoration is a screenless call box. Apartment 2B is clearly labeled with the first initial and last name of its occupant. Another strike against the building, in my book. Ingold might not be the most unique surname, but one can never be too careful. Anyone with an internet connection can learn that *the* Brian Ingold and his wife, Catherine—née Newhouse of, yes, *those* Newhouses—have an only child attending Berkeley. I'd hope that Alice's friends know better than to give out her exact address, but someone might reveal her general area.

I press the call button and wait for the intercom to crackle with my daughter's voice. Seconds later, the line sizzles open.

No one speaks.

"Alice?" I struggle to keep my voice in Glinda-the-Good-Witch range. "It's Mom."

A dead bolt clicks.

Passing through the inside door results in a stairwell. Fluorescents flicker the way to the second floor. No doubt I'll be told the shoddy wiring is all part of the aesthetic. Horror-film chic. Retro Argento.

I forge ahead to apartment 2B, forcing a smile. If there's one lesson I've learned in nearly twenty years of parenting, it's that criticism alone rarely yields results. I'll need to feign interest in this place. Alice picked here for a reason. Knowing why will sharpen my arguments for an alternative.

The second-floor landing opens to a hallway with two apartments. 2B is roughly four yards to the right. When I raise a fist to the door, I hear someone walking on the other side. The building evidently lacks soundproofing. Third strike.

A scraping noise echoes the footfalls.

"Alice?"

No answer.

I knock. "Allie?"

The slurp of a breaking seal sends me backward. Light escapes through the new opening, cutting a gash onto the concrete floor. For a second, I'm the babysitter in a slasher film—the ingenue who inexplicably heads *toward* trouble.

"Alice? You in there?"

I push back the door and step inside. Street sounds attack my ears: car horns, male voices, bass from a distant radio. Brightness blinds me.

I morph my hand into a visor. Sunlight invades from a wall of casement windows.

"You made it!"

My vision adjusts. Before me is the face I know like my own reflection, despite a lack of resemblance. Alice is pert nosed and pouty lipped, beautiful in a way that doesn't require qualification. I'm all sharp angles, more apt to be called *striking* than *pretty*. Several gossip blogs have quipped about how fortunate I was to land Brian—emphasis on the *fortune*. Without my money, they imply, the *striking* compliment might be downgraded to *severe*.

I pull Alice into a hug, tempering my annoyance to relish the warmth of her slight torso against my chest, my heart back where it belongs. "Had to see where you'd be living, didn't I?"

Alice pulls away, reacting to some note of disgust I've failed to resolve in my tone. "Lots of places have camps for the unhoused, Mom. They're literally everywhere now."

"Really?" I maintain a saccharine smile. "Guess I haven't seen many."

"Well, you don't come across a lot in Sausalito. It's all rich people."

I mentally warn myself not to engage. Stick to the plan: discover what she likes about the place, then offer a better option. "So, this is it, huh?"

A single support column, no doubt a drywall-wrapped heating duct, separates the main living space from the bedroom area. I spy a book-stacked nightstand and the duvet I gifted her last Christmas draped over a mattress that lacks both box spring and bed frame. Silken fabric spills onto the dusty floor. Mere feet away, a curtain hangs from a wire jammed between two beams. A toilet peeks from behind the drapes.

Resisting the obvious quip about separating shitting and sleeping areas, I turn my attention to the bedroom wall. A corkboard is dotted with pushpinned Polaroids. There's Brian and me, smiling on the boat—a happy Saturday when he'd stolen a few hours from the office. If I squint, I can make out his laptop on the neighboring seat. Displayed more prominently are pictures of Alice's friends. I spy girls from high school, along with Monica, her former college roommate. There's a boy as well, though his nose hides behind my daughter's neck.

"Allie, who is—"

"What do you think?"

Alice beams beside a table set with her grandmother's dishes. The flow-blue bowl at the center beckons, a multifaceted sapphire in a Formica setting. For the first time, I detect a smell. It's mild. Wheaty.

"You cooked?"

"Followed a recipe," Alice crows, grabbing a serving spoon.

The logic of her white tee and leggings is suddenly apparent. We're not going out.

I approach the table in my restaurant-ready slacks, throat tightening with politeness. Whatever rests in that bowl deserves praise, no matter how unappetizing. For a child raised with a chef, cooking's an achievement akin to earning a driver's license.

Alice reaches for a dish. "I'm guessing it's just us."

Two more plates sit on the table. She's set a place for her father, even though she should know better than to expect him on a weekday—or weekend, for that matter. Though it would have been nice of him to try.

"Oh, honey. You know his work."

"I know his priorities."

She bows over the food, a curtain of blond hair covering her expression. Still, I hear the frustration, the bitter hiss of her *s* emphasizing disappointment.

"He loves you." The words escape before I consider how empty they sound given the circumstances. At this point, defending my husband is all reflex.

"Whatever."

"Changing the world is a full-time job, honey."

"Catering to his ego is a full-time job." Alice stares at me as she says the last part, anger electrifying her blue eyes. "Why do you keep making excuses for him? After everything this past summer?"

I am not getting into this. Not today. Not again. This afternoon is about enjoying a nice lunch, after which I will convince my beautiful, vulnerable, stubborn teenager to move back into the safe, secure, and, quite frankly, more sanitary dorms. When her father and I granted her permission to live off campus, we clearly didn't mean here.

I lean over the table, peering into the serving bowl at its center. Asparagus tips poke out from a mountain of cream-covered fettuccine. Brown bits fleck the ski-slope noodles, moguls of . . . meat!

"Pasta carbonara! Wow!" My enthusiasm isn't simply to change the subject. When Alice announced her veganism in late August—badgering me about cow flatulence while I attempted to enjoy a fillet—I assured myself it wouldn't last three months. Here we are. Not even four weeks later.

Alice sets down her plate and gestures to a stool. "Wait until you taste it."

I settle onto the designated seat, reminding myself to deliver three compliments before launching into my reservations about the apartment. The first should obviously concern the food.

"This dish looks lovely."

Alice grins as she doles a heaping spoonful onto my plate. One accolade down.

"It's so nice to see you using Mom's china."

"You noticed." Her smile widens.

Two. Check.

I scan the room, seeking a third point of approval that can segue into the coming conversation. "The light in here is truly *something*."

Not quite three, but it'll suffice.

Alice pulls out her own chair. "It's a perk. This building was converted from a factory."

I pick up my utensils. "Hmm. That explains the lot next door."

Again, Alice stares at me, pupils shrunken to pinpoints thanks to the unbearable brightness. "This is ten minutes from school."

I feign interest in finding the perfect noodle. "Why commute in the first place?"

"The dorms are small and stuffy."

"They're protected by campus security."

"Police patrol here."

"Really? I didn't see any."

"They can't park themselves outside." She gestures to the windows, as if it's possible to see anything through that glare. "That'd be harassment."

I press my lips together, suffocating a quip about preferring harassing officers to nonexistent ones. College kids are like Wi-Fi signals. Overwhelm them and they'll drop the connection.

"Well, everything smells delicious." I twirl my fork into the pasta. "I can see why you like this unit. I'm sure we can find something closer to the academic buildings with similar amenities."

She palms her cutlery. "Not for this price."

"Saving money's honorable, Allie bear." Her nose wrinkles at my term of endearment. "But you don't need to live like a pauper."

"You know this place is far beyond what most people can afford."

"That's irrelevant."

Alice grimaces. I've offended her by acknowledging the obvious.

"I can't rely on you and Dad my whole life," she mumbles. "I don't want to."

I set down my loaded fork. This studio isn't about spite but self-reliance. Since the unfortunate conclusion to her summer job, Alice has no doubt returned to her first career goal: writing. She's attempting to live on a starving artist's salary. It's considerate. Admirable, even.

It's also utterly out of the question.

"I can't have you slumming it."

Alice winces.

Tomato emoji?

I try again. "Besides, in several years, you'll have access to your trust."

Her eyes roll. "A permanent dependent of my robber baron great-grandfather."

I open my mouth to retort, then think better of it. Sometime during Alice's sophomore year—no doubt after attending a politics lecture or two—she began spouting her disdain for generational wealth. Thanks to her professors, I've become a cow sucking from the teat of my ruthless forebearers. Well, so what? Whether she likes it or not, she's gulping from the same tycoon trough, as are all the PhDs evidently filling her head with contempt for her inheritance. If people like me couldn't pay her tuition, how could schools employ people like them?

I reclaim my fork and knife. "How about being thankful that we've money for college *and* decent accommodations?"

She considers me, eyes more pools than flames now. "It's not that I'm ungrateful. I just . . . I want to make my own way. *Add* value, you know?"

A year pre-graduation is early for post-diploma jitters. I attempt to quell them all the same. "You will. I found a way."

She shoots me a withering look. "Your charities?"

Though my instinct is to defend my work—to argue that my fundraisers bring in donations far exceeding any entertainment spend—I stop myself. The truth is, galas have never been what gets me out of bed. "Caring for my family."

She sighs, a serrated knife scraping my skin. "Nana's gone, Mom."

The blade goes in.

"Dad spends most nights at the city apartment."

It sinks deeper.

"Plus, I'm nineteen. Twenty this year." She twirls her pasta onto her fork. "You need another passion project."

And there's the twist.

"I'll wait for you to graduate first," I quip, swallowing the insults I could add to spice up my bland comment. For good measure, I fill my mouth with food. Alice will not goad me into an argument. Not after our last one. Maintaining focus is my special sauce.

Alice's special sauce is . . . something else. Her attempt at carbonara coats my tongue, creamy and decidedly *off*. Though the texture's right, there's a strange tang to the cheese. Did the milk spoil?

Alice's brow lowers. "You hate it."

I cover my mouth with my napkin, fighting the urge to spit. "It's flavorful."

She scoops up an impossibly large bite of her concoction. "Blended cashews. That's the secret. And plant-based bacon." She covers her mouth with a hand, chewing and talking. "Oh, and nutritional yeast for the Parmesan. Can't even tell the difference, right?"

Between listeria and yeast?

I drop my blessedly unused napkin to pierce an asparagus that has avoided the fungal slurry. "I bet there are apartments walking distance to vegan groceries, or a Whole Foods. Those are in safe areas."

Alice stares into her pasta like it's tea leaves. "It's not that I want you to worry."

"Then don't make me, Allie bear." Said it again. Darn it. "Given it's your last year, I can rent something off campus—with a real kitchen."

Alice points at the wall. "What do you call that?"

She's referring to an electric cooktop plopped atop a granite counter like a builder's afterthought. Instead of a backsplash, wallpaper lines the adjacent wall. The whole thing's a fire hazard if ever there were one. Which gives me an idea . . .

"I doubt any of *that* is up to code."

Alice detects the threat in my statement. Her eyes widen from slivers to saucers. "You're not going to call anyone?"

"I'm your mother. I need to make sure you're in a healthy environment."

"Other people live in this building, Mom."

"All the more reason for it to be inspected." I indicate the ceiling. "Who knows what's up there? Asbestos?"

"Mom!"

"Alice!"

"You know, I knew you'd do this. But I hoped . . ." She trails off and pushes her chair from the table. "Guess that's it, then. This area isn't zoned residential, as I'm sure you're aware. Not like I can stay and get my neighbors kicked out."

"I'll help. Hire movers." I gesture to her plate. "Sit and eat. You went to all this trouble."

Alice collects her dish. "This is Simon all over again."

Simon, the big-talking philosophy major who would have had my daughter living in a desert commune, financed by her trust fund, wasting her twenties in dirty skirts, discussing a revolution he was born fifty years too late to start. I hated Simon. Fortunately, Alice realized—with a push from me—that the boy was beneath her. She'd mistaken a free-love stoner for an erudite idealist.

"I'm your mother. It's my job to help you see what's best."

"You make me wish I didn't invite you."

It's not the first time Alice has said such a thing, so I'm surprised by how the words sting. Nineteen, I realize, is dangerously close to the age when I'll need an actual invitation. As it stands, I won't be on my daughter's list of regulars.

"I suppose you didn't have much choice," I retort, "seeing as I *am* the guarantor and essentially paying for the place."

Alice puts her plate in the sink. "Dead people pay for it, Mom. Both of us should thank Nana."

This barb does more than sting. If my mother were alive, I'd be doing the opposite of thanking her. But she departed without warning, a party guest who'd enjoyed one too many and opted to sneak away before anyone might comment. She never told me she was sick. I'll never know what miracles a properly motivated Sloan Kettering might have manifested.

I rise from the table. "I'll hire a van. Have everything packed."

"Mom. I'm—"

"You can commute from home until I hear about the dorms." I grab my purse and head toward the exit.

"Wait. I'm sorry." Alice presses three fingers to her lips, no doubt stifling some qualifier. She drops her hand. "This isn't the way I wanted lunch to go."

I swat at the kitchen. "Look at this place. What way *could* it go?" I turn back toward the door. "Start packing, Alice." I pull it open but stop myself before storming out. As angry as my daughter makes me, she's still my only child.

"I love you, and I'll see you early next week," I add. "With boxes."

"Mom!"

My title follows me into the hallway. Before taking the stairs, I hesitate, giving Alice a chance to rush out with excuses, or at least a proper send-off. Instead of footsteps, I hear the faucet. Evidently, she's decided to do the dishes.

Well, they'll need to be clean to box up. I smooth my blazer and stride toward the staircase, telling myself it's all fine. Some things are worth months of icy teenage resentment and eye rolls. Safety is one of them.

My kitten heels clack on the hard floor, growing louder as I descend the stairs. I've got an eerie feeling that I'm being watched, but I chalk it up to the unfortunate lighting. I'm simply not made for abandoned warehouses.

Neither is my daughter.

I reach the exterior door and pull it back. Behind me, a flickering bulb goes out.

ALICE INGOLD

DIARY ENTRY ONE

My first kidnapper smelled expensive. I'm guessing this detail isn't too helpful, given that detectives only travel with scent hounds in prison-break movies and my olfactory senses aren't sufficiently honed to identify the exact perfume. But I've walked through enough fancy department stores to recognize the complex mix of florals and fruit oils that define high-end spritzes. And it's the best I've got. I'm still unsure of my assailant's gender. Since taking me, heeled boots have blurred her (his?) height. Bulky sweatshirts have hidden her body. She hasn't shared anything personal, let alone how she identifies. I haven't seen her face. I've yet to hear her real voice.

Writing demands pronouns, however, so I'm sticking with female ones. *She* gave me this diary, along with a couple of flimsy pens and the instruction to tell "our story" shortly after locking me in the windowless cage I now find myself in.

I haven't decided whether writing makes her more or less likely to kill me. I'm staking my life on less. And I need to live. There's so much I want to do, so much I haven't had a chance to fail at yet, let alone accomplish.

When she arrived, I was hand-washing plates. The chore was by choice rather than necessity. My mother, I'm sure, is telling police that my apartment is one step up from a meth den. Mattress on the floor inches from an open-air toilet? Truth is, I was kidnapped from a spacious yet-to-be-legalized warehouse conversion, the kind of apartment that's all over Instagram thanks to original casement windows and an open-plan layout. The kitchen, admittedly, appears a rush job, possibly done under cover of night when no one would notice cabinet installers in front of a property zoned for commercial activities. But it's equipped with all the necessary appliances: stovetop, sink, microwave. Dishwasher.

Still, my grandma's heirloom china couldn't be trusted to a Kenmore. So after having my mother over for lunch, I placed Nana's plates in the sink, turned on the hot water, and began rinsing.

Trendy or not, the building's plumbing *is* temperamental. The temperature instantly shifted from lukewarm to scalding, burning my hand. I switched the faucet to the coldest setting and ran the stream over the red bloom between my thumb and index finger, cursing myself for letting frustration make me careless.

In the short time I've been in this cell, I've wondered how things may have unfolded differently had I not been washing the dishes. Had the attempt at proving my self-sufficiency over lunch gone surprisingly well and my mom had offered to, say, take me out to buy dish towels. Or had my dad decided to join her, for once. He'd have been there when my assailant arrived. Would that have changed everything?

The water's rush covered any initial knock. I didn't realize someone was outside until a Morse code message blared in my apartment. Buzz. Buzz. *Buzzzzz.*

I hurried toward the door, absentmindedly bringing a dish. Such frantic bell ringing could only be my mom, I thought, and her return—so soon after departing my place in a huff—indicated an emergency. Smash-and-grab was the likely culprit. Someone had probably broken her car's passenger-side window to check for portable electronics. She'd returned to wait for the cops and complain, again, that my neighborhood is a crime-ridden cesspool.

"Mom?" I opened the door. "Everything alright?"

"That depends."

A stranger shoved me from the threshold. As I stumbled back, the wet plate slipped from my hand, exploding on the ground like the last scene of an ASMR compressor video, the ones intended to release anxiety via images of destruction. The scene was just as consuming for me, though not at all calming or *satisfying*. I forgot to dodge the shrapnel—forgot, even, about the invader in my home. I thought only that I'd never be able to replace my grandmother's dish. Even if I found another at an auction, it wouldn't be the one held by the woman who'd hosted me each summer in her Newport home, bragging to anyone who'd listen about her granddaughter, the writer.

I heard the door shut. "Don't you want to know what it depends on?"

The voice was odd. More robotic than human. Every word was followed by a tinny reverb, as if auto-tuned flat. I whirled toward its source, expecting to see some sort of microphone or tracheal tube.

A stranger's sweatshirt billowed over bootcut jeans. I looked toward the face framed by the cinched hood.

There was no face.

In place of a nose, mouth, and eyes was a black expanse. Not a mask. Balaclavas give the impression of human features: the bump of a nasal bridge, cutouts around the orbital sockets. Rubber masks have plastic prosthetics. This was a void, scarier than any Halloween monster. I stared into an abyss.

"It depends on whether you cooperate," she continued.

As I tried to process what was happening, she waved a gloved hand in front of the space beneath her fleece hood. Two red circles materialized, along with a glowing grin. I was being robbed by an LED jack-o'-lantern.

"Get out of my apartment!"

My order, delivered while backing away from her, was far less emphatic than needed. In retrospect, I should have yelled it while ramming into her chest. At a minimum, I should have taken my own advice and run past her into the hallway, shouting for my neighbors.

Some mix of fear and self-preservation stopped me from going on the offensive, though. While I guessed my uninvited guest was female, she was still bigger than I was. And judging from her digitized expression, meaner.

"That's the plan." She waved in front of the screen again. The animation changed to a Pac-Man-style ghost with googly eyes and a wavy line for a mouth. "But you're going to come with me."

Her cartoon lips trembled as she spoke, a visualization of a sound wave. Logically, my attacker's new face made her no less threatening. Yet the sight of an uncertain mouth emboldened me. "I'm not going anywhere. You think because you went to Party City that I'm intimidated?"

I didn't wait for an answer. My phone sat on the kitchen counter. I strode toward it, arm outstretched.

"Don't." A click added the full stop to her command. I froze, a battery-operated toy whose power switch had been flicked off. In the corner of my eye, I caught a glimmer of metal between gloved hands. She was aiming at my torso. "Open the window."

My stubborn streak immediately turned yellow. I did as directed, moving toward the wall of casement windows and cracking open one of the panes, all the while assessing my likelihood of walking away from the two-story drop to the street. It seemed survivable, but barely. I'd have to jump exactly right.

"What do you want?" I asked.

Ghost Face answered by raising the gun until it pointed between my breasts. "We're taking the fire escape down."

Her tacit promise not to kill me won my compliance. I approached the open pane and pulled it up farther, revealing a metal staircase.

She gestured to the first step with her head, keeping the gun focused on my vital organs. "I'll be right behind you."

I stepped over the windowsill onto the grate. The metal staircase shuddered with my new weight, an ice sheet in the sun. I grabbed the railing and peered over the edge. If I intended to jump, it was now or never.

A Toyota idled in the alley below. Anyone passing would have figured that a rideshare driver was waiting for a passenger. The only difference I could see between the car and an Uber was a drug-dealer tint on the front window. Seeing through it was impossible.

Metal pressed through my sweatshirt into my spine. "Let's go."

Never go to a second location. The warning resounded in my head. Wherever Ghost Face and her waiting partner intended to take me would give them the advantage.

I gripped the banister more tightly. "I—I can't move," I stuttered to sell the lie. "I'm afraid of heights."

My attacker pushed the barrel farther into my back. "Better get to lower ground, then."

I refused to budge. "Why are you doing this to me?"

The question was a stalling tactic, as the answer was obvious: *money.* Someone had spotted "that shipping socialite" or "the AI guy's wife" and realized that Catherine Newhouse Ingold was visiting her daughter.

"Get moving, bitch," Ghost Face replied.

The voice changer turned her epithet jocular. I looked over my shoulder, half expecting to see the mask removed and one of my (soon-to-be former) friends laughing about "getting me good."

The digital face was different from before. In place of the ghost's wide eyes and uncertain mouth were two neon *x*'s and a sewn-shut smile. "Only two ways out of this." The voice lowered to a mechanical groan. "Down the stairs or over the side."

I maintained my position. "I can pay. My phone's inside. If you'd let me call my mom—"

A laugh erupted from the voice changer, far more frightening than the foulmouthed Siri I'd been speaking with. "Poor little rich girl. Money can't solve this problem."

I descended one step, creating distance between me and her gun. "Then what can?"

Again, I felt the cold metal between my shoulder blades. "You'll see," she said. "They all will."

CATHERINE NEWHOUSE INGOLD

THE DAY OF

Love is patient. Love is kind. *Love* is parking a burnished gold Bentley across from a housing encampment to visit someone who will be nothing but hostile the second you question her decision-making.

I love my daughter.

Of course, when I left my car curbside in this garage-forsaken neighborhood, I didn't fully consider how the buildings would cast barred shadows onto the asphalt, transforming the pavement into a two-dimensional jail cell. I never imagined the clack of my red-bottomed heels calling all criminals as I approached a vehicle that surely costs more than Alice's apartment, if not most of the units on the block.

I've nothing to protect myself with. In my twenties, I would have threaded my keys between my fingers like brass knuckles. My car's plastic fob is a poor weapon in comparison. Its only support is a panic button that will set off my sedan's screeching alarm, alerting people to danger without truly calling the cavalry. I wonder if engineers considered female self-defense when they changed the standard equipment. What made them so confident digital keys were an upgrade?

Remote unlock doesn't feel that useful when I hear the footsteps. At first I assure myself that the person behind me is simply heading down the same street. It's not until their tempo matches the click-track of my heels that I accept I'm being followed.

A glance over my shoulder reveals a man in sunglasses and a ball cap—pulled low. His chin's angled toward the ground, hiding his expression. I read his intent from the position of his muscled arms, puffed from his sides.

I'm about to be robbed.

I mentally riffle through my purse. There's a wallet with my AmEx and Visa, either of which can be canceled in seconds, and my debit card, which will likely get me escorted to the nearest cash machine. No money, of course. I handed my remaining singles to last night's valet, and I'd been surprised to have those. Even my hairdresser takes Venmo.

I've no bills to throw. Nothing sharp.

Screw modern conveniences.

"Excuse me." The voice is polite. Still, male. I force myself to move faster on my two-inch pegs. "Excuse me."

The car is still a couple yards away, sandwiched between two older American brands. Even so, perhaps the alarm will serve as a deterrent. I pull my purse in front of my chest, only to realize that I can't unzip it without stopping.

"I'm sorry!" I shout, refusing to slow. "I don't have any money."

"I'm not begging, Mrs. Ingold."

My name whirls me around. Though my stalker's head is raised, his face is obscured by the aviators and his cap's long brim. I study the little I can for a future lineup. Straight nose. Complexion ruddied by dirt and sun. Handsome, from what I can see, but in the generic, near-androgenous way of a catalog model. There's nothing remarkable about this thief's appearance. No scars or face tattoos.

"Mrs. Newhouse Ingold." He refers to me the way the society pages always do, though leaving off their typical addendum: wife of tech visionary Brian Ingold.

"Do we know each other?" I ask, though I'm certain of the answer. This guy's young, but not enough to be Alice's peer. It occurs to me that maybe, hopefully, he's a beneficiary of some board I've served on. Perhaps he's here to thank me.

"I have a message for you."

Or he's a mentally ill man determined to make the nightly news.

"I—I, well, I'm afraid I don't have time. I'm late for an appointment." My statement demands movement, though I don't run. This stranger is in sweats and sneakers. My shoes are good for little else besides raising my pant hem off the ground.

I shift my gaze to his hands. He pinches an envelope between a thumb and forefinger. It's white rather than the mustard hue I associate with legal filings. Still, I consider the possibility that I'm being served. With great privilege comes a great number of petty lawsuits.

The man extends the letter. "You'll want to read this."

"Why?"

A shrug. "They said so."

"Who said?"

He nods toward the encampment before shifting his attention back to me. "Take it, okay? I can't be standing out here all day."

"Tell me whom it's from first."

He releases the envelope. I watch it flutter to the concrete. Part of me wants to leave it on the sidewalk, let it decompose alongside the gum and unidentifiable detritus. But he knew my name. Somebody had to tell him that.

"Who pointed me out?"

The stranger doesn't answer. Instead, he beelines to the encampment like he's the one late for an appointment.

I watch him disappear before returning my attention to the hand-delivered mailing. The front lacks a name or address, which makes it appear less official than a legal notice. Kicking it over doesn't yield additional clues. The other side is also blank, and nothing rattles or sifts when it's moved.

Not anthrax, then.

I pick it up like it's a firecracker, holding it as far away from my face as possible. Slowly, I tear it open. Nothing explodes. The edge of a folded paper peeks out from the envelope.

Keeping my arms extended, I withdraw the loose leaf, watching for powder. When none falls out, I run through all the inane reasons why a strange man might hand me an envelope-encased note. Some sort of penis picture is the front-runner. A degenerate in the tents could have recognized the lady from the local magazines and decided to draw me a present. What I hold might be the poor man's version of AirDrop-ing his eggplant emoji.

I unfold the paper. Three sentences, each typed, are centered on the page. Sunlight and ten-point font make reading them difficult without my glasses. I bring the letter closer and squint hard.

> Dear Mr. and Mrs. Ingold,
> We took your daughter.
> Call the cops. Alert the media.
> Await further instructions.

I spin toward Alice's building. The entrance is empty, as is the stoop. We said goodbye minutes ago. She was fine. Her building locks. She's still fine, has to be. This is some ridiculous plea for attention. *Alert the media.* Who says that?

My mental assurances don't stop me from exchanging the note for my cell. "Call Alice."

An AI assistant echoes my command. "Calling Alice."

Instead of phoning, I wish the voice was connecting to Alice's smart-home devices so I could view a live video of whatever's happening inside her apartment. But Alice doesn't have Nest cams. I curse that fact as her recorded message answers. "You've reached . . ."

I hang up and try again while sprinting on my micro-stilts toward my daughter's stoop. Her voicemail answers once more.

When I hit her steps, my left heel catches in a cement crack. The red sole snaps as I yank my foot toward the landing, forcing me to peg-leg it into Alice's vestibule. Once inside, I tear off both shoes and press the buzzer.

"Alice! Alice, it's Mom."

There's no answer. I slam my palm into the button. "It's Mom." My voice has risen an octave. "I know you're mad, but it's important."

No intercom hisses. No bolt unlocks.

I lean on the button harder. "Alice!"

She's in the bathroom, I tell myself. Her phone was on silent so as not to interrupt our lunch. She must have left it in the living area. Any minute, she'll respond.

A second is all I can bear. I smack both hands against the call box, simultaneously connecting to multiple apartments. The lock disengages as a scratchy male voice instructs someone to "Leave the food by the—"

The door's slam cuts off the intercom. I take the stairs two at a time until I'm back on Alice's floor.

"Alice?" Her name announces my presence as I knock on her shut door. It opens.

She left it open.

My heart drops to my bowels. I barge into her apartment, fighting the g-forces on my internal organs, silently bargaining with God. If I find my daughter safe, I'll give even more to the poor. I'll find real religion. I'll donate a kidney.

What I see stops my bartering.

My mother's dish lies in pieces, a warning from beyond the grave. A window's open. Not cracked—wide open. I hear car tires spin. Someone's peeling out of somewhere. Fast.

I run toward the racket. An open window connects to a fire escape bolted to the building's exterior. I slip through and step onto metal grates.

"Alice!"

A silver streak swerves from the alley below onto the street. The car's taillights are off. I don't catch a license plate, couldn't even guess at a make and model.

"Alice!"

Frantic, I withdraw into the apartment and scan the room, praying that I somehow missed my daughter lying on the floor, the victim of a hit to the head or punch to the stomach. Battered and bruised from a break-in, maybe. But here. Safe.

Aside from the shattered plate and the dishes in the drying rack, Alice's place is inspection-neat, as if she was preparing for company—or trying to impress her mother.

I look back at the note still gripped in my right hand. Tears blur the words, but I know the first instruction regardless. I punch three numbers into my cell.

"9-1-1. What's your emergency?"

My voice barely produces sound. "It's my daughter. Alice Ingold. She's been kidnapped."

ALICE INGOLD

DIARY ENTRY TWO

Maybe I'm too young for my life to flash before my eyes. When my assailant pressed her gun into my neck at the base of the fire escape, no highlight reel of firsts or lasts played. I didn't see my parents' smiles or flashes of friends. My grandmother's ghost failed to resurrect. There was only the stranger's command to *get inside* and the sight of a wide-open trunk.

A different version of me—someone more like my mom or Nana—wouldn't have done it. That girl would've dared the woman to shoot and alert the whole neighborhood. She would have assured her would-be kidnapper that taking her would result in hefty charges and then name-dropped her friendship with such and such judge.

But I didn't inherit my mother's bravado. So I didn't fight when Ghost Face grabbed my wrists with her free hand, even though it left her gun vulnerable to being knocked away. I didn't move while she pulled a zip tie from her sweatshirt pocket and looped it around my touching palms. I *watched* as she tightened the plastic, robbing me of evolution's second-greatest achievement after the human brain. My greatest chance of survival.

My courage returned only after the gun was gone. I kicked the locked trunk's interior until I feared my foot would fracture. I screamed until my voice cracked. It wasn't until the car picked up speed that I gave up on someone hearing. Whatever sound emerged from the racing vehicle would no doubt get lost in the rumble of tires. Instead of continuing to yell, I switched focus to figuring out our direction.

Every turn forced me to the opposite side of the trunk, painful proof of Newton's third law. I mentally tracked each tumble, whispering to myself the new heading. For a while, I was sure we traveled east. Then we went through what I assume was a roundabout, given the way I was jostled, and I completely lost my bearings.

I lost all perception in that trunk, really. Once we got on the highway, the compartment turned into a sensory deprivation chamber. I stopped hurtling and became lost in the darkness. Time and location no longer existed. I almost drifted off . . .

Then the car stopped.

Parking meant she'd be coming for me soon. I inched toward a corner, pushing off with my feet and extending my body, an earthworm seeking a hidey-hole. If I positioned myself right, I figured I'd have a chance at leaping out when Ghost Face arrived. At the very least, I could attempt a surprise shot to her stomach with my linked hands, a *Star Trek*–worthy double-fisted punch.

As I crawled, my thigh brushed hard plastic embedded in the carpeting. This was new. I ran my conjoined hands across the material, feeling for a lever or a pull, something that might fold down the back seats and let me slip out via a rear passenger door.

A line traveled through the plastic like the seam of a battery pack. Tracing it revealed a crescent-shaped cutout. I dug my fingers into the space and pulled. The plastic popped up.

I felt for whatever hid behind the tab, touching a cool metal slab with bolts on either side. When I lightly pushed them, they pressed in.

Somewhere outside, a door opened. As I hadn't pinched the bolts hard enough for a response, the reaction was a coincidence. A male voice—normal, albeit muffled—erupted to my right. "You sure? It's going to be a long night watching her."

When Ghost Face had forced me from my apartment, I'd suspected she had an accomplice in the car. This was my first confirmation.

If my female kidnapper responded, I didn't catch it. The sound of another door opening told me all I needed to know. My captors were switching drivers, readying for the next leg of our lengthy trip.

It was now or never.

I braced myself and pushed both buttons.

The trunk cracked open at the same instant a door slammed. Light slipped inside along with the scent of pine and dried leaves. I pushed the trunk an inch higher with my tied fists, revealing a rectangle of dark, empty road. Pavement blurred beneath the vehicle's taillights. My new driver was testing the pickup from zero to sixty.

Jumping was going to hurt. At a minimum, I'd have road rash. Worst-case scenario? I'd break a leg and be shot dead trying to crawl away.

But at least I would have tried to escape. The papers had long branded my intelligent, witty mother as "shipping socialite" Catherine Newhouse Ingold, "wife of visionary tech CEO," as if all she were good for was primping for parties and catering to my father's ambitions. I'd no doubt be dubbed "kidnapped heiress Alice Ingold" for the remainder of my life—however long that would be. There was no way I'd let the media also portray me as a hapless victim, someone too money-coddled to even attempt to fight back. If it came to finding my body, there were going to be scratches.

I crouched beside the opening and then, with my linked hands, tossed the trunk upward. Wind smacked my face like I was at the top of a roller coaster.

I shut my eyes and dove forward.

In films, people tuck and roll when escaping a moving vehicle. Unfortunately, I only remembered that after hitting the ground knees- and hands-first. Grit tore into my palms and through my spandex leggings as I tumbled sideways on the pavement. Friction seared my skin. I felt my pants cling to fresh blood.

Nothing seemed broken, though—at least not then, with my adrenaline pumping and my heart going off like an EDM song before the drop. I pushed myself to standing with my tied tripod arms and took off.

Whatever my injuries were, they made sprinting impossible. All I could manage was a hobbling jog, aided by flinging my shoulders forward in lieu of pumping my arms. I wasn't sure where to go. A browning hill rose on one side of the road. Opposite it, a chain-link fence operated like a bumper in a bowling alley, keeping cars from skidding into an adjacent forest.

Behind me, the sedan screeched to a stop. I heard the door unlock, followed by a screamed "Shit!"

"You didn't tie her up?" The man's voice was so high and panicked, he almost didn't sound human.

Footsteps beat the ground. I tried picking up speed, but my knees were unhooked safety pins linking my calves to my thighs. There was little chance of me beating my male captor on a straightaway, and no way I could take the hill. I shifted toward the fence. There was even less likelihood I could climb over four feet of chain-link, but it was possible that I could reach the end of the barrier and slide down the embankment.

The footsteps behind changed from sporadic thuds to steady drops on pavement—a storm coming closer.

I remembered the gun.

It's more difficult to hit a target while moving, and even more so if the target is erratic. I angled away from the fence, intent on zigzagging, but a sharp pain sent me straight back to the barrier. The end was only a few yards ahead. I had no energy to waste.

"Alice!"

My name barely registered before fingers latched on to my shoulder. In my mind, I insisted the man let me go as he pulled me into his torso. I demanded to know why he and his partner were doing this, what they wanted. But my mouth and tongue couldn't translate any of those thoughts into intelligible speech. All that came out was a single screamed word: "No!"

The stranger hoisted me under his arm like a package and began carting me back toward the waiting car.

"Please!" I finally managed to shout through my sobs. "Please, I'll pay you."

My second offer generated about as much interest as the first in the apartment. The man dropped me into the trunk face down. Pain shot up my leg as my battered knees hit the carpeted interior. Though I tried to rise onto my haunches, thick hands pinned down my shoulders. As I struggled, I heard the high-pitched whine of an approaching car.

"HELP ME!" I directed all my energy into my volume. "HELP ME!"

Plastic pressed around one of my ankles.

I kicked, a bronco determined *not* to be ridden. My foot connected with fabric and something soft. A loud grunt responded, along with a hissed "Don't make us shoot you."

The threat might have been empty. My face-down position prevented me from seeing beyond the man's torso. For all I knew, the gun was safely in the front seat.

But it was also possible that Ghost Face had joined in and was aiming at my gut.

I ceased moving. My feet knocked together. Before the trunk slammed, I heard the zip of the plastic tie pulling into place and the whiz of a passing car.

And that was that. The trunk slammed, and I was plunged back into a void. In the darkness, nothing indicated our heading or what might become of me. I felt only the ache of my knees, heard only my ragged breaths. All I could see was the swirling quality of the space around me, blurred by my tears.

Soon, I didn't even see that.

CATHERINE NEWHOUSE INGOLD

THE DAY OF

This can't be Oakland's finest. Four male officers hover in the apartment, each between the age of twenty and thirty, all ill-equipped to deal with any crime more serious than speeding. Short of demanding that I repeat what I told the dispatcher, they've done little but mill around with their hands on their holsters. Only one seems to care that Alice was taken into a car, and he expressed his interest not by sending out an APB but by excusing himself to find the building's super.

He's back now, listening to an elderly neighbor go on in the hallway like a running blow-dryer. The woman has already proved herself full of hot air, swearing she saw Alice in the stairwell and then describing a completely different girl: tall, brown-skinned, raven-haired, dark-eyed. Despite this, Good Cop thinks interviewing the senile more valuable than searching an outdoor drug den for the man who delivered the note.

"Excuse me. Has anyone checked the tents yet?" I'm careful to control my tone as I direct the question to the three policemen. Though I've already deemed them near useless, revealing my opinion won't encourage more effort. And I need much, *much* more from these armed individuals. "I said the guy came from that encampment. About six foot. Sunglasses. Ball cap."

The tallest of the trio nods, acknowledging I've mentioned this already. His partner chimes in. "I'm sure Detective Frazier will get you with a sketch artist."

It's the umpteenth time I've heard some version of "when the detective comes," and it no longer has any calming effect. I'm not Estragon content to wait for Godot until I'm ready to hang myself. Sherlock needs to show up now. With a SWAT team. Helicopters.

"I'm sorry, but we're losing valuable minutes. My daughter could be in there."

"He'll be here—"

"What if she's being assaulted?" I lower my voice instead of screaming. Emotional women are easily dismissed. My husband despises when I get hysterical. "Right now," I whisper. "What if that's happening?"

The officers don't respond.

If the guys with guns won't look for Alice, I have no other choice. I step toward the door.

The tall one blocks the exit. "Ma'am, I'm going to need you to stay here."

"You can't expect me to sit while—"

"We have a unit canvassing the neighborhood, Mrs. Ingold."

For a moment, I wonder how the officer has managed to speak without opening his mouth. He steps to the side, revealing the true source of the voice.

A towering Black man stands on the threshold. There's something solid about his energy, as if he's been silently here all along, monitoring every word and action.

"Detective Devon Frazier." He locks eyes with me while accepting an evidence bag from the smallest officer. "And police have been through the encampment."

It's the first I'm hearing that the cops have looked in the most obvious place. I glance at the law enforcement trio for some sign that they knew—*and withheld*—this crucial piece of info. They betray nothing, staring only at their superior.

I return my attention to the detective.

"Unfortunately, Mrs. Ingold, we doubt your daughter's still in the area." Frazier opens the evidence bag and withdraws the note. It occurs to me that Alice's cell must be in another container. I saw one of the officers pick it up.

"A corner store has security cameras," he continues. "They caught some of the fire escape. It appears two women descended from Alice's apartment."

"Her kidnapper's a woman?" Hope rather than confusion lifts my voice. Men rape and murder. Women negotiate.

The detective's head movement is noncommittal. "The footage is from a considerable distance, so we can't discern much more than physical outlines. Judging from the assailant's stature relative to your daughter, that's our guess. The camera also captured a car pulling out of the alley shortly after."

"Did you get a license plate?"

The detective takes a moment to read the four-line letter. He doesn't answer me until he's slipping it back into the Ziploc. "We called a digital forensics team. They'll have a look at all the security footage in the area. Full plate's a tall order. With luck, they'll get a make. Model."

"What about the boy who gave me that note?"

"Checking everything will take time."

"We don't have it!" There's no controlling my voice anymore. I'm shouting over a ticking clock with each second marking more space between my daughter and me. "What's that they say about the first twenty-four hours? If we don't find her, Alice could . . . she could . . ."

My knees buckle before I complete my thought. The detective grasps my elbow, saving me from the floor. He leads me to Alice's couch and releases me onto a cushion. I drop into the plush fabric, my stomach suddenly gurgling like a filled pot over high heat. Lunch bubbles into my throat.

The detective shouts for an officer to bring a bowl. As I empty my insides onto the floor, I hear him demand that they hurry. "We need to preserve the crime scene!"

Though more acid fills my esophagus, I swallow it. Somewhere amid the dust and broken dishware could be a hair traceable to Alice's captor.

"I'm sorry." My voice could be featured in a *smoking kills* commercial. "I'm sorry."

I cough out more apologies between sobs, unsure for which of my sins I'm asking forgiveness: vomiting, refusing to be more understanding toward my child earlier, failing to demand that she leave this dangerous area immediately, or still staying inside the apartment rather than scouring the streets.

The detective hands me a huge mixing bowl. "You need to understand that we're dealing with a sophisticated crime, Mrs. Ingold. And that's a good thing. These kidnappers are aware of your family. They know you're of means, and they've announced their intent to give you instructions. They want money. They've got to know that you won't pay without evidence that they have Alice and that they're caring for her. The first step in any kidnapping is providing proof of—"

"Have we found my daughter?" The sight of my husband surprises me, though it shouldn't. Only a monster wouldn't cut a meeting short under such circumstances.

He stands in the center of the room, his laser-blue eyes scanning the interior, feeding information to the outsize brain behind his broad, square forehead. Brian's very presence reinforces the terrifying scale of our problem. During a TED Talk, he once boasted about keeping his work entirely separate from his homelife. When at the office, he bragged, his house could catch fire and he'd still maintain focus on whatever was on the screen in front of him.

This is worse than our house burning down.

His gaze rests on me. I can guess what he sees: my face bloated from tears and sweat, leaning over my expelled lunch. Another person *not* helping this situation.

I expect disgust to flare his nose. Instead, I see my own feelings mirrored back at me: Anguish. Fear. Desperation. The sight is a source of both relief and terror. He's not angry with me, but he also doesn't know what to do. Brian's genius mind, with its lauded ability to process information, is stuck in an infinite loop. For the first time ever, he's frozen.

"We still don't know where she is," I explain. "I received a note promising demands."

Brian's programming finds an exit. He regains his composure, closing his wrenched mouth and grasping his hips. "The officer said as much on the phone. So what do they want?"

"They haven't said."

"Understood. No price . . . yet." He zeroes in on Detective Frazier. "Is this like in Mexico? With that MS-whatever? How much do these gangs usually ask for? Do we counter?"

I look up, unsure whether I heard my husband right. He couldn't have said *counter*, as if we've been thrust into some sort of business negotiation rather than the fight of our lives. "We can't bargain for Alice. Whatever they—"

"We don't know what they want!" Brian shouts.

Frazier holds up a palm, a traffic cop signaling for Brian to stop. "I can imagine how scary this is. But it's important we remain calm."

Brian's volume isn't only about fear. He's accustomed to me agreeing with him and annoyed that I've dared raise any public objection to his reasoning. People smarter than I am respect his authority. What does it say if his wife doesn't?

I look to Frazier, lowering my voice. "It must be money. As you said, this man knew who I was. My family name. They must want—"

"There are things more valuable than money," Brian interjects.

He's right. And Alice is one of them. I would give our every dime for her safety. Though I know our daughter isn't what Brian refers to. He means his baby, Zelos AI, the company birthed Athena-like from his own cranium.

"We have to be strategic, Cath."

My nickname's unnerving after all these years. It dates to when we were young and deeply in love, back when I was an idealistic college sophomore entranced by the brilliance of an older boy with an awkward earnestness and uncool penchant for khaki slacks and blue button-downs—a boy so intent on changing the world that he'd go days in front of his computer, forgetting to eat anything besides potato chips and cold Pop-Tarts, yet somehow remember to send me flowers on Fridays or wish me luck on an upcoming exam. My name acquired syllables as our romance faded. I've been Catherine for most of our marriage. I can't recall the last time Brian didn't use my full name.

The moniker, I suspect, is a form of emotional manipulation. Brian wants me on his side in case Alice is being used to leverage his corporate information.

I maintain focus on the detective. "How much do you think they'll want?"

Frazier gives me a look like he knows but won't share the answer. "It's advisable to establish how much you have in liquid assets."

I can tell when someone is being diplomatic. Frazier's holding back to avoid spooking Brian and me, but he has an idea. What he wants to say is *everything*.

ALICE INGOLD

DIARY ENTRY THREE

Sleep must be a stress response. How else to explain my drifting off inside a locked trunk while kidnappers took me to an unknown destination? Or coming to with a flashlight aimed at my eyes?

The glare shrouded my captor in shadow. I blocked it with my tied fists and strained to identify something—anything—about my surroundings. Metal glinted behind a human outline. A wall? My brain was emerging from its REM haze, a stoner from a sweat lodge. Since when were walls made of sheet metal?

Since never. Because I wasn't looking at a wall.

A retractable door, the kind in truck-loading areas or ship docks, shone behind my assailant's shoulder. Seeing it sharpened my senses. Bay doors have automatic openers and pull releases for emergencies. If I could free my legs. Find the switch . . .

"Put out your hands." It was the male voice again, though filtered through whatever device the woman had used earlier. His fist entered the flashlight beam, followed by a sharp snapping sound.

A switchblade caught the light. I pulled my lashed legs to my chest, shielding my organs armadillo-style, though my bird bones were no reinforced shell. The flashlight lowered to the lip of the open trunk, switching my view from extreme brightness to blackness.

"Hold still." As he moved forward, I tucked my head behind my linked arms, a subtle attempt to see his face. A fluorescent glow obscured his features. My eyes weren't fully adjusted to the darkness. I assumed the neon was like those spots that materialize after staring at a bright light.

He grasped my ankle, separating it from its mate. The act wasn't rough, but I yelped and squeezed my thighs together anyway. If this guy intended to return my mobility, it wasn't to help me leave.

"My mom will realize I'm gone soon," I pleaded, following the advice of FBI profilers on every serial killer show I'd ever seen: *Personalize yourself. Make them see you as a fellow human.* "She'll be so worried. She'll look for me."

"I bet she already is." The voice changer filtered out any feeling—if there was any in the first place. "Now, hold still. I don't want to cut you."

The statement was a threat. He didn't *want* to cut me. He *would.*

I ceased flopping and went straight to dead fish. Better for me to submit to a rape than be sliced to ribbons. What could I do, anyway? I was zip-tied in a trunk.

Metal brushed my calf. I closed my eyes, wishing I could somehow summon my father. Regardless of the reality, every daughter wants to believe her daddy's a Liam Neeson character. Deep down, though, I knew Brian Ingold's presence would only make things worse. This stranger had football-carried me to the car like I weighed less than half of whatever he benched. My dad, on the other hand, burned most of his calories through his brain. And there was no guarantee he would ever fight for me.

The zip tie snapped.

My defenses kicked in. I planted a freed foot on the trunk's carpet and shifted to a crouch. Though my knees throbbed, the pain was worth the possible leverage. My vision was finally calibrating to my surroundings. I could jump out, find the garage opener.

"Give me your hands." A faux face looked down on me. Arched brows glowed over blue-outlined eyes. An illuminated mustache and goatee framed the mouth. Lite-Brite Guy Fawkes. "I'm sorry it worked out this way," he said, head turning toward my cut-up knees. "We never wanted you to get hurt."

V for Vendetta reached toward my torn pants. I scrambled backward. "Don't touch me."

His hand rose in mock surrender. "I'll get you some hydrogen peroxide and bacitracin."

Despite the offer, Fawkes didn't move. Again, I caught sight of the garage door. Maybe he wasn't leaving because he knew I could escape?

I relaxed my posture, slumping into a seated position and extending my legs until they dangled over the concrete floor. Pins and needles pricked my calves as I assumed the new position. I played on the pain, wincing and gritting my teeth as though the cramps were far more excruciating than my very real fear.

"Please," I gasped. "It hurts. It hurts so much. I need a hospital."

Fawkes exhaled through his voice changer, producing an echoey vocal fry. "I'll get you something. You'll stay here?"

I kept my tone high and breathy, the way I imagined one might if agony made inhaling difficult. If he thought I had a collapsed lung and broken ribs—even better, a shattered rib piercing my lungs—maybe he'd let me loose. "I don't"—gasp—"even know"—gasp—"where here is." GASP. "How can I leave?"

He dropped his free hand onto the switchblade and pushed the knife into its holder. "Don't move, okay?"

I hung my head like a beaten puppy, all the while watching my assailant round the vehicle. As soon as he turned the corner, I stretched my bound hands toward the flashlight. As the car door unlocked, I linked my fingers around the light's barrel, holding it like a bat.

A compartment snapped open somewhere behind me. In my mind's eye, I could see Fawkes leaning over the front seat, his head down as he sifted through the car's center console.

I ran.

Every step was a blow. I shuddered from absorbing them as I headed toward the sliver of wall abutting the steel garage door. Though I hadn't seen the controls, that didn't mean they weren't there. It was the logical location. In my parents' house, the manual controls were by the door itself. And I couldn't make out much of anything given the flashlight's awkward angle in my zip-tied hands. It was aimed at two o'clock when I needed it pointed two hours later.

"Alice!" The metallic shout lacked any tenderness. Dr. Jekyll had morphed back into Mr. Hyde.

I stopped inches from the wall and jostled my fingers, lowering the flashlight another degree. It illuminated a patch of blank cement.

"Alice!" The call was closer. I whirled around, bringing the flashlight with me. Its beam highlighted the man's torso. His advance was slow, as if he were no longer worried that I would escape. Clearly, I'd picked the wrong wall. "You promised to stay put."

I'd made no such pledge. But how could I argue with a psychopath?

I raised the flashlight to his masked face, hoping to both blind him and spotlight the far wall. For a moment, the beam got lost in the high ceiling above. It soon reflected off a metal duct. What was this place?

There was no time to figure it out. I lowered the light, refocusing it on the wall behind Fawkes's shoulder. It glinted on the knob of a second door and something else . . .

A plastic panel!

My glow-in-the-dark captor blocked my direct path to the garage controls. I sprint-shuffled ahead anyway, a battered running back charging toward the end zone. What I lacked in speed, I made up for in small stature. I was a tiny target. With luck, I could find a hole and squeeze past.

Fawkes mirrored my movements, covering double the distance with each step. I wasn't even at the fifty-yard line before he was on top of me. Pivoting didn't work. My knees were shot, and he was a far more effective lineman than I was any sort of athlete.

He grabbed my arm. Instinctually, I swung the flashlight into his ribs, switching the sport to one that might suit me better. I hoped to hear a crack.

Fawkes groaned. The sound was his only reaction. He didn't recoil. Didn't release my arm. Instead, he grabbed my linked wrists and yanked me toward his chest, simultaneously swatting away my only weapon. I heard the light hit the concrete floor. The sound of its fracturing plastic case recalled a breaking skull.

I screamed and pushed against Fawkes's chest, but his grip was a constrictor knot, tightening with my struggle.

"Alice. Stop. Stop. Let me explain. It had to be you." Fawkes kept a hand tight around my trapped wrists. "Or someone like you. No one would care if one of us disappeared. Well, maybe a parent or friend, but we'd barely make the news. You, though . . ." He raised his free hand to my cheek but stopped short of touching it. "You're special. Pretty. White. On track to graduate from Berkeley with honors."

The perfect victim?

"Wealthy," he continued.

And there it was. Money: not the root of all evil but surely the source of all greed.

"You want a ransom from my parents." My female assailant had claimed this wasn't the case, but I suspected she'd lied. She simply wanted more than my parents could easily withdraw from an ATM on short notice.

The voice changer hissed with a sigh. "Everyone thinks money's the only motivator. But you know what really drives people? Purpose. Wanting to matter, to feel like our days are worth a damn . . ."

Fawkes continued talking, but his voice became the drone of a background appliance—a fridge's hum or filament light's vibration. I wasn't listening so much as planning my next move. How could I get to that bay door? My captor knew now not to trust me when I claimed to be in pain, and he seemed impervious to a two-pound metal cylinder slamming into his ribs.

"You're not listening." Even the voice changer couldn't mask Fawkes's frustration.

"There's only one thing I want to know: When can I go home?"

"It depends," he said, echoing his partner's earlier quip. "But I won't hurt you. Promise."

"Tell that to my wrists and knees."

He looked down at my hands and released his grip. Regrettably, I took a second too long to register my freedom. Before I could step toward the garage door controls, the switchblade was back in his hand.

"May I cut the tie?"

May I? The politeness from a man holding me at knifepoint did not compute.

"Give me the knife and I'll do it," I offered.

The glowing goatee changed directions as Fawkes cocked his head. "That's not an option, I'm afraid."

Oh, he's afraid.

Though I considered pointing out the hypocrisy, the back-and-forth was only sapping my adrenaline. I needed to concentrate on getting out. And, as much as I didn't want this man holding a knife anywhere near me, my chances of escape were better with free hands.

I extended my arms. "How long were you two planning this?"

Fawkes ignored my question, propping my hands onto one of his open palms instead. "The trunk was a bad idea." He slipped the blade between my palms and pressed it to the plastic. "We thought it would look more legit. In case we were caught on camera."

The zip tie snapped. My wrist pulsed from the sudden lack of pressure.

"Let me go," I demanded, aware that the knife was still in striking distance. "Please. Nothing unforgivable has happened so far. We can forget all of this."

Fawkes sighed again. This time, the voice changer turned the sound almost musical. "We've come too far."

I stepped back and to the side, pretending to seek distance between my captor and me rather than a clear path to the far wall. "I understand you want the press involved," I said, continuing the conversation in the hope that it might distract from my positioning. "But I'm not a celebrity. I'm just a girl with school tomorrow."

Fawkes slipped the blade into a back pocket. "You don't know your power, Alice. You can help change the world."

"I can't." I shifted my weight to my toes. "Not like this."

I took off again.

Fawkes didn't move to stop me, though he could have. For a moment, I believed my protests had gotten through to him. He was giving up. Letting me go.

The thought had me giddy as I slammed my palm into the garage controls. Gears strained. I whirled around to see the bay door rise half an inch . . . and crash to the cement floor.

Cursing, I pressed the controls again. The door repeated its pathetic attempt only to bang back to the ground, a WWE wrestler slammed to the mat.

Fawkes strode toward me, shaking his masked head. "It's chained and padlocked on the outside."

The admission threatened to sap my fight. I ignored it, marshaling the strength I had left to attack the interior door beside me. I grabbed the knob and twisted.

It didn't turn.

Hope morphed into rage. I yelled epithets and kicked the wood. Once. Twice. Each time, the impact rattled my spine. I didn't care. I needed to hurt something. Do something!

A last kick sent me flying backward. I braced for my tailbone to fracture on cement. Instead, I was caught midair. My kidnapper lowered me to the ground, brushing back the hair tear-glued to my cheeks.

Though I hate to admit it, I couldn't help but appreciate his tenderness. Everything ached: my feet, knees, wrists. Pride. I'm not a fighter by nature. The slight kindness made me revert to my inherent state, a rabid dog transformed back into a pet.

"It's okay, Alice," Fawkes cooed in his android voice. "It'll all be okay."

He pulled me into his chest and rocked.

And, despite everything, I let him.

CATHERINE NEWHOUSE INGOLD

THE NIGHT OF

I've no need to close my eyes to see my daughter's face. Staring into space makes her materialize. I can picture Alice's every detail: the slope of her nose, angle of her jaw, arch of her brows. She comes across so clearly that I could draw her ribbon-mouth tied into a smile.

Wherever she is, she's not smiling.

That fact is a speculum forcing me to stare, *A Clockwork Orange*–style, at the faces in front of me. Instead of photographs, pencil portraits are arranged in an on-screen grid. Individual features light up as my cursor passes over them. For the past hour, I've sat in this police station in front of Detective Frazier's computer, plucking attributes from various visages and dragging them onto a blank oval in an attempt to sketch the man who delivered the kidnap note.

I've yet to approximate a good mug shot. My problem is the sheer number of choices. The noses alone number in the dozens: aquiline, Romanesque, downturned, beaked, pointy, upturned, short, narrow, wide, high, flared, and every variation thereof. None seems to fit. Each time I pull one onto the picture, the Frankenstein assemblage doesn't sit right with what I saw under those aviators and ball cap.

"Maybe the nose isn't my problem." I say it more for myself than for Brian or the detective flanking me. "Could it be the placement?"

My husband rubs his forehead. Watching me fail has given him a headache. "This would be much faster with my software. It'd put together photorealistic examples, not these *Wall Street Journal* hedcuts. You'd find a match."

Detective Frazier leans forward in his chair, looking around me to focus on Brian. "This program is better for our purposes. AI has some *problematic* ideas of what a criminal looks like."

Brian's eyes narrow. My spouse may not believe in prayer, but he worships his technology. Frazier has blasphemed his messiah. "How is a drawing better than a photo?" Brian's tone emphasizes the rhetorical nature of his question. "I'm telling you, she describes the face to my AI—in words, not even text—and we'll have this guy." He snaps his fingers, adding an arrogant exclamation to his assertion. "Like that."

Frazier's expression is the opposite of impressed. He turns back to me. "We don't want another real-looking face to replace the image in your memory."

"That's ridiculous," Brian counters. "San Francisco PD is trying it out."

I feel a twinge of annoyance. Now isn't the time for Brian to sell his software.

Frazier points to his screen. "Perhaps the glasses sat lower on the man's nose."

As much as I want to curry favor with the detective and agree, Brian is *Brian*. Creator and CEO of Zelos. The man dubbed "The Brain" by business journalists and billionaires. If he says that his technology would do a better job, it's worth a try.

"Tell your AI to create a face half-covered by sunglasses with a straight nose, maybe Roman, and a strong jaw. The face should be shaded by a baseball cap, and the skin color should be ruddy, like this guy spends a lot of time outside. Or he did this past summer. And his hair? Dark. Kind of wavy."

Brian raises his cell and hits a button. "Say that again for Zelos."

"A young man with a ruddy complexion. Straight nose—"

"Let's call it, yeah?" Frazier interrupts, ending this exercise before Brian's results poison my recollection. "We can resume in the morning."

Part of me wants to heed his advice. Tired doesn't begin to describe my state. It's as if I've been sprinting across a noonday desert without water. I want to collapse. Bury myself in the sand.

But I can't. Alice's life could depend on finding this guy. "I'll grab us more coffee."

"What you need are fresh eyes." Frazier reaches across his desk, unplugging my cell. It's been charging with the ringer on blast in case the kidnapper calls.

He hands it back to me. "Our monitoring software's been installed on this. When the kidnapper phones, we'll know."

Accepting my device is saying goodbye. I can't release the lead detective on my daughter's case that easily. "The kidnapper told us to alert the media. Have we done that? I can call ABC. I have a contact. They covered my last charity event."

Frazier suddenly seems like he's trying to ignore a bad smell. "The kidnappers want us running around, chasing false leads."

This had occurred to me, albeit with another worse thought. "What if they get angry that we're not following directions? What if they take it out on Alice?"

Judging from Frazier's face, the foul scent has ripened. "I understand your concern. But the longer we can hold off the press, the better our chances of maintaining control in this case." He pushes back his chair and stands. "We've stationed units at your home. Go, get some sleep."

He might as well order me to bake a cake or sing a show tune. Either task is more likely than me napping while Alice is out there.

Brian rises, evidently eager to work on our facial composite. I don't follow suit. As powerful as Zelos's technology is, the police are sitting on real clues: security tapes, physical evidence. I remember that they have Alice's phone. Surely what's on it will be more helpful than a rough sketch of a half-disguised man. It'll contain recently called numbers, contacts who may know her new address. At the very least, it could provide a way to trace her laptop, which the police did *not* find in her apartment. Presuming the kidnappers took it, we might be able to use the phone's Find My app to locate my daughter.

"Did any of those passwords open Alice's cell?" I ask.

Frazier stifles a yawn. "No. And I don't think we'll try more tonight."

Brian stiffens. It occurs to me that he didn't realize the cops have Alice's phone. They'd bagged it before he arrived and then asked for passwords during my private interview.

"Give it to me," he orders. "I'll have my software crack it."

Frazier shoots him a look that I recognize all too well. It's the same stare I bestow upon charity folks when they ask me for more money than I'm willing to spend. "It's evidence, Mr. Ingold. We can't install new software on it. We don't know how your program might interact with what's already there. What if it changes the record of her locations or erases—"

"That would only be a problem if you think I'm hiding something," Brian snaps. "Or you believe I have some reason to cover up Alice's whereabouts."

Frazier pats the air, smoothing the atmosphere's raised hackles. "We've asked for a warrant. Once the judge signs off, the company will turn over her password. We'll get in *without* disturbing anything or compromising potential evidence."

"Every second counts," Brian retorts.

"We'll have it tomorrow." Frazier nods to emphasize his certainty.

Brian transfers his scowl to me. Frazier probably interprets the look as exasperation, but twenty years of marriage have allowed me to better translate my husband's expressions. He's admonishing me. Alice is my responsibility. I've let this happen. Now I'm *sitting here* while the police stall. What kind of mother am I? This is how I do my job?

"Waiting that long is unacceptable." I stand while attempting the authoritative tone Brian slips on like a silk jacket. "Why do we need a warrant? For court? All we want is our daughter. The best way to find her is to track her missing laptop and, if that doesn't work, go through her contacts and photos to see who might have visited her new apartment, or at least who knew the location."

My new attitude doesn't intimidate Frazier. If anything, he appears to feel sorry for me. "Alice provided her address to the college. We checked. Anyone with access to Berkeley's system could have seen it."

Blood rushes to my head. Shouting releases the pressure. "SO? DO SOMETHING! Phone the school administrators. Wake up the judge. Get the warrant for Alice's phone. FIND HER!"

Detective Frazier suddenly wraps his hand around one of my own. His thumb creates a warm spot on the inside of my left wrist.

The touch seems too intimate, especially given my behavior. I bring my arm to my side, forcing him to release my hand. As he does, I realize the reason he grasped it in the first place. He believes I'm about to be sick. *Again.* His fingers were pressing my Neiguan point, the one squeezed by anti-nausea bands.

Frazier considers me anew. "We have a whole team working on this."

His tone is different, less sympathetic. I've surprised him with my rudeness, or maybe I've simply confirmed what he's always guessed about wealthy white women: We assume the world works for us, that every public servant serves at the behest of our tax dollars.

I don't think that. Not really. Until today, I considered the police employees of everyone else. People like my family present an outsize risk that we couldn't possibly place on the system. It's why I've always had top-of-the-line home security and my mother employed a butler with a military background until the end of her life. It's why Brian bought a gun.

I'm realizing, however, that money determines outcomes more for perpetrators than victims. Though I can afford a private investigator—an army of PIs, perhaps—it's doubtful any ex-cop Columbo will find my daughter faster than the detective in front of me. Frazier's already searched Alice's apartment and subpoenaed the neighborhood security footage. Plus, he's holding her cell in an evidence locker. He has all the pieces that a PI would need. Despite my wealth, I'm like everyone else: at the mercy of the cops and their resources, their timetable, and their caseloads.

The revelation makes me lightheaded.

Frazier indicates my prior chair, urging me to sit. "I understand you're upset."

He *understands*. There's no way he has any idea what this is like, what it's done to me. Gone is Catherine Ingold, an individual with goals and dreams, loves and hates. I'm now a simple machine with one directive: *Save Alice*.

I don't sit.

Brian looks me up and down, satisfied if not impressed by my belated display of aggression. Anger isn't a trait I show often. The stress of Brian's job has put a premium on me making family time pleasant. Moreover, a wealthy, demanding woman is branded a b-i-you-know-what by the world. My mother taught me to communicate *no* with silence, *yes* with attention and compliments.

One glance at Frazier's tense jaw and my upbringing kicks in hard. I soften my tone. "Let me try to break into Alice's device. I know there are a lot of combinations with her birthday and social. Still, one of them will work."

Frazier grimaces like I've claimed that two plus two equals negative five. I've never been great at math, but even I know "a lot of combinations" is more like tens of thousands.

"Please." I'm back to begging. "This is my *child*. Could you rest if she were yours?"

I don't know if the detective has kids. The way his eyes go fuzzy, though, makes me believe that he not only has them but feels guilty returning to his when my baby can't come home.

"Alice bought her own phone, you said . . ."

I'm not sure if he's asking a question or making a statement. "Yes. She's very responsible. Works every summer. She wants to make her own way in the world. She's studious. A good girl. A great girl."

I'm rambling. Frazier can think what he wants about me, but I need him to sympathize with my kid. "This last summer she interned for Zelos," I continue. "She—" I stop myself from rattling off all her responsibilities. Alice's access at her father's company would only underscore her nepo-baby status. Although being the boss's daughter didn't provide the benefits Frazier might assume—especially not at the end. "She pays many of her own bills," I add.

It's technically true, though the money in Alice's account has largely been gifted to her over the years. From the way Frazier's brow wrinkles, he suspects as much. "And Alice has always been responsible for her own phone?"

Brian looks to me, as unsure of the answer as the detective. "No," I admit. "We pay for her plan."

"So you brought her to the store and put her on a family account?"

"Sure."

Frazier returns to his chair and scoots in front of the computer. The clacking of keys is suddenly so loud, I could believe he's on a typewriter.

"My ten-year-old, Jay, got his first phone for Christmas." Frazier talks over the clatter. "I needed to create a new account for him under mine. I'm his recovery contact."

I resume my seat. An iCloud webpage replaces my last facial composite. Frazier scrolls down a list of password-reset instructions.

Brian remains standing. "Even if Catherine's email is Alice's recovery address, I'm sure the information is protected by two-factor authentication. We don't have my daughter's laptop, right?"

Frazier nods before pointing to the cell in my hand. "Might as well try."

He reads the directions aloud as I open settings on my phone that I barely knew existed. Just as Frazier suspected, I'm the recovery contact for Alice. I tap her name and receive a code.

Brian's frown erases any momentary excitement. "To input that, we need a device where she's already logged in. Those numbers are useless to us."

Waterboarding must feel like this. Every time I breathe, I invite drowning.

Frazier isn't giving up. He opens another Apple site, this one cheekily named iForgot.

He slides the keyboard to me. I drop my phone and take over the computer controls, clicking a password-reset button. Immediately, I'm directed to another page asking me to enter Alice's phone number and prove I'm not a robot. After verifying my human ability to identify warped letters, I'm asked for the email associated with Alice's account. As a clue, the first letter of her ID, *A*, and the initial letter after the @ symbol, *g*, have been provided. It's her Gmail.

Brian crosses his arms. "The instructions will go to her Google account, which we also can't access."

He's probably right. He's always right. I should be pleading with Frazier to release Alice's phone and let Zelos do whatever dirty work it can. Brian has told me that his AI's capabilities far exceed what's been publicly disclosed—not that he's shared any details.

Even so, I have hope. I type in Alice's email, click "Continue," and silently pray. For once, dear God, let my husband be wrong.

The page refreshes with an announcement that reset instructions have been sent to all of Alice's "trusted devices." Brian clears his throat, readying an *I told you so.*

My tears—or Frazier's look—keep him quiet.

I blink at the ceiling, desperate to clear my vision, to not be the useless, emotional woman that Brian must think I am right now. "What else can we do? Please. I need to *do* something."

Frazier sighs as he rises from his desk. "Do you have numbers for Alice's friends?"

I stop crying. "A few. Her old college roommate's cell, in case of emergency, and a high school pal or two. Mostly, I have contact info for her friends' parents."

Frazier gently pulls back my chair, the police station equivalent of a bar turning on the brights. "You really *should* rest." He glances at Brian, making clear the instruction is for both of us. "And, Catherine, you really *shouldn't* look at a bunch of AI photos. But I can't stop you from calling around, asking if anyone has been to Alice's new place."

He's suggesting the job so that I don't lose my mind, not because he thinks I'll find anything useful. Still, the task is a lifeline. I stand and grab my phone. "I'll get on that right away."

Frazier winces. "Don't reveal that Alice has been kidnapped. The spread of nonpublic information could compromise the investigation. You can ask what her friends think of her new neighborhood, play the overprotective mom."

It's a role I don't have to research.

"I can do that," I assure him. "What I can't do is sleep."

ALICE INGOLD

DIARY ENTRY FOUR

The second exit wasn't an escape. My rave-worthy assailant revealed this after gesturing toward the door I'd attacked and assuring me I'd be fine in there. They'd "made it up nice."

Fear glued my feet in place as he fished a key from his pocket and slipped it into the lock. Nothing about having my own place was pleasant. It meant they intended to keep me for some time.

The door screeched open. Fawkes's LED face dipped into the dark. I tracked its halo until it was swallowed by the black hole. For a moment, I had the fleeting sense that maybe none of this was real. This nightmare would soon switch to some other anxiety dream: me, naked, presenting an unwritten thesis to a packed lecture hall. Or worse, showing up at my dad's company only to hear that he wants to speak with me in his office.

Then Fawkes turned. His glowing face advanced toward me, bobbing in the blackness. A hand reached through the void into my space and slapped something on the wall. Overhead lights blinked on inside the room. "I always forget the switch is on the opposite side," he said.

In the new hospital glare, I saw a mattress atop wooden pallets. A reading lamp stood on a gray box, along with a cardboard water carton and a paperback. Seeing the book made my eyes well. They'd thought to give me something to occupy my mind in solitary confinement. These accommodations were *definitely* extended stay.

"You can rest in here while I get something for your legs." I guessed that Fawkes fancied himself the good cop. Sure, he intended to lock me in this cell, but he was being cordial about it. Either that or he was the self-appointed host of this Bates Motel. *Mother* was the other one. "Come on," he said.

Instead of moving toward him, I looked behind me to the car. It was a sedan—not the semitruck required to ram through a chained garage door—and its keys were likely in one of my captors' pockets. Still, it was a vehicle. If the garage ever opened, I could drive it out of there.

"I can sleep in the car."

Fawkes moved back into my space, bringing his glow-in-the-dark smirk with him. "Not an option, Alice."

"I—"

"You need disinfectant for your cuts. We can't afford an infection, okay?"

I doubted anyone would suffer the consequences of sepsis aside from me. His use of *we* was false fellowship.

"You could take me to a hospital," I said, testing his good-guy act on the chance that I was wrong. "That's the only way to ensure my wounds heal."

"Alice." My name emerged as a growl. He'd either done something to alter his tone in the voice changer or had spoken so low that the device couldn't properly pick up the sound. "I understand you're scared. So let me tell you how this is going to go. You'll chill in that room until we say it's time to leave. We'll bring you water and food. You won't die of thirst. You won't starve. Then, at some point, we'll ask you to read something for us, which we'll record."

My mind flashed to the terrorist-taped "confessions" of war journalists and aid workers—the ones made moments before their beheadings.

"Why do you need me to record anything?"

Fawkes's hands fell to his sides, but not before his right one dug into a pocket for the switchblade. He palmed it with the quickness of a pickpocket. "Get in the room, Alice."

I started the forced march into my cell. Though I told myself I'd tried everything, it felt like the trunk all over again. As soon as I got inside, I'd think of some escape plan that would have been possible just outside the door—something I was missing right then.

The room was cool, and it had an odor. Sawdust mixed with . . . something else. Something organic. *What* exactly didn't compute before the door slammed and the dead bolt's click obliterated any further thought about scents. My mind immediately returned to remaining alive. What did I require to keep my heart pumping and lungs inflating? Brain firing?

Food and water, first and foremost. I marched over to the gray box turned bedside table and grabbed the water container on top. The thin cardboard squished in my hand, advertising that I couldn't use the carton as a weapon, not unless I managed to fill it with cement. It had a recognizable label. The cap's seal appeared intact as I popped it off. Even so, I sniffed the contents before putting the carton to my lips. It smelled like water. Odorless. Clean.

My first sip seemed to confirm it. There was no flavor aside from the acid in my throat, and that had been there ever since I was tossed around in the trunk.

Water, then. I wouldn't die of thirst anytime soon. At least not if I rationed this.

Though he didn't say it, I knew Fawkes's promise to keep me hydrated and fed was conditional on him getting whatever he wanted out of my captivity. Same as his promise to let me go.

Only he didn't *actually* swear to release me, I realized. He'd said I would chill here until it was time to leave. He'd never said *how* I'd be leaving.

My stomach turned. I slowed my breathing, trying to suppress the need to retch. If I vomited, there was no guarantee that anyone would clean it up. I'd be stuck with the stench and whatever vermin it might attract.

I scanned the small, windowless room, taking inventory of what was there, what I might be able to fashion into a shiv. Aside from the flimsy cardboard water container, there was the mattress, the wooden pallets supporting it, a pile of what appeared to be folded linens, the gray nightstand, the lamp. The book.

I balanced the reading material in my palm. The book's title suggested it was about human beings adapting to technology—not that I cared about its subject matter. Its weight was the important feature. It seemed a pound, perhaps a few ounces lighter. I could throw it as a diversion, but it wouldn't provide much more punching power.

The lamp was more promising. I tossed the book onto the mattress and picked up the light, praying it was more club than baton. Gripping it took zero effort. The body was hollow. Worse, it was battery powered. An electric lamp would at least have a cord that could be wrapped around a neck. In a fight, this would be useless.

I fought an overwhelming urge to throw the light at the wall. Destroying something would have felt like progress. But I had no idea how my fake friend might respond to my rejection of his hospitality. Instead, I released my frustration by slamming the lamp down onto its table.

The surface of the cube folded in on itself as if it were a pop-up laundry basket. Confused, I grabbed an edge and yanked it back up. The hollow frame re-expanded to a box shape and clicked into place. When I pressed the lid a second time, it didn't collapse, though I could see from the seam that it wasn't permanently attached.

I dug my fingers under the lid and pulled up. Again, the lid clicked into place, though this time it transformed from a solid cube into a sort of chair, with the lid serving as a back and a hole in the center of the seat. Every horror image I'd ever seen filled that empty space. I peered into it, hoping not to glimpse something I'd never forget: the head of my captors' last guest or rats intended as torture tools.

Inside was an empty bucket.

Instinctually, my chin retreated to my chest. The gray box wasn't a nightstand at all. It was a personal porta potty like what campers used, or so I assumed. I'd only gone camping once. When I was nine, my mom took me cross-country to my Nana's estate in Newport, Rhode Island. The two of us stopped in national parks along the way, but we never set up a tent. Instead, the whole trip was in a tour bus turned luxury RV, complete with a driver. It was nice. Though, as relaxing as sleeping in a real bed was, sometimes I wished I'd been in a beat-up sleeping bag on the ground, staring up at the stars. There are things in this world one can't appreciate without getting a little dirty.

But this was another level. My kidnappers expected me to poop in a box.

Under different circumstances, a scatological sense of humor might have kicked in. I might have laughed at the idea of my jailers emptying my chamber pot like I was a queen rather than a captive. Exhaustion and fear kept me from seeing anything funny, however. This was literally a shit situation. God only knew how long I'd be in it. How this room would smell in a few days. Months?

Without warning, my lunch rushed into my esophagus. Before I fully understood what was happening, I found myself leaning over the toilet's open circle, spewing creamed cashews. The vegan carbonara I'd made for lunch tasted far worse coming up than it had going down. I saw a flash of my mom's face during our meal hours earlier, her nose shrinking at the food.

Suddenly, I *was* laughing. The sound exploded from me, as violently as my stomach's contents had moments before. My gut contracted. Tears filled my eyes. Mom would have lost it, too, if she'd seen her face as I'd explained what was in my faux carbonara. My polite society parent, the one who so prides herself on her ability to hide her emotions and merely imply distaste, had been totally unable to mask her revulsion. She'd looked like someone had snotted in her soup.

I laughed so hard, it felt like crying. Then I remembered that my disgusted mother had been willing to try my food anyway.

And I was bawling all over again.

The stress of the day had stripped me of emotional control. I was rapid cycling—hysterically crying, *in hysterics*. Back and forth, a pinball at the mercy of the strangers pressing the buttons.

Thinking of my kidnappers somehow manifested them. I looked up from the blob my body had formed on the concrete to see pants-clad legs—four, not two.

I scrambled away from the toilet, as if additional distance would add doubt as to who'd made the mess inside it.

"Shit," the woman said. Her tone was normal. Apparently, she'd removed the voice changer.

Though not the mask. The same LED-lit ghost peered from her hooded sweatshirt. The room's overhead lights rendered the image slightly less frightening than Guy Fawkes's mask had been, though it was still unnerving.

"That's what we got it for." The man spoke with the same processed tone as before. In the light, the wires outlining his cartoon features were visible. They recalled the glowsticks I'd used as a kid—the pink, blue, and green ones that required cracking an interior glass vial filled with hydrogen peroxide so that it could mix with the phosphorescent chemicals and turn luminous. We'd tested how they work in one of my high school chemistry classes, which was a ridiculous thing to remember with my life in danger.

I had the insane urge to laugh again.

"I'm not throwing it out." The woman brought her hand to where her nose hid behind the mask, unwittingly changing the face to the scarier x-eyed, sewn-mouth version.

"I got it." Fawkes turned toward me. "Glad you figured this out. I didn't show you."

As much as I wanted to yell at him to stop all the Mr. Nice Vigilante stuff, the act was better than the alternative. His coconspirator wouldn't even acknowledge me as a human being.

"I brought the creams." He waved his cupped hands. Bacitracin and gauze pads were stuffed into one palm. The other was entirely taken up by a large bottle of hydrogen peroxide.

There was no room for his knife.

I couldn't shake that thought as I followed his instruction to stretch out my legs. My mind was a skipping record, the needle returning to that lyric. *No knife. No knife.*

Fawkes didn't necessarily need a weapon, of course. Even if he couldn't stab me, he could smash my head against the concrete floor. If he was too tenderhearted to beat me to death, his partner appeared happy to do it for him.

He poured hydrogen peroxide onto a pad and pressed it to the scuffed fabric stuck to my right knee. "I think I might need to get beneath the pants," he said.

Because the mask hid his eyes, I was unsure whether he'd spoken to me or his partner. She answered from her position by the closed yet temporarily unlocked door. "So do it."

"Maybe she'd feel more comfortable if you helped."

She barred her arms across her chest. I imagined the frown beneath her mask's laced grin. "Or we could stop playing doctor and give her privacy to clean up her own shit."

Fawkes turned back to me. "Would that be better?"

I nodded. Verbally agreeing with Bad Cop felt too much like a coerced confession.

He dropped the medical gear beside me. In addition to the gauze, there were self-adhesive bandages, the kind that go over the knee. Either my captors had stashed a medical supply kit, or the girl had gone to a pharmacy specifically to address my injuries. The latter indicated a town close by. We hadn't been at our new location *that* long.

"There you go." She looked at Fawkes rather than at me. "Let her do it herself. She'll manage."

As much as I wanted to hope for a town, I couldn't imagine my female captor doing me any favors. They probably had a medical kit for their personal use.

"Okay, then," he said.

She unfolded her arms to reach into her sweatshirt pocket. I braced for the gun. Instead, a square paper appeared in her fist. "We'll leave you to that in a moment. But first—"

The guy stood. "Now?"

She unfolded the sheet and held it out toward him, keeping her back pressed against the door. "The longer she's here, the more we risk."

I rose from my spot. "Then let me go."

If the mask's eyes could have rolled, they would have. Instead, the woman tilted her head in Fawkes's direction.

He strode over and took the paper. "You brought the phone?"

The girl patted a bulge in her sweatshirt pocket.

Fawkes extended the scrap toward me. "Read this a few times while I clean up."

"What is it?" Though my question was the obvious one, my captors turned to each other as though neither knew how to respond.

After a moment, Ghost Face shrugged. "It's what you'll be saying on camera." She chuckled. Even without the voice changer, her laugh sounded hollow. "Our manifesto."

CATHERINE NEWHOUSE INGOLD

THE NIGHT OF

I'm driving alone. Brian and I took two cars to the station, so I shouldn't be surprised. Really, it was foolish of me to expect my husband to deviate from his schedule any more than he already had. He's not a man who changes methods in a crisis. Brian believes in optimization, finding the best way to proceed and sticking to it. During the workweek, he sleeps in the San Francisco apartment, and this night could be no different. As he explained, the day's events had wrested him from the office. He had emails to answer. Instructions to deliver. Code to approve. Employees, corporations, governments—all depend on him to do these things. Plus, he had to get Zelos's AI working on that facial composite. Better for him to be a block from his office than stuck in the suburbs, a traffic-clogged bridge away from his firm's nerve center.

I told him I understood. Saying anything else would have struck Brian as needy, and as far as he's concerned, there could be no less attractive quality in a woman. Besides, I signed up for this. I'd married a genius, then funded his brilliance by providing Zelos's start-up capital. The role "wife of visionary tech CEO" requires a measure of self-reliance and an ability to tolerate loneliness.

And I have my own work to do. Regardless of how news sites refer to me, my chief title will forever be Alice's mother.

My first call is to the friend I like the least. Monica, Alice's former roommate, is more opinionated than the tech gurus Brian used to bring home to dinner. Those guys would dominate the conversation with futuristic visions featuring their respective businesses, scorning any challenges from wives unenamored with their utopias. But they never personally faulted me and my forebearers for handing them the sad world they'd been market-called to fix.

In Monica's eyes, my ilk has ruined everything. Global warming? The result of soccer moms' carbon emissions, of course—what, with all the scooting around in our gas-guzzling SUVs instead of fuel-efficient golf carts. The wealth gap? The world's Rockefellers bribe Congress through political action committees to maintain favorable taxation rates, don't you know? Even undeniably positive developments such as the rising stock market are somehow evil schemes of the rich, scams invented by the investor class to fleece workers out of profits.

Greta Thunberg and Elaine Brown rolled into a tart, that's Monica. There's no debating her. She possesses a gunslinger's speed on her cell. Say anything, and she'll call up some paper or study refuting your point in nanoseconds. It's like arguing with the progeny of ChatGPT and the American Civil Liberties Union. And she's not even prelaw. She's a computer science major.

She's also a heavy partier, which is why I know she'll be up at this hour. Monica prides herself on *having stories*, most of which precede her stumbling into the dorms on the dark side of the morning with a Mad Libs–worthy stranger. I'm sure she's not in bed before midnight.

Ten till glows on my dashboard as I head over the Golden Gate. The tires crossing the bridge's joints create a rhythmic rumble that I associate with returning from the city. Did Alice's kidnappers take her over this bridge? Did she hear the sound and think, *I'm so close to home?*

Tears well as I search for Monica's number in my contacts. The soupy vision adds extra difficulty to driving while scrolling. Accidents happen like this.

I take the first exit and pull into a lookout point. A streetlight shines over a sign for hiking trails. Alice and I visited this national recreation area at least once a month in her younger teens. We'd hike along the Marin Headlands, taking in the view of the bridge and bay from a different angle. Sometimes we'd attempt the extralong loop of the Tennessee Valley Trail, rewarding ourselves with midday sunbathing at the beach. We never talked much on these excursions, though I listened, and when Alice had something to say, she'd share. That was parenting a teenager, making myself available so that when my daughter was ready to open up, I'd be around to close any wounds.

When she comes back, we'll do the long hike, I promise myself. Alice will tell me what she suffered, and I will heal her. Me, the Pacific breeze . . . and her best friend.

I park the car and dial. Coyote howls punctuate the rings. Since I don't expect Monica to answer an unknown number, I begin formulating my message. Frazier's instruction *not* to mention the kidnapping ties my hands, removing the urgent reason for Monica or anyone else to return my call. But his argument makes sense. The police need to focus on real leads, not crackpot theories or pundit analyses.

I've settled on "Alice had an emergency" when a voice answers.

"New phone. Who dis?" Monica's tone is playful, a tad naughty. She slurs the final *s*. In the background, there's conversation. Music.

"Monica, this is Alice's mom, Catherine Ingold."

"Oh? Catherine Ingold, is it? *The* Catherine *Newhouse* Ingold?" She echoes me in a singsong tone. "To what do I owe the honor?"

The sarcasm surprises. Though I'm certain that Alice has complained about her *snob* mom, Monica typically wouldn't mock me to my face. She must be very drunk.

"It's about Alice." There's no melody in my inflection this time. "She's in danger."

"What sort of d*ah*nger?" Monica drags out the *a*. She's imitating me, I suppose, given the way she snorts with amusement.

"Monica, this is serious."

"*Sahrahous*, really?" Monica dissolves into snickers. "Oh my God, Allie, the impression's insane." She catches her breath. "You have the Boston Brahmin thing down pat. Totally her."

"Monica." I raise my voice. "This is *not* Alice. This is her mother. Alice has been . . . She's had an emergency. There's nothing funny about it. She could . . ." My stern tone melts into tears. "Please." I swallow a sob. "I have to talk to you."

There's still laughter, though only in the background. A sharp inhale pierces the speaker, followed by a rush of words. "I'm sorry, Ms. Ingold. Alice's mom. I didn't mean. I thought—"

"I need your help." I overenunciate to cover the crying. "That's why I'm calling."

When Monica speaks again, her words are clear. "What's wrong?"

The background noise grows louder. Someone turned up the speakers.

"Where can we meet?"

———

I take the Richmond Bridge back to Berkeley. The route requires passing San Quentin Rehabilitation Center, home to death row inmates, though the state doesn't execute anyone anymore. When the governor announced a halt to all lethal injections, I applauded the move. Surely everyone is capable of rehabilitation and deserving of forgiveness. "Vengeance is mine, saith the Lord" and all . . .

Now a stranger—perhaps more than one—is doing God knows what to my child, and I'm reconsidering my whole position. Maybe mothers should decide who is worthy of forgiveness—juries of women who've given life, who've nurtured seeds inside our bodies until they split us open, then planted them in the centers of our worlds, watering and feeding them with our energy until their branches spread far beyond our reach. Maybe we should have a say in who gets cut down.

Once I'm over the bridge, it takes another fifteen minutes until I see Sather Tower, a lit beacon calling all liberals. For Berkeley students, the structure's the equivalent of Paris's Tour Eiffel. If you're lost, it's the natural place to go.

But my daughter isn't lost; she's trapped.

Monica waits for me on a bench illuminated by the tower's base, sipping from a thigh-sized water bottle. As she sees me, she sets it down. The liquid's half-gone.

She stands as I draw closer. Her miniskirt and blouse, cut deep enough to show her bra's lace, advertise the night she'd anticipated having. Her hair confirms it, worn in a messy curly ponytail that cascades over half her forehead to cover one eye.

But she's not strutting for a date tonight. She's on a bench trying to sober up enough to help her ex-roommate, even if it means suffering through a conversation with a woman whom she clearly regards as stuck-up, out of touch, and callous. I've no doubt that she calls me "Karen" Newhouse Ingold behind my back.

Maybe my daughter's right to love this girl.

Monica gives me a half-hearted hug by way of greeting. The minor show of affection almost breaks me. My entire body trembles with the effort of remaining upright, of keeping my voice steady as I thank her for coming, and I realize I'm not strong enough to hide the truth of what's happening. I'm too desperate for answers. I need Monica as motivated to find Alice as I am. "What I'm about to tell you can't go further than here, okay? Alice's life could depend on it."

Monica's expression morphs from wary curiosity to an almost exaggerated show of worry, like the animated crying-face filter. She nods for me to continue.

"Alice was taken from her apartment earlier today," I say before correcting myself. "Yesterday afternoon. Hours ago."

Monica's hands fly to her mouth. "Taken?" Her palms muffle the words.

"Kidnapped."

She shakes her head, instinctually rejecting my assertion. "How? Why would anyone—"

"Alice hasn't been in the new apartment long," I continue. "Two weeks. I have to find out who else knows her address."

Monica pulls her phone from her pocket. "She must have gone somewhere for the weekend. I'll call her."

"It won't work," I say. "The police have her phone."

Monica lowers her cell. She considers it a moment, debating whether to believe me. Another moment passes before she swaps the phone for her water bottle, taking a short sip.

"Who else knew where she lived?"

She squeezes the bottle's plastic case, filling the silence with a crinkling noise. "I helped her move," she says finally.

"Who else?"

Monica either struggles to think through her hangover or weighs whether to reveal something. She looks vaguely constipated.

"You're not betraying her confidence. All that matters is getting Alice home safe."

Monica seems unconvinced. Again, she sips from her water bottle, an old debate team trick. Drinking's a convenient excuse to think before answering a question.

I can imagine only one reason for Monica to consider her response so carefully. "What about that boy?"

She swallows hard. "Sorry?"

"The young man in the photo she has pinned above her bed. Her boyfriend?"

Monica straightens. I can almost see her willing the alcohol from her system. "You know she broke up with Simon. She said she told you, and you were over the moon. You thought he wasn't good enough, that he'd spend all her money on Coachella tickets and weed."

I dole out enough judgment that I recognize the condescension in Monica's last statement. She thinks I disliked Simon because he wasn't wealthy. I feel the need to defend myself. "That boy was aimless. It was only a matter of time before Alice got bored."

Monica shrugs. I realize she hasn't actually answered my question.

"But there was someone after Simon," I prod. "Someone she recently began seeing, whom she didn't yet want to introduce to her parents."

Monica directs her attention to the bottle cap. She screws it on and off, as if the twisting will wring the remaining alcohol from her brain. "I don't know of anyone serious. Maybe she made a friend during the summer or something. But no one here."

I lean in, a detective putting the screws to a perp. "In the picture, he was kissing her."

Monica's kohl-lined eyes are suddenly sharp. "I don't know what you want me to say, Ms. Ingold. The semester hadn't started. Alice was getting settled. She wasn't having people over. There was me. She mentioned inviting you to lunch. That's all I know."

Her surety saps my fight. I'd prayed that Monica would have a list of potential suspects.

"I understand. I'm sorry. I'm so . . ." My voice breaks. "I'll let you get back to your night."

I start from the bench. Before I fully stand, Monica grabs my arm. "There's no going back to my night. Are the cops showing Alice's picture around? Have they told the press?"

"They don't believe that's a good idea."

Monica jumps from the seat. "Why not? We need people looking for her—searching apartments, checking in neighbors' windows, peering into parked cars. The TSA should have her photo so no one can take her drugged up on some plane."

That risk hadn't even occurred to me. "I don't think they can get her out of the country like that," I say, more to quell my own fears. "I have her passport."

Monica's face flashes disapproval. I know Alice complains that I control her—with my money, the age limit on her trust fund, the executor who will approve large purchases even after she receives her share of the family fortune at twenty-five.

"We should still contact the media," Monica says, shrugging off this latest data point of my enemy status. "We need to organize search parties. Get students to comb the campus."

She's fired up. Again, I'm reminded why I can't argue with her.

"The police don't think it's a good idea."

Monica scoffs. "You trust the cops?"

It was only a matter of time before I hit a Gen Z trigger. "What choice do I have? The police are trained in what to do, and the detective was adamant that news coverage will only complicate matters. The cops are calling the shots."

Monica reaches for my arm again. This time her hand falls onto my shoulder. "With all due respect, Ms. Ingold, you're wrong. The police are *not* calling the shots." She looks me straight in the eye. "The kidnappers are."

ALICE INGOLD

DIARY ENTRY FIVE

The diary was a reward for the recording, a treat given to a dog after a good sit. My kidnappers bequeathed it along with a few plastic pens, the kind convenience stores sell in packs of sixty, too flimsy to inflict physical damage, save maybe to an eye. And unfortunately, my captors' masks protect those.

Their face coverings also rob me of much-needed insight. My inability to read their expressions is a form of blindness, which I'm sure is intentional. They want me off-kilter, unable to guess what's coming, clinging to their gifts like buoys in a storm. It's how they'll train me.

So far, it's working. I immediately wrote in the diary, as suggested. Afraid to sleep, I opened the notebook and put down everything that happened, in case anything happens to me. I didn't close the book until noon the following day, or so I assumed. At the time, I knew nothing of the hour. I was simply aware of my cramping hand and the lack of new details to share. The period between filming my kidnappers' cryptic message and setting down my pen can be summed up in one sentence: I wrote.

Afterward, I read. I would have preferred a romance novel, something to allow my mind to wander. Barring that, I'd have appreciated some of my schoolbooks so that I wouldn't fall behind in my reading. There wasn't another option, however, and I couldn't shut off my brain. For me, sleep isn't a fatigue symptom so much as a routine. My skiff to Nod leaves on an exact schedule. Missing the boat means waiting for the following day to drift off. I couldn't shut my eyes, despite the silver dollars weighing on my lids. My choices were to pick up their chosen reading material or stare at the wall.

The book's cover featured a translucent male torso comprised of ones and zeroes slowly dissolving into a DNA-like double helix constructed of the same binary code. The back boasted praise from Elon Musk and Stephen Hawking. "Compelling." "Thought-provoking." Translation? Smart, rich people owed this author favors.

I sat on the mattress edge and turned to the inside flap. The author's bio included a photo of a professorial Rob Lowe and his credentials as an MIT physicist, which explained the Stephen Hawking endorsement and why I'd likely pitch this paperback across the room. In high school, I'd tried to get through Hawking's *A Brief History of Time*. A quarter in, I'd capitulated and pushed it to the back of a bookshelf. Geniuses often earn their titles because their brains work spectacularly well in specific areas, not because they do everything better than average. Take my father, for example. IQ: 160. EQ: 40, if I had to guess. I'd never know for certain. Brian Ingold would never take a test for something he couldn't ace. Or, at least, he'd never disclose the results.

Whatever skills had made the author a lauded theorist likely didn't translate to penning an entertaining read. Still, I flipped the book over and opened the first page.

It started with a question about superhuman AI, asking if I thought such technology would be created during my lifetime. The answers it offered were binary: yes or no. If yes, I was to continue to the next page. If no, skip to a following chapter.

As a kid, I loved those Choose Your Own Adventure books in which chapters end in cliff-hanger decision trees: "If you open the box, advance to page 3. If you leave it closed, turn to page 5." For someone as sheltered as I'd been growing up, it was nice to feel a world of choices at my fingertips.

I considered the page's question again.

Neither answer appealed to me. I didn't know enough about artificial intelligence to choose. To honestly respond, I needed a third option. "If you haven't given this question much thought, turn to page . . ."

Evidently, the MIT professor had assumed anyone reading his book would already possess a firm opinion on AI's future. He hadn't envisioned his audience as a college English major trapped in a windowless room trying not to die of boredom.

"Well, that makes two of us," I muttered, turning to the next page. I was never the type to skip around or read the ending of a book first. Why change now?

I was barely through the first paragraph when I heard the arguing.

At first I assumed my captors were in the neighboring room. Their voices—not whispers but not full volume either—spurred fears of a sneak attack. I bolted from my springless mattress, clutching the thin blanket they'd left as though the fabric were Kevlar, not cotton.

The door stood closed. I looked to the knob, straining to pick up movement in the desk lamp's meager light.

It didn't turn.

"Why haven't they alerted the media?" the girl asked.

"Cops must have told them not to."

A man answered, though he lacked Fawkes's reverb-laced baritone. For a moment I feared a third coconspirator. Then I reminded myself that I'd only really heard my male kidnapper speak through a voice processor.

"And they're just going to obey?" the girl asked. "What rich person takes orders from the police?"

Their debate emanated from somewhere to the right of the door. I rose from the bed, careful not to make much noise. If I could hear them, chances were they could hear me.

As I stood, my leggings pulled at fresh scabs. I regretted putting them back on. Disinfecting my cuts had required removing my pants to apply peroxide-soaked cotton. I'd pressed the wet pads to my wounds until the dried blood had fizzed and my skin had burned white. Afterward, I'd slathered on bacitracin and tried slapping on the bandages left by my attackers. They wouldn't stick with all the goop, however, and I couldn't wait in my underwear for my skin to dry. I didn't want Fawkes seeing me half-naked. Though he fancied himself a gentleman, any man who would keep a woman against her will couldn't care *that* much about consent.

"It doesn't matter," said the guy I presumed was Fawkes. I followed his voice across the room.

"Of course it does!" The girl's retort echoed above me through an air vent. "We need the press to carry the video, follow them around."

"We'll get the media."

"And how do you—"

Steady beeps interrupted. I heard a door—maybe a cabinet—open and shut.

"Where are you going?" the girl shouted.

"It's nearly noon," the guy replied. "She's probably starving."

I took the time as gospel. Since they didn't know I was listening, they had little reason to lie about the hour.

Footsteps moved across the ceiling. A door slammed.

I hurried back to the bed, trying to strike a balance between silence and speed. Being able to eavesdrop on my kidnappers was a literal gift from above. I couldn't let them see me using the air vent like a cup-and-string telephone.

The door opened as I slipped back beneath the blanket. Fawkes entered carrying a tray. My stomach dropped. I hadn't expected him to come in with his hands essentially tied. Had I remained where I was, I could have pushed past him and through the door.

"I brought soup." His voice was robotic again.

He kicked the door closed behind him and carried over the tray. A vegetal scent wafted above the chlorine-pool smell that had permeated the room since he'd cleaned my porta potty. I'd managed *not* to use it since, though I'd felt the urge.

I continued to ignore my bladder as Fawkes brought a bowl of thick, bubbling liquid into view. The substance was bright orange, the color of creamed carrots or toxic waste cannisters.

Hunger pulled my hand toward it, yet fear stopped me from picking up the bowl. Soup could hide anything. Rat poison. Bodily fluids. I saw what Tyler Durden had done in *Fight Club*.

"It's sweet potato," Fawkes said. "Try it."

"Um. I'm . . . I'm vegan," I stuttered.

Given my situation, announcing any dietary restrictions was ridiculous. My captors were not short-order cooks. But I was all too aware how dairy could impact an uninitiated digestive system, and my only toilet was a bedside bucket. Plus, I really didn't believe in harming animals for my meals. At least, not since August.

"It's okay." Fawkes pushed the tray in my direction. "This is made with cashew milk."

My stomach turned at the thought of ingesting anything close to what I'd spewed out earlier. I scooted closer to the wall. "I'm not hungry."

"You have to eat, Alice."

"I'll eat after you let me go. My parents will have an entire SWAT team working on that riddle you gave me to read. Though I don't understand the reason for being cryptic. You can tell them what you want. Negotiate."

Fawkes shifted the tray to one hand and picked up the spoon with his other. "Do you know why online games are so addictive?"

I guessed where he was going. "You want to rile people up by having them puzzle over the answer."

"We want to direct their attention." He swirled the edgeless utensil in the liquid. "This is a little hot but good."

I flashed to Brad Pitt's Durden "seasoning" mushroom bisque. "I don't know the ingredients."

Fawkes brought the tray closer. "It's that Whole Foods brand. Cruelty-free. Vegan approved."

Again, he dipped the spoon in the bowl. This time, however, he brought it toward my closed lips, a parent attempting to feed a reluctant toddler. "You have to eat."

Gloppy liquid dripped from the spoon's edge. Bile rose into my throat. "I don't want it!"

I swatted the spoon from my face. As the utensil hit the neighboring wall, my hand dropped, smacking the tray. The bowl sprang from its plastic perch. Hot soup splashed Fawkes's mask. He yelped and grabbed his face, sending the tray tottering to the ground. For the second time in as many days, I heard ceramic shatter.

Fawkes doubled over. I took advantage of his distraction and pounced from the bed onto the floor. The exit didn't lock from the inside. If I could get into the garage, I'd have another chance at getting out. My assailant had gotten in somehow. Surely there was another door.

Something hit the floor. Though I feared it was my captor's switchblade, I didn't check. Instead, I grabbed the knob and began to turn.

Hands gripped my shoulders. A warm dampness pressed against my back as Fawkes pulled me into his stained shirt. "Alice."

"Stop!" I yelled.

His arm barred below my clavicle. An inch higher and I'd be trapped in a rear choke hold.

I whirled around, beating my fists against his torso. "No. No!"

"Alice, please. Allie."

My palms froze against the drum of his chest. This voice was familiar. It belonged to the man upstairs, not the masked assailant who spoke to me through a mechanical processor. Had the liquid shorted out some wire in the vocal device?

I raised my chin, expecting to see glitching LEDs, or perhaps no lights at all.

Dark eyes looked down at me from beneath a mop of brown hair. A five-o'clock shadow softened a youthful jawline. This face was handsome but not alarmingly so. Fawkes was the kind of guy most of my friends would concede was nice looking, though some might quip he wasn't their type. Not that I knew what type he was. Generic white guy, I supposed. Put him in a baseball cap and he'd blend in at any Delta Kappa Epsilon party.

His eyes narrowed as I examined his face. Too late I realized that committing his features to memory lowered my chances of being set free. The guy had worn a mask for a reason.

I shut my eyes. "I'm sorry. I didn't realize. I didn't see—"

"Damn it, Alice," he snapped. "This changes everything."

CATHERINE NEWHOUSE INGOLD

THE DAY AFTER

Alice calls for me.

I hear her, though I can't make out much in this dense forest. Redwoods the width of Smart cars block my vision. Their canopies filter the light, pushing the time from twelve to twilight. Light patches speckle the shadowed ground, a wisp trail through the dark. I navigate from one to another, shouting her name.

They lead to a clearing. As I step inside, something glints in my peripheral vision. I run toward the shimmer, drawn by the promise of metal, something man-made.

I'm nearly on top of the structure when I skid to a stop. Before me, a web worthy of Wes Craven spreads between two steel poles. Bloodred ropes stand in for silken threads. In the center sits Alice.

Her gaze is distant. Haunted. I'm unsure if she sees me.

"I'm coming!" I grab the bottom rope. It feels strange in my palm, more carbon fiber than fabric. The material slices into my skin as I scramble up to the spider's lair.

When I reach my daughter, she's changed. In place of a young woman is a child of three. Blood trickles from a gash in her chin.

Toddler Alice opens her mouth, releasing more fluids. A gurgle emerges from deep inside her throat. It morphs into a blaring BEEP.

I'm awake.

Dappled light bathes my office floor. It dances toward the sofa where I apparently fell asleep after emailing the umpteenth parent to whom I haven't spoken in ages. I only meant to rest my eyes long enough for my vision to cease blurring.

So far, I haven't added any more of Allie's friends to my contacts, though I expect I'll receive responses over the next several days. I decided my best chance at obtaining information—without revealing the kidnapping—was to claim that I intended to throw Alice a surprise graduation party. I wanted her old pals' numbers and email addresses to send the digital invites.

Only one person emailed back before I fell asleep, a mom who wanted to know if my message was a phishing attempt. She noted how "unusual" it was to receive an email from me, out of the blue, at three in the morning.

Phishing fears may be why none of Allie's friends have responded to me on Facebook or Instagram. A message from Alice's mom must seem odd, especially given that Alice wasn't active on either site. She had a few photos up on each platform, but she rarely posted. Brian's doing, I suspect. He's repeatedly warned us against sharing much online. More than most, he knows what tech companies can do with that information.

My nightmare's beep emanates from the cell gripped in my right hand. The time shines on the screen above a photo of Alice and me from years earlier. Her hair is several shades lighter, youth rather than dye. It's five a.m.

I bring my phone to my face like it's an oxygen mask. The home screen unlocks, despite the tears and smeared makeup altering my appearance. I haven't washed since yesterday morning. All I've managed in the way of personal hygiene is a brief toothbrushing, which I accomplished solely to spare others the rancid smell of my post-sick breath.

A number one is appended to my text icon. One message.

I click. The sender is unknown. I brace myself and click again.

No words, just a web address.

I wish Brian were here. I need a hand to stop mine from shaking.

This link could lead to my daughter. Or it could open a back door into my life, allowing access to my personal information, contacts, and financial passwords. Of course, I may have already let the police in such a door with the software they downloaded. Do the cops already know about this message, I wonder, or does their spying program only work for phone conversations?

Again, I wish for Brian. He'd know.

I click.

A circle appears—Apple's pinwheel of death, but devoid of color. Something's downloading, no doubt a worm that will eat into my apps and absorb all the necessary information to clone my bank cards. I'm tempted to hit the power button, but hope keeps my finger off that trigger. There's a chance I'm installing software that will connect to a live feed of whatever dungeon holds my daughter.

The desaturated Trivial Pursuit piece earns a wedge. Whatever this file is, it's big. I watch the pie fill, my thoughts drifting to my dream—or fictionalized memory, as it were. The only time Alice ever went to the ER.

She'd been playing in a public park. The kids' area had been renovated with climbing walls, seesaws, swings, and shock-absorbing wood chips. What my three-year-old loved best, however, was the new rope spiderweb. A hole in the middle was the catbird seat. Kids fell all over themselves crawling up the spokes, aiming for the arachnid hub. And Alice wanted nothing more than to be Charlotte in the center.

I stood behind the apparatus as she climbed, arms outstretched should she fall through the toddler-sized spaces between the ropes. No matter how hard I tried *not* to imagine it, I pictured Alice clutching a little arm or limping toward me after slipping through and smacking into the mulch below. The very thought made my bones ache.

But my anxiety found no sympathy with my daughter. "Go, Mommy!" she shouted, her squeaky voice a comedian's impression of a child. "Go, Mommy."

I assured her, of course, that I had every confidence in her ability to make it to the main circle. Still, I maintained my position.

Other moms—those content to chat on benches as their children risked life and limb—side-eyed me like I was the poster child for helicopter parenting. Parents were supposed to let their kids make mistakes. Wasn't that the prevailing wisdom?

I didn't care. Alice—then, as now—was my world. Not that I had planned it that way, for her to become its center, to morph into a black hole in which all my ambitions and desires spun around, aiming to be absorbed. Twenty-four-year-old me would have sworn I'd be helping Brian expand his company, charming would-be investors and providing the social grease to get things done. As it turns out, when an invention is truly life changing, such soft-sales tactics are unnecessary. Brian simply had to show Zelos's software to businesses, demonstrate a few of its capabilities, and then let their owners' imaginations sell them on how his technology could be exploited. People ended up pitching *him* on applications they could create, begging to give him cash, to partner with and train his AI software to assume needed assignments. Brian had created technology that would learn and grow from its inputs, that could discern the optimal solution to a problem and then execute it. He was a tech god. Thus, his universe exponentially expanded as mine shrunk, squeezing down to a singularity, a few divided cells in an ovum. And I called her Alice.

As my baby stretched toward the web's center, I continued to shadow her every move, standing on my tiptoes while encouraging her grunts of exertion and squeals of success, reminding myself that her joy was worth my increased heart rate. By the time she was finished, I was so relieved to have her on solid ground that I slumped onto a nearby bench to watch as she ran to a water fountain.

That's when it happened. She tripped on the wooden rail cordoning off the wood chips and fell face-first into a spear-tipped splinter. The shard pierced a hole in her chin so deep that bone peeked through the blood.

Parenting doesn't come with a manual, but it does have autopilot. Without thinking, I scooped up my daughter and carried her, screaming, to the fountain. There I flushed the wound, pulled a napkin from my purse, pressed it to her chin, and then ran with her against my chest to my car, her blood soaking the shoulder of my blouse.

I sped to the nearest hospital, expecting to be seen immediately. The injury was to her face! Surely doctors would shuttle her into an operating room for stitches.

That didn't happen. Emergency rooms operate by a different hierarchy than the real world. Women and children receive no preferential treatment. There's no paying up for priority seating. When we arrived, old men with chest pains and teenagers with twisted legs waited on plastic seats steeped in sweat, bodily fluids, and industrial antiseptics, all shuffling in line according to the seriousness of the next arrival's injury.

Alice and I waited for what felt like hours. In the end, a plastic surgeon stitched her up while I held her tightly against my body, barring her arms and legs with my own so that my already hysterical daughter wouldn't be strapped into a straitjacket. Three-year-olds aren't often put under anesthesia for non-life-threatening injuries lest they never wake up. As with my place in the ER line, there was no amount of money I could pay for a better option. Alice wasn't Alice Newhouse Ingold in that hospital. She was another little kid with a split chin. And I was just another mom.

When I look at Alice's face from a certain angle, I see the thin white scar on the underside of her jaw, and the whole day comes back to me. I feel my frustration and guilt, the helplessness while I waited for the plastic surgeon to grace us with his presence. Money will never make those feelings go away.

So what are all my millions good for? Putting a target on my daughter's back? Buying her freedom, which was only stolen because of that target?

The on-screen pie fills. I wait for something to happen. For a moment, it seems nothing will. I've been watching a virus develop without symptoms. It will infect my accounts, but only after I've forgotten all about this exposure.

The screen goes black.

Panicked, I triple-tap the seemingly dead device. A video play button materializes. I press it.

Alice appears. She stands in some sort of basement. The wall behind her is blank cement. If there's natural light from windows, I don't see it. Overhead bulbs emphasize dark shadows beneath her eyes. She's not crying, though. Her stare is defiant, challenging the viewer or whoever holds the camera.

"My name is Alice Ingold. I'm the daughter of Catherine Newhouse Ingold, heir to the Newhouse shipping fortune, and Brian Ingold, CEO of the artificial intelligence firm Zelos. On September ninth, 2025, I was kidnapped."

She clears her throat. "I acknowledge that I've enjoyed a life of immense privilege and wealth. And I want to return to my life. I want to go home." Her voice breaks on this last word. And that hiccup breaks me. I hear a crack, my heart separating like a shattered windshield. "I will go home." Alice's voice steadies. "If you find me."

The final phrase doesn't fit with a ransom demand. I watch as Alice picks up a piece of paper from a gray nightstand. She repositions herself in front of the camera and reads.

> In a clean room near . . .
> Behind a curtain of air
> Folks grow sick and die

Our flesh far too weak
We willingly go offshore
But the remains stay

People want more and *mores*
How to fix all those who need?
Remove their engines

Put them in barracks
Shelter, though the view be bleak
Is what I see now

She stops and stares at the camera, waiting for a response. Her kidnappers' approval? The defiant spark in Alice's eyes has been snuffed, replaced by a watery gleam. She smiles weakly. "Mom, Dad. I don't want you to worry. These people have promised me I'll be alright, provided you play along. Use the media. Crowdsource the answer. Find me. Please. I love you."

The screen goes dark.

The loss of her image feels like watching the kidnappers drag her away. I poke the cell's glass face, desperate for Alice to reappear. The play button comes back on-screen. I rewatch the video in its entirety. Rather than pay attention to the words this time, I look for signs of injury.

Only Alice's torso and head are visible. No bruises shine on her cheeks or arms. Her eyes are tired but not bloodshot or blackened. Her pupils don't shrink or shiver with fear. She isn't cowering.

They haven't assaulted her—yet. Perhaps they're saving that for when we fail to decode their cryptic nonsense. "In a clean room near"? Are Alice's captors trying to convey that she's not being kept in squalor? Is that their version of an assurance? And "behind a curtain of air"? What does that mean? The earth's entire atmosphere is air! So she's on the planet. How is that helpful?

Alice's video tells me only two things: There's more than one kidnapper, and they're worse than I feared. "These people," as she'd said, are not criminals out for a quick payday. Her captors fancy themselves the new Zodiac Killers.

I pocket my phone and rush into the kitchen. My keys sit on the table along with my purse. I grab both, determined to get to Brian. He might be too important to sleep at home during the week, but if anyone can solve this puzzle, it's him. This is his daughter. He owes her. After all these years of subordinating my wants and needs for his career, he owes *me*.

My broken kitten heels wait by the mudroom door, in the same place I kicked them off earlier. I push them aside to pull a pair of sneakers from a closet. Never again will I make the mistake of prioritizing fashion over mobility. From now on, I'll be ready to race.

I do exactly that, rushing to my garaged car and jumping into the front seat. I hit the automatic door opener and turn on the engine. Brian's on the north end of the city. I'll be at his door in twenty minutes, barring bridge traffic.

As the door lifts, lightning flashes stop me from peeling out onto the street. I pull down the visor and struggle to make sense of the sudden electrical storm. The sun is rising.

People clog the road in front of the gate. Some have signs, but most carry microphones or cameras. As the garage door hits the ceiling, the crowd begins to move, segments of a centipede snaking toward me. Cameras point in my direction, compound eyes focused on my windshield. Questions screech through unseen speakers.

"Mrs. Ingold? Where is Alice? What have they done with her?"

The kidnappers wanted me to alert the press. There's no need. They're already here.

ALICE INGOLD

DIARY ENTRY SIX

I should have eaten the soup. My stomach grumbled as I stared at the orangey blob shining on the floor like a sorority dare. *How much are you willing to degrade yourself for what you want? How hungry are you?*

I'd not yet reached the lick-substances-off-a-floor level of calorie deprivation, though I considered that I would. Unmasked Fawkes had warned that seeing him changed everything. No doubt he was referring to keeping me alive. Kidnapping and blackmail are federal crimes on par with murder, and he's much more likely to face punishment now that I can describe him.

Should my dad read the above sentence someday, I'm sure he'll blanch at my frankness. I can picture him shaking his head, lamenting yet another poor decision by his regrettably sensitive, artsy only child, thinking me illogical enough to give the kidnappers ideas. This diary, after all, is no more secure than this room. My captors can access it whenever they like.

Despite what Brian Ingold might assume, however, I'm not pouring out my thoughts without any concern for my safety. It's just that, regardless of what he believes, some things matter more than physical or material well-being. I, too, care about my legacy. As bad as my current circumstances are, my fear of being remembered as a victim is worse.

I know the media will paint me as a poor little rich girl, too spoiled to fend for herself, a zoo-raised lion waiting for her keepers to deliver the next meal despite gazelles in the enclosure. Whatever happens, it's important to me that people know I fought. I argued. I *tried*.

Still, I'm guessing my jailers will read this, so I'm not sharing anything that they don't know. Even my ability to listen through the vent isn't a secret—at least, it hasn't been for the past few writings.

After Fawkes left, I listened beneath the vent, waiting for him to discuss my fate with Ghost Face. By the time I stood up, my backside throbbed as though hours had passed, though it was possible that little time had gone by at all. The mattress, thin as it was, was hotel grade in comparison to the cement ground. And I wasn't used to sitting on a floor.

I headed toward the bed, weaving around ceramic chips. One side of the soup bowl had shattered while the other remained intact, as if a desperate chicken had pecked itself free of its eggshell. Most of the shards were too small to cause more damage than a splinter, but one piece appeared promising: a triangle fragment with one rounded edge and a sharp point.

I plucked it from the mess and then swept the rest of the shrapnel into the corner with the side of my sneaker. I'm sure folks on Reddit will argue that I should have fashioned all the broken pieces into some sort of booby trap, road spikes to pierce my kidnappers' boots, perhaps. For them I'll note that there was no way to get the fragments to stand pointy end up without adhesive. Stepping on a pile of bowl, I'm sure, would only have annoyed my assailants, not disabled them.

The triangle piece wouldn't do much either. Still, I felt better holding it. At a minimum, I could cause a distracting flesh wound, provided Fawkes didn't snatch my weapon during my first stabbing attempt. Unfortunately, there weren't many places to hide the thing. Beneath the covers might have been a possibility, but I feared rolling onto it by mistake after falling into an exhausted stupor. And I'll remind dear Reddit escape experts that under the bed wasn't an option. The mattress was propped atop pallets.

My gaze rested on the book. It could hide my Stone Age spearhead.

I slipped it inside the pages like a bookmark and then plopped on the bed. Just as I was putting my feet up, a door opened.

"Back so soon?"

I turned to the entrance, expecting my female kidnapper to be standing on the threshold. The door was closed. All I saw were blank walls leading up to the ceiling vent.

"I went to the store." A voice, heavy as wet snow, tumbled down into the room. "There was an accident."

"What do you mean?" My female captor sounded concerned. I figured her care was more about providing proof of life along with an eventual ransom demand. She'd made her feelings about me all too clear.

"She tossed soup on my mask," Fawkes said. "It got all in the eye slits."

"And you went for cleaning supplies?" the woman asked. "You know we have—"

"She saw me."

Silence.

"I didn't mean for it to happen." Fawkes's voice was raised, a defensive response to whatever disappointed glare his partner was no doubt sharing. "My eyeballs were on fire."

Footsteps paced the ceiling. "She barely saw you though, right? I mean, how great a description could she get in a few seconds?"

"A good one."

The footsteps stopped. "You didn't immediately cover your face?"

"I had to keep her from getting out."

"The garage is locked." The quiver in my female captor's voice became a seethe. "Who cares if she—"

"She could have come up here."

"AND?" This word popped through the surface. "SO?"

If Fawkes responded, I couldn't hear it. I stood on my tippy-toes, straining to make out a mutter or whisper.

"I've worked it out," he said finally, his voice at regular volume. "It'll be a bit more difficult if my description is out there—"

"Oh, a bit?"

"It's not like she took a photo," Fawkes retorted. "If the eventual sketch is good, there are other ways out of the country. We can rent a boat. I'll bleach my hair, get contacts. Grow a beard." Heavy footsteps emphasized this last statement. "You always liked me with facial hair."

"I don't know."

"We'll disappear," Fawkes continued. "Same as planned. You, me, and a glittering sea. Swaying in a hammock . . . by our beach bungalow. Killing time, the way we like . . ."

The pauses in his cadence confused me. If Fawkes had been wearing his voice changer, reverb would have explained the need for extra space between words. Without it, there was no echo to wait out.

"Stop." The woman's voice no longer threatened to boil over. I moved toward the vent, trying to figure out what was happening. Was he restraining her? "Stop." A playful giggle accompanied the command. It occurred to me how Fawkes had lowered the temperature of their argument. They were making out.

More footsteps sounded. I considered that he had led her toward a bed. I'd have to listen to them get it on, aroused by the possibility of absconding to a beach bungalow with my parents' money. Maybe I had reached sorority pledge–level depravation.

A door opened.

"Wait, what are you doing?" Fawkes asked. "I thought—"

"It's alright. I'll fix this."

The door slammed.

I scurried to the bed, again determined to hide my ability to listen in. A moment later, I changed course. I'd blown a chance to escape Fawkes earlier by not being near the door, and if my female captor was coming down, it was likely for one reason. Hiding was no longer an option.

I grabbed my bowl shard from its book hiding spot, rushed back to the exit, and then stood beside it, back against the wall. My plan was about as baked as an ice cream cake, though I had the shape of it. When the woman entered, I would shove the door back at her, slamming it into her head and knocking her gun out of her hand. Then I'd charge forward to whatever exit she'd used, ideally before Fawkes could block the way.

I held my breath, feeling for vibrations through the drywall: the shake of a door slam or the thud of footsteps. Only the thumping of my heart came through, its rhythm so fast I feared passing out.

A click interrupted my ragged breaths. The doorknob turned. I rotated ninety degrees, raised my hands to my chest, and directed all my energy into my triceps.

The door pushed back.

I reacted too soon, slamming my hands into the wood before it had picked up any momentum for me to return. An *oomph* responded, followed by a more forceful push that knocked the ceramic shiv from my hand.

Weaponless, I drove my shoulder into the retracting panel, hoping to hear the crunch of damaged plastic on the other side. Instead, I heard the bowl shard splinter beneath my sneakers and a dull thud. I hadn't even broken her LED mask.

She shoved the wood back in my direction. There was no winning this match of tether-door. I rounded to the opening, ready to throw fists for the first time . . . ever.

The woman stood before me, rubbing her forehead. Adrenaline kept me from registering that the space framed by her hood wasn't black plastic but tan skin. I was too focused on the emptiness behind her, the darkness that had to be an exit.

I rushed forward, checking her shoulder as I headed into the garage. The black opening was ten yards at most. I could make it. I had to.

Fawkes's large body suddenly filled my escape hatch. "How she'd get out?"

I whipped around, a rat searching for another tunnel. Brown eyes stared back at me, uncovered by black netting. Ghost Face had removed her mask.

"She was waiting for me," she said, still rubbing her forehead. "She must have known I was coming down. The walls here lack soundproofing. I bet she can hear us."

The revelation of my eavesdropping might have scared me had I not already been frantic. My female captor no longer cared if I could describe her. There could be only one reason.

"Alice." Her raised voice urged me to look at her. "We'd like to talk."

I averted my gaze to the floor. "Just let me out. Let me go."

"We will," she said.

The promise compelled eye contact. Ghost Face's real visage was striking. Irises the color of cognac. A full, shapely mouth. There was no lineup in the world where she wouldn't stand out. She'd be a celebrity posing for a mug shot.

"I don't believe you," I said.

A heavy hand landed on my shoulder, emphasizing my point. Fawkes wasn't going to guide me to the exit.

"Well, I can understand that," Ghost Face replied. Though, without her mask, the moniker didn't really fit. "But by the time you leave here, you will. What's more, you're going to believe in what we're doing. You won't want to turn us in."

My captors liked manipulation games. This was no doubt another one: assuring me of my safety so they could more easily hurt me later.

"I won't turn you in." I looked my female captor directly in the eye. "I won't say anything if you open the garage. I'll hitch a ride home, tell everyone it was all a joke. That crazy riddle."

"It's no joke." Her expression grew stern. "You'll understand."

"I don't want to understand."

I shrugged off unmasked Fawkes's hand. His mitt fell on my bicep and closed tight, a literal handcuff placed too high. He began walking, pulling me with him. "It'll be okay."

In front of me, the woman held open my cell door. "I know the Matrix has been good to you, Alice Ingold. But it's time to wake up."

CATHERINE NEWHOUSE INGOLD

THE DAY AFTER

How many FBI agents does it take to answer a kidnapper's riddle? More than one, apparently. For that matter, it also requires more than a genius technologist, multiple law enforcement officials, bleeding-edge AI software, and a desperate mom.

Four of us are gathered in my second-floor sitting room: Brian, Detective Frazier, Special Agent PJ Lee, and myself. Our superhero-sized detective entered along with Lee's 125 pounds of federal force about thirty minutes after I phoned the station, ten minutes after the cops guarding my house from across the street repositioned themselves in front of my door. Despite Lee's slight stature, he barged in like he owned the place, marching around closing blinds and shutting off lights, ordering me back from my windows.

I'd been monitoring the press from behind gauze curtains in the second-floor hallway. Minutes earlier, I watched a tide of reporters engulf Brian's Tesla Roadster. At first the crowd largely ignored his sports car, perhaps assuming he was already in the house. Then someone recognized the rectangular face and unkempt hair, and the media crashed upon his vehicle, a polluted wave of bodies and broadcast detritus.

Leaning on his horn did little to make anyone disperse. It wasn't until Frazier appeared, blue light whirling on his Dodge's dashboard, that the sea parted, allowing Brian to turn into the driveway. Even then, it took a siren's wail to truly drive back the human flood surging toward the garage.

"People want more and *mores*." Lee mutters the kidnappers' lines as if they're catchy lyrics. He's not talking to us—at least, not directly. There's no eye contact. Since watching the video, he's kept to himself in the corner, staring out the northeast-facing windows.

The view of our local yacht harbor was a selling point. Before all this, I could spend hours staring at the docked vessels, imagining where they'd been and still would go—entertaining myself with the possibilities while waiting for Alice to return from school. The sight now has the opposite effect. The water's an endless expanse, growing darker as the day moves on. It could hide anything.

Lee finally faces the group. "Why the *s*? Was she slurring the word or changing it?"

"She didn't seem drugged," I say. "Right, Brian?"

Brian looks up from his laptop. On his screen are diagrams tying phrases in Alice's speech to other words. Without my glasses, the graphs resemble a PET scan of brain synapses, a neural network lighting up with possible solutions to the kidnappers' cryptic poem.

So far, none of Zelos's suggestions have been remotely feasible. Among the top proposals? Alice was trapped in a Japanese facility manufacturing clean-air systems for the electronics industry. Brian's software had focused on the "clean room" phrase and the poem's haiku structure rather than the logistics of smuggling a reluctant English-speaking woman out of the United States. Alice couldn't enter another country sans passport or pass through airport security in an obviously inebriated state. Moreover, a naturally blond, blue-eyed girl in distress wouldn't exactly go unnoticed in Japan, where 99 percent of the population is Asian.

Even so, Brian placed a call to Airtech's CEO and the American embassy in Tokyo. He wasn't willing to accept that, when he needed it most, his greatest invention's advice was worth less than his wife's commonsense considerations—even though Agent Lee agreed that Alice was most likely being held within driving distance, in the state or in Oregon. Maybe Canada.

"Forget the riddle." Brian shuts his computer. "It's nonsense to distract us. At the end of the day, this is about money, or leverage to ask for proprietary info that will make them even more money."

"I don't know." I touch his hand, a silent signal that we're in this together, though I'm about to disagree and probably upset him. "These guys want publicity for some sort of message. Why else tip off the media?"

Frazier leans forward in the armchair across from us. "We don't know that they did."

"Who else would have?" I ask.

Frazier exchanges a glance with Lee, seeking approval to share something. A chin bob grants permission. "You contacted her friends," Frazier says.

I sense blame. "And you knew I intended to do that. We wanted to find out who knew where she lived. I didn't go around telling people she was kidnapped."

Frazier regards me like I'm the patsy, unwittingly involved in a crime above my pay grade. "You really didn't mention to anyone that Alice was in danger?"

My cheeks grow hot. "I, well, I told Monica. But she's Alice's best friend. She wouldn't say anything."

Lee looks at me like I've testified to the accuracy of an influencer's Instagram photos.

"She wouldn't," I insist. "She loves Alice."

Brian pats my hand—no doubt to lessen the impact of his coming criticism. "How the press found out is irrelevant," he says, surprising me. "What's important is finding out what they want—and if it's money, which it hopefully is, paying off the right people. We need to get a message to these guys, tell them we're willing to negotiate for our daughter."

Lee transfers his disapproving expression to Brian. "Paying these folks won't guarantee Alice's safety."

"Sure it will." Brian rises with his hands on his hips, assuming his CEO stance. "If the number is big enough, and we set the right conditions, why wouldn't it?"

I hate the idea of bargaining for my daughter, treating her like an expensive piece of real estate to bid upon. However, my husband has a point. These people didn't pick Alice up off the street. They knew who she was. Who *we* are.

"I can go to the bank today," I offer. "Determine how much of the family trust is liquid."

Lee finally decides to fully engage. He approaches the room's center, passing a money tree in a golden planter. Karin, a Chinese American friend, gave it to me as a fortieth-birthday present. I've nurtured the plant for years, watering and pruning it, plying it with extra minerals and attention, ensuring it has the ideal mix of sunlight and shade to thrive. And it has. Its braided trunk resembles intertwined arms. Its leaf clusters are long waving fingers shimmering with sweet sap, a green hand dipped in a honey jar. It's beautiful. Healthy. But Lee could pick it up and toss it out the window right now, and I'd be powerless to stop him.

"The position of the United States government is that we don't negotiate with terrorists or kidnappers." He makes eye contact with both Brian and me individually. "Every person who pays encourages more criminals to see American citizens as ATM cards. Take one and name your price."

I stand alongside my husband. "They *can* name their price. I'll pay anything."

Lee rubs his neck. "Anything? A million? Ten? A hundred?"

"Whatever it takes," I retort.

He raises his eyebrows as if I've said something shocking. "Terrorists can do a lot of damage with ten million dollars."

I gather that Lee is thinking of the attacks on American soil: 9/11, the Oklahoma City bombing, the Boston Marathon explosions. Alice's life must seem insignificant to him in comparison to such carnage. Saving Americans is his job, however. Saving my daughter is mine.

"Then don't let them use the money." I look first at Lee and then turn my attention to Frazier. "Make sure you catch them."

Frazier nods sympathetically, though his words are anything but. "And if we don't?"

Worrying about atrocities exceeds my current bandwidth. I can only care about my kid.

Brian employs his do-as-I-say boss voice. "Make sure you track them down."

Love for him suddenly washes over me, flushing out any lingering resentment for his abandonment last night. Everyone always assumes Brian's genius is the attraction for me, and that's sort of true. The appeal isn't so much his brain, though, as the influence his intelligence allows him to wield. It's intoxicating being with someone who not only dreams of getting things done on a grand scale but *does them*—has the *power* to impose his will. And now, finally, when it counts most, he's leveraging that power on behalf of our family.

Lee straightens to his full height. The fact that he's squaring up at all shows confidence in his position. Brian may have superior size and wealth, but Lee has the strength of US bureaucracy. "Paying a ransom is a violation of—"

Frazier rises, his overwhelming stature silencing his federal counterpart. "This is all premature. We don't even know how to contact these people yet. The video didn't include an address, and the message came from an unregistered pay-as-you-go phone. Those things are largely untraceable. Even if we could track the burner down, I'm sure the kidnappers weren't so naive as to send a message from wherever they're holding Alice. So far they've shown a level of sophistication in planning. They knew enough to turn off her laptop's location-sharing and disconnect it from the internet."

Brian directs his boss energy at Frazier. "What do you suggest, then? It's not like the riddle has real clues. If it did, my software would have solved it. I mean: 'willingly go offshore but the remains stay'? What is that? What remains?"

The answer must dawn on him, because Brian covers his mouth rather than voicing our worst fears. "It's gibberish," he mutters.

As much as I wish I could agree, I can't. The Zodiac Killer's cipher wasn't gobbledygook. Someone cracked it after fifty-one years.

Of course, I can't wait that long.

"The kidnappers want this riddle solved." I grasp for Brian's hand, forcing him to look at me. "They know these words will mean something to somebody. We need to crowdsource the answer, like Alice said."

Brian shakes his head. "There's no logic to this."

"We'll hedge our bets," I respond. "We'll ask for help *and* add incentive, tell the press we're willing to pay for any information leading to Alice's safe return."

Lee groans. "You can't pay a ransom."

"Not a ransom. A reward." I hold up a hand, silencing any further objections. "Either someone will figure this out and lead us to our daughter, or the kidnappers will turn her in themselves."

ALICE INGOLD

DIARY ENTRY SEVEN

Leaving the Matrix was better for Neo. Sure, he awoke to discover himself trapped in a pod with plugs connected to his naked body, another organic battery for superintelligent computers. But he was soon picked up by friends and informed of his great purpose to outthink the machines and save humanity.

I, on the other hand, was forced back into a windowless room by two zealots intent on brainwashing me. Instead of expanding my worldview, they wanted to shrink it to fit their own.

They requested the "opportunity" to explain themselves and join me in *my* room. The sudden obsequiousness was a tactic, obviously. Still, I used it to my advantage. If they wanted my permission, I said, they could get me more soup—in a closed can this time.

How long had passed since they'd left for Campbell's, I didn't know. Time was a theory inside my concrete box. Fawkes's mention of noon could only orient me so much. Had my latest escape attempt taken an hour or mere minutes? Had they driven to a distant store or rushed upstairs to a cupboard?

My stomach's grumble suggested it was nearing dinnertime, though it could easily have been announcing a desire to break our forced fast. I burrowed beneath the blanket atop my bed, trying not to think of my hunger or the riddle video or my survival chances now that I'd seen both of my kidnappers' faces. Instead, I conjured mental meditation images—waterfalls of light, stars twinkling in black holes. I tried contemplating the universe and my insignificant place in it, giving myself over to a higher power. My mom can complain all she wants about Simon—my peace, love, and pot-smoking ex-boyfriend—but he would have been pretty Zen in this situation. Just saying.

I was not Zen. My visualizations all dissipated before fully materializing, sand sculptures in a storm. Mindfulness is *not* an area of strength for me, nor most people my age. I hail from a generation raised with pocket computers capable of answering any question, or at least suggesting a solution. My peers and I don't ruminate. We zone out to thirty-second-long dog-and-cat videos.

A knock interrupted my attempts at inner peace.

"You decent?" It was my female captor's voice but with added sugar.

"Does it matter?" I shouted back, determined not to be fooled by the saccharine act.

"I thought we might talk," she said. "Like we discussed."

Let the indoctrination begin.

I refused to give my torturers the satisfaction of an invitation, but I did lean over to shut the porta potty's lid. After they left, I'd succumbed to nature's call. The scent of urine wafting from the bucket was bad enough without stomaching any comments.

The door cracked open as I pushed the lid into place. I returned to the mattress and pressed my back against the cement wall, bracing for whatever methods my new friends had in store to break me down. Sleep torture was an option. The light switch for the room was located outside. They could pretend to forget about shutting off the overheads, making it impossible for me to reach a state of rapid eye movement.

Lack of dreams could be fatal. I'd read an article once about a government study charting the relationship between REM sleep and death. Losing just 5 percent of one's dreams correlated with a 17 percent increase in the chances of dying young.

She entered, arms extended. "My version of an olive branch." In one hand was a butcher paper–wrapped cylinder. "It's the veggie delight," she explained, coming closer. "Lettuce, tomatoes, green peppers, onions, and olives."

Saliva built in my mouth, but I refused to become Pavlovian. "I wanted soup. In a sealed can. Remember?"

She glanced over her shoulder at maskless Fawkes behind her. He stepped forward, reaching into a pants pocket. Gone was his all-black bank robber ensemble. A green sweatshirt had replaced his prior hoodie, though he still wore black cargo pants with enough pockets to fit all the urban male's emergency tools: wallet, condoms . . . utility knife?

Something metal flashed between his fingers. A snap followed.

I winced, expecting the switchblade.

"It's a can opener." He dug into another pocket. A small can of minestrone soup emerged in his palm. "The sandwich is probably better, though."

The woman pushed her offering toward me. "Swear I haven't opened it."

Precise wrapping testified in her favor. Though it was possible she or her boyfriend had learned food prep techniques while working some service job, I couldn't picture either of them behind a deli counter. Neither seemed the type to cater to others.

Then again, John Wayne Gacy had volunteered as a hospital clown.

I pointed to the silver peeking from Fawkes's palm. "I'll open the soup. I don't trust you doing it."

The guy considered the can opener. It was about three inches of stainless steel, the kind doled out to military members in World War II but purchasable on Amazon as a nostalgia piece. It wasn't exactly a knife, though it was better than nothing.

"I'll open it right here," he said. "In front of you."

I gave them my best offended expression. "The masks are off, and you want me to believe whatever you two have to say, but you won't let me open my own can?"

They exchanged a look. With their faces exposed, I could read it: *How much are we invested in this trust exercise?*

The girl's gaze darted to one of Fawkes's pockets. I read that glance as well. *You have the gun?*

Fawkes tossed the can onto the bed. It bounced as it landed beside me, emphasizing the mattress's lack of give. I held out my hand for the opener.

He slipped it to me, standing back as soon as it was between my fingers. "Careful with that thing."

I turned my attention to the sandwich. "On second thought, I'll eat that first."

His counterpart looked to the wrapped cylinder in her hands as if she'd forgotten all about it. When her eyes met mine again, they were narrowed. "We wouldn't want you going hungry," she said, extending her carrot while making clear a stick was behind it. Her threat wasn't subtle: *Use the can opener as a weapon and no more food.*

I accepted the veggie delight and peeled back the wrapper striptease-style, slowly, so as not to reveal how much I wanted it.

"May I sit?" she asked.

Rather than answering, I finished exposing a corner of bread. Lettuce peeked out from between two sourdough buns. I noted cucumber slices. I love cucumber.

"Is that alright?" Again, she gestured to the mattress.

I tore off a piece of bread and popped it into my mouth. For a moment, I didn't chew, instead letting my saliva soften the starches, savoring the flavors of dough and oil. There was a vinaigrette of some kind.

The girl formerly known as Ghost Face took a seat on the bed's corner, even though I hadn't granted her permission. "I know this is difficult, Alice. If you hear us out, I really think you'll feel differently about everything. You won't see this time as us holding you against your will. You'll see it for what it is—"

"An extortion attempt." I was chewing, so my tone lacked the intended bite.

She glanced toward the door, where her man had retreated, a prison guard resuming his post. "A chance to wake up the world," he said. "If it were about money, don't you think we'd have asked for a ransom?"

I met his eyes. "I don't know what you'd do. If I did, I'd have gotten out by now."

She faced me. Her position on the bed's edge recalled a friend at a middle school sleepover. This was a girl primed to gossip. "I want to tell you how I came to be here."

I took another bite. "You drove."

"Actually, I drove," Fawkes said.

"Really?" I feigned shock. "Hard to tell locked in a trunk."

My female captor visibly stiffened. I chewed, silencing any more quips. Testing their politeness, throwing them off their game, made me feel somewhat in control of the situation, or at least of my mind. Deep down, however, I knew they had all the power. Somewhere in this room—likely in the guy's pocket—was a pistol. My life was at their discretion.

"I get what you mean," I mumbled.

The woman took a deep breath. "I was the first in my family to go to college," she exhaled. "My parents were immigrants. They moved here for my education, so I could go to one of the schools in American movies." She smiled to herself. "And I did."

"They must be so proud." I delivered the line as deadpan as possible, turning my congratulations into an insult.

Her smile went wan. "Yeah. Anyway, I earned a finance degree. It came with about a hundred thousand dollars in debt, but I was sure I'd be able to pay it off. I'd be working for Goldman or BlackRock analyzing securities, right? Picking winners. Shorting losers. A few years ago, that's where the money was, you know?" She chuckled to herself. "So that was my dream. Work hard. Earn a good living. Buy my parents their own house."

I glared at her. "Figured kidnapping was a faster route to success?"

Her expression darkened. She walked over to Fawkes, wanting his support, or maybe to emphasize that the muscle was on her side. "I was never going to get that house. The job I was studying for—the one I went into debt for—doesn't exist. These billion-dollar investment banks, they're not estimating EBITDA and interviewing CEOs anymore, making decisions on who's likely to succeed or fail. They're trading based on momentum. They all have some dude with a data science degree figuring out patterns in stocks' movements; what goes up a basis point in a minute tends to rise two basis points in a minute and ten seconds. Stuff like that. This quantitative analyst then writes code to buy and sell based on his formula, which doesn't give a crap about the company whose shares it's trading. What firms do, whether their employees are smart—that's all irrelevant to these programs. And soon the data guy won't even have a job. AI will identify the patterns and write the algorithms without any human intervention. Just ask your dad."

For a moment, I felt something approaching sympathy. Then her boyfriend squeezed her shoulder, and I was reminded of how he'd dragged me back to the car. Neither of these people deserved my pity.

"Finance has never been a field about fairness or altruism," I shot back. "It's about risk. You made a bet in the hope of making a killing. It didn't pay off. Happens. When it does, people don't become kidnappers. They find another way to contribute. Learn another skill—"

"With what money?" she snapped.

I bit off a chunk of sandwich in case my lack of *understanding* was punished by her snatching my food. "Someone moved your cheese." I chewed while talking. "Maybe the world's better off having smart people choose other careers."

She smirked. "Oh, like the arts?"

Apparently, she'd done her research. The realization turned the bread into paste between my teeth. "How long were you two planning this?"

It wasn't the first time I asked. The woman's smirk widened into something truly Regina George–worthy. "People think our generation has the attention span of a squirrel, always darting to the next thing. But we can see what's coming."

She grabbed the doorknob, turned it, and then paused, fighting with herself about something. A moment later, she was facing me. Again. "Maybe you can't understand what it's like to *need* to work. Your basic income has been guaranteed since birth. You don't know what it's like to be stuck with college loans for a useless degree, forced to choose between driving an Uber or doing rich people's grocery shopping while you try to figure out what you can possibly be good for."

I swallowed hard. "You think I've had it so easy, huh? That I don't worry about what I'll do after college? I want to be a writer, and it's been made clear to me that there's little future in that. I'm no good at prompt engineering or telling the software what to do and how. I worked for my father for less than three months, and he . . ."

My throat closed before I could finish. It's funny how you can think you've gotten over something—think you've put it into perspective, digested the other side's arguments, and swallowed the whole affair—only to discuss it and have all those sour emotions come bubbling back up.

Ghost Face wasn't listening anyway. She pulled back the door, oblivious to my becoming upset or, more likely, unwilling to stick around and develop any sympathy for me.

Seeing that door open—knowing it would soon close without me on its other side—sent me into a panic. In a bid to preserve my sanity, I'd chosen the wrong strategy: fighting my captors when I should have been pretending to buy their arguments. If this woman and her partner thought me impenetrable, they'd lock me in this room to rot. I was only getting out of here if they believed I wouldn't turn them in.

"You're right. I don't know what it's like to worry about money. But I realize it's not easy to change course when the career landscape is constantly shifting."

She rolled her eyes. The polite veneer was slipping. "You don't know yet. I know you don't. You will, though. Because wealth is a wall, but it's not a dome."

I kept staring at her while sliding my hand along the mattress, feeling for the can opener I'd dropped for the sandwich. If she changed course and came after me, I needed to be armed.

Her gaze flitted to the movement. I pretended to fidget with the blanket. "Wealth is not a dome. Is that another riddle?"

She chuckled. "More of an analogy. Because you know what happens when the rest of us—the rest of the hoi polloi—get frustrated and depressed from too little opportunity? From a system tailor-made to concentrate wealth among the people born having it all?"

The opener's metal tip pricked my forefinger. "You eat cake?"

She smirked, possibly at my Marie Antoinette joke, though more likely at my obvious attempt to conceal a weapon. If the gun was in Fawkes's pocket as I suspected, she'd have little reason to fear a can opener.

She cocked her head. "We come for people like you."

The coldness of her words robbed me of my fight. I was not built like this woman. I couldn't steal a person's freedom and then mock her about it. Can opener or not, I wouldn't win a physical altercation with someone this ruthless.

I watched her stride out, head held high with the confidence of having made her point. Fawkes gave me a slight wave and turned as well.

I shot up from the bed. "Wait—"

He slammed the door behind him.

My heart thudded against my rib cage. Neither of my captors had indicated when they'd return. All I had was half a sandwich, a soup can, a metal opener, a few swallows of water, and shards of a bowl that could maybe be used to scratch tally marks into the wall. I doubted I'd carve more than seven days before I stopped being lucid. Could they leave me in here that long?

Though I hadn't managed to picture a waterfall of light earlier, I could imagine myself dying of thirst. I could visualize my skin becoming dry and flaky. Hair shedding. Lips cracking. Eyes sinking back into their sockets, burning from a lack of tears.

I palmed the can opener. The tool might not be capable of removing the doorknob or threatening my captors, but it did promise options.

In the end, I'd have at least one choice left.

CATHERINE NEWHOUSE INGOLD

THE DAY AFTER

After this, I'll have to move. My house has become a television studio. Someone, no doubt one of the producers rearranging my living room, lowered the shades to block the daylight. Sunshine is no good for news, apparently. Head-sized lights have replaced the natural glow. They shine through translucent screens, casting the room in a somber gray tone. It looks like rain.

The setup fits the story I've pledged to share—or, more accurately, the one Lee promised his source at the national news desk that I would tell. I haven't spoken much to the journalist who will interview me, though I've gone over bullet points with her "bookers."

Cameras point at a swivel chair moved to face a white sofa. Brian and I will take the love seat, I assume. The anchor, Evelyn Diaz, hovers by the equipment, her face vaguely familiar even though I haven't watched the news in years. I recognize her from gym televisions and doctors' waiting rooms. She's been a background actor in my life for decades. I never imagined she'd become a supporting character.

She flashes an awkward smile as I approach. We've been formally introduced, though I gather she doesn't wish to talk until we're filming.

Her producer insisted that they capture my "spontaneous reactions"—a.k.a. my tears. Repeating the same story too many times, they fear, could make me stoic.

They needn't worry. Every time the underground spring of my emotions seems tapped, I picture another indignity Alice might be suffering, and the aquifer refills. It'll take all my willpower *not* to blubber through the entire interview.

I nod at Diaz and make my way to the hot seat where Brian's already claimed a cushion. He stares ahead as a pink-haired makeup artist attacks his T-zone with a fan brush. His nose fails to squinch as powder sprinkles its ski-jump tip. Since Zelos went public, Brian's become a regular on the business broadcast channels. He's inured to women painting on tans, I suppose, transforming the boyish engineer I married into an alpha-male specimen befitting his CEO and founder titles.

CEO. Founder. I always knew Brian would have those labels. I just thought they could coincide with other ones: Husband. Father. I've since learned that a human being, even a genius one, can only hold so many positions, and a man truly focused on changing the world can't trouble himself with something as small as the operations of his own family. That's why I'm the COO and CCO—chief caregiving officer—of our little unit: Alice and me. I'm an engineer of sorts, too, albeit a social one.

Once Alice was born, I dedicated myself to helping Brian and her connect. My success rate hasn't been stellar. Brian was always too busy to care about Alice's grades, or writing competitions, or track meets. And after a while, Alice stopped seeking his attention or approval.

At some point last year, she changed her mind. Alice asked to intern at Zelos. Her desire was a shock for both Brian and me. Technology had never particularly interested her. But with graduation on the horizon and friends like Monica vying for jobs at big firms it made sense that she'd want to give the corporate world a shot. I think she also realized that she'd soon be out of our house for good, and out of Brian's sight and mind. She must have considered a summer job at his company some sort of last-ditch bonding effort.

In retrospect, I should have warned her against working for him. However, I was also hopeful. Alice was nearly an adult, and a smart one. I thought that might be enough for Brian—that *she* would be enough.

But nothing is ever *enough* for my husband. Not his success. Not Alice. Certainly not me. The world itself doesn't even measure up. Why else would he be so intent on changing it?

The thought of Alice's last interaction with her father threatens tears. I assume that the makeup artist notices because she shifts her attention from Brian to me.

"Sit for a touch-up?" She gestures to the couch, a weak smile on her bright-red lips. If I hazarded a guess, I'd put her at Alice's age. A rash of acne peppers her forehead, though she's covered it with skin-colored pimple patches nearly the same shade as her foundation. "Real quick?" she asks.

Objecting would take more energy than acquiescing. I plop down beside Brian and submit to the same powder brush. The woman applies so much to my nose that it seems like she's trying to erase it from my face. I imagine I'll resemble some sort of Kabuki performer when she finishes.

"Really, I'm fine," I say.

"You're a little red, honey." She indicates the lights. "And these add glare and heat. We can't have you sweating everything off."

"I might cry it all off."

She gives me a pitying smile and pulls a spray bottle from the black apron covering her clothing. "Not if I can help it. Close your eyes."

Again, I do as I'm told. A mist coats my face as if I've passed the open door to a steam room.

My makeup artist talks as she sprays. "I lost my job for a while during COVID," she says, revealing that she's older than I'd assumed. "In news, the makeup department's all private contractors, so it's easy for them to end our employment. I spent a lot of time crying about that. I was going on job interviews, though, so I needed to look bright eyed and rosy cheeked. This spray. Boy." The droplets stop hitting my face. "Lifesaver."

I open my eyes to see a handheld mirror. My reflection is me, only older. Fear and lack of sleep have sapped the filler from my face. I appear more my age than I have in years.

The young woman smiles at me, searching for some signal that I'm satisfied with her work. I try to return her expression, but it must not reach my eyes. Her face falls. "You don't like it?"

"It's fine," I respond. "Thank you."

The woman offers another smile before slinking away, revealing Evelyn receiving the same treatment from another makeup artist. Unlike me, however, the reporter isn't silent as her face is patted and drawn upon. She talks to the producer who'd preinterviewed me over the phone. "This will lead the hour," she says, ignoring the gloss tracing her bottom pout. "Has to."

The producer taps a pen against a clipboard. "Only competition's the piece on the housing crisis. Oh, and Elon Musk added a billion to his wealth today. Something to do with Tesla beating earnings projections."

"This has to top business, wouldn't you think?" Evelyn focuses on my ceiling as her makeup artist applies mascara to her lower lids. "I mean, you've seen the photos."

"Pretty blond doesn't hurt," the producer concedes. "But they didn't ask for a ransom."

Evelyn glances in my direction, sensing my glare. My daughter isn't just some "pretty blond" who might lead the hour and boost Evelyn's career. She's Alice. My Alice.

"She's on track to graduate with honors, you know." My voice trembles with rage. "She's a writer. The stories she could tell you. I wanted to be a writer once, too, though I never had her talent. The poetry in her language. Beautiful. Like her heart. Alice has always been concerned with others around her, how they're doing, whether they need anything. When she was little, with the toys. If she had something, she wanted her friend to have it too. And if they couldn't have it also, she'd give it up right away. A tiny kid and still that . . . that . . . selfless."

Brian squeezes my hand. His stern expression warns me to stop my tirade.

I turn the heat of my gaze onto him. "You know that about her, right? When she worked for you, you must have seen how much she cared about the other employees around her. The way she would take time to listen to people. Not simply nod along, waiting for her turn to interject. Really listen. *Listen.* Did you see that? Did you?"

Brian looks away. "We're going to start soon."

"Apologies for the shoptalk." If Evelyn's truly embarrassed for her earlier remark, I can't tell as I'm blinking up at crown molding, trying not to ruin my freshly done makeup. I couldn't care less how I look, but I'd like to avoid a second powder-puff attack.

"We'll get started in a minute," she says.

Sixty seconds is more like six hundred. I take deep breaths to compose myself and fidget, rubbing my knuckles while watching the camera crew slap the final touches on their setups. Though Brian sits next to me, his stiff body language and far-off gaze convey he's not up for conversation, at least not with me. He's punishing me for yelling at him, I expect. We've already discussed anything worth saying, anyway. If he's having second thoughts about our game plan, he won't share them in front of live mics.

A skinny man tapes a micro-receiver to my lapel as a phone rings. The sound engineer looks to my pocket before shifting focus to Brian. "We'll need quiet on—"

Brian doesn't let him finish. He pulls the offending cell from his jacket pocket and answers with a loud "This is he," and "Good. *Arigatō.*"

The background noise fades as Brian heads to a corner, out of the direct line of mics and lenses. Everyone eavesdrops. They assume Alice's father wouldn't take a call minutes before going on national television if it weren't important. It could be the kidnappers.

"Konnichiwa, Shimizu-san," he says.

I guess that Brian's speaking to the clean-air company he phoned earlier. As much as I don't believe its executives will have anything useful to say, I scoot over to better hear the conversation.

"Chotto matte kudasai," Brian says, tripping on the double consonants, running them together like he's telling someone about Peter Piper's pickled peppers.

Brian pulls his phone away, squints, and then jabs a finger at the screen. He then fishes a case from another pocket, flicks it open like an agitated smoker, and pushes an earbud into his left ear. "Thank you for returning my call," he says.

His sentence is followed by a low-toned singsong that my American ears interpret as music rather than speech, though I realize it's the phone's software translating his words into Japanese. Brian presses a button, and the electronic voice ceases to emanate through his cell's speaker. Announcing, "That's better," he continues explaining himself in my mother tongue, apologizing for bothering the man and admitting that he knew Alice's presence in his factory would be unlikely. "I won't take up any more of your time."

I expect Brian to hang up. Instead, he nods and paces, listening. His brow furrows. I wonder if Zelos's translation app suffers from the same commonsense blind spots as the software Brian used to decode the riddle.

"Perhaps," Brian says. "Thank you."

He hangs up and then turns to the crowd. No one pretends *not* to have been watching. We all stare: the cops, the news producers, the anchor. Me.

"Any updates?" Evelyn asks from across the room.

Brian strides back to his seat. "I'm not sure."

Before he settles down, the producer holds out a hand for his phone. "Can't have it ringing when we're live."

Brian regards the woman like she's asked him for a blank check. He makes a show of turning off the ringer and then slips the device back into his pocket. "It's a work phone."

Giving up, the woman turns her attention to the cameramen and assistants all hovering around equipment. "Alright. Places, people. We begin in five."

I lean in closer to him. "What did he say?"

Brian turns to me, nose brushing my neck. His position tickles like a memory. When was the last time we nuzzled? For a second, I forget that he's simply trying to cover his lip movements with my hair.

"He reminded me of something. Semiconductors. They need clean rooms and air showers."

"Air showers?" I picture a faucet streaming purified oxygen. In my head it almost looks like— "A curtain," I say.

Brian nods. "We design chips here on the West Coast, but nearly all the fabrication takes place in Asia now. It's too expensive to run fabs here because of foreign subsidies. Plus, there are environmental and safety considerations."

I hear Alice's voice. "We willingly go offshore," I whisper, repeating her words.

"Yup." Brian's breath strokes my neck "And there's the 'mores' thing Lee pointed out. I don't think Alice was slurring. She was referring to—"

"Moore's law."

Brian's eyebrows rise. He's surprised I know this, though he shouldn't be. The belief that the number of transistors in a circuit double every year, allowing chips to shrink in size while improving processing power, is a basic commandment of the tech industry. Tech is mostly what Brian's talked about these past twenty years.

"Okay, people. Sixty seconds." The producer shouts the instruction from behind a cameraman. Evelyn stops hovering to take her seat across from Brian and me. She's HD flawless, thanks to the inch of powder atop her skin. I'll be talking to a real live filtered human.

The producer makes a hand motion reminiscent of a pit crew sending off a race car driver. Evelyn nods at me before turning her attention from my eyeline to a camera behind Brian's shoulder.

"Tragedy has struck an iconic American family." She speaks directly to the at-home audience. "Alice Ingold, the nineteen-year-old daughter of Zelos CEO Brian Ingold and his wife, shipping heiress Catherine Newhouse Ingold, is in grave danger tonight after being kidnapped from her Oakland, California, apartment by unknown assailants. We are *live* with the Ingolds, who, hours ago, received *not* a ransom demand but a *riddle* concerning her whereabouts. A riddle Alice herself encouraged them to share with the media."

Somewhere behind me, I hear my daughter. "In a clean room near . . . Behind a curtain of air."

Alice's words have meaning for the first time. She's in a room related to semiconductor fabrication. Though if Brian's right and the US offshores most—if not all—of its chip manufacturing, I don't see how she'd have gotten to such a place in a day. Without an airplane?

"How to fix all those in need?" she continues.

The references to car engines and military barracks are still confusing. Is Alice hinting that these computer chips are destined for military vehicles?

"Though the view be bleak," she finishes, "is what I see now."

I picture her staring out a window, eyes filled with frightened tears, worrying that the chances of us finding her are slim. My own lids grow heavy.

A pressure on my palm stops me from crying. Fingers lace through my own. I turn to see Brian staring, silently urging me to be strong—or at least not embarrass him.

The video finishes, and the anchor makes eye contact. "Thank you for speaking with me during this difficult time."

Brian's perpetually downturned lips pull in at the corners, a PR-trained attempt at a neutral expression. "We want our daughter home safe."

"And you're seeking the public's help with this . . . riddle," Evelyn adds.

Brian nods rather than responding. He hates to admit this. "We believe some of it relates to semiconductors. Clean rooms and Moore's law."

"Arguably, you have access to some of the most powerful generative AI software at your fingertips," Evelyn says. "You must be using it to solve this puzzle."

Brian turns into Rodin's *The Thinker*, chin dropping to a closed fist. He needs to choose his words carefully. Admitting that Zelos has offered *nothing* useful will result in the front page of every business section blasting his supposedly superhuman software's intelligence. If he oversells his firm's contribution, then the whole interview will be moot. The at-home audience will assume we don't need their assistance.

"We're exploring all avenues," I pipe up. "We're also offering a reward to anyone who can help us. Ten million dollars."

Evelyn's head moves forward an inch, a turtle popping from its shell. She didn't know the amount because, before this moment, Brian and I had only discussed it with each other. Lee suggested a paltry sum, no more than five figures. Anything larger, he said, and the police wouldn't be able to handle the volume of tips.

But Brian and I don't care about the cops' ability to work the phones. We want the nation knocking on doors. And we want her captors facing the worst prisoner's dilemma of their lives: continue their game for an uncertain payout or accept millions for ratting out their coconspirators.

"Ten million to solve the riddle?" Evelyn blinks rapidly.

"For information leading to Alice's safe return," I clarify. "It's not a one-off. We'll pay that to anyone who provides information resulting in Alice coming home, whether that's answering the riddle or sharing a sighting that leads to her whereabouts. Or finding her themselves."

As I speak, I catch sight of Lee behind a cameraman. He gestures emphatically toward Frazier. The detective, to his credit, appears calm, like he expected me to do this. As an officer who deals with the public, he's probably more accustomed to people lying and flouting authority than an FBI agent is.

Though Evelyn can't see Lee behind her, she must sense his agitation because she addresses his complaint. "You're not concerned this money will result in false leads?"

I shift my attention back to the anchor, even though my words are meant for the men behind her. "Of course we're concerned. But Alice is our daughter. Like any parents, we'll use whatever means we have at our disposal to get her home safely."

Evelyn adjusts her position in her seat, preparing to ask another question. Before she does, I turn my attention to the camera. The lens stares back at me, a vortex leading to other dimensions: private living rooms, phone screens, maybe even the kidnappers' house.

"Please," I say, breaking the fourth wall. "Anyone out there with any information, please help bring Alice back to us. She's a kind girl. Conscientious. An honors student at Berkeley. She volunteers. I'm certain she's scared and . . ." I trail off, unable to complete my thought without giving power to my worst fears.

Brian picks up where I left off. "She should be at home with her mother. She needs to come home."

Evelyn nods as if she sympathizes. The gleam in her eyes, however, tells a different story. I brace myself for a *gotcha* question.

"Why do you think Alice was targeted?"

"We assume because of our finances," I say.

"Yet the kidnappers didn't ask for a ransom."

Brian takes this one. "We believe they haven't gotten around to it yet."

"If they do, you'll pay it?" she asks.

Brian stares over the anchor's shoulder, challenging the officers behind her. "We've been advised against paying any ransom. The government is concerned about what these people might do with the money."

"But what would you do?" she asks.

I am not the strategic thinker that my husband is. Still, I can anticipate a few moves ahead on a chessboard. We can't answer this question. If we say no and the kidnappers intend to ask for a ransom, they could kill Alice. If we say yes, we're admitting that we would risk others' lives for our child's safety.

Again, I look directly into the camera. "I want to say to the kidnappers, please don't hurt my baby. She's a good person. If you knew her at all, you'd know that. She deserves a chance to—"

I start crying. The act isn't controlled enough to be conscious manipulation, yet I'm aware that my tears are furthering my objective. With me bawling, any combative questions from Evelyn will appear like she's bullying a distraught mother. Moreover, who can't sympathize with a woman willing to be reduced to a sniveling mess on national TV?

Evelyn turns to the camera over my shoulder. "A parent's love is priceless. Now back to Bill with a statement from the superintendent of police."

She's cutting short the interview rather than losing more control over it. That's fine with me. Brian and I have done what we intended.

Evelyn approaches and shakes my hand, promising to follow up and asking that I phone her with any developments. Her words fade into the background. Begging for my daughter's life has brought the threat into high relief again. I can think of nothing else.

The camera crew starts packing. I watch without moving, waiting to take direction from Lee or Frazier or anyone who'll give me some idea of what happens next.

A hand brushes my shoulder. I reach for it, expecting to feel Brian's thick fingers. Instead, I touch long nails. Brian, I realize, is already speaking to the detectives in front of me. Behind the light, I see his hands grasping his hips, prepared to lecture the officers poised to admonish him.

I turn to see the pink-haired makeup artist from earlier. "I'm so sorry you're going through this."

I nod, simultaneously grateful for and embarrassed by her pity. My brain flashes to me onstage, calling up the latest recipient of some need-based scholarship endowed by my family trust. Is this how they felt? Honored but ashamed?

"I know this may not be useful or whatever. But just in case . . ."

I nod again, albeit more stiffly than before. This is what Lee was warning about. I'm about to receive my first nonsense tip.

"When I was unemployed like I mentioned—in need, I guess—I stayed at a shelter for a bit. In Santa Clara County, of all places."

I want to be anywhere but on the receiving end of this woman's ten-million-dollar Hail Mary. Brian is feet away. I start to excuse myself. "I'm sorry, my—"

"The shelter was made up of these temporary structures," she continues. "Like barracks."

I step back, retreating toward Brian and the cops. "I should—"

"In the parking lot," she adds, raising her voice to cover the added distance between us, "of a former semiconductor factory."

I stop backtracking. One similarity could be mere coincidence, but two? A homeless shelter made of military barracks *and* an old semiconductor manufacturing plant?

I grasp her hand, clinging to this lifeline. The woman shakes as if we're sealing a business deal. "So if it's helpful . . ." She trails off rather than demanding ten million on the spot.

I drop her hand. "I'll need the address of this shelter."

ALICE INGOLD

DIARY ENTRY EIGHT

Loneliness is a form of torture. The Pope, various US presidents, and the American Senate have proposed banning solitary confinement in prisons due to the long-term psychological effects. After my kidnappers left, I shouted this through the door. Since they saw themselves as revolutionaries, I figured they'd be horrified to be equated with human rights violators. They might bring me a television or something.

But they didn't return. For some time after, I alternated between sitting on the bed and pacing. All the walking in circles made my bruises throb. Eventually, I decided my frustration required release in some form other than physical. I sang to myself. Talked to myself. Read my diary aloud.

In some of my entries, I sound annoyed with my parents. On some level, I guess I am. I realize how ungrateful that makes me seem, given all they're probably doing to save me—all I hope they're doing. I love them. Of course I do. Though I can't help but feel upset that I'm here more because of who they are than who I am.

Ghost Face's tirade betrayed the real reason she and her boyfriend picked me. It wasn't simply that the media would cover the disappearance of a wealthy, white coed. She hates me because of my folks. I'm the offspring of a prominent AI tech CEO and an old-money American heiress, the financial beneficiary of job-displacing software and a tax system that allows wealth to concentrate at the top like mountain snow. Or maybe ice caps are the wrong analogy since they melt to form rivulets that fill rivers, lakes, and public aquifers, and much of my family's money sits in the markets, swelling with the steady rise in American productivity, collecting dividends.

My family's fortune has convinced my kidnappers that I deserve this. If money buys happiness, then I've had more than my fair share. I can afford to suffer. Karma's a bitch and all.

Inherited wealth hasn't granted me the vault of joy that they think, however. There are downsides: unwanted attention from strangers who I wished never noticed me, too little attention from people I wished did. As privileged as it sounds, family money is a burden as well as a boon.

Take, for example, my dad's private plane. When I was little, it flew my mom and me around the world, usually to snag lunch with my father between meetings at this or that conference. I saw Paris and Tokyo before I saw the inside of a classroom. But that same plane took my dad away from me on birthdays and recitals. Track championships. Graduations.

I'm supposed to get my diploma next spring. I skipped a grade back in elementary, the result of my mom's supplemental homeschooling and, she claims, the Ingold genetics. I'm only sure about the former. In another life, one in which Catherine Newhouse hadn't signed on to run Brian Ingold's family affairs, she might have been a CEO herself. In this one, she poured all her type A energy into me.

Last summer, I tried showing my father the results of her hard work, and my own. I got an internship at Zelos—no doubt thanks to a reluctant boost from the boss. I'm sure he didn't love the idea of inviting me into his inner sanctum, but I couldn't see how else to spend quality time with him before permanently leaving the nest. And, truth be told, I was curious about the company he so clearly preferred to me. So I expressed interest, and my mom worked her magic, as always.

At first, I think my dad and I enjoyed the time together. I was awed by his work, and he reveled in seeing me speechless. Though my mom always said Dad was changing the world, I'd never really understood *how* until going behind the scenes at his company. Before then, my experience with Zelos's AI had been the same as the average American's, limited to free apps that primarily helped people complete tasks tangential to their core competencies and responsibilities. I knew it could write a decent essay for, say, a mathematician, but I wouldn't have wanted to hand in its work to my English professors. Sure, influencers used its AI filters on their posts, but real magazines would never employ its catfishing "enhancers" on their cover models. And yes, occasionally, more unnerving Zelos creations would go viral: a song that sounded exactly like a certain artist or a convincing fake celebrity endorsement. However, such works were usually revealed to be heavily influenced by skilled experts—real music producers, marketers, and editors who'd expanded upon Zelos's initial offerings.

The tech Zelos sold to companies was capable of far more than what I'd seen. My internship's first two months consisted of following my dad to meetings where Zelos's division heads showed off AI applications that could do everything from scan billions of cells for defects to predict demand for products based off real-time internet chatter, all without much, if any, human intervention. For the first time, I understood how my father's AI could cure cancer and upend entire industries. Brian Ingold, I realized, was *actually* a visionary.

And he was *my dad*. It was the latter relationship that encouraged him to take me to lunch one day toward the end of our summer. Mom had booked us at an omakase sushi place, no doubt because she'd wanted to ensure the experience lasted at least an hour.

The food was Michelin starred, though our conversation spoiled it to such a degree that the sight of raw fish—of any plated animal, really—now turns my stomach.

After greeting the chef in Japanese, my dad switched to English and interrogation mode, asking what I planned to do after college. In retrospect, I think he thought me sufficiently impressed by everything I'd seen to beg for a job at his company. He'd been encouraging me to sneak behind Zelos's curtain and watch what levers the great and powerful Oz was working so I could determine which ones I might wish to pull myself.

But my goal had never been to land a real job at his company. I told him of my intention to be a writer. As money wasn't a necessity, I explained, I'd buckle down and turn my upcoming thesis into a publishable novel. "I want to create something that speaks to the human experience," I said. "Makes people think."

My dad plucked a blob of sea urchin from his plate. He chewed it slowly, debating my career choice. For a moment, I thought he might offer some encouragement.

"No good, Alice." He motioned to the chef to bring the next plate. "Zelos will make writers like rock stars. A few authors—we're talking a dozen people, *maybe*—they *might* create something that'll be widely read. But most folks won't buy books in the future. They'll be too busy with personalized stories created by Zelos's AI just for them. Whatever entertainment an individual feels like consuming, Zelos will generate it."

"My stuff will be better than whatever a computer comes up with," I insisted.

He smiled then. Not because he believed me, but because he was thinking of his technology's power. "You'd be surprised." He leaned forward to be heard over the background conversation, loath to raise his voice in a public space and risk revealing corporate secrets. "AI art, whether visual or written or 3D sculpted, draws upon centuries of human creativity in seconds. Zelos's paid software can compose the stuff of Pulitzer Prize winners on whatever subject is grabbing headlines. You need only give it the right prompts."

"It can't feel genuine," I protested. "A computer can't capture the human soul."

My father reached for his briefcase then. He pulled out a laptop and set it on the onyx sushi bar, right beside a new plate of firefly squid sashimi. The creatures were bioluminescent and glowed when alive. On our plates, they were a dull gray.

"See for yourself," he said. "Give me a genre."

I blurted out the ones that I was most likely to write. "Romance, or maybe mystery."

"And a protagonist. You can pick one from another book."

I thought back to my reading list from the prior year. "The second Mrs. de Winter."

My dad's eyebrows rose. "That's the name?"

"She's a main character in *Rebecca* by Daphne du Maurier," I said, pleased that I might have added a complication his software wouldn't be able to handle. "She's never named exactly."

He shrugged and typed. "And what writer do you admire?"

There were too many to pick one. Stephen King was the first who came to mind, but I wanted to prove my point by making it as difficult as possible for Zelos's AI to create something special. King and du Maurier both employed elements of atmospheric horror and psychological suspense. "Hemingway," I said, mostly because his style was so different.

My father smiled. "Fine." He keyed in another command.

I knew from his expression that I wouldn't like what was about to happen. My dad was aware that I was trying to stump his software, and he found it funny. "Write a short romantic mystery story," he said, reading aloud his typed instructions, "in the style of Hemingway starring the second Mrs. de Winter from Daphne du Maurier's *Rebecca*." He looked up at me and winked. "But call her Alice."

He turned his attention back to his plate. "Give it a minute."

Zelos might have taken two seconds. I couldn't even consider whether to try the squid before my dad triumphantly turned his laptop to face me.

On-screen was a ten-page short story about a young woman named Alice who was engaged to a wealthy man with a secret past, despite her longing for adventure. As Hemingway was the author-inspiration,

Alice expressed her desire mostly through describing the claustrophobic setting of her wedding. Ultimately she uncovered her husband's secret—he'd come into his wealth by staging the drowning of his first wife, very much like the husband in *Rebecca*—and she took off to be a war reporter.

The story wouldn't have won the Pulitzer, but I could picture it in Berkeley's student literary magazine. It was at least that good. In many ways, it was far better than one of my first drafts. And those took me weeks. Months, even.

As I read the screen, my heart shrank two sizes. This was nothing like the writing I'd seen from the free apps. I looked up at my father's smug (proud?) expression and was overwhelmed by an emotion so strong that I initially mistook it for anger. But I wasn't enraged. What I felt was so much worse than uncomplicated fury. I was *jealous*. My father's preferred child, the one he spent all his time and energy on, could do what I dreamed of better and faster than I ever would be able to. Worse, better and faster than the literary titans I most admired.

Pressure built behind my eyes. "Why would you do that? Why would you code something to rip off artists? Plagiarize human beings?"

"Plagiarize?" My father pulled the laptop back toward him as if I no longer deserved to see it. "Hardly. You asked for a story in the style of Hemingway. It's derivative, but all art comes from somewhere."

I drummed my chopstick against my plate, my nerves creating a tingling triple-time beat. "This has to be illegal. Copyright law—"

"Only covers the expression of an idea," my dad interrupted. "And this is a new concept that Hemingway never wrote about, so there's no violation."

"Oh, there's a violation!"

My father looked offended. He'd taken my dream and torn it to pieces as if it were tissue paper, something decorative and meaningless laid on top of a far more substantive present. But I didn't have another dream inside me. Yet *he* was offended.

"This is the future of art." His tone was matter-of-fact, as if he were merely stating the undisputed answer to a simple equation. "Photographs, essays, books, films, architectural designs—they'll all be bespoke, computer-crafted to satisfy whatever an individual wants, tailored to that person's exact tastes. Feeling like a buddy comedy starring Garfield and Odie with the plot of *Bad Boys*? Sure. Throw in Will Smith's voice while you're at it. Or you want a new house and love Russian avant-garde architecture? How about a 3D-printed building in the style of Zaha Hadid?" My father's eyes shimmered, as if he'd donned augmented-reality glasses and could see all the glorious eventualities projected in front of him.

As I struggled to stomach what he was saying, the chef set down two plates of shrimp, heads still on. The deshelled bodies shone like raw wounds. Their whiskers twitched.

My dad waited for the chef to move to another pair on a business lunch before resuming his speech. "And Zelos won't only transform the so-called creative fields." He leaned toward me, lowering his voice conspiratorially. "In the world *I'm creating*, everything—and I mean everything—will be customized. Health care will be tailored to a person's unique genetic makeup. Physician advice and prescriptions will come from AI medical concierges capable of interpreting full-body scans. Your doctors will all be in your phone, so no need to see a specialist. The AI is the specialist! It's the specialist in everything. Imagine having a Zelos AI assistant capable of not only providing endless individualized entertainment but also answering any question and solving nearly any problem, no matter how great or mundane. No need to worry about what to wear in the morning. Your Zelos AI stylist will select outfits based on your stated preferences and order clothes off e-commerce sites or 3D print them for you. Your Zelos AI business manager will file your taxes and prepare rote legal documents, or even write more complex arguments, should you need them. Not that the courts will be relevant, given how easy my technology will make adjudicating disagreements. Everyone will be able to see how a Zelos AI judge would rule once they put the facts into the system, so people will settle their complaints without ever stepping foot in a courtroom. No need to pay overpriced lawyers. And financial markets will finally make sense. Zelos's software will have them running at maximum efficiency thanks to processing formerly impossible amounts of data. My AI will decide the ideal allocation of capital to fuel global GDP. Oh, and dating. Zelos will revolutionize that too. People will have AI companions on their phones and, as robotics advance, in their kitchens and bedrooms. No more bad dates or incompatible matches. I'm almost there, Alice. You've seen what's already possible, and every month—every week—Zelos gets closer to making the future our reality. In five years, the world will be a different place. Picture it: a life where everything is optimized and made just for you."

He wagged his index finger at me as he said the last part. I think he was tempted to boop me on the nose like a little kid or a dog. His pupils swelled with his vision, this utopia he was ushering in that would enable people to silo themselves in their own personal computer-generated havens where they'd never want for anything—save, perhaps, for a job, a purpose, and real human connection.

"What if I don't want a computer to make things for me?" I protested. "What if I want to make things for myself and others? If I want to—"

The laptop shut with a sharp clack, cutting me off. "You don't get it."

"I do get it, Dad. That's the problem." Anger raised my voice a decibel over what was fancy-restaurant appropriate. "And if more people knew your plans, they wouldn't keep using Zelos and feeding it information, training their replacements. Who wants everything at their fingertips if it means they *do* nothing?"

My father shushed me as he slipped the laptop into his briefcase. "This is proprietary technology that I've shown you as an employee. You're aware of that, right?"

I ignored his question, posing one of my own. "How will people even pay for all these Zelos services? Your technology will make most of us obsolete!"

He picked up a wriggling shrimp and ripped off its tail. "Open your eyes, Alice. Most people *are* obsolete. They contribute nothing." The shrimp's shiny body pulsed as he plopped it into his mouth. He chewed as he continued talking. "They should be thankful to get a small basic income—no doubt paid by Zelos's taxes—and to have our free AI-generated entertainment amuse them."

"While you and a small number of your friends take all the wealth?"

My father made a face, as if he'd realized how unappetizing live shrimp really was. He then transferred the look to me. I felt he was seeing me for the first time, and he found me horribly small and ugly and stupid. "You don't get how business works. How progress works."

"I get how fairness works."

He snorted. "Fairness? You think you got this job on your merits?" He stood and slung his briefcase over his shoulder. "It was a mistake to let you intern for me, Alice. Don't come back to the office." His tone hinted that he wasn't simply giving me the afternoon off.

"Are you firing me?"

"Go back to your mother." He pulled out his wallet. "I'll get the check."

I did as told, though not because I was following orders. My mom was the one who always made up for whatever injuries my father inflicted. I wanted to go home so she could heat up something from the kitchen and remind me of my strengths, make me feel like less of a failure. Less afraid.

When I walked through the door of our home, she immediately began following the expected playbook. She welcomed me inside and, seeing my tears, pulled me into her chest. After a long hug, she brought me into the kitchen, where she put on a kettle. For my mom, chamomile is to emotional pains what Vicks VapoRub is to colds: a cure-all.

As she poured hot water into mugs, I poured my heart out, sobbing about Dad terminating me because I disagreed with his intentions for his technology.

My mother shook her head. "Oh, Alice. You know how he is about his work." She plopped a tea bag into a mug. "Why did you challenge him?"

I couldn't believe the question. "You're taking his side?"

"You two were bonding. He was revealing something he probably doesn't show many people, letting you see his vision. You threw it in his face, honey."

"*I* threw it in *his* face?"

"He was trying to impress you."

"He was trying to show me up!" I shouted, finally free to yell. "He wanted to prove that his technology was better than me. Better than I'll ever be. Better than anyone."

My mother played with the tea bag, lifting and lowering it into her cup like she was trying to fool a fish. "I'm sure that wasn't his intent. Why would he do that?"

"Because he's an egotistical, narcissistic sociopath!" I shouted. "He doesn't care about anyone but himself."

My mom stopped fussing with her drink. "I know Brian hasn't been a present father. And I'm sorry about that, Allie. I wish I could have changed it, made him stay longer, take more of an interest in us. I don't know. Maybe wanting Brian to be a more available husband and father isn't fair to the world. He's working to improve things. To—"

I had to cut her off. "For who?"

"Sorry?"

"Who is he working for? Who's he trying to make things so much better for?"

"Lots of people, honey. Everyone. He's giving people tools to improve their lives."

"Whose lives? What he made certainly won't improve mine."

Again, my mom shook her head. "Alice, not everything is about you."

If I didn't feel small enough already, her words were like a potion in Wonderland, shrinking me to mouse size. I picked up my car keys. "Well, not everything is about him either," I said, marching to the front door. "Other people exist. And we matter too. What we want matters. It has to!"

I slammed the door behind me that day. And I didn't talk to my mom much after that, at least not until our lunch. When the kidnappers came, I still hadn't spoken to my father.

If this journal ever gets out, this story will probably seem out of place. It's not about my kidnappers or their tactics or an escape attempt. But Ghost Face thinks I'm too spoiled to worry about the future, and she's wrong. If she ever reads this, I want her to know it. I, too, am part of the generation trained for a life that may no longer be possible. I may always have a roof over my head, but I can still feel lost. I don't deserve this like she thinks I do.

Plus, the truth is, a lot of this kidnapping has been me sitting in a room, alone, trapped with a pen, paper, and time. Writers are supposed to write what we know. Since my kidnappers locked me in here, this has been what I've thought about. In some ways, it's been on my mind since August.

Maybe Zelos's AI would tell my story better. It would pen it in the style of du Maurier, replete with eerie details, or make it like Hemingway, leaving the reader to guess at the subtext. But this will never be a computer's tale to tell. It's happening to me.

So I keep filling the pages of this journal. I keep hoping, with every word I scrawl onto its lined sheets, that it's not all for naught. And I pray that this diary—and I—might see the light of day in the future.

CATHERINE NEWHOUSE INGOLD

THE DAY AFTER

The shelter was in San Jose, just ninety minutes south of Sausalito but enveloped in a completely different culture and climate. My little town has always been something of a bohemian escape for San Francisco expats. Sausalito's winding roads, thick with vegetation, snake past the gabled roofs of hill-nestled homes positioned to overlook the bay's yacht clubs, houseboats, and occasional film crews. My place, centered in the fog-free Banana Belt, enjoys high seventies and sunshine throughout much of the year, even while the city remains shrouded in sweater weather.

San Jose, on the other hand, is hot. Omnipresent office buildings fuel the heat, much like computer servers in an un-air-conditioned room—or so Brian has said. All I know is I find it stifling, even though we're arriving at the coolest time of the day.

The sun sets through the police vehicle's passenger-side window. I watch it drop toward browning hills buttressing sprawling office parks as we head down a four-lane highway, all silent. Frazier drives. Taking his unmarked sedan made sense, given its back-off blue light and state-granted speeding permissions. Agent Lee called shotgun, or he opened the front passenger-side door so there could be no debate about who would assume the role of navigator. Not that map reading will ever again be required of a front passenger. A screen, big as the one in Brian's Tesla, shines on the Dodge's dashboard. There's a strange keyboard below, its buttons marked with law enforcement hieroglyphs. Microphone. Short wavy line. New riddles I can't solve.

It's better that Brian and I are in the back. Here, we're cocooned in window tint, safe from the cameras that protrude from passing press vans. The moment we entered Frazier's unmarked car, the reporters followed suit, retreating from my gate into their vehicles—an army regrouping for some future offensive. We lead a caravan of satellite trucks and cheap sedans, a hearse guiding hazards-blinking mourners.

Still, I wish I were driving. In the perp position, there's little to do but wait for whatever comes next. No signs or guided turns distract me from my fears. Brian's not talking. Instead, he scrolls through his cell, amassing information in a bid to feel some control. My husband has always inhabited a world in which the smartest person has the power. I'm not sure we live there anymore.

"It's a Superfund site," Brian says as the car turns left. "Partially remediated, which is why they can install temporary structures. Any digging would be problematic, so developers haven't snapped it up."

Lee looks over his shoulder at us. "The remains stay. Could be a reference to chemical remains. Poisoned ground."

I picture Alice—hungry, trapped in some basement, being offered God only knows what to eat. "The 'flesh far too weak' line. Do you think someone might have been hurt by pollutants or had a relative injured by them? Maybe they want to call attention to that. If someone has cancer and they're angry, blaming big tech—"

"If anything," Brian interrupts, "these folks are environmental freaks. America should abandon the silicon and lithium mines, beg resources from China. Bet they wouldn't give up their cell phones, though."

Brian turns to me, seeking a grunt of affirmation. I've no idea whether he's right or not, nor do I care. Our daughter might be locked in a poisoned building, inhaling toxic fumes. Her kidnappers' reasons for putting her there don't matter.

I pose the only relevant question. "Do you think they'd hurt Alice to prove a point?"

Lee frowns before he points to the windshield. "Here we are."

We approach a property-long fence. Cheap and chain-link, it taunts visitors with a clear view into a seemingly off-limits area. There's a van-sized break in the metal, which we turn in to, entering a decaying parking lot. Weeds peek through crumbling asphalt. The most intact pavement stretches toward what appears to be two massive ducts, segmented like the aluminum conduits in my attic but sized for a skyscraper machine that doesn't exist.

Frazier turns off the engine. "It's a pop-up shelter. They're like tents, but bigger and with electricity."

The structures *do* recall military barracks, as referenced in the video, though not the brick-and-mortar ones on a permanent base. These are the kind erected by troops sent abroad for long campaigns in hostile territories, forced to dig in.

Frazier exits first, telling us to wait inside until he returns. He may as well tell me to cease breathing. Now that we're stopped, adrenaline has rushed to all my extremities. I'm ready to run through this place screaming Alice's name and yanking doors off hinges.

I pull the handle as Lee joins Frazier outside the vehicle. My door doesn't move. I jimmy the release again. Nothing. My heart races like a greyhound that's spied a rabbit. When I told Frazier and Lee about my pink-haired makeup artist's suggestion, they'd insisted on coming to check it out. I realize now that they wanted to keep Brian and me from investigating the place ourselves.

The feeling of being trapped is excruciating, and my pain isn't a fraction of the dose delivered to my daughter. Brian and I both know Frazier will let us out eventually. Alice has no idea of her kidnappers' true intentions.

Through the window, I see the reason why Frazier locked the back doors. Press vehicles have pulled up behind our car. He orders them back with hand gestures, a beat cop directing traffic. "Private property," he bellows. "Police business."

Agent Lee joins his calls for space. "Outside the fence." Lee holds something up. Though I can only see the backs of both men, I gather it's his FBI identification. The cameraman swiveling his lens toward it is a dead giveaway.

"This is an active investigation," Frazier continues. "Units are on the way."

"Is Alice Ingold inside that shelter?" The voice sounds like a TV reporter, the way it poses the question without the tone underscoring the punctuation.

"We will work with stations that cooperate with us," Lee responds. "Anyone still on this property in two minutes lands on my *no comment* list."

Maybe it's because Lee previously handpicked the outlet to interview Brian and me, but the reporters behave like they believe him. People scuttle back to their vehicles as Lee and Frazier head toward the main structure.

Once our escorts disappear inside the center barrack, I grab the edge of the driver's seat and pull myself across the bench toward the computer console. My jeans slide across the faux leather as if a cop car's back seat were oiled to push people around. I prop my knee on the cupholders, avoiding the fancy keyboard in front.

"Catherine," Brian whispers, as if the vehicle's bugged. "What are you doing?"

"Child locks won't keep me in here." I hop my other foot onto the console's plastic, an unbalanced yogi assuming the warrior position. Momentum sends my knee into the driver's seat, which is exactly where I wanted it to land, though not so hard.

Brian points to the tents. "Alice's kidnappers could be in there."

"Alice could be in there!"

Before my other leg makes it into the driver's seat, Brian's hand lands on my waist. "These guys could have guns." His eyebrows form an upside-down *v*, a circumflex accenting his fear. As I note it, his gaze drops to his hands. "We're not armed."

"That's why we need to be in there. We don't want Alice involved in a shoot-out. We've got to *talk* to these people. Negotiate a price, like you said."

I've uttered the magic phrase. Brian's jaw hardens as he nods his agreement. I've given him a way to contribute that doesn't involve outshooting professional criminals.

I slip into the front seat and hit the unlock button, pressing twice to disengage the back. Brian slides over so that we exit the same side of the car. He marches past me toward the tents.

"Wait!"

Brian turns, annoyed rather than confused. "Hurry. Before they—"

"If we pass Frazier and Lee, they'll take us back to the car," I hiss.

"We'll explain we want to bargain."

"We did explain, Brian, and they don't want us paying anyone for information. We need to talk to people ourselves. Offer rewards. It's not like her kidnappers will have her out in the open. We'll need someone to tell us where she is. What room."

Brian continues toward the bulbous building. "Do these things have private rooms?"

I can't answer until we're nearly at the tent's sidewall. Windows are punched into each metal segment, though there are no doors. Peering inside a pane reveals a mess hall with long tables and rows of cots, each topped with a white pillow and thin blue blanket. People sleep on some, but not nearly as many as the shelter could accommodate. Given what I've read in the news about homelessness, the vacancies are a testament to folks' reluctance to bed down with strangers.

"What are you doing?"

I whirl around, expecting Frazier or Lee, even though the slurred voice doesn't sound like either man. Instead, I see a stranger. He wears a camouflage jacket that might be military grade or simply the style. The garment appears too worn to have been recently purchased. A ball cap sits on his head, its brim peaked as if the person breaking it in pressed too hard on the corners.

The hat keeps me staring. Alice's note was delivered by a man in a cap.

"I asked what you're doing."

"Peeping" is clearly the wrong answer, and I gather from his furious approach that he's in no mood to hear about my missing daughter. "I was, uh, checking to—"

"Like hell!"

The shout serves as a power switch, turning on the electronics of the media behind us. Voices swell. Cameras click into position. A paparazzo's lens can apparently see into space.

Brian glances at the crowd and then steps in front of me, blocking the man's direct route of attack. "We're with the police."

This stops the guy. From behind Brian's shoulder, I examine the man's sunken eyes and skeletal cheeks. It's possible that he's the same age as the guy who gave me the letter, but that's their only similarity.

The stranger catches me staring again. The moment we make eye contact, I switch my gaze to the pavement.

But it's too late.

"What you looking at?" He shifts around Brian, glaring at me like I gave him the finger. "You think you better than me, bitch? You think you—"

"Hey." Brian extends an arm, gating me behind him. "Don't talk to her like—"

The man clocks him in the jaw. Brian stumbles back, blinking rapidly. I'm certain that he's never been really hit before. For that matter, I've never been struck either. I don't know if I can still say the same for my daughter.

The thought awakens some feral instinct. While the man rears back to strike Brian a second time, I charge from the side, slamming my hands into his face as hard as I can. His hat flies off. The fist intended for Brian switches trajectory, aiming for the top of my skull. I kick my right leg forward, shooting for the stranger's groin. But I'm too close and inflexible. My foot slams his shin instead.

The blow hurts me more than it does him. My body responds like a tuning fork, vibrating and throbbing while the man barely flinches. He rears back his right fist. On reflex, I shut my eyes.

The man doesn't make contact. When I look again, I see that Brian has the stranger's raised arm bent behind his shoulder. I seize the opportunity, jumping back so fast that I stumble and fall.

As my tailbone hits the dirt, I hear Brian grunt. I look up, fearing the man's fist has landed someplace important. Instead, I see my brainiac husband on top of the guy, whaling on the man like he's in an octagon. One fist lands, then another. There are no rules. Brian's aiming for whatever he can strike.

I watch as he reaches for the stranger's neck. "Where's my daughter?" he yells. "Where's Alice? Where is she?"

If the man knows, he can't answer. Brian's hands are wrapped around his opponent's throat. The attacker's bleeding face goes bright red.

"Brian!" I yell as I attempt to stand. "Brian. Stop."

He doesn't listen. For twenty-four hours, Brian has felt as powerless and emasculated as he's probably ever been in his life. This man's punch was the straw that broke the proverbial camel's back.

I move toward him. "Brian. That's enough."

Still, he squeezes. A vein pops from the man's forehead. Blood trickles from his nose.

I rush over and touch his shoulder. "Bri!"

An elbow drives into my thigh. Again, I stumble back, unsure how the choking man managed to get a shot in.

But he wasn't the one who hit me.

"What the hell is happening here?"

Frazier hurries forward, flashing his badge. "Police."

This gets through to my husband. He releases the man and rises, his hands in fists should the guy get up. The stranger rolls onto his side, coughing, a barking sound that's thankfully more dry than wet. He wipes the blood from his face, then points up at Brian. "He attacked me."

"You hit him first." I turn to Frazier. "He was going after me."

"Lying bitch." The man rises to standing position. "Fucking poverty tourist."

Frazier looks to Brian, a principal deciding how to mete out a punishment between bullies. My husband shudders. Whatever spirit had possessed him leaves his body. I see his shoulders round. His face pale. For a moment, I fear he'll fall to his knees.

Brian didn't mean to hit me, I tell myself. Adrenaline made him crazed. In a way, he was protecting me, trying to drive me away from danger.

I rush over and wrap my arm around his waist. My narrow shoulders aren't much of a ballast, but they're all I have to offer. "He went after us first," I reiterate.

"I told you two to stay in the car," Frazier grumbles.

"They were looking into windows!" the man shouts, delighted that the police seem to be on his side. "People don't want to be stared at like goddamned zoo animals. They think—"

Frazier holds up a hand. "Enough." He turns to Brian, body language more friendly now, or at least resigned. "Do you want to press charges?"

Brian shakes his head no. Frazier turns to the guy. "Go, before he changes his mind."

The man walks off, spitting blood and epithets, mostly aimed at me—the "rich whore." To drown them out, I ask Frazier a dumb question. "Did you find Alice?"

If he had, she'd be here. And if Frazier had discovered something terrible, he wouldn't be standing over us with such a scolding expression.

"It's only men in there." The explanation emanates from Lee. He walks up behind Frazier, partially hidden by the expanse of the larger officer's torso. "The director said they have a few families in the back units, most with young kids. One girl's around Alice's age, but she doesn't match the description."

The universe could not have brought us here simply to beat us up. I refuse to believe it. "We should check."

"It's not her," Lee insists. "This woman's known to them. She's been in and out of here before. Local addict."

Though Lee continues talking, I'm no longer listening. I stride past him, arm still around my spouse, guiding Brian to a structure I've only now noticed. In the back of the property, semiobscured by the main tent, is a line of RVs. They're all some version of beige with faded red, green, and brown stripes, a color scheme as seventies as corduroy and tube socks. There's no way they're still operational.

"Remove their engines."

Brian is close enough to hear my whispers. He picks up pace, freeing himself from my supportive grip. I match his steps. In seconds, we're both running.

"Alice!" I shout. "Alice."

Footsteps thunder behind us. Frazier and Lee are closing whatever gap existed from our seconds head start.

As I draw closer, I spot wet clothes dripping from a laundry line. A woman crouches behind a leaking pair of jeans, digging into a plastic basket for more sopping garments. One of Alice's kidnappers is a woman.

"Hey!" I shout. "Excuse me."

The woman considers me like we might be prior acquaintances. Her smile is embarrassed. "Yes?"

I pull my cell from a pants pocket and bring it to my face. It opens to a picture of Alice and me. "Have you seen this girl?"

The woman pins up a crop top. "You're looking for someone?"

Her confusion puts me more at ease, though it shouldn't. Anyone can fake being puzzled. I bring the phone within an arm's length of her basket. "My daughter."

Adding *kidnapped* would only complicate the situation. If this woman is involved, she'd know that already anyway. "Alice Ingold," I add. "She's nineteen. A student. I think a woman may have brought her here."

This woman squints at the screen. She's in her late twenties, if I had to guess, with a grown-out blond dye job that betrays her sandy-brown roots. "I haven't seen her."

Disappointment cinches my vocal cords. I pocket my cell, fighting tears.

"Are any of these trailers unoccupied?" Brian asks.

The woman points to one in the back corner with a green stripe. "A girl came in yesterday, but she only used the place to crash. Left the next morning."

Girl sounds promising. "Blond?"

"Black girl," she says.

Not Alice. I'm about to cry when Detective Frazier's voice sounds behind me. "Which trailer did you say she went to?"

I force my tears back into my throat. We're playing a game, I remind myself. Even if Alice isn't here, her kidnappers may have left a clue.

Frazier takes over, leading the way to the trailer with the green stripe. Calling it *green* isn't exactly accurate, however. I'm rewinding time, guessing its original hue from the faded olive blur before me.

Before Frazier opens the door, Lee hurries forward, gun in hand. Frazier takes the cue, cop-knocking the door. The strength of his fist sends it careening backward. He pulls his gun and shoots me a severe look: *Don't even try to follow.*

They disappear inside. A second later, they pop back out, announcing the space is "clear." Frazier looks down on me. "We found something addressed to you."

I grab his outstretched hand and hop into the RV's interior. It's my first time in a true mobile home, but it looks as I've imagined. There's a foldout table where the passenger's seat should be, and a Murphy bed behind it. An electric stove/sink combination lines one wall.

What has my attention, however, is the counter space. An envelope lies atop the Formica. My name is scrawled on the front.

"Let me open it," Frazier says. "It's evidence."

It's already between my ungloved hands. I peel back the triangle closure and withdraw folded notebook paper. Faint blue lines traverse the surface. The edges are frayed where the paper was ripped from its brethren. Holding together the sheets is a metal clip far larger than needed. It clinks on the countertop as I examine the first page.

How much is a daughter worth?

The cruelty of the question brings tears to my eyes. It's rhetorical, clearly. They must know the answer is *everything*.

Brian's hand lands on my shoulder. "What does it say?"

My vision's too blurry to read. I pass over the pages. He clears his throat and begins:

> How much is a daughter worth?
> What decides?
> How much someone can pay?
> A quant estimating potential?
> Or is it all momentum?
> Go where the real traders move the markets.
> I'll be held there long as they hold their shares.

Brian sets down the paper and stares into the distance, looking beaten. The forlorn face doesn't compute, however. This clue seems easy. Everyone knows New York is the world's financial capital. "It's Manhattan, right?" I whisk away tears with my knuckles. "They want us to go to a big bank's headquarters or a hedge fund. Which financial institution moves markets the most? Who has the most assets?"

Before Zelos went public, Brian traveled to New York on an investor "road show." I'm sure he knows the answers to these questions. It's the kind of thing he could rattle off at a dinner party. *J.P. Morgan has the largest position in Alphabet. Soros is consolidating his shares of Microsoft.* Whenever he's home, Brian always has CNBC on.

He rubs his forehead. "It's not about banks. The *real* market movers are machines, algorithms in colocated servers constantly buying and selling, providing liquidity."

"Okay, but that's still in New York, no?"

Brian doesn't answer. The money clip on the counter calls his attention, tinfoil attracting a bluebird. He picks it up. For the first time, I realize there's a symbol on its face, a thick line drawing of a clenched fist.

Brian taps the clip against his open palm. "I don't think she'll still be there. There might be a clue."

The last thing I want to hear is that this game might have multiple rounds. "Brian, tell me where we're going. Is it New York?"

Brian passes Frazier the money clip. "Not New York. New Jersey."

ALICE INGOLD

DIARY ENTRY NINE

Fawkes returned with a stolen computer. I know because I'd swear it was mine. The MacBook Pro was the same size and featured a bear-shaped tacky spot in the corner reminiscent of the Berkeley mascot sticker I'd slapped on my own machine.

"Is that my laptop?" I asked.

He shot me a look, which I could read now that he'd ditched the mask. It wasn't so much offended as bemused. *Of all the things you have to worry about,* he seemed to ask, *you care about a computer?*

He brought the device closer. "This has been wiped and completely quarantined from the internet. So don't get any ideas."

The laptop was open. A video player was set to full screen and queued to start. He suppressed a smile. "You should see this."

I braced for footage of my teary parents pleading for my safe return. Never did I expect to see my dad's head snap back as a fist connected with his jaw. And I couldn't ever have anticipated his reaction.

Smart money would have been on the shelter resident. My father has the quintessential dad bod, rounded in the middle but developed on top thanks to weekly personal-training sessions in his office gym. He isn't a small man, but he sure isn't a fighter. The unhoused individual, on the other hand, recalled the inside of a coaxial cable, muscle fibers braided into a hard shield.

Yet, before my eyes, my father transformed from Bruce Banner into the Hulk. Not the professor-monster at the finale of the *Avengers: Endgame* movie either. The childlike version from the earlier films. *Hulk smash!*

"Does he kill him?" I asked, mentally assuring myself that this couldn't be the case. No internet meant the footage wasn't live. Fawkes couldn't be so sadistic as to show me a snuff film.

He pulled forward the video player's tracking bar, skipping the bloodiest parts of the fight. "Your mom stops him. I really wanted you to see the footage afterward."

My kidnappers had cut together a highlight reel of the news. Pundits' reactions fell along political lines, as expected. Outlets on the left lamented the sight of a corporate bully literally beating a downtrodden man, acknowledging only in passing that my dad had been sucker punched. On the other side, conservatives branded my father a paladin. Brian Ingold was a successful guy who could handle himself in the boardroom or the boxing ring. To hear Fox commentators tell it, my dad had taken down a system-milking meth head while searching for his daughter. He was Superman endowed with Lex Luthor's business savvy transported into a *Taken* movie.

The truth is always buried beneath the viral headlines. I suspect the stranger's violent response had less to do with any Robin Hood chivalry than with inhibition-reducing drugs coupled with knee-jerk fury at the sight of a woman wearing diamond earrings worth more than most people's annual rent. The world's bias had been displayed in high relief. He couldn't simply stand there, admiring the facade.

My dad's reaction, too, was more complicated than any fuck-around-and-find-out narrative. Brian Ingold had been backed into a corner that he never knew existed. After collecting all the capitalist Infinity Stones—knowledge, health, money, success, influence, connections—he was supposed to be safe in his power. Yet here he was, facing off with a man who couldn't afford a roof over his head. And that made him afraid, and *angry*.

To anyone reading this in the future, I say be careful about the news. Look for the facts between the "analysis." Heroes and villains get the engagement; social media algorithms spread the stories people interact with most. Nuance takes mental energy. It's not an easy click.

My male kidnapper knew that the fight would be catnip to a mewling media. I suspect that's why he'd entered looking so elated about my father's altercation. This story was tailor-made to go viral. If there was one thing my captors wanted, it was attention.

Still, I felt guilty. I never wanted anyone to get physically hurt over me.

Marbled tears fell down my cheeks, swirling with the remains of my makeup and dirt. I hadn't washed my face since arriving, and I didn't even want to consider what was happening with the more odiferous parts of my body.

"Hey." Fawkes closed the laptop. "Your dad's okay, you know."

I wiped the tears, hating the fact that his modicum of concern made me feel better. "I want to shower."

"What?"

"I have wounds that need cleaning," I said, ignoring the full bottle of hydrogen peroxide beside my bed. "I'm covered in grime. I'll get sick. I can't live like this."

He considered me like a frugal pet owner debating whether Fluffy *really* required another trip to Bark and Splash. Whatever he saw made him press his lips together and nod. "Fair."

"Like, now." I struggled to keep my voice from turning a statement into a question.

"I need to talk to . . ." Fawkes stopped speaking rather than reveal his partner's name. He started toward the door. I followed, spurred by the fear that, if he made it outside, I wouldn't get another opportunity. I'd upset my female captor by ignoring her story. She'd probably relish me stewing in filth.

"I promise," I shouted after him. "I'm done fighting. I only want . . ." I trailed off. I wanted so many things: to go home, to sleep in my own bed, to know I'd make it through this alive. Asking for any of those, however, would have been the equivalent of wishing on a lamp for more wishes. "I can't feel like this anymore," I said. It was the truest thing I'd uttered since being locked away.

He raised two fingers in the air like a Boy Scout. "We'll do something about it. Swear."

He left, taking my stolen laptop with him. I retreated to the bed. This man was no Boy Scout. What were the promises of a thief really worth?

CATHERINE NEWHOUSE INGOLD

TWO DAYS AFTER

We're taking the plane. The visual of Brian beating up an unhoused man only to hop aboard a private jet won't do his personal brand or company any favors, but we're beyond caring about sideline commentary. We've been drafted into this game, and we intend to use whatever is at our disposal to win. Zelos's Gulfstream G650 can take off within an hour's notice.

We should be wheels up by ten p.m., with an estimated touchdown in Newark, New Jersey, at four a.m.—seven Eastern. Frazier is staying behind with the Oakland PD. Since our TV interview, the tip lines have been blowing up. Someone needs to sift through them all. Agent Lee and the power of his FBI badge are coming with us.

I watch as Lee looks up at the plane, its white fuselage opalescent beneath the tarmac lights. If he flies private, it's not often. He checks out the wingspan as though he intends to ask Brian how many miles per gallon this thing gets.

The ladder is already down, manned by a suited first officer. I've never met this one before. Captain Luke is our regular pilot and, after all these years, something of a friend, as much as one can have a pal on the payroll. I use the term loosely to mean that I have his personal cell for last-minute transportation emergencies. His first mate has always been whoever's available. This guy's young. Handsome in the shaggy-haired Gen Z fashion. I gather he understands the reason for our sudden trip by his downcast gaze.

Brian boards first, leading the way to the meeting room. We pass a long couch and a series of single seats before entering the semiprivate quarters. Here, four chairs face one another train-car- style, with a table in between. I'm the only one who sits.

Lee announces his plan to settle in the other seating area and call his East Coast counterparts. He doesn't want us listening in, though he's sensitive enough *not* to state the obvious. "We need to secure proper clearances," he says by way of apology. "Getting in there won't be easy."

Brian nods like he understands, so I don't bother to ask questions. Instead, I watch him take the chair diagonal from me and flip down the table, removing the barrier between us. The act reminds me of when Alice was young, before her school schedule became such that I couldn't easily pull her out to accompany her dad to Europe or Asia. With the table down, the four facing seats convert into a full-size bed. I once slept in this very spot beside my husband. Alice always took a jet bed toward the front.

"Why all the security at this place?" I ask as Brian adjusts his chair.

He settles in and gestures for me to buckle my seat belt. "Where we're going is basically Fort Knox. Money's more digital than physical now, and this data center houses the computer servers for the New York Stock Exchange, the world's largest trading platform. More than 28 trillion dollars are on these machines. Trillion."

The reason for the company's name suddenly becomes clear. Brian had said the fist logo was the symbol for Fortix, a tech firm. All the technology companies I knew had names derived from scientists, mathematical concepts, or, as in Brian's case, Greek gods. Fortix sounded more like a play on *fortress*. Clearly intentional.

"If it's so secure, how could kidnappers get Alice in there?"

Brian leans back into his semireclined seat. "They couldn't."

"But—"

The presence of a stewardess silences me. Like the first officer, she's also new to the crew. She's younger than the prior woman I remember from my trip last Christmas when I flew to see Brian in London. Prettier too.

She slinks over, a tight smile on her face. "Hello, Mr. Ingold and Ms. Newhouse."

Her use of my maiden name prickles. It's *Newhouse-Ingold*, been that way for decades. "Ingold," I correct. "I'm old fashioned. Changed my name when I signed the marriage certificate."

That smile pinches at the corners. "Can I get you anything to eat or drink?"

Brian raises an eyebrow at me. "Silver Oak?"

It's my go-to de-stressor—all the flavors of a good meal with a silken finish and enough alcohol to warm the insides. I can't let myself go all gooey, though. Not now. "No. We need—"

"We can't do any good at ten thousand feet, and I *need* some sleep." Brian turns to the new stewardess. "If you'd bring the bottle, Jen. Thank you."

Jen looks to me, waiting for an objection. I should decline. Who drinks good wine while her daughter could be dying of thirst? But Brian clearly doesn't want to talk to me—or anyone—and I don't see how else I'll quiet my brain enough not to bother him. Alcohol is as good a shut-up pill as I'm going to get.

"Thank you, Jennifer," Brian repeats, his tone dismissive.

Hurt flashes in the stewardess's eyes, and not the sympathetic kind. I'm not a jealous woman by nature, but neither am I oblivious to the possibility that Brian's been unfaithful over the years. He travels often and keeps another apartment. I'm sure he's been presented with opportunities. As we've aged, our relative values have inverted. When we married, I was a wealthy heiress who, if not classically beautiful, wasn't hard on the eyes. Brian was a brilliant albeit geeky guy with a ton of potential but without a penny to his name. Now he's a rich and powerful fifty-year-old who had a glow up sometime after his company went public. I've become his older housewife.

If it weren't for my money and the cachet of my name, I might have been his starter wife. Sometimes I wonder if I'd have been happier that way, divorced with a little kid, having to start over. On nights like the prior one, when I've (again) gone to bed by myself in that big house, I can't help but consider that I've invested too much in the title "wife of visionary tech CEO." I like what people think it says about me—that I'm the right-hand woman and confidante of someone changing the world—more than what the position really entails. I'm expected to be home, raising Alice, while Brian does whatever the hell he wants.

Jen turns around and strides toward Lee. Her uniform features a cropped gray jacket over a pencil skirt that highlights a toned behind. To his credit, my husband doesn't watch her go. At least, not obviously.

"The riddle is to bring *us* to Fortix," Brian says, resuming our prior conversation. "They all but revealed Alice wouldn't be there in the last line."

He's said as much before, and his assertion is as unwelcome this second time. "The line is 'I'll be held there,'" I protest.

"'Long as they hold their shares,'" Brian quotes. "Where we're headed—this data center—it's also where algorithmic trading firms colocate their servers so they can obtain information fractions of a second sooner than the rest of the market. The time matters, because these guys hold their stocks for less than a day, sometimes less than a minute. And they're behind much of the market's momentum, constantly trading."

I shake my head, not because I don't understand how these conditions satisfy the riddle but because I don't get why I'm here. If Alice won't be at Fortix, then I shouldn't be on this plane. I should be with Frazier, running down local leads. "What if their plan is for us to jet all over the place looking for clues so we don't notice what's right in front of us? Whoever took Alice knew her address."

Brian glances over his shoulder, perhaps looking for his new girl, punishing me for challenging him by diverting his attention to a more pleasant woman. "That's a dead end." He employs the same tone with which he sent away Jen. "The school had Alice's address. These people are probably hackers. Getting into Berkeley's system can't be that hard. They could be anyone."

"It's still worth checking out," I counter. "We should be—"

"I think this is the right bottle." Jen cuts me off. She carries the wine with its familiar silver label. Two stemless glasses are pinched between her fingers. I watch as she sets the lot down on the counter beside Brian and pours a taste into one of the glasses. Rather than passing it to him, she offers it to me.

Brian reaches for the bottle and the empty vessel. "That'll be all."

As Jen hands it to him, a pink blush spreads from her cheeks to her neck. I tell myself that my heightened emotions are encouraging me to read too much into her behavior. She could simply feel awkward given our horrible circumstances. It'd be easier for me if I believed that.

Brian resumes speaking as she stalks off. "Alice is a pawn in all this." He pours himself a drink and then places the glass in a cupholder before reaching for mine. I fail to object as he fills it more than a quarter of the way. "They picked her to prove a point."

"About?"

Rather than answer, he places the bottle in another cupholder and turns his attention to the window. I sip my wine and wait for him to finish. The liquid goes down as expected, honey in a raw throat.

Brian swallows from his own glass and then sighs, still gazing out the window. The view is blackness, save for the distant glow of a tarmac light growing dimmer as we move.

"What's their point?" I ask, finally.

Brian sighs. "Doesn't matter."

"They picked her because of our money," I say. "Our wealth made us a target. It made Alice a target."

Brian drinks. His turned head keeps me from seeing his face, but I wonder if his sudden quiet is the result of deep thought or a desire to keep his feelings in check. Wine is Brian's emotional lidocaine.

It's my antianxiety medication, though it's not working. My stress requires something stronger. Questions scroll through my head, credits at the end of a movie that's already run long. "Why haven't they asked for a ransom? I don't get it."

Brian faces me. "We should rest. Once we reach cruising, I'll take out the jet bed."

Again, I'm reminded that our seats transform into a full mattress. This will be the first time in three weeks that I've shared a bed with my husband. He was in Asia the prior two weeks and at the apartment these past five days. The first decade of our marriage, we slept in the same bed every night when he wasn't traveling. We *slept* together a third of that time.

Those days seem so long ago now. Sleep seems so long ago. Since receiving the kidnapper's letter, I haven't gone to bed so much as fallen unconscious for an hour or two. In my husband's arms, I think, maybe it'll be possible, provided I don't think about stewardess Jen. Or our daughter. Or maybe my entire marriage.

Brian smiles weakly and again returns his attention to the window. I follow suit, taking a long sip as the plane lifts off.

———

I wake to a familiar yet strange heaviness around my torso. Brian's arm drapes over my stomach. It's found the groove above my hip bone, like a dowel slipping into place. After everything that's happened, it feels like déjà vu, something barely remembered. Brian snores behind me. The noise, a whistling from his deviated septum, evokes the same feeling of temporal distortion. When was the last time Brian and I cuddled on a plane?

The sun got me up. It peeks through the oval windows, an eye struggling to focus. Judging from the light, it's a little past dawn. We should be landing within the hour.

The FBI agent is already awake. I see him buckled into an upright chair, staring out the window. He's watching the sunrise, perhaps. Either that or running through scenarios of what awaits.

I'm well aware of what will be greeting me on the tarmac. I slip from beneath Brian's arm to visit the nearest bathroom. Unlike the facility at the front of the cabin, the suite's bathroom has a shower stocked with hotel toiletries and items I've forgotten in drawers. Perfume. A blow-dryer. I don't put on a full-court press, but I do freshen up. I know reporters will be pointing their cameras when we land, and I want to look presentable and rational, like someone who'll get her daughter back.

By the time I exit, Brian's sitting up in what had been our bed. Breakfast has been served—eggs, by the smell of it. Coffee. The wine bottle from the prior night rests in a cupholder, about a third of the liquid remaining. Jen might have left it to ease a hangover, though I can't help but wonder if she's subtly admonishing me. I was drinking while my daughter was somewhere scared, probably starving. I'm a terrible mother.

"Please take your seats." Jen speaks through a loudspeaker. "We'll be landing shortly."

———

Fifteen minutes later, the four of us are rushing past TV cameras' long lenses. We see the news vans up close as the town car pulls out of Teterboro Airport, en route to the New Jersey Turnpike. As before, we lead a caravan down the highway.

This one, however, doesn't have to follow us for more than twenty minutes. We pull up to Fortix's headquarters before I've fully registered my surroundings. The rectangular building in front of me looks . . . wrong. Surely this place can't store trillions.

Fortix resembles a five-year-old's LEGO creation—a blocky box attached to another box. There are no visible windows or logos. No army of guards. The exterior is cordoned off by a concrete fence on one side and a chain-link version on another. The only indications that something truly important lies inside are the omnipresent telephone poles and undisguised cell towers lining the parking lot.

There is a check-in desk, however. As we pull up to the gate, a guard asks for our information. Lee collects all our licenses and an extra card from Brian, then exits to talk to the man. Whatever he says must suffice, as Lee is back inside within five minutes, telling the driver to park up ahead.

The walls block prying eyes *and* news cameras. I'm certain that television crews are amassing on the other side of the concrete barrier, but they've yet to send drones or helicopters over the fences. At least, I don't hear any.

Still, I hurry to the front door. Lee beats me there. Again, he flashes his FBI ID, this time at a stout man with brown skin and a Sikh turban. The new individual introduces himself as Arun Sethi, director of facility operations. From the way he regards Brian and me, I can tell he knows exactly why we're here.

"We've conducted a thorough search," Arun says. "I'm sorry to report that your daughter isn't in the facility."

Brian steps forward, slipping the man the card that Lee had shown earlier. "I have a key. And we're not looking for Alice. We're looking for—"

Lee interrupts. "We need to search for anything the kidnappers left. You're welcome to follow us."

Though Arun's jaw tightens, he opens the door, allowing us into a vestibule. One side is blocked by thick glass, presumably bulletproof. A guard, this one with his gun clearly visible, sits inside the enclosure like a museum artifact. *This is what security looked like in the 1900s.*

But it's 2025, so the guard isn't the half of it. We pass beneath round black cameras punched into the ceiling, following Arun to a massive blank wall. In front of it is a door affixed with a black electronic panel. As we approach, the screen turns on. A looped video shows where to stand for the retina scan.

Arun indicates Brian. "He can go through as an authorized client."

I glare at my husband. This is how he recognized the company logo on that money clip.

Brian reads my expression. "We have servers here."

Before I can ask why he didn't reveal this seemingly important detail, Lee pipes up. "As I said, you can escort me, but I need to be inside as well. If anything was left for Mr. and Mrs. Ingold, I must ensure it's handled correctly and that a chain of evidence custody is established."

Arun indicates Lee's badge. "I understand your position. Without a warrant—"

"Please." I step forward. "You can search us, do whatever you want. My daughter's missing, and her kidnappers have directed us here. There must be something they want us to find."

Though Arun shakes his head, he withdraws his key card and presses it to the screen. Afterward, he stands in front of the retina scanner and opens his eyes wide. Light illuminates the red in his brown irises. Finally, he punches a code into a keypad.

The door opens.

Arun motions us all through. Brian is first, followed closely by Lee. I trail behind, watching the three men disappear into a blue haze on the other side before entering myself. The door slams behind me.

I'm bathed in light from blue LEDs. They illuminate a cavernous warehouse of sorts, divided into storage units by ten-foot metal grates. The porous walls enable visitors to peer inside at black cabinets housing motherboards and mainframes. I notice electronic panels and PIN pads, presumably more locks. A low hum fills my ears. It smells like air-conditioning, vaguely syrupy.

It doesn't feel cool, though. Heat blasts my ankles as I step into an aisle between the walls of cordoned-off servers. Computers expel their used air into the hallways, I realize. Above me, a circuit board of colored ducts segments the ceiling, no doubt pumping cold air into the pods themselves. This place must consume enough electricity and gas to power a midsize city, maybe a small country.

"I really don't know how there could be anything that was left," Arun says. "As you can see, we have state-of-the-art security. If kidnappers or *anyone* unauthorized came in, we'd know."

"We don't know that the person would be unauthorized," Lee quips.

Arun reacts like Lee has insulted his child. "Our employees are vetted to the—"

"Mr. Sethi," I interrupt, "did you see our television interview? The video of my daughter?"

His brown eyes soften, answering the question.

"We don't know what game these people are playing," I continue. "But we're sure that they've planted clues. It's possible they want us to find something that they know was in here already. We're praying that, if we walk through this place, something will stand out to us. Something will make sense. Please."

Arun looks from me to Lee, who has his phone in one hand and badge in the other. If the man doesn't like my argument, Lee's prepared to make a different case.

"Okay," Arun nods. "I can take you on a short tour."

The air grows warmer as we follow Arun down an aisle. "Each individual unit is locked," he explains. "No one can enter without a badge *and* the code recognized by that particular pod, and only engineers who service the units and the servers' owners themselves have both."

His voice echoes, bouncing around the double-height walls. This place is miles and miles of closet-sized homes for machines and the infrastructure to keep them temperature controlled and off-limits. Everything else is open space.

"For our engineers to access an individual unit," Arun continues, "we need permission from the company." He glances at Lee. "Or a warrant requiring it."

I imagine the FBI's application for that. We have no evidence that anyone connected to my daughter is or was here, only a note hinting at the possibility and a money clip. Can a judge sign off on a hunch? "May we talk to employees?" I ask. "See if anyone saw anybody strange?"

Arun clears his throat. "Nobody will have seen anything the cameras didn't. There's been no one, save for our employees and technologists from other firms arriving for scheduled maintenance and due-diligence visits. We checked in advance of your arrival."

Lee isn't buying it. "We'll still need the names of those visitors to run background checks."

Again, Arun looks offended. "I assure you, we ran those same background checks."

Brian gazes down the corridor, as I did moments earlier. He must be thinking the same thing I am: We came here for nothing. The kidnappers probably couldn't even gain access to leave a clue.

"Did anyone come for Solucian Capital?" Brian asks.

The question clearly takes Arun off guard. He has the look of a raccoon caught in a porch light. "Oh. Well, I'd have to check the logs. Did you send anyone?"

I turn to Brian. "What's Solucian Capital?"

He lowers his voice. "Zelos's AIvest product. Our artificial intelligence trades stocks through it, analyzing the data in real time, guessing what's coming next. It's completely autonomous. The algorithmic trading firms still have people trying to figure out patterns and program the software. Our AI crunches the data and writes the instructions by itself."

His voice ticks up a notch as he says the last part, pride fueling the extra decibel. "It's a new business unit."

"Which you don't want your finance friends and hedge fund investors to know about," I add, filling in his reasoning for not mentioning this earlier. "They wouldn't like Zelos trading sans human intervention. Competing with them."

"It's more a proof of concept." Brian strides in front of me. "The finance community knows better than anyone that AI will be integrated into all industries. Hedge funds were among the first to try out early versions of my software. They helped train it." He turns to Arun. "Let's see if there's anything in my pod."

Arun lets Brian take the lead, bringing up the rear so he can monitor Lee and me. I'm sure he trusts that we're who we say we are, that we're not here on some supersecret spy mission to infect the stock exchange servers with a computer virus. But his job is to be vigilant. I make it easy for him, keeping my hands at my sides where he can see them.

We reach the locker for Brian's company. As with the outside of the building, there's no discernible logo, only a number and a keypad, as well as an ID sensor. Brian places his card on the pad and punches in a PIN. The door opens.

It's far colder inside this room. Goose bumps erupt on my skin as if tectonic plates beneath my arms have shifted, creating a sudden mountain range. It's also loud. The computers and air-conditioning resonate at an uncomfortable decibel level. I place my hands on both sides of my head to muffle the sound as I watch Brian circle one of his server cabinets.

He comes back holding an envelope. "This was on the floor."

Arun's face falls. "It's someone from your company. Or someone whom you'd given access. It's the only way. We wouldn't let anyone in here otherwise."

Brian shoots me an admonishing look. "See? I told you Alice was a pawn."

ALICE INGOLD

DIARY ENTRY TEN

My kidnappers are either experienced backpackers or off-grid survivalists. How else to explain having a portable shower and a pop-up privacy tent on hand? Then again, they could simply be perfectionists who planned my reluctant stay down to the last detail.

The shower resembled a sleeping bag tucked into its carrier. When I first saw it, I feared that Fawkes had decided to camp out next to me. I'd overplayed my fears of getting sick; now he intended to monitor me for night sweats or other signs of infection.

He set the duffel in the corner before removing a disk-shaped bag from his back. An unzip later, he was struggling with a mini tepee, wide as a tree trunk. His arms could barely get around the puffy green vinyl as he tried getting it to stand up.

As he wrestled with the tent, I should have made a run for it. My door didn't lock from the inside, and it was possible he'd left an exit open somewhere. Unfortunately, that thought—like most of my best ideas—didn't occur to me until later. Instead, I watched as he reached into the duffel and pulled out an attached hose.

The sight of a shower nozzle erased any inkling of making a break for it. In that moment, I wanted to wash more than escape. The mixture of dirt, blood, and sweat—made more rank by fear—had turned me into an animal, twitching with the urge to run or hide or fight. I needed to feel human.

He threaded the hose through the tent's top. "This will keep the water from getting everywhere. Just pull up the front flap, and there you go—a shower as good as any on a private plane . . . Not that I'd know."

I caught the bitterness in his tone. He knew I knew.

"My parents will pay a ransom." It was at least the third time I'd offered on their behalf. I hoped the media attention on my dad might help change my captors' minds about keeping me any longer. The press was well aware of my kidnapping and their riddle. What else did they want?

Fawkes withdrew a travel-sized baby shampoo from a jacket pocket and tossed it onto my mattress. "I already told you, this isn't about money."

If I hadn't been so intent on keeping my shower, I would have called him on his bullshit. Yes, my captors wanted me because of who my parents are, but also because of *what my parents have*. No matter what they said, money would come into play at some point. It always does.

Though I was silent, my expression must have betrayed my skepticism. Fawkes's frown deepened as he looked at me. "We want to change the future," he said, "make folks see how this world prioritizes technological convenience at the expense of enabling people to have real careers. Real lives! And we want to wake folks up to the way governments continually pander to corporate interests, further consolidating wealth at the top. The rich just get richer, regardless of what they contribute. And I'm betting these technological advancements on the horizon—the kind of stuff your dad is doing at Zelos—will only widen the distance between the haves and have nots. Unless there's regulation, a way of equitably redistributing the wealth so more billionaires don't turn into trillionaires, passing down the GDP of countries to their kids."

My shower was mere feet from my bedside. If I managed to stay silent in the face of this provocation, I could be inside in moments, feeling (hopefully) warm water cascading down my scalp and spine. But my kidnappers thinking of me as a symbol of unearned wealth, instead of an individual, was part of what had gotten me into this mess.

"I don't control government policy," I retorted. "I'm a student, soon to graduate and jockey for a job like everyone else."

Fawkes glanced at the ceiling. "'Like everyone else.' Sure."

I was tempted to go into my father firing me, but a long story would only delay my shower. Plus, I'd just finished writing all that down. At some point, maybe Fawkes would steal back my notebook and read the whole thing.

Instead, I stood from the bed and grabbed the shampoo, talking as I headed toward the tent. "I was born with affluent, connected parents— you're right. And I assume that you were born in the United States, with all the access to free education and democracy and our country's vibrant, admittedly flawed economy. Others are born in places where there's not clean water or food. What if someone kidnapped you to hold you up as an example of American privilege? How would you feel then?"

Fawkes stepped toward me. "Privilege is relative. We didn't only choose you because you have so much more than most. You're part of all this in a way that I'm not."

I gestured to my surrounding cage. "What control do I have? Why do I deserve to be in here any more than you?"

His nostrils flared, an angry bull readying a charge, though he didn't take another step toward me. I credited his restraint to my stench. My BO was an armor of sorts, an olfactory chastity belt protecting against sexual assault or close contact of any other kind.

"I studied technology." Fawkes changed course as he spoke, putting himself between me and the most direct route to the door. "Did I tell you that?"

"You're a hacker? That's how you found my address?"

He waved, not admitting anything so much as dismissing the question. "I intended to be a programmer. That's where the jobs were, right? I mean, since our country outsourced most of its manufacturing labor to machines and poorer countries so Americans could focus on higher-level thinking positions. We were supposed to be the designers and architects, the people who controlled the computers."

Fawkes pointed at me. "I applied for a job at your dad's company, in fact. I thought I'd help search get better and faster. Didn't realize that they don't need new comp-sci grads for that. The software has been taught to improve itself by crunching ever-larger amounts of data and refining its own algorithms. The only job I could get at Zelos was maybe helping code the interface or user-experience stuff, the peripheral parts that make it easier for us to interact with the machines doing the real work."

As he spoke, it occurred to me that I didn't have to sit and listen. The can opener was hidden at the side of my mattress, resting on an inch of pallet pressed against the wall. I could wait for Fawkes to be distracted and then strike, one quick plunge to the jugular. Or, if I wasn't strong enough to puncture his neck, a thrust into his eye.

I slumped back onto the bed as if settling in for a long story. "I'm guessing my dad didn't hire you."

"For the best," he sighed. "Zelos doesn't even pay enough to afford a city apartment. They were offering all the code monkeys spots in these tiny prefabricated units—like pods from *The Matrix*, only equipped with kitchenettes."

I nodded along, slipping my hand behind me into the crack between the makeshift bed frame and the wall. "You chose me because you're upset at the way my dad's company treats employees?"

Fawkes cocked his head. For a moment, I thought he'd caught me fishing for a weapon. Quickly, I adjusted my position so it might appear that I'd grabbed the edge of the mattress for leverage to sit straighter.

"It's not only about your dad," he said, *not* moving from the door. "Zelos's example will make it easier for other companies to do the same thing, particularly as its technology becomes more prevalent. Why pay people enough to live near their office if you can simply buy better software to reduce your workforce? The people left will be so happy to have any job, they'll take whatever salary you're offering. Live in a closet."

I returned to feeling for the can opener. A moment later, its point pricked my finger. I pinched the cool metal between my index and middle digits and began pulling it toward the mattress edge. "I have nothing to do with my father's company," I argued, continuing the conversation as both a distraction and a defense. "Your grievance isn't with me."

"Didn't you work there?" he asked.

Bro had done his research.

"I interned for a summer, but I want nothing to do with that place. Believe me. I'm still hoping to become a writer."

"It doesn't matter," he quipped. "You benefit from his company. You live in an apartment it pays for."

Though I wanted to argue that I paid the rent on my Oakland loft, the fact was that my checks came from an account funded by my parents over the years, and my mom was the unit's guarantor. Without her name on the lease, the landlord wouldn't have accepted mine.

Instead, I admitted the one grievance Fawkes couldn't dismiss. "I don't *only* benefit," I said, giving him the much-abridged version of my diary entry. "Growing up, my dad spent way more time with his company than my mom or me. He never came to anything I did—no sports matches, no recitals. I got the lead in the school play once. He said he'd stream it, and he didn't even do that. My stuff didn't matter to him. Only his work."

As soon as I finished my spiel, I regretted it. This guy was my jailer, not my friend. He didn't care about my first-world problems. If anything, my complaining only solidified my poor-little-rich-girl stereotype. "Point is, I understand your frustration with Zelos," I mumbled. "But you shouldn't take it out on me."

He rubbed the back of his neck. "All the more reason you should sympathize with what we're doing."

"I don't understand what you're doing."

"People need to see what's coming—for their jobs, for their dreams. We'll all feel like you soon. Shunted to the sidelines."

Agreeing with this guy wasn't going to get me released, I realized. It was time to change tactics. Maybe defending Zelos would make Fawkes see that kidnapping me wasn't necessary.

I channeled my father. "Zelos will do great things for the world, too, you know. I'm sure you've read all the articles celebrating what the company is working on, how Zelos's AI will ultimately identify disease factors that we never realized. With all the data it can process, it could end up curing cancer, Alzheimer's, Parkinson's. It could save us from the next pandemic."

"Or start it." Fawkes pointed at my makeshift nightstand. The AI book rested on top. "If you had read that, you'd know that AI is making it easier to edit DNA. Governments could use it to create biological weapons."

I palmed the can opener. "Or solve the problem of the BRCA gene. My grandma died of metastasized breast cancer. You wouldn't be so cavalier about technology that could cure diseases if someone you loved had suffered."

Something close to contrition flashed across Fawkes's unmasked and, regrettably, not-unattractive face. In movies, the would-be victim always finds it easier to kill the vampire when he's a bat-eared beast as opposed to in his forever-young form. Fawkes would have been easier to stab in the mask.

"Nothing is ever all bad," he admitted. "There needs to be balance. Folks should understand how they'll be impacted—so workers can get the right protections, so we don't all end up consumers on subsidized basic incomes, feeding off ad-supported tech, unaware of how anything we use works, how to fend for ourselves. Think for ourselves. Buying what we're pointed at, believing whatever stories the algorithms surface, each generation getting dumber and dumber as computers become increasingly intelligent. No longer able to fix the code or even understand it, let alone make a difference."

Make a difference. It was the magic phrase that united Fawkes and me, what I'd wanted to do with my writing and what he'd hoped to do with coding. "I really do understand. I don't know what I'm going to do with my life either. I wanted to be an author."

Fawkes offered a sad smile. "Yeah, maybe you do." He groaned. "God, I could use a drink."

The admission made me feel even more aligned with my male captor. He, too, was tired and frustrated and wishing he could escape— if not physically, then chemically. "You're not the only one," I quipped.

His smile brightened. "When we get out of here."

I clung to the implication. "You see a future where I'm enjoying a cocktail?"

"I hope you'll be enjoying a drink or whatever you want in the future."

Hope was not a promise. My grip on the can opener tightened. "Why wait? Let me go."

His eyes went all guilty puppy. "People are only now catching on to the point of all this. Folks like me—people who understand and have studied tech a bit, who've tried to work at companies like your dad's—we know more about what's going on. But regular people need to see what's happening right under their noses, that this tech isn't only about making it easier to do their jobs. Zelos's AI is taking those jobs. We need to give the public more clues that bring them to places where Zelos's influence is undeniable—and terrifying."

Fawkes wanted me to ask for details. The blaze in his brown eyes said as much. Listening to all of Zelos's "bad deeds" wouldn't help me escape, however. I only cared about how long he intended to keep me here.

"How much do you plan to show them? How many more riddles do you have?"

Rather than answering, Fawkes pointed to the shower. "It should be warm. The nozzle has a button to help conserve water. Faucet only runs when you press it." He turned toward the door.

The metal can opener burned in my palm, dry ice melting my skin. It was now or never. Fawkes believed I wanted the shower too much to risk losing it. He wouldn't be expecting me to pounce on his back and drive a metal point into his throat.

I rose from the bed as he grabbed the doorknob. *Breathe,* I told myself, shifting my weight to the balls of my feet, preparing to lunge.

"I'm Hugh, by the way."

The introduction pushed me off course. "What?"

He turned to face me, slowly enough that I had the necessary second to hide the can opener behind my back.

"I didn't tell you before because I thought you wouldn't want to know. That you'd think it meant you were in more danger since you could tell it to the cops." Hugh met my eyes. "But I know it's a lot to ask that you trust us when you don't even know who you're talking to." He waved, a shy gesture more befitting a kid in a kindergarten class than a grown man. "So, Alice, my name is Hugh."

My fingers loosened on the can opener. "Hi?"

Hugh flashed a real smile, a boyish grin with shiny teeth peeking from beneath full lips. The look was inviting, almost flirtatious. "Nice to meet you." He pointed to the portable water heater attached to the shower hose. "Guess I should leave you to it."

"Hugh" turned toward the door, giving me his back. I watched him palm the knob, wondering if it was at all possible that he'd shared his real name. Such a damning detail was more of a sign of overconfidence than a trust exercise. Hugh believed so deeply in his cause and his ability to convince me of its righteousness that he didn't fear me ratting him out to the cops.

He opened the door. At the same time, my shocked fingers unwittingly released the can opener. The metal slid from my sweaty palm and smacked the concrete with a sharp ping, loud as cutlery against crystal. I watched in horror as the weapon skidded in front of me toward my captor.

In the doorway, Hugh stiffened. I could almost see his hackles rise below the sharp line of his crew cut. He knew what had caused that sound.

I froze. I'd fashioned the man's olive branch into a shiv. Any second, he would whirl around, grab the can opener, and drive it into my own neck.

Hugh's hands curled into fists.

Every synapse in my body fired with one direction: Run. But where to? My much larger male kidnapper was blocking the only exit.

"I, I . . ." The excuse I had yet to invent wasn't forming on my tongue. "I—"

"Have a nice shower." Hugh stepped into the neighboring room without turning around. I watched, panting, as the door slammed shut behind him.

CATHERINE NEWHOUSE INGOLD

TWO DAYS AFTER

A concrete wall can't keep out the press. We exit the data center to helicopter blades battering the air. The resulting wind transforms the parking lot debris into shrapnel. Grit attacks my face, adding injury to myriad insults as I run to the idling town car. I'm tempted to look up and shake my fist at the long-lens cameras. Maybe flip the bird.

But I was raised to genuflect rather than flash my middle fingers. I keep my head down and slide into the back seat. As unsatisfying as my restraint feels, I know it's for the best. We need the media right now. The envelope retrieved from Brian's pod didn't contain a calling card in the form of a logo-stamped money clip. All we have is another cryptic poem.

> What happens to a truth ignored?
> Does it make a sound
> As a felled tree in a wood?
> Or go quiet amid the clicks
> of viral opinion?
> And what of the fact finders
> The questioners and querants?

When bots summarize stories
for ad-supported blogs?
Do they lose their voices
Screaming for attention?
Or reach for a match?

The kidnappers were evidently Langston Hughes fans. They'd attempted to ape the style of his poem "Harlem" with its famous first line, though they'd failed to get the rhythm right or conjure the same visceral images. Still, not a terrible poem for their purposes.

The front passenger-side door slams. Our driver puts the car in gear while Lee whisper-reads the words. I catch him turning the syllables on his tongue like a strange food he's unsure he wants to swallow.

"It's about the media," he says, perhaps to himself.

The statement isn't any revelation. "Fact finders" and bot-summarized stories gave away the subject of the clue. The question is the destination. More than a thousand daily newspapers exist in the United States, along with even more magazines. The Zelos search app on my cell revealed that fact in nanoseconds. Visiting each one would be impossible.

"Is there a paper that gets summarized the most?" I ask. "Or any particular publication that's had an issue with blogs or bots?"

Brian rubs his right thumb across his left knuckles, an anxious habit that I'm somehow only now recognizing. Is it possible I've never seen him really nervous? "We should head across the river," he says. "New York's the mecca of media. *Wall Street Journal.* The *Post.* The *Times.* We can start with the *Times.* God knows these idiots are lefties. Marxist liberals, most likely. Morons."

I could do without Brian's political commentary. He has an unfortunate tendency to brand anyone who doesn't agree with him as stupid. If I shared my opinions, he might say the same about me.

Whoever has Alice isn't dumb. They've stumped us so far. "The *Times* probably has the biggest circulation," I add, thinking of its international scope and online Wordle players. "Though there must be something in the poem that points to a particular paper. Something we're missing."

Brian leans between the seats to address our driver. "There's probably no point visiting the papers in person until we know which one. Take us back to Teterboro."

Though the man nods, he doesn't make eye contact. I belatedly realize it's because he's busy evaluating the coming obstacles. Beyond the security gate awaits an army of journalists and camera crews. We advance toward them, not so much driving as rolling, a projectile headed into pudding.

As the gate rises, the human glob spills toward the car. Questions emerge from the mass. Though it's impossible to see the individual querants in the crowd, we hear them clearly enough.

"How did they get in?"

"Was there another note?"

"Where's Alice?"

Lee turns to the back seat. "We can't reveal that someone entered your firm's personal unit," he tells Brian. "It'll let the kidnappers know we're onto them."

I shoot my husband a look. *Can you believe this guy?* As much as we might wish things were different, everyone in the car knows that we're not *onto* anyone. Whatever we've deduced, Alice's captors wanted us to figure out. They wanted to show Brian that they can access Zelos's secure spaces. If Alice's kidnappers believed leaving the note at the data center would lead us to them, they surely wouldn't have done so.

Brian averts his eyes from mine. "Blow the horn," he says.

Though the driver does as told, the crowd barely moves from Brian's side of the vehicle. Journalists aren't scared off a story easily. They've been trained to face down danger to get needed information . . . which gives me an idea.

I lean over Brian to press the button lowering his back window. The glass descends, increasing the volume of the shouts. "We received another letter," I yell to the crowd.

The car ceases its forward crawl. Conversely, the journalists stop crowding. Instead, they point their cameras toward the open window and await my next words.

"We don't want the public knowing everything," Lee hisses, pinching the letter between his fingers. "If we get these guys, we need unreleased information to trip them up."

I snatch the paper from his hand. "All I care about is getting Alice."

"Catherine," Brian whispers, "we should think about this."

What my husband means is he wants time to consider what implications the note may have for his company.

Before Lee or Brian can say anything else, I begin reading. The journalists go silent, no one daring to ruin the sound bites. It seems that even the helicopter blades hush, as if the networks have called off their aerial dogs now that I'm cooperating.

As soon as I finish, the crowd starts up again, computers rebooting. "Where do you think she is? What do you think it means?"

"We're hoping the public can help with that," I shout.

"Do you think it concerns the media?"

"Is it a threat?"

"Is the mention of 'match' an allusion to an intended arson?"

A male voice resonates above the din of questions. "A match could be a reference to a labor strike. You strike a match."

I stretch farther out the window to see the one person giving information rather than demanding it. The crowd doesn't shift to let me see the speaker, though. He doesn't push through.

A female journalist speaks up. "The *Washington Reader*'s staff are picketing as we speak. They've shut down the paper."

Unlike the mystery informant, this woman makes eye contact. She wants to be certain I'm aware of her contribution. If there's a future scoop to be had, I know who to call. "Shelley Maxwell, ABC," she says before continuing. "The Washington paper's cutting jobs for the third time this year. Replacing some of the writers with AI."

I look to Brian, hoping my expression communicates the question: Is Zelos involved?

Instead of answering, he lifts a hand in thanks and raises the window. He won't tell me. Even now, with our daughter's life on the line, he's prioritizing his work.

Before the window completely closes, I hear one last question: "Mr. and Mrs. Ingold, where are you going now?"

I don't respond, though I finally have an answer. First we're headed to the airport. Then, as soon as we land, we're marching straight to the Capitol.

ALICE INGOLD

DIARY ENTRY ELEVEN

The water tank had enough for ninety seconds, give or take a drop. I peeled off my clothes beside it, watching the door for Hugh to reappear with a weapon of his own, something to punish me for plotting his murder. After a minute without a visitor, I stepped inside the green cocoon and zipped myself inside. Being surrounded by neon vinyl had threatened to make me claustrophobic. Instead, there was something comforting about standing inside the alien embryo. I could almost pretend I was safe.

As I grabbed the showerhead, I gave myself a mental pep talk. Undercarriage, face, wounds, and hair—all needed a good scrub. Without touching my head, I could tell that my locks were matted. Something about the weight of the mop. The way it plopped onto my shoulders and down my back like gloopy dough. Washing it was worth the risk of running out of water and leaving soap on my skin.

The showerhead was a spray nozzle. I held it to the top of my skull and pressed the lever, bracing for an icy blast. What emerged was lukewarm, the temp of tea left on a counter. Not delicious. Not wholly unpleasant.

Rather than letting the water trickle from my scalp to my back, I quickly spritzed my head and then misted the rest of my body.

Afterward, I set down the shut-off nozzle and began working the baby shampoo over every damp surface, creating a slick if not a lather. I concentrated on the four areas of interest, taking extra time with my cut-up knees, peeling off the Band-Aids and working the soap into the scabs. The suds didn't sting nearly as much as the hydrogen peroxide, which I took as a negative. Wounds must hurt to heal.

I was rinsing when I heard footsteps. The door had apparently opened and shut without my noticing, a consequence of the sopping hair covering my ears. Rather than stopping, I moved the spray over my body twice as fast. Hugh could reclaim his gift any minute. Though he'd let me shower after hearing the can opener drop, I doubted he was feeling especially magnanimous toward me.

"Got you a towel."

The voice belonged to Ghost Face, whose real name I still didn't know. My guess was that I didn't know Fawkes's either. I doubted "Hugh" was on any birth certificate. Still, he'd at least given me something to work with.

Either *Hugh* was too angry to bring towels himself, or he was trying to preserve my dignity and prove he wasn't any kind of sexual threat. I hoped for the latter.

I started to say thank you, but the pleasantry caught in my throat. Ghost Face was the mean one. I hated being at her mercy.

"And some fresh clothes," she added.

Do they have prison stripes? I thought but didn't say.

"We're about the same size, I think," she continued. "Small."

As much as I didn't want to wear my captor's clothes, putting back on my blood-stiffened leggings and sweat-soaked top would negate many of my shower's benefits. I gave my underarms and undercarriage one last blast of the shower nozzle and then let the remaining water trickle into my hair for good measure. When the drips stopped, I squeezed the tangled mess into a rope that squeaked as I tightened it. After, I unzipped the tent's front flap, just enough to push my hand through.

"Pass them to me." I felt her knuckles and then rough terry cloth, which I immediately reeled through the hole I'd created. The fabric was thin, the bath towel equivalent of single-ply toilet paper. They'd probably stolen it from a roadside motel.

I ran the towel over my body anyway, whisking away the water droplets rather than absorbing them. Afterward, I wrapped the damp terry cloth around my hair. It wasn't long enough to cover much more than my chest, so why try?

Again, I slipped my hand through the hole in the vinyl. "May I have the clothes?"

"You'll need to open the tent more."

I moved to the tent's side, stretched toward the zipper, and widened the hole another half inch.

"More." Exasperation seeped into her tone.

Any more and the flap would fall forward, exposing my nakedness. I was reluctant to reveal myself for two reasons. One, modesty. The second, safety. All I knew about my female captor was that she'd been willing to put a gun at my back and force me into the trunk of a car. Though she was acting nice now, she could still be a sadist who'd relish the sight of my skinny, unclothed body shivering in my rapidly cooling shower pod.

"You have the clothes?"

"I can leave them on the bed, if you'd prefer," she said. "Come back later."

Her offer didn't seem particularly sadistic. I pulled the zipper until the door flapped forward and extended my arm through the space. A moment later I held a pair of folded sweatpants, a hoodie, and a plastic-wrapped pack of cotton panties. Seeing the undies was a new relief. Anyone who'd taken enough care to make certain I had clean undergarments couldn't intend to murder me, right?

As I dressed, I realized that the woman was correct about us being the same size—a surprise since we wore our weight so differently. Ghost

Face was shapelier, with a backside that might have filled out these gray sweatpants.

She stood in front of me holding out a pair of socks. "No point giving you these in there. You'd only get them wet."

The gesture deserved an audible thank-you. Hugh had no doubt instructed her to bring me fresh clothes. Wanting me to have dry feet, however, had to be all her. "Appreciate that," I said.

The socks were warm, maybe fresh out of the dryer. Slipping my feet inside them made me feel like the house-elf in Harry Potter. I was free!

But I wasn't. And while I was dressing, my first kidnapper had positioned herself in reach of the door. Her hands were tucked into her sweatshirt's front pocket, adding two lumps to the distinct bulge in the center.

Her cat eyes caught me staring at the gun's outline. She redirected my attention to the toilet/nightstand, pointing to it with pursed lips. "I left you that too."

Atop the nightstand was a new paddle brush, complete with paper around the plastic bristles. It's never-used nature was both blessing and misfortune. A new brush meant no lice, though an old wooden one would have made a better weapon. This was more valuable serving its intended purpose.

I snapped off the paper and then pulled my hair to one shoulder, working the brush up from the ends.

"Feel a bit better?" Her expression was a strange combination of sheepish and hopeful. Some people expressed guilt with sadness, others with a crooked smile.

"You don't want to keep me here," I said.

She leaned against the closed exit. "Of course I don't *want* to keep you here."

I indicated the door. "Nothing's stopping you from stepping aside right now."

She widened her stance. "Folks are still arguing that we're doing this for the environment. I mean, we send them to a *homeless shelter* on the site of a former computer chip plant, and the media turns it into a story about groundwater pollution. Really? They go to the second derivative rather than the obvious juxtaposition of technology impacting the labor force. So much for setting the tone."

I pulled the brush through a tangle. "Why not write out your grievances in plain English and have my parents read those to the press?"

She snorted. "People are done being lectured to by elites. Like we said, they want to engage. Solve the puzzle themselves."

I sympathized with the logic, though it wouldn't help me get out of here any faster. "People will draw their own conclusions, then," I sighed.

My female captor echoed my heavy breath. "The internet's amateur sleuths are on the case, tracking down all the companies that have space in that data center. They'll put it together."

"You put the last clue in a data center?"

She reached behind her for the doorknob. "It doesn't matter."

"It does to me. Where do you have my parents going now?"

The woman chewed her bottom lip.

"You're torturing them, you know." The accusation came out louder than intended, part whine, part shout. It pierced her emotional armor. I could almost see her sarcastic cloak falling away, as if the muscles in her face had been held by invisible SPANX and were now tumbling back into their gravity-stricken shape.

"Hurting your folks isn't our goal. But they're emblematic of the problems we're talking about. And someone has to sound the alarm, even if . . ." She trailed off with a long exhale. "People need to care enough to demand that we direct AI technology to fields where it benefits the entire human race, where it helps *people* do their jobs rather than take their jobs. We need to contain AI with laws and regulations. At the very least, we've got to figure out how to properly tax the use of it so that the wealth it creates is redistributed to all of society and not concentrated among corporate owners while the rest of us live off some paltry government assistance. And making companies pay for their data centers' carbon emissions isn't a bad idea either."

Hugh had already made many of the same arguments. Clearly, neither he nor his partner would be swayed by sympathy for my rich AI-owning parents. I resumed brushing my hair.

"Is there anything I can get you that might make the next few days a bit more tolerable?" she asked.

Pride demanded that I insist she stop visiting until my parents have finished her ridiculous treasure hunt. But I couldn't let my ego win. Solitary confinement didn't suit me. I'd gone from living with my parents to dorming with a roommate to sharing an apartment. I didn't know how to be alone. Plus, the more I talked to my captors, the less of a symbol I became. Destroying a symbol is easy. Much more difficult to attack a soul.

I scanned the room, seeking something to request that would be useful in an escape without being obvious. This girl wasn't going to bring me a ladder to access the ceiling vent. I needed to find something subtle. My gaze landed on my few visible possessions: the book, the toilet box and its interior bucket, the hydrogen peroxide bottle. Not exactly the stuff of chemical warfare.

I faced her. "The toilet smells. Do you think I could empty it out and get some bleach to counteract the scent?"

"Sure, we can take care of that for you."

"Great."

She pulled open the door.

"Oh. And nail polish remover."

She turned back around. Brow furrowed. "Nail polish remo—"

I waved my broken nails. "I snapped a bunch jumping from the trunk. And the paint's chipping, which makes me pick at it. Blame OCD. If the polish is off, I'll have to find another fidget that won't tear up my hands."

My explanation was too long. Liars overexplain.

Her brow remained furrowed for another second as she stared at my sorry manicure.

"The little things make us feel human," I added.

Her tan skin smoothed out. "Sure. I'll see what I can do."

I watched the door shut behind her and resumed brushing my hair. Good. She would see what she could do.

And so would I.

CATHERINE NEWHOUSE INGOLD

TWO DAYS AFTER

Traffic doesn't only stall cars. The one-hour flight from Teterboro to Dulles International will cost us three times that due to clogged airways over Newark and Queens, or so says Captain Luke. An express train would take the same time, though we'd be hassled by journalists riding in an open car. Since I talked to the press, Lee hasn't stopped lamenting that he can't trust us to "preserve the integrity of the investigation" . . . a.k.a. *shut our mouths.* He insisted on waiting for the plane.

As a result, I'm glued to a leather couch, attempting to keep busy rather than staring through a two-story wall of windows at our grounded jet. Teterboro's interior recalls an upscale medical waiting room, the sort of place where people might fill out paperwork for elective surgeries. Its fancy yet sparse furnishings suggest purgatory on the way to paradise. One can only hope.

I don't exactly know what to do with myself. When we arrived, I immediately got to work tracking down the number for editors at the *Washington Reader.* Fortunately, the PR firm I used for my last charity event had the executive editor's cell. Within a half hour, I was listening to a Marianne Gradisher shouting over call-and-response protests from strikers. Though the woman hadn't heard from Alice's captors, she couldn't be certain that they hadn't reached out. None of the journalists had been at their desks in days. Mail was piling up. For all she knew, the next clue to Alice's location was yellowing in a storage closet.

I secured a promise from her to check the mail and then hung up, turning my attention to Brian. He sat in an armchair catty-corner from my couch, whisper-yelling into his cell. For over an hour, he's grilled Zelos's employees, trying to figure out who'd accessed the data center from his firm. From what I've overheard, only Brian, the CTO, and the firm's director of infrastructure had their retinas on record and the relevant key cards/codes.

"Well, you know what happens when you assume," Brian growls into the receiver. "I don't care. I want those tapes." He hangs up, neck flushed from restraining his volume.

"They still don't know how someone got in?" I ask.

"They get notifications whenever someone enters the pod. Yet they didn't think to tell me I'd been logged over the summer." Brian clenches one hand over a fist. Someone's getting fired over this. "They figured I'd stopped by for a surprise check while on East Coast business. Didn't say a damn thing. Idiots."

The assumption that Brian dropped in on a business unit doesn't seem like a terrible one. Given how difficult the data center makes entering, it stands to reason that anyone who'd accessed Zelos's room was the rightful owner of Brian's key card. Moreover, Brian has a reputation for spot-checking business units. Anyone can prepare for a big presentation, he's always said. The measure of an employee is how they perform when the day isn't important, when they're amid another interminable week with a longer-lead deadline. Are they still motivated to work? Or are they hanging out at long lunches, grabbing a quickie with a significant other?

To me, it's more believable that Brian visited the data center and forgot than someone successfully impersonated him. "How would anyone get your retina scan?"

Brian grimaces like I've suggested he's suffering from Alzheimer's. "You got in without one."

"Only because it was an emergency," I counter. "I was also accompanied by you, the FBI, and the head of facility operations."

Brian rubs his knuckles. "Point is, it's not impossible."

Though still improbable. "And how would someone get your key card? Are ID cards hackable? Can you print them or—"

"Let me Zelos that for you," Brian snaps.

I'm tempted to retort but opt to give the rudeness a pass. Brian prides himself on being able to answer any technical question imaginable, including how people steal digital identities. Someone swiping his key card is an attack on his sense of self. It means Brian Ingold, AI guru, was robbed in his own house.

The more I think about it, the more I suspect he might simply have been robbed. I can't imagine Brian clicking on a spam link or letting a worm past all his corporate safeguards.

"Do you have a backup ID for the data center?"

"Not lying around." Though Brian's tone remains annoyed, his expression betrays some doubt. He pulls out his wallet and begins sorting through his cards, sliding them up with the base of his thumb from the leather folds. All the while, he continues audibly convincing himself that his backup key card must be in one of the flaps. "When I was here over the summer, I didn't even visit the data center. I was busy taking meetings."

The quip recalls something Alice said about flying to New York with him toward the end of her internship. Her exact words, I believe, were: *Yeah, he takes me everywhere, but he barely speaks to me. I spent the whole time being babysat by his chief technology officer.*

The thought scratches at my throat. Brian was so terrible to her over the summer. Alice made the effort to get to know him on his terms, at his place of business, which is more than he's ever done for her. Yet he couldn't appreciate it. He couldn't take one lunch meeting and make it about her rather than about him—couldn't let her leave on a positive note.

And now she's trapped somewhere because of his company.

I'm struck by the urge to slap the wallet out of his hand and scream at him for failing to pay attention to the important things. His precious key card. His infinitely more precious daughter. But what would be the point? He'd only accuse me of being hysterical, blame my behavior on stress and our daughter.

"Alice mentioned that trip," is all I say.

Brian moves on from the wallet's flaps to its inside zipper. "I'm surprised." He scoffs, not looking up. "She couldn't have been more transparent about her lack of interest in working for me. Meanwhile, her friends are nose to the grindstone, lining up careers with real companies. Real prospects. You know her pal Monique?"

The name is unfamiliar. I'm about to say no when I realize that Brian must be mistaken. There's no way that, in the little time he's spent with our child, he's been introduced to a friend I've never met. "You mean Monica?"

"Brown eyes, uh, darker skin color? Studying computer science."

"Monica, yeah. Her college roommate for *three years*."

Brian doesn't pick up on the implied admonishment. "I ran into her at the end of the summer when she came in to see Alice," he continues. "She'd had an internship at RenCap—big algo trading firm in New York. Kid was only on the infrastructure team, but that's at least a stepping stone to financial coding. Meanwhile, here's Alice, relying on me to let her shadow folks, despite not having the slightest inclination to absorb anything, find something at Zelos that she could be passionate about."

Even now, with Alice possibly fighting for her life, disdain saturates Brian's tone. He likes to pretend that he'd coined Spider-Man's Voltaire-cribbed motto: *With great privilege comes great responsibility.* Alice, in his estimation, has never lived up to those words. And he definitely let her know at the end of the summer.

"She's passionate about writing and literature." My voice trembles, whether with anger or nerves, I can't tell. "Ever since she was little, Alice has read everything she could get her hands on. Remember how she loved comics in the beginning and then moved on to fantasy? She devoured all the Lord of the Rings books before ending elementary school. Then there were her sci-fi and dystopian stages in middle school with *The Hitchhiker's Guide to the Galaxy*, *The Handmaid's Tale*, and the like. Even movies. She had me watch all the old Matrix films with her. In high school it was thrillers and romance, *in addition* to the assigned reading. I swear she went through a book or two a week. Then in college, she got immersed in American poetry and British lit. I can't recall a time Alice didn't have a book on her nightstand and another on her phone. You know she's always scrawling away in a notebook."

Brian doesn't make eye contact as I speak. If he knows any of this, he doesn't care. He's ignoring me, as usual, as he ignores everything that doesn't involve his ego or business or legacy. As he's done to Alice most of her life—until the moment when he *fired her.*

The truth is, I helped him do that. I kept trying to bring him and Alice together. I pushed him to hire her. Why? Why did I put my daughter in the impossible position to please him?

Because I couldn't face the man whom I'd married. I wanted to believe Brian's obsession with his work was, at its core, a form of self-sacrifice and altruism. I didn't want to see who Brian had become with all his success, maybe who he's always been: a self-centered, egotistical workaholic, laser-focused on his own importance. Then, when Alice came to me for comfort—when she told me what I already knew, deep down—I blamed her rather than ruining my fantasy of him.

"Well, writing's not exactly a growth industry, as I told her." Brian snaps his wallet shut and then rotates it in his palm, a magician about to perform a trick. Abracadabra and the key card will appear. "The spare must be in an office drawer," he mumbles.

"You know Alice only took that job to get to know you and give you a chance to get to know her. And you blew it." Rage adds vibrato to my voice. "You fucking blew it."

"Catherine." Brian turns my name into a warning. I'm sure no one has cursed at him in a very long time. Brian believes profanity is a sign of low intelligence.

I don't care anymore. "Our daughter is an amazing person. Did you give a fuck, though? One iota of a fuck? You didn't even try to see that, did you? You measured her against your custom yardstick, judging an artist—a *humanist*—by her desire to climb the corporate ladder."

Brian glances behind him, checking who might be listening to my tirade. He lowers his voice to a growl. "I gave her a chance—"

"You fired her!" I shout. "She came to bond with you, and you fucking fired her. Sent her home crying, feeling like a complete failure, like her own father thought she was worthless."

Brian stands. "You should never have asked me to hire her. You made me think she would be impressed—"

"Not everything is about you!" I stand, too, though my voice cracks, undermining my own power pose. It's not anger rubbing my vocal cords raw but restrained tears. Brian is right. It's my fault too. I've enabled him for years.

Brian blinks at me like he doesn't recognize the woman in front of him. His nose is flared as if I've morphed into something disgusting: a troll or a troglodyte or a business interviewer asking him a *stupid question*. "You should get a glass of water. Take a breath. You're stressed."

I glare at him. He's not the only one disgusted. "I'm upset. I'm also awake for the first time in so long. I should have said this a long time ago. I should have stood up for Alice."

Brian returns his wallet to his jacket pocket, ignoring or dismissing my realization. "I'm sure the key card is in my office," he mutters, changing the subject. "It's more difficult to break in there than it is to get into that data center. I don't allow anyone to hold the door open for *friends*. No one could . . ."

He trails off. I catch a shiver in his eyes, lightning in a passing cloud. He's made a connection of some kind.

"What?"

He shakes his head. "No. Nothing."

What he means is, nothing important to our daughter's disappearance. He's probably figured out something to do with a work problem, some other business taking up his mental computational power when all he should be thinking about is getting back our only child. "What do you mean, noth—"

I'm interrupted by the sound of running. Our plane's first officer hurries over to Brian and me, looking us square in the face for the first time. Green eyes shine from beneath his cap. The color is arresting, a saturated jewel tone contrasting with the dour navy of his uniform and the airport's neutral decor. It's clear from the intensity of his stare and stride that something has happened. Something bad.

"Mr. and Mrs. Ingold," he says, "you should see the TV."

I scan the room. A flat-screen is mounted on a far wall. "Where's the remote?"

The television flickers on in response. A glance reveals Captain Luke talking to an airport attendant behind the counter. Both look toward the screen. The station changes from CNBC to cable news. Without my glasses, I can't make out the corner logo. The female anchor, however, I recognize.

"Now our top story," Shelley Maxwell says. "A new development in the kidnapping of nineteen-year-old Alice Ingold, daughter of AI technologist Brian Ingold and his wife, shipping heiress Catherine Newhouse Ingold. And this latest suggests Alice's captors are motivated not by money but by concerns about the very technology that Alice's father is spearheading at his firm, Zelos AI. For more on the story, we go to Washington correspondent Tasha Murphy."

The TV flashes to a younger female reporter standing in front of a cement-and-stone building. Behind her, men and women march in an elongated oblong. They hold signs with slogans such as AI, BYE BYE and HAL 9000 DIDN'T TELL THE TRUTH.

"We're in front of the *Washington Reader*'s offices, where staff have been on strike over proposed employment cuts and the adoption of Zelos software that many here argue would replace reasoned journalism with PR-influenced, computer-generated articles. It seems that Alice Ingold's kidnappers may agree with that argument."

I shoot Brian a look. As I thought, his software is involved here too.

The reporter turns her cheek to the camera, encouraging the operator to widen his shot. The camera zooms out to encompass an imposing older woman standing beside her. A chyron beneath this new character identifies her as Marianne Gradisher, the *Reader*'s executive editor.

"Ms. Gradisher, you found something today in the mail room."

The woman removes a folded paper from the pocket of a slate-gray blazer. She adjusts Buddy Holly glasses on her nose. "This was sent to me and our technology reporter. Apparently, it came from a New York address. We found it today after being prompted to enter the building and look through the mail room."

"What is it?" the reporter asks.

"A poem, it seems. Of sorts." The executive editor turns to the camera. She raises the paper to right below her chin, a singer holding a score so that it doesn't block her projection.

"America," she begins, before lowering the paper. "Like the start of that Walt Whitman poem, which you'll see this borrows from." Footnote delivered, Gradisher resumes reading. "Centre of equal daughters, equal sons, All, all alike endear'd, grown, ungrown, young or old, Strong, ample, fair, enduring, capable, rich, Perennial with the Earth, with Freedom, Law and Love."

Gradisher clears her throat. "This next part appears to be influenced by Langston Hughes," she says, looking at the camera again. "America was never *that* America to me," she continues. "Corporations all, all alike endear'd as equals to citizens. Money held in the same tight fists;

new kings created by the progeny of that same *grand*mother who once abolished them. Our elected knights have rendered us techno serfs, destined to live in boxes, organic batteries for capitalist machinery. The privilege is living in a palace and not seeing it is the selfsame box, a pittance bequeathed by those in power. But eureka! Treasure still lies within this city of opportunity. For what else is a daughter?"

Gradisher lowers the paper, indicating that she's finished. The reporter pushes a microphone closer to the editor's mouth. "What do you think it means?"

"Our business-page editor has suggested that the beginning references wage stagnation among the middle class, due in part to automation and outsourcing. By and large, these forces have pressured the majority of American workers while fueling immense wealth for top earners."

"What about the box in the city of opportunity?" It's the question that the journalist should be asking, though I'm the one who shouts it at the television. "Where should we go?"

"City of opportunity," the journalist says. "Do you think that's a clue to where Alice is?"

Gradisher sucks her teeth. "Given that her kidnappers are quoting poems about America, I assumed 'city' was another analogy for the United States itself. The authors are taking poetic license, bringing country down to the digestible size of a city."

"You don't think it's a clue to where Alice is being held, then?"

Gradisher looks down at her hands. "I hope she's still being held. Statistically—"

"Shut it off!" Brian yells.

". . . kidnap victims who aren't found within the first twenty-four hours are—"

"Shut it off!" he roars again.

The television goes black. Though the end of Gradisher's thought wasn't broadcast to those of us in the terminal, we can all mentally fill in the blanks. Alice might not be alive. These clues may be encouraging us to run around aimlessly, proving some political point on behalf of Alice's kidnappers while her body decomposes in a shallow grave.

The thought squeezes the air from my lungs. I react like a heart attack victim, reflexively pressing my hands to my left breast. Though my lips part, I can't inhale.

Beside me, Brian notices my distress. He doesn't reach out, try to hold me. "Don't be dramatic, Catherine. It's fine. I know where Alice is." He's bragging, as always, pretending he has all the answers.

I still can't breathe.

"That half-witted woman doesn't know," Brian says. "But I do. We should go."

The instruction to move somehow unfreezes my brain. I gasp. "How? How do you know?" My voice sounds as if I'm speaking underwater.

Brian smirks. "Because they're my boxes."

ALICE INGOLD

DIARY ENTRY TWELVE

My manicure request made my female captor suspicious. I could tell because she brought Hugh along to deliver the nail polish remover, even though carting bleach, a pack of cotton balls, and a bottle of acetone required two hands at most—certainly not four. Hugh's extra mitts were for trouble. She wanted backup in case I tried anything.

What I was attempting, I don't think she knew. As I'm about to get on with it, I might as well admit that her instincts were right. By the time my captors get this notebook—if they get it—I'll have either succeeded in escaping or . . . well, I don't want to write the alternative.

If it comes to that, though, I hope my parents find this and show it to the media. It might be my only chance at achieving any of my dreams, even if, well . . .

And if my kidnappers find it, I want them to understand that I'm not trying to hurt them. I understand their frustration with technology sapping their purpose. I share their anxiety about how my father's AI will impact my future. I'm sorry that the system is unfair. But I, like them, was born into this system. I deserve to die because of it no more than they do.

Buying into their promises of me surviving this would be foolish. Anyone willing to kidnap a person to make a point must be willing to do far worse. What if a police officer shows up at this place? Would they really leave me to testify against them after having seen their faces?

I can't stake my life on it, which is why I asked for nail polish remover.

The item seems harmless enough. A household ingredient on the shelf of nearly every woman's vanity. By itself, a bit of acetone doesn't do much more than strip off some varnish. Mixed with bleach, however, it becomes chloroform, a liquid whose fumes are powerful enough to knock out a grown man—or worse. And nearly everyone knows bleach plus a little hydrogen peroxide becomes a bomb.

How do I know these things? Not from any chemistry class, that's for sure. I know because Tyler Durden knew them in *Fight Club*, a classic film that I initially watched with my best friend sophomore year for Brad Pitt's bod but rewatched because it suggested that the average dude was becoming so frustrated with our country's income inequality that he was literally willing to punch himself—and anyone else—in the face. That resonated. I could see that simmering sentiment on the streets of Oakland and San Francisco, in the way folks looked at me as I waltzed into my boho-chic loft. *Entitled brat. Undeserving nepo baby. Capitalist piglet suckling on generational wealth.* Even good friends assume that my parents bought my way into Berkeley, despite my skipping a grade and having high marks. No one really believes a trust-fund baby earns her keep.

My penchant for thrillers filled in the rest of the chemical recipe. Amazing what writers can search online without ending up on an FBI watch list. If the average person googles "how to make chloroform," they better be prepared for a visit by some badges. Someone with a book or two—or pursuing a creative writing degree—gets a pass.

When I saw my captors enter together, I feared they'd gleaned the same information from books and cinema that I had. Hugh's insistence on cleaning my toilet bucket for me, despite my feigned embarrassment, seemed suspicious. However, his reasoning had logic.

"You don't have a sink down here," Hugh said, his good-natured tone masking any distrust. "Least I can do."

As he began to cart away the bucket, Hugh's partner handed me the nail polish remover and a pack of cotton balls. "I might be able to find a pink or red," she offered.

The suggestion seemed so genuine that, for a moment, I forgot she was my jailer. This girl could have been another college-aged peer suggesting we get ready for a Saturday night. If money hadn't separated us, maybe we would have been friends. I wondered if she thought that too. Could she imagine another sliding door where she and I were both at a financial firm, complaining about our fifty-hour workweeks during Friday happy hour?

"Maybe later," I said. "I only need to remove the polish."

She stood in front of me, a sommelier waiting for my wine order. Or, more accurately, a store clerk watching so that I didn't nick the merchandise. I opened the bottle and dabbed some acetone on a cotton ball.

"I have gels," I said, an obvious lie given the lack of sheen on my fingertips, though only detectable to the initiated. Her nails were bare. "Gel paint can take half a bottle to remove," I explained. "I'll have to soak these." I emphasized the point by pressing a cotton ball to my index finger.

She eyed me for a second before backtracking toward the door. "I'll get dinner."

Her promise served double duty as a warning that she'd be back. I told myself then that I'd wait until her return, hopefully sans Hugh, to put my plans into motion. Until then, I'd have to amuse myself with reading . . . and writing.

As she started to exit, Hugh returned with the bucket. Though I could smell the bleach wafting from what he carried, he no longer had the bottle in hand. Still, the bucket was better than nothing. I thanked him and then, to usher them both along, suggested I might need to use my recently cleaned facilities sooner rather than later.

"I'll rinse it once more after dinner," Hugh said.

He was never going to give me the cleaning spray.

"Thanks," I replied. "Could you maybe give it an extra spritz of bleach when you do? I'd rather feel like I'm in a hospital than a latrine."

Hugh grimaced. "Sure. Already did in there."

My rank urine was a bonus, apparently. Again, I thanked him and then watched as he exited through the door that his partner held open. Her nonchalance about keeping the exit unsecured seemed almost like a challenge, though one I knew I'd fail. Even if I took them off guard, say by splashing nail polish remover in their eyes, they knew I couldn't make it past them both. And certainly not their gun.

The door shut behind them with the sharp click of an engaging lock. Since I couldn't hear footsteps, I counted to 120 Mississippis before getting to work. As promised, there was a thin film of bleach in the toilet bucket. I dropped a handful of clean cotton balls inside to sop it up. Afterward, I pulled them apart into a weblike fabric and drenched it in acetone, creating my own chloroform-dipped material. Whatever bleach Hugh left on the second go-round would be the catalyst for my explosive reaction.

Part two would have to wait until after dinner. I needed my kidnappers off guard, going through the motions of giving me my meal and nighttime speech. Surprise was the main weapon of any guerilla army. And I was Che Guevara.

I picked up a cotton ball and began rubbing the paint from my nails. I'd bide my time. After dinner, I'd be ready to entertain.

CATHERINE NEWHOUSE INGOLD

THREE DAYS AFTER

Brian's boxes are more rectangles: two cubes of connected lumber and particleboard, fifteen feet wide and twenty feet long in total. They resemble shipping crates lined up along both sides of the mile-long warehouse in which I stand. "Prefabricated apartment" seems a questionable description for them, though each of these three-hundred-square-feet "micro-studios" is meant to house people rather than packages.

All have cutouts for doors and windows. Peering inside one reveals drywall slabs as thin as poster board. The interior shrinks "tiny house" to a new level. There's room for a single bed, toilet, and tabletop microwave, or maybe one of those camp stoves with a cook surface that doubles as a heater.

A woodburning stove is an odd image for me to conjure, as I've never actually seen such an appliance aside from on TV. Alice took up camping recently, so maybe she mentioned it. The warehouse's scent is what really brings it to mind, I think. The air's thick with the remnants of a campfire: charcoal, sawdust. The lingering tang of smoke. Nothing in this room appears singed, but I'm not imagining the odor. I feel it in my sinuses, an unscratchable itch that puts me on the precipice of sneezing.

I exit my current box to investigate another one. This second apartment features the same empty interior. Same dusty plank floors. No footprints. No sign that anyone has ever been inside.

I step back onto the warehouse floor. "You're sure we're in the right place, Brian?"

Rather than answering, he peers inside the cutout window of another unit. Brian already took me through his logic on our return flight. The kidnappers name-dropped the "city of opportunity," a onetime nickname for Vallejo, California. A former state capital, Vallejo earned that moniker thanks to a shipyard and, ultimately, a naval facility that constructed fighting vessels. It was a place Americans could secure good, pension-paying government jobs. I vaguely remember my family having shipping ties here. To what exactly, I couldn't say.

The clincher for Brian was that Vallejo was almost dubbed Eureka, as hinted at in the poem, though the city was ultimately named after the Mexican general who'd helped integrate newly annexed California into the United States. This bit of trivia was in Brian's mental bank because his company is a primary investor in the outfit that owns this very warehouse. The Factry—*o* deliberately excluded—makes affordable living spaces. Its vision is to Lincoln Log–stack them and then unite the whole structure with an external fire escape. The firm's marketing materials even tease the city's history, claiming that the Factry's founders had their own "eureka" moment and decided to tackle the housing crisis head-on: creating opportunities for homeownership from the "city of opportunity."

Brian removes his head from a hole carved into a neighboring crate. "It's the only place that fits the poem's clues that's also connected to my company and isn't teeming with people. As I've said, this is all about attacking me, stirring up bad publicity for Zelos."

He detailed that argument on the plane as well. Alice's kidnappers want to hurt Zelos by drawing media attention to some of its "newer" business units without providing the "necessary context," thus scaring people into protesting the company. Why else, Brian said, would they highlight Zelos's moves into tentpole industries in the American economy—finance, media, and real estate—if not to incite a backlash?

Who "they" are, Brian doesn't know. He claims that a Zelos competitor's the most likely culprit, some corporate entity with ambitions to do what Brian's already doing who wants to stall his progress. Though the theory *is* possible, I think it stretches credulity that a rival business would resort to kidnapping when TV news networks are all too happy to have competing CEOs take shots at one another *live* on camera. Whoever kidnapped Alice needed her notoriety to attract reporters.

But Brian's clearly right about the kidnappers' motives. This last clue made it more obvious than ever that these people are angry about Zelos's business practices. Knowing that has only fueled my newfound fury at my husband—and with myself. All this time, I encouraged Brian's ambition at the expense of our family, thinking his resulting power was beneficial to all of us and the world. Instead, it was pissing people off and endangering our child.

What keeps me from blowing up at him again is the task at hand and my own culpability in our current situation. My ego played a large part in this. I enjoyed how Brian's position elevated my status beyond "socialite." I liked being adjacent to greatness. What I never considered was how much power I might have wielded on my own had I not spent so much time and energy compensating for my husband's absence and catering to his needs. If I'd had an equal partner, what decisions might I have made differently? Would I have taken my Stanford environmental studies degree and spearheaded climate change initiatives, as I'd initially planned? Would I have written books pointing out the environmental cost to train Zelos's AI models? Would it have been some other CEO's kid standing in front of a cement wall, lit in chiaroscuro, reading a poem about curtains of air and begging her parents to find her?

Sliding doors. Paths not traveled. Imagining other realities is pointless. The only dimension that matters is this one. Here I must channel my rage into finding my daughter.

I peer into a new unit, suppressing the desire to call Alice's name. So far, all the locations have only held clues to her whereabouts. There's little reason to believe this time will be different.

Instead, I shout at Brian. "How would someone who hated your company know about this place? It doesn't look like anyone works here."

"Maybe they saw the marketing materials," Brian yells from somewhere behind me. "This shop isn't scheduled to go online for another year or so. The commute from the city's too onerous. Until they get more of the very thing that they build, they're still manufacturing in San Francisco. That will change once they start 3D-printing these structures. For now, though, this place is only used to store nearly finished units until they really get up and running."

He keeps talking as I peer into another identical apartment. "The press will swarm this warehouse like termites now!" Brian shouts. "I'm sure they'll take issue with the units' sizes—what I think is acceptable housing for people—completely ignoring that there are no real affordable living spaces for low- and no-income workers in the first place. What do they expect subsidized units to look like?"

He's readying arguments for the near future. Reporters have yet to enter the building, though Brian's not wrong to anticipate that they will. Thanks to websites that track private airplane emissions, the media knew the moment we landed at Buchanan Field Airport. As this isn't where Brian usually keeps Zelos's plane, they immediately guessed we were on the trail of another clue.

News vans idle outside the front gate, blocking the Factry's movie studio–sized parking lot. It's only a matter of time before the helicopters arrive, as they had outside the data center. They might be here already. This warehouse has some level of soundproofing. Nature sounds from outside are silenced within these walls. There's no wind. No birds. The loudest noises are Brian's grumbling and the clomping of Lee's FBI-issue boots as he steps from the cement floor into one of the crates and then back down again, a participant in a slow-motion cardio class.

"It's ridiculous," Brian says, still debating with an imagined interviewer. "Thanks to my technology, our country will produce trillions more over the next decade without *any* additional labor costs. People will likely be gifted these units by the government, courtesy of the taxes paid by businesses like mine. What do Alice's kidnappers want? The United States to abandon all this possibility while China plugs along? They want us all to work for authoritarian governments?"

Rather than answer his rhetorical questions, I peer inside another box. The wooden walls mute Brian's diatribe. It's silent. Dark. I imagine Alice held inside a place identical to this one, sitting on a mattress shoved in a corner. Walking in circles for exercise. The poem indicated she'd been here at least for a few hours. "Treasure . . . For what else is a daughter?"

Remembering the line recalls the remainder of the poem. Alice's kidnappers referred to techno serfs living in boxes. In their view, this micro-studio isn't an opportunity for homeownership. It's a coffin, a place where dreams go to die.

I shudder, not from fear but from my barely contained anger. For a moment, I feel what Alice's kidnappers must have experienced knowing Brian's plans for these cubes, their fury at the filthy-rich CEO with multiple homes and the audacity to believe this should be enough for the likes of them, who sees it as some sort of charity.

I exit the box to find Brian peering into another unit while muttering to himself. His voice is gravel abrading my skin. Suddenly, I can no longer contain my feelings. He should be paying the price for his callousness. Not Alice.

"You need to fix this!" I shout.

Brian whirls around. "What?"

My hand flies out as if I'm spasming rather than indicating my surroundings. "These people are incensed that you're building people these . . . these hobbit holes to live in while creating technology that does white-collar jobs."

Brian looks at me like he's Julius Caesar in mid-March. "I'm making it so businesses can remain competitive. They'll use this technology—"

"Who will use it, Brian? Workers or business owners?"

"Both."

"Bullshit."

He hesitates. "Both."

The hiccup makes me want to slap him. "How many jobs will your tech replace?"

"It'll create jobs too."

"Really?"

"Really."

I don't believe him. Though I want to. "Well, then you need to get on camera and say that. Make a case so they stop taking out their frustrations on our daughter. Go out there and tell the press how this will add jobs, and which jobs—"

Brian throws up a hand. "I can't do that."

"Why?"

"I don't know which jobs will be added. The market always adjusts. That Goldman Sachs report about three hundred million—"

"It'll add three hundred million jobs?"

"Well, they said subtract. Globally, of course. But there will be other jobs. Worldwide GDP is expected to be through the roof thanks to generative AI technologies. Folks will figure out how to use this software to do things even I haven't imagined." Brian's face is red. I see the same color creeping into the whites of his eyes. "Think of every technological innovation that we've had in our lifetimes. Phones. Computers. 3D printers. The cell phone meant that we didn't need telephone operators, but we got people who design phones and cases and program software for palm-sized supercomputers. The average person now has more technology in their pocket than it took to land on the surface of the moon! Think of that. Think of how efficient people have become because of those devices. Able to work from anywhere and everywhere. Think of Zoom and how it's meant that you can meet face-to-face with people across the globe. How it got us through a pandemic! Technology saves lives. It changes things for the better. On the whole, people figure out how to use it for the better. At least, the *important* people do. The relevant ones."

I consider the cell always in my pocket or purse, how it's enabled me to communicate from anywhere, find any place on a map. If Alice had her phone, I'd know where she was right now. Overall technology has certainly changed *my* life for the better.

But the daughter of the Newhouse shipping fortune was never going to be a switchboard operator. Or a secretary, for that matter.

Before I can respond to Brian, Lee shouts from the other side of the room. "I've found a door."

Logically, I know a new door doesn't mean Alice is any more likely to be in this warehouse. Still, I run toward his voice. Brian's footsteps thud behind me, then in front as he sprints ahead on his longer legs. He yells our daughter's name. "Alice! Alice!"

Lee has already disappeared through a double-wide opening in a far wall. It was behind one of the prefab apartment blocks, which explains why I didn't see it first. Brian disappears through the space with me on his heels. Suddenly, my sneakers squeak against a rougher cement surface. We're on a new factory floor, I realize, only this space is smaller, perhaps the size of a three-car garage. Though I can't see much without the lights turned on, it appears meant to fit a long-haul truck. Even in the dark, I can see a metal bay door and sense the vacuous space above my head. The ceiling is at least a story high. Maybe two.

"Lee, where are you?" My question echoes in the rafters.

He responds a moment later. "In here."

Brian and I both follow the sound to an open rectangle punched into the corner of the room's left wall. A spotlight shines inside, no doubt the flashlight that had hung on Lee's belt. As I approach, the scent of smoke grows stronger. Someone burned something in here.

The thought twists my insides. I force myself not to think about what was set ablaze.

Lee's flashlight beam swings toward me as I enter, coming to rest on the open door. "See the char there," he says. "Someone lit a fire."

I pull my cell from my pocket, flick on its flashlight, and then aim it where Lee directs my attention. An entire edge of the door is burned and broken, as if someone set it on fire and then kicked until it came loose from the wall.

"Alice!" I shout, directing my phone's flashlight into the room.

The beam catches on a triangle of green cellophane. I jump back. It looks like a chrysalis for some sort of alien bug. "Alice?"

Lee marches over to the cocoon. As he does, his own light clarifies what I'm looking at. It's a tent. A flap hangs open.

"Looks like there's a showerhead in here," Lee says.

"And a bed over here."

Brian shines his phone light on a mattress left on the floor near a stack of pallets. I start toward it. "She was here," I say, more to convince myself. "This is where they were keeping her."

A thin blue blanket lies on the ground beside it. I pull it up, searching for the next clue, a poem or a letter. Maybe a ransom note. As I do, a ring shatters the tense silence.

Alice's kidnappers left a burner phone somewhere in this room! They're calling it, ready to deliver their instructions for a money-prisoner exchange. I strip-search the mattress for it, running my hands over the thin sheet. Digging into the pillow.

Then I hear Brian's voice.

"What do you have for me?" Whatever the person on the other end of the line says does not make him happy. "I don't care that they had my PIN code!" he shouts. "I obviously didn't hand it over." Though I can barely see him in the darkness, I can feel his anger. Hear it in the way he paces behind me. "Well, then, some moron did," he snarls. "And there's no reason for anyone to ever release that info, or even have it. I don't even give it out to—"

He stops.

"Brian?"

He doesn't answer.

"Brian, what are they saying?"

"I'll call you back," he says. The anger has fled his voice, replaced by slack-jawed shock.

"Do they know who accessed your pod?" I ask.

"What?"

"In the data center. Do they know who broke into your pod?" Lee repeats my question.

"No," Brian mutters.

His company's lack of explanation seems to affect Brian more than our daughter being kidnapped. Instead of searching for a clue, he stands in place, hands curling into fists. A vein pulses in his neck. Something about his expression is even more threatening than when he was choking the man at the shelter. Brian Ingold looks like he could kill somebody.

"Hey, come on." I try to redirect his attention to the task at hand. "The kidnappers must have left something for us here. They left something every other time."

I yank the mattress back, exposing the floor below it. Nothing's there. I turn my attention to the pallets, pushing them back and accidentally hitting a gray box in the process. Something thuds to the floor. Instinctually, I drop to my knees and feel around for it. My hands touch cement. Grit. Something sharp—a glass shard, perhaps. Thankfully, it's too large to become embedded in my palm.

I point my cell light at the pointy piece. It's white. Part of a plate or bowl. This would rattle, not bump, after hitting the floor.

The source of the sound lies behind the broken ceramic. There's a notebook—one of those black-and-white marble ones that Alice was required to have for certain high school classes. I pick it up and aim my flashlight beam on its pages.

Text fills the first sheet. The writing is Alice's penmanship. I'd recognize the careful, tiny letters and loopy *s*'s anywhere.

"My first kidnapper smelled expensive."

"What do you have there?" Lee asks.

I turn toward the agent's dark outline against the tent's illuminated green. "It's from Alice. I think it's a diary."

PART II

Alice Ingold

Three Days After

On to the tale of my daring escape! How I wish this story could be in the diary, but detailing my death-defying getaway in its pages would arouse all sorts of suspicions: When did she write this? How did she manage to make a break for it *and* leave a record behind?

I'll tell it on the talk shows, I suppose. After emerging from the woods and taking the requisite recovery time, I will muster the courage to share my harrowing ordeal with TV audiences—how I employed common household ingredients to free myself from not one but *two* armed assailants. It promises to be an exciting story, laden with the threat of me blowing myself up or being discovered.

Of course, the really juicy bits I'll save for the book.

I already have a first draft of the climactic chapter. After my captors left, I relieved myself in the "facilities" and then waited for their return with chloroform-soaked cotton tucked into the pockets of my borrowed sweatpants. My female kidnapper didn't take long to deliver dinner—another sandwich, this one soggier than the first, likely due to stewing in a fridge somewhere. As soon as she gave it to me, I began complaining about the scent of urine. True to his word, Hugh showed up minutes later to remove my bucket. He brought it back within the hour, a bleach film in the base.

That last bit of bleach was the final ingredient in my plan. Once my captors departed a second time, I flipped my mattress onto the floor and rested it on its side, creating a barrier between me and my planned explosion. Next, I set the bucket with its half inch of chlorine bleach beside the locked door and then poured in the remaining hydrogen peroxide. One good kick to disturb the contents was all the catalyst required. I dove behind the mattress and lowered my head to my knees, bracing for a boom.

It came within a second. The sound was more intimidating than the fire itself, which did little more than poison the air with an acrid scent and irritating smoke. Through the vent, I heard a feminine yelp and Hugh declare that he'd check out the noise.

I tracked his heavy footsteps as they crossed my ceiling. Moments later, he flung back the door. And I was ready for him, pressed against the wall with my makeshift anesthesia rag in my palm, a James Bond assassin sans sexy getup. I'd pulled my borrowed sweatshirt over my nose and mouth, cinching it tight to keep myself from inhaling any airborne chemicals. As Hugh stepped inside the smoky interior, I threw myself at him, shoving the heel of my hand into his nose as though intent on breaking it. Though he grabbed my wrists, he seemed more focused on keeping me from clawing his face than stopping the cotton from being pressed into his nostrils. He kept asking what had happened, as though I'd been driven into a frantic state by some accident.

As he didn't immediately pass out, I did my best to play into his distressed-damsel fantasy. I told him there'd been an explosion, and I was certain the air was dangerous.

"The whole room is filled with asbestos, or God only knows what!" I shouted, handing him more of the damp cotton. "Put this in your nose. It'll filter out the bad stuff while we get out of here."

Hugh didn't help me escape, however. Despite believing that the room was poisonous enough to keep the cotton up his nose, he held my arms close, preventing me from fleeing while attempting to find the explosion's source. By the time my culpability began dawning on him, he was stumbling around with my wrists held tight, struggling not to pass out, still unaware that the cotton I'd supplied was responsible for his fading consciousness. He kept the material in his nose the entire time, asking me what I'd done until he could no longer make sense of the question, let alone my confused response.

The sound of his fall brought his partner running, albeit not fast enough. She entered to see Hugh comatose on the ground with the can opener at his neck—the same one he'd heard drop but hadn't taken, no doubt in some sort of bid to preserve our false trust. His mistake.

"Give me the gun!" I screamed.

"What?" The question was a stall tactic. I could tell by the way she moved her hands to the front pocket of her sweatshirt. "I left it upstairs."

"Give it to me or I'll jam this into his jugular." I pressed the can opener harder into Hugh's neck, pricking him just enough to draw blood.

I doubt my female kidnapper truly believed a spoiled trust-fund baby was capable of murder. But she loved Hugh too much to take the chance.

"Alright. Don't hurt him." She held up one hand in surrender. With the other, she pulled the gun out of her sweatshirt. Barrel-first.

"Slide it over to me!" I shouted, my fist still wrapped around the can opener.

"It's not even real." She emphasized her point, tossing the weapon on the ground. "It's a prop. A toy."

As she said it, I spied the stopper in the barrel. Black marker had been used to paint over the orange rubber, though the underlying hue still showed through at the edges. No doubt she'd gotten this item from the same store that sold the light-up masks.

Toy or not, I demanded she kick the prop gun over to me. I didn't know enough about fake weapons to be sure this one couldn't do any damage. Rubber bullets might not kill, but they can blind. And they can certainly create enough of an impact to break a rib or stop a runner.

My weapon still aimed at Hugh's main artery, I used my left foot to hook the gun, pulling it into me. Then, with one hand, I reached into Hugh's pocket for what I knew was the real prize: the switchblade.

"You have to get him out of here," I said, holding my breath so my voice would sound stuffed up. "Smell that? Its poisonous gas made from the chemicals you left. Without fresh air, Hugh will die."

I was pretty certain my every word was rubbish. Hugh was a young man in good shape, and chloroform was supposed to knock people out, not kill them. But I wasn't positive that he wouldn't suffer a heart attack if the material wasn't removed from his nose in a timely manner.

"You have to get him out of here and make sure his airways are clear," I clarified, swapping the can opener for the more lethal knife.

Her wide eyes took in the blade. "I thought you understood us. We're trying to save our future, yours and mine. We're showing people what your dad and others are doing right now with AI—pushing them to demand regulations before we're all living on some pittance in shoebox houses while the elites running this technology buy their third and fourth mansions."

I winced. My parents had our Sausalito residence, the San Francisco penthouse, and a Hawaii vacation home that sat empty for much of the year, as well as the Newport estate my mom inherited after my grandma's passing. Still, I couldn't sacrifice my freedom to atone for my parents' excesses.

"You have two choices. Save him or come for me." I gestured to my female captor with the switchblade. "And if you choose me, I'll fight you with everything I have. You might win. But he won't. Not if he's here breathing poison."

She cupped her hand over her mouth. "Go!" Her palm muffled the scream. "Just go!"

I stood, still brandishing the knife, and shuffled toward the door. All the while, I kept my back toward the wall and my eyes on my enemy. It wasn't until my female captor ran to her boyfriend and dropped to the ground beside him that I sprinted into the neighboring room.

Moonlight rained down through second-story windows. For the first time, I could truly see where I'd been held. It appeared to be the loading area of a warehouse. The setting explained the cement floors and the bay door, though not the apartment above my quarters. I'd intended to escape to my captors' lair and then exit whichever way they'd been going in and out. But there wouldn't be a residential unit over a factory floor.

There would, however, be offices. A glance back at my cell's open door confirmed that my kidnappers had been occupying a second-floor workspace. A glass wall lined the warehouse's left side, reflecting the moonlight from the above windows. The office was a loft of sorts, overlooking the loading dock. My apartment back in Oakland might have been like it once.

Aside from a fire escape, there'd be no way out upstairs. I scanned for another door or, better, the car—ideally with its key left inside. The vehicle had been stashed here.

It wasn't any longer. As far as I could see, there was only open space and, at the far end of the factory, the retractable metal wall. Hugh had chained it from the outside before, but it couldn't be secured like that anymore. My captors would have needed the bay doors working to move their car. Surely they hadn't bothered to chain everything shut *before* returning their vehicle for the night.

I pulled the sweatshirt from my face to better breathe and ran toward the garage control panel. It was plastered on the wall closest to my cell. En route, I heard my female kidnapper grunting, no doubt struggling to pull Hugh into this larger room. As I hit the garage door opener, gears squealed to life, followed by a male groan.

Hugh was waking up.

There was no more chloroform and no more time. I took off, forcing myself to forget the throbbing in my legs and the acids burning in my throat and stomach. Only one thing mattered. The metal door was two inches in the air and still rising. I could get outside.

Behind me, I heard another male moan, louder than the first. Hugh was definitely coming to. "Baby!" the woman yelled. "Honey, wake up. I need your help. Wake up."

She wasn't done with me. A glance over my shoulder confirmed it. Ghost Face had dragged her partner into this loading bay. She held him in a seated position, braced against her kneeling figure. "I need you!" she shouted.

I watched *Hugh* place a hand on the ground and start to rise, Frankenstein's monster getting up from his gurney. No way I was risking the same fate that befell Mary Shelley's villagers. The bay door squinted at me from the end of the space. I picked up speed, my heightened fear coursing like nitrogen through my legs, forcing the pistons to rotate faster. A moment later, I was diving beneath the half-retracted exit into a gravel parking lot.

Behind me, two sets of footsteps sounded, one quick and one lumbering. In front of me, a sea of pavement stretched into the darkness. I noticed metal on my left, a chain-link fence guarding more pavement on its other side. On my right, cranes stretched over a black expanse that I could only assume from the sulfuric smell was the end of a river, its fresh water turning brackish as it mixed with the ocean.

I headed the only way I could: straight. Surely the pebbly asphalt would turn into a road at some point, a proper thoroughfare with drivers who'd wonder what a skinny, scared young woman was doing out in the middle of the night sprinting like a horror movie's final girl.

I ran toward my best chance at freedom. My breath's steam was the only indication of temperature. Adrenaline and activity kept me from feeling any cold. I noticed only the hardness of the pavement beneath my feet, the rhythm of my steps. There was no syncopation accenting my footfalls. Maybe they'd given up.

Before I could allow myself to hope, I heard the car. It was faint, a distant screech followed by a low rumble, a fox being devoured by a bear. As much as I wanted to blame the sound on wildlife, the omnipresent pavement made it clear that my predator was mechanical. Animals could not survive in this fenced-in concrete wasteland.

Two choices presented themselves: keep running or hide. My tired legs begged for the latter, but I couldn't see any place capable of providing cover. There were a few shipping containers near the cranes, but that'd be the first place my captors would search. If my kidnappers found me, I'd have no choice but to fight. Though I had a knife, they had size and numbers. My switchblade wouldn't beat Hugh's bulk in extended hand-to-hand combat, let alone with his partner getting in shots.

Behind me, I sensed headlights. They weren't on me yet. Still, I could see the sky's black thin into a deep purple, as if someone had dropped a dollop of water on an ink pad. I sprinted from the center of the road to its side, running alongside the fence to keep out of the coming car's direct line of sight.

Behind me, wheels crunched on gravel. They were moving onto the road. Soon they'd be on top of me.

Tears blurred my vision. I was stuck in a *Groundhog Day* scenario, running on a street only to be caught by Hugh's thick hands. Again. Of course, this time he might not be so gentle when he brought me back. Poisoning him had no doubt killed off Mr. Nice Vigilante. Whoever was resurrected in Hugh's body would be far more dangerous.

As the headlights brightened, I spied something to my right: a break in the chain-link, not so much a hole as a section that was cut and bent back, as if someone had snipped the wires to sneak in. I dropped to the ground and pushed against the torn metal, peeling it back as I passed through. The exposed edges caught my sweatshirt sleeves and raked the back of my neck.

Even so, I made it. My new sweatpants held up against the mix of gravel and vegetation on the fence's other side. This area was not as paved as the part before had been. I looked up to see a tree line and a large wooden sign. The material reminded me of the notices I'd seen on hikes around Marin County with my mother. There was a trail in that wood.

I hobbled over to it, keeping my back bent and my head low so as not to be caught by the coming car's lights. They shone at the edge of my peripheral vision, illuminating both the road and the sky behind me. My kidnappers had put on the brights to improve their search.

But they were too late. I rushed past the sign into the woods and then continued onto the trail, determined not to stop until my legs gave out. The sound of the car grew distant. The headlights faded. Soon all I could see was moonlight slipping through the spotty overhead canopy, dappling my path forward. I silently thanked God for the late summer weather we'd been having. Fall had not yet stolen all these trees' leaves. Their branches could still provide cover and, with luck, shelter. I'd seen redwoods with holes in trunks big enough to house a moose, let alone little me. Surely I could find somewhere to hide. Rest.

My legs screamed for respite. After slowing to a jog and then a hobble, I couldn't go on any longer. I was sure no footsteps followed me. Even so, sleeping out in the open wasn't possible. I'd traveled a few miles, at most. If my captors followed the same path, they could stumble upon me before morning.

I scanned for a large tree or bush to hunker down behind. Instead, I spotted a human-sized brown rectangle camouflaged between two oaks. Had it not been for the moonlight glinting atop its metal roof, I might have missed it. The structure was too small to be a home or even a shed. I moved toward it anyway, hoping for some kind of emergency phone booth left for lost campers.

It was an outhouse. I tried the door, and it flung open. Inside smelled of dead wood and whatever feeds off it, but not excrement. Even if it had, I wouldn't have cared. Here was a shelter. And it locked—from the *inside*.

I collapsed onto the toilet seat and closed the door. With luck, I figured that I could rest inside for a few hours until sunrise. In the daylight, I could get my bearings and head toward the nearest highway or residential area. This was America. We had great wildernesses and national parks, but few places were truly uninhabited.

I comforted myself with that thought as I rested my head against the structure's sidewall and shut my eyes.

And . . . SPOILER ALERT!

I made it to the highway two days later and was rescued. Meanwhile, my captors vanished—never to be found, despite the efforts of local police, FBI, and a nationwide manhunt. Two days is simply too long to keep a trail toasty when dealing with folks using fake names who lack any connection to the victim and don't abscond with money or other traceable evidence. It's why police stress the first twenty-four hours in a random abduction. Any longer and they lose the scent.

All in all, I'm happy with the way my story is shaping up. It's virtually engineered to go viral. The necessary ingredients are there: money, privilege, intrigue, and, if I do say so myself, a plucky, pretty protagonist. Plus, it's true crime.

Of course, none of it's *true*.

But what is truth in a world where computer programs pen the news off press releases and online commentary? Where we can't tell if a picture is real or if a video is a deepfake? Sure, there's no Hugh. No female kidnapper in an ever-changing LED mask. No poor little kidnapped heiress *surprised* by her father's ambitions. There is, however, my dad's AI and the threat it poses to my generation and those who follow. That's all too real.

That's the story I want to tell. To do it, I've written a tale with all the choice bits of a social media meal. And when people gobble it up, they'll have no alternative but to unwittingly consume the vitamins I've snuck into the ice cream: my real message. *Unfettered, unregulated technological advances are chipping away at our collective purpose.*

Instead of making us smarter, Zelos and its ilk threaten to render us complacent and lazy, dependent upon devices whose effects on our collective mental health and institutions we have yet to study. It risks making us redundant, taking our jobs—and not the labor we'd all gladly outsource, like sorting junk mail. Believe me. I've seen the utopia my father intends to roll out. The future 3.0. It's a dystopian nightmare for many of us, with AI writing our books, news, and music, developing our computer code, deciding our legal disputes, trading stock in our businesses, acting in our movies, flying our warplanes. Deciding when and where to drop bombs.

But we can still change my dad's vision. If we all peer behind the paywalls, assess what this technology is truly capable of, and then demand regulations, we can have a different future. Maybe even one in which AI augments rather than cannibalizes our capabilities.

I was complacent before, but no longer. *We the people* must have a say in what intellectual property is protected from Zelos's insatiable lust for information and what's fair game, which uses for its AI will help us advance as human beings and which seem certain to destroy our potential. Because we the people—we of flesh, blood, bone, and brain—are the rightful heirs of a million years of human ingenuity. Not programs. And certainly not my asshole dad.

This should be my time, not his. However, I can't reach my potential alone. Individuals do not fix systems. They inspire the collective to demand change, to insist on safeguards, and—perhaps most important—to equitably share the wealth.

Sadly, my character is not up to the task of demanding any of this. Alice Ingold is a serviceable victim, a well-meaning young woman whom people hope will survive, as we all want a lost dog to find its way home or a hatched sea turtle to make it to the water. But what more is she? What sacrifices has she made for her dreams? What privileges has she traded for her ideals? She couldn't even get her own father to listen to her concerns.

That's why Alice cannot be the protagonist of my actual story. Thus, my name, my chosen name, like the nom de guerre adopted by so many revolutionaries before me, is Elizabeth. Nickname Liza. Liza Ring.

And my purpose is to sound the alarm.

CATHERINE NEWHOUSE INGOLD

FOUR DAYS AFTER

The diary doesn't contain another clue. At least, none that I, the police, the FBI, Brian, or Zelos's superintelligent software has found in the past twelve hours. As soon as we returned to Sausalito, Agent Lee suggested we scan Alice's writing and upload it to Brian's laptop, enabling Zelos's AI to search for patterns in sentences, codes in capitalization, or odd turns of phrases that could be a tip-off to *something*.

It surprised me that Brian didn't suggest using his AI himself. He cooperated with the plan, taking cell photos of the diary's pages and then sending them to Zelos's cloud-based brain. But he didn't hover over the computer as he had before. Instead, he left his laptop on his office desk and slumped into a rocking chair in the front parlor.

He's there now, a jittery knee pushing him back and forth as he stares out a window. I don't think he blinks. It's as if he anticipates Alice walking up the front steps at any moment, and he's determined to greet her before she reaches the door.

If I didn't know him better, I'd think Brian has lost faith in his technology. But my husband would never forsake his work so easily.

The addition of bad corporate publicity to Alice's disappearance has simply forced him to take a time-out. He's finally overwhelmed.

I watch him from the kitchen, unsure of how to help—unsure whether I want to. Doting wife is not a role I've played often in our marriage, mostly because Brian rarely stays home long enough to be doted on.

Chamomile tea always made my kid feel better. I put on a kettle and grab two mugs. One bears Alice's face, though I don't notice until after I've dropped in tea bags and set them on the counter beside the stove. The kettle's curved copper reflects and distorts her nine-year-old image, elongating her face into something more adult while preserving her smile. It's like being visited by a ghost.

Though only for a moment. Blue flames soon lap at the kettle's sides, smoking its exterior. Alice's reflection begins to vanish.

It's all too much.

I crumple to the kitchen floor. Sobs shake my shoulders. I'm bawling, but soundlessly, a drowning woman bobbing in the waves.

My rescuer enters the kitchen within seconds. I hear heavy footsteps and, for a moment, think they might belong to Brian. He's feet away in the foyer.

The hand that squeezes my shoulder is too large to be his. The touch is foreign, firm but gentle, not completely unknown. My wrist pulses with the memory.

"She's a smart girl, Catherine. I can tell from the diary." Detective Frazier's voice is hushed, which keeps the other officers from rushing in and witnessing my breakdown. "If she didn't escape, she'll have reasoned with them. They wouldn't—"

"You don't know what they'd do." Sobs subdue my own voice. "She couldn't have fought them."

Believing otherwise would be an act of blind optimism. Alice isn't built for battle. She's small. Thin. Vegan, for God's sake. Moreover, she lacks physical aggression. When she was younger, my child refused to even consider peewee soccer despite half the town signing up because she couldn't imagine kicking a ball *away* from someone, nor risking driving a cleat into a peer's shin or taking one to her own. She could never have bested a grown man and his female accomplice—even with chloroform, which I doubt she could have made successfully. Nail polish remover and bleach do combine into a poisonous gas, but Alice would have no idea of the correct chemical proportions.

"Hurting her doesn't help their cause," Frazier says.

I look up at him, wanting to see if his expression shares the certainty of his tone. His salt-and-pepper five-o'clock shadow outlines the determined set of his jaw, but his brown eyes are soft. Sympathetic. His left hand is on my shoulder. Though I don't mean to notice, the ring finger lacks a wedding band.

He offers his right hand to help me up. I take it, rising from the floor. "You think because the kidnappers want to turn public opinion against Zelos that they'll keep her alive? They need to maintain sympathy, so they'll have to give us another clue."

"We're all done with clues."

Brian enters the kitchen, shaking his head at us like a college professor who's overheard students arguing over the wrong answer.

"You think the reward will work, then?" I cannot accept that the game is over. It's our only connection to Alice. "It's got to, right? So far there's nothing, but someone will see something. For the kind of money we're offering, they'll have to say something. Or the kidnappers will turn on each other."

Brian rubs his forehead as if he's provided an answer that I'm too dense to understand. I need reassurance, and he's giving me exasperation.

"Or something will come of this search?" I try again.

Frazier offers the lifeline. "Something will have to. In a few hours, police, FBI, and local volunteers will comb through every inch of the Vallejo woods. They'll find something."

Though I know he means a clue, *something* has a more ominous connotation. It could mean a body. That's why Lee has asked that Brian and I *not* participate in the search. He doesn't trust that we'd be able to stop ourselves from touching Alice's lifeless form.

He's right—about me, anyway. Though, I'm still going to the woods. Nothing could keep me away.

Brian cups a hand over his mouth, hiding his expression or maybe restraining himself from being too frank. "I doubt anything will come of the search." He drops his hand. "The woods aren't that big. If Alice ever was in them, she's not there now."

It's not what I want to hear: another problem rather than a solution. "Then where do we look? Where's the next clue? Is there something to the data center? Whoever hacked it would need special skills, right? Skills you could only get at a fancy college or working for a big tech giant. We can go through employee rosters and—"

"Catherine." Again, Brian turns my name into a warning.

"Or your people can trace the hack." I turn to Frazier. "Or the government. The FBI. They do that, don't they?" I sound desperate. I am desperate. The mere thought of my daughter's death is a thousand-degree coal, burning right through whatever it touches. I can't hold it in my head. There'll be nothing left.

"Catherine." Frazier says my name this time. It sounds like a prayer.

But I'm no longer on my knees. I need action. "Tell me what to do!" I yell. "Please, Detective, tell me what to do. I have to be able to do something. I love her so much, and she was so mad at me. She was so mad. You can tell. In the diary. I only wanted her safe. She didn't understand—"

Half my words are unintelligible. Frazier doesn't ask for clarification. He clasps my hand, steadying me as my husband rotates toward the stove and turns off the flame on the hissing kettle. "We'll find Alice," he says flatly.

The lack of emotion reads as confidence. I want to believe him.

"How do you know?" I ask. "Did the software indicate . . . Did she leave a location somehow? In code?"

Brian pours the steaming liquid into the cup bearing Alice's face. "I know because I know what her *kidnappers* will do next. They're going to ask for a ransom."

LIZA RING

FOUR DAYS AFTER

This moment calls for champagne. As much as I hate flaunting wealth, I've brought a good vintage. Armand de Brignac, courtesy of my parents' often ignored liquor cabinet. The brand is known for the ace of spades emblazoned on its burnished gold bottles, each bright enough to be spotted across a crowded club so that folks in the know can see you've got a grand or so to drop on bubbly. I assume that's why a guest brought this to my mom's last holiday party. *Merry Christmas! I'm rich too!*

Or maybe it's simply delicious.

Cynicism isn't an attractive trait in a nineteen-year-old, so I've been told. In my defense, it's difficult to remain Little Lord Fauntleroy when your benefactors insist on maintaining the aristocracy.

As I'm already kneeling, I hold the bottle between my jean-clad thighs and pull the cork. Applause follows the ceremonial pop.

"Honest opinions now. You know I won't be offended." I pour the pale gold liquid into white wineglasses. The stemware's not flute-fancy but *is* the proper goblet for aerating and tasting champagne, as I've learned from the many bartenders at my mother's charity functions.

Four glasses grace the picnic blanket that we set up outside our two-person pop-up tent. I start filling the second, rotating the bottle upright exactly when the liquid hits the hips of the pear-shaped goblet. Six ounces and a splash, just as the bartenders showed me.

Sean chuckles while pinching my butt. "Yes, folks. Don't feel obligated to swallow this swill."

I pass him a half-full glass. "Not everything expensive is good."

He rises from his semireclined position to accept the champagne. "That hasn't been my experience."

"Well, Alice would know," Monica chimes in. "She's had much more exposure to the *finer things*."

The comment could be a tease, but Monica's tone is a bit more biting than it should be for kidding. Something about Sean rankles her—the old-school manliness, I think. Though he's only twenty-six, he seems plucked from a different era, one in which boys grew up wanting to be fighter pilots and police officers and firefighters, heroes worthy of nineties films. Sean actually was a fighter pilot, though he left the air force as soon as his mandatory five years were up. He wanted to be in the sky, not navigating drones from an office.

He smirks at Monica. Sean doesn't adore her either. In his mind, she was intent on becoming part of the AI problem until she realized coding financial algorithms would be among the first jobs outsourced to superintelligent software.

I pass the next glass to her. "Notes of peach, apricot, vanilla, honey, and lemon, with red berry aromas and a touch of toasted brioche, or so say the tasting notes."

"How one tongue can discern all that," she quips, passing the glass to the pink-haired woman seated on her left.

Monica's girlfriend, Demi, was a late addition to our group. Initially I was skeptical about bringing on my bestie's lover, as Monica's relationships tend to expire faster than fresh berries. I couldn't have our plan become collateral damage in a breakup. Monica's convinced that Demi's the one, though. And her conviction convinced me. That and Demi's considerable acting chops.

The role of makeup artist turned out to be an inspired choice for sneaking into my parents' house and tipping them off about the first clue's answer. To hear Demi tell it, she waltzed in with the team of journalists, a bag loaded with her own cosmetics on her arm, asking for "Mrs. Ingold" as if she'd been summoned. The news producers assumed someone of mom's stature would have her own cosmetologist for press events, and my mom figured Demi was working with the station.

Though watching my parents plead for me on television was difficult, I must admit, Mom's makeup did look good.

Though Demi accepts the glass, she doesn't seem to be in a celebratory mood. Her smile's strained, and she's certainly talented enough to turn mild satisfaction into pretend elation. I'm tempted to remind her of the promised ten million from my parents for directing them to the homeless shelter, but it probably would only bring up how much she stands to lose by being here. It's one thing to impersonate a makeup artist, quite another to be toasting with the nation's most wanted kidnappers and their victim. The former's a misdemeanor, maybe two. The latter's life in prison.

I gesture to our surroundings as I pass Monica the final champagne glass. "Don't worry. We're in the middle of nowhere."

Sort of. Skyline Wilderness Park is hardly off the map. It's barely a twenty-eight-minute drive from the search-party site. However, it's a world away, as far as the police would be concerned, as I could never cover the twenty-mile distance in two days on injured knees. Plus, Sean and I set up camp a good distance from the visitor parking and RV lot. We're tucked away in a copse of trees set back from a pond. I've yet to see a hiker come close.

Sean picked the place. He's a veteran camper, one of the only traits he shares with fictional Hugh, whose personality is more Monica based. My female captor was modeled after a pseudovillain from one of my favorite thrillers, though her ruthless streak might mean she has more in common with me than I care to admit.

These past few days have been my first time really roughing it—though the glass of several-hundred-dollar champagne in my hand probably disqualifies me from saying such a thing aloud. I raise it high. "To sounding the alarm."

Sean's glass clinks against mine a moment before the others. "And to a bestselling diary."

"Don't jinx it." I lower my glass before taking a sip. "It's bad luck to drink to anything that hasn't happened yet. Besides, I don't need the diary to be a bestseller. It'll be enough if it hits the news and does its job. No way anyone can read it and continue to misunderstand the kidnapping's purpose. People will have to start talking about what Zelos has planned."

Never one for superstition, Monica drinks. "I'm on it," she says, post-gulp. "I'll see your mom at the search in a couple of hours and press her about what they found in that warehouse. Then I'll say how people need to know what you went through in your own words and yada yada."

"If she says no, you can always leak it to the press like you did last time," I add. "That journalist thinks of you as part of the family's inner circle."

Monica gestures to Sean with her glass. "Or the first officer can do it—say he heard your folks discussing it on the plane ride back."

Sean sits up straighter. "I can't hear anything in the cockpit."

I slip my free arm around his waist. "Plus, no one knows Sean's my boyfriend. They'll wonder why he's so interested. He already drew enough attention to himself squawking about the newspaper strike in that media gaggle. Just because my parents didn't see him doesn't mean a reporter or cameraman didn't notice."

Rather than agreeing, Monica drains her glass and turns to Demi. "We should probably go. If Alice were really missing, I'd be early for the search."

"Aw, love you too," I coo, adding for Demi's sake, "my sister from another mister."

I finally drink some of my champagne, both to toast my friendship and encourage Demi to have a taste. Her glass is nearly full. "Not bad," I assure her. "I'm getting the honey."

Demi takes a cursory sip. "You're positive no one will see when Sean drops you on the highway?"

"We've scoped it out. There aren't any cameras on that stretch of road, and it backs up to the wetlands. If I were wandering around the woods and turned north, I'd end up there."

Demi darts a glance at Monica, asking for permission to keep up her interrogation. "Why wouldn't the search party have found you?"

The question's fair, and fortunately I have an answer. "The abandoned navy yard there is littered with empty buildings; we're talking bunkers no one has touched since the 1960s. I'll claim I was hiding out in one and fell asleep, then say I got turned around at night and ended up back in the woods. If they ask why I didn't hear the search party, I can always say I was conked out or thought it was my kidnappers looking for me."

My plan must satisfy Demi because she finishes her champagne. Monica clearly hasn't told her about our other, potentially bigger problem, though she hasn't stopped calling my burner phone to remind me of it. I guess she doesn't feel the same need to stress out her girlfriend.

I'm anxious enough for all of us, I suppose. Though I refuse to wallow in worry today. No plan is ever foolproof, and as of right now, everything's working the way we wanted. The media's poring over how the locations of our clues are tied to Zelos, and the pundits are opining about my dad's AI in the right terms. Instead of gushing about his AI curing cancer in the far-off future, they're discussing its nearer-term impacts on the labor market, admitting that existing regulations are not up to the task of protecting human capital and intellectual property. Moreover, they're asking what happens when coders themselves are phased out and no one can understand how to fix the software should it make harmful or incorrect associations. And X is all atwitter about where I am, who I am, and whether my kidnapping is a terrorist act or the natural result of a system that promotes vast wealth inequality. In other words, whether I *deserved* to be taken.

All in all, things are going well. I'm sipping champagne with my best friend and beau beneath a warm sun in air heady with the smells of ripe grapes and greenery while helping to reveal my dad's real plans to change the world and, hopefully, stop him. So who cares if some people say I deserved to be kidnapped? They're right, in a way. Alice Ingold was spoiled and ignored, a combination for a bitter vintage. I get the distaste for her. Liza Ring, on the other hand, is like the drink in my hand: bubbly, complex, and full of promise. She did what she came to do. She created my story.

Now I need the world to swallow it.

CATHERINE NEWHOUSE INGOLD

FOUR DAYS AFTER

Everyone wants to find Alice. People crowd the main route to Mare Island Woods, a two-lane road squeezed between rusted tracks and a barbed wire fence posted with trespass warnings. Folks of all ethnicities and ages are gathered, though more faces bear youth's roundness rather than the angles of middle age. Navy windbreakers emblazoned with *Cal* in bright gold are polka dotted among the monotone fall coats. Berkeley's out in force. News of the search must have reached one of Alice's friends—most likely Monica. Rallying Alice's campus would be easy. Berkeley has attracted activists since the 1960s, and the prospect of press attention surely wouldn't hurt.

Still, it feels good to see all these folks here for my daughter.

Frazier isn't pleased with the turnout. The rearview mirror reflects his deep frown as he drives more slowly than a shopping cart through a grocery aisle. He's providing the volunteers with plenty of time to notice his flashing blue light and shuffle into the scrub grass beside the abandoned freight line.

"Lots of people." His tone emphasizes that he's anything but impressed.

"It'll make covering ground easier," I say, trying to inject optimism into our silent, depressing ride from Sausalito. Only Frazier and I are in the vehicle, and he insisted on me sitting in the back. The window tint would keep the paparazzi at bay.

Brian should be here. He insisted on heading to the office in the hope of tracking down leads related to whoever broke into Zelos's AIvest server room. I can't help but think he also wanted to help manage the PR crisis caused by the kidnappers' anti-Zelos treasure hunt. I would be on the phone, yelling about his lack of concern for our daughter, if I didn't think I'm probably better off without him here. I don't want to be around anyone who isn't a thousand percent focused on finding Alice.

The agency and local cops are interviewing the searchers to ensure they don't have any ulterior motives. It's possible one is a kidnapper. Perpetrators like to keep an eye on the investigation, Frazier explained. Alice's captors might be the sort to risk returning to a crime scene. Though it's more likely that those without noble intentions are simply rubberneckers. My family is a totaled Maybach dangling off a meridian. Who wouldn't break for the carnage?

I suspect that's what has Frazier uncharacteristically surly. In his mind, this search is the latest event in the media circus making his job immeasurably more difficult. He no doubt blames Brian and me for fueling the frenzy with our insistence on sharing the kidnappers' Son of Sam–inspired notes and chumming the waters with a multimillion-dollar reward for information. Engaging in a meme-worthy fistfight didn't help either.

"I'm sorry for all this," I say. "You're working round the clock and not seeing your family. I know how hard that is." My voice breaks. In the mirror, I see Frazier's jaw soften.

"Don't worry. My son's with his mom this weekend anyway." He forces a smile. "Hopefully this turns up something."

"Some*thing*," I repeat. "You don't think we'll find Alice here?"

I brace for the answer that I know is coming, even if Frazier bites his tongue: *Not in any state we'd want to find her in.*

Mentally, I've been preparing for burns, gashes, and broken bones, for seeing Alice's face bruised and swollen. Her body mangled. The whole of Mare Island is roughly eight square miles—ten including the wetlands that would require canoe navigation. As much as I'd like to believe Alice has been sheltering in an abandoned kayak, a teenage Moses bobbing among the reeds, I know it's unlikely. If Alice hasn't made it out of the woods yet, it's because she can't walk to the road.

Frazier sighs. "I think there's no choice but to look."

His statement's a conversation ender. I turn my attention to the passenger-side window, watching the crowd shuffle both out of the way and toward our heading, heads all bent toward cell screens. To ensure no volunteers slipped in without IDs, the police set up a barricade at the northwest end of the island, at the juncture where the highway meets the two roads into town. There, they took names and addresses while handing out QR codes. Volunteers were then directed to one of three lots belonging, respectively, to a scrap yard, an abandoned factory, and a visitor center for migratory-bird watchers. After parking, they were told to report to the GPS location revealed on their cell by their individual QR code. That would be their personal search territory.

The entire undertaking seems very efficient and high tech. Though it doesn't change the fact that Frazier and I must roll past everyone to meet the FBI team at the end of the island. If Alice is here, she's most likely to be near the housing factory where she was held. The professionals have been assigned accordingly.

It takes another thirty minutes or so to make our way down the four-mile stretch. I pass the time by rereading Alice's diary, every page of which was scanned and stored on my phone. As with every other read, I see no new clues. But it doesn't matter. Her writing allows me to hear her voice. It's a small comfort, even if most of what she says is not.

Finally, Frazier pulls into a lot. I exit with a long, deep breath. The bay-scented air settles my stomach after reading in a moving vehicle, though the smell isn't particularly pleasant. Wetlands have a distinct odor, like roses left in water a few days too long. Not exactly fetid, but certainly not fresh. This whole island is surrounded by marshes.

I spot Lee near a long folding table topped with Gatorade jugs and paper cups. The setup recalls water stations at races. There's also something reminiscent of a neighborhood 5K in the way the searchers are spread out: backs to the road, each focused on the stretch of grass before them. Their similarities with weekend warriors end there, though. These participants all have jackets with *FBI* on the back, not to mention gun holsters and military boots. They're in a league of their own.

How I fit in is an open question. I didn't get a QR code. "Agent Lee," I shout, "where should I start?"

Lee motions for me to join him by the table. "We have you all set up."

As I come closer, I see that my designated area isn't a patch of land but a green folding chair, the type in which fishermen lounge while waiting for a bite. "I want to help."

"That's understandable," Lee says, though his suggestion makes it clear he lacks any such understanding. "Unfortunately, we can't have you in these woods."

"You're afraid I'll damage evidence. I know. If I find anything, I swear I won't pick it up. I'll call it in like all the other volunteers. I understand it's important not to leave fingerprints or—"

"It's important to keep you safe," Lee interjects. "As Mr. Ingold mentioned, the kidnappers appear upset with Zelos and your inherited wealth. We can't know whether Alice is bait to lure a bigger fish."

"Brian?"

"Or you. Alice doesn't have direct access to your family's funds. You do. You could transfer millions with a phone call."

He may have a point, though not one I'm willing to entertain after coming all this way. "If they wanted money, they'd already have demanded it. These people want publicity. Either Alice has already escaped them and is hiding in these woods, or they've recaptured her. If that's the case, we must find clues to her next location. We need to rescue her before they decide she's no longer generating the social media views or *engagement* they want."

It's the first time I've expressed my fear so bluntly. Alice's value is directly proportional to the media's interest. Without new cryptic clues, press attention will wane, along with the kidnappers' incentive to keep my daughter alive.

"I assure you, we're all working on finding Alice," Lee says. "If she's hiding, she'll want her mother as soon as she comes out. We need to know you'll be right here waiting for her."

For the first time, I realize Lee must have training in psychological manipulation. He's offering my greatest desire: *Stay here, and we'll bring your daughter to you.*

Lee points to the chair. "Right there."

I take the seat. The vinyl provides poor back support, forcing a ridiculous recline. I place my elbows on my knees to counteract the give, pushing my weight forward and the chair back upright. It's not comfortable, but that's the point.

A whistle blows. The agents respond like slow-motion hunting dogs: step forward, sniff around, repeat. Their movements disturb the browning grass, rippling it like wind on muddy waters. There's a quarter mile of this terrain before hitting a wall of bushes and brambles, barren forsythia bushes transformed into stick porcupines for the season. Alice couldn't have pushed her way through those without a machete.

"Is there a path anywhere?" I yell the question in Lee's general direction. He's several yards in front of me, barely visible in front of Detective Frazier's back.

Lee shouts around the big man. "Agents are on it."

Psyop training or not, he fails to hide his exasperation. Alice had the same problem, becoming visibly annoyed whenever I dared ask a question or make a statement about anything she found obvious, as if I were disparaging her intelligence with the mere mention.

Lee walks toward the woods, out of earshot of the cheap seat. I've been relegated to the balcony section in an arena without screens. The show is barely visible, let alone the stage. Though, I can hear the agents. The air's filled with a chorus of "Alice. Alice Ingold."

I rise, determined to sneak into the floor section, after all.

"Ms. Ingold," a female voice calls out.

At the same time, a deeper male voice asks, "Do you know this girl?"

I turn to see Monica standing in reach of a uniformed policeman. The crest on his jacket says *City of Vallejo*. Alice's case is roping in cops from every district in the Bay Area and beyond.

"Monica," I say, indirectly answering the cop's question, "I expected you to be with the other students."

She shoots the police officer a *told you so* glare and steps toward me. "Yesterday the local news was reporting from outside a factory at the tip of the island. I figured they must have followed you all there. So if Alice is anywhere around this place, it would be here—near that site."

The police officer also takes a step. "I explained this area is for FBI and family."

Monica whirls on him. "And I told you I'm Alice's best friend. We were roommates for years. That's family."

The officer glances at me, seeking verification. Though I wouldn't call Monica "family," she's not wrong to believe that she meets Alice's criteria. I'm certain Monica knows more about my daughter's life leading up to the kidnapping than I do. "It's alright." I gesture to the seat I just vacated. "She can keep me company."

Monica doesn't hide her satisfaction. She smirks at the officer for good measure and then strides over to me, head held high. This is a sad club to want admission to, but Monica's proven she's a VIP member.

She checks out the camp chair for a nanosecond and then opts to remain standing. "You were here, right? In that factory behind us?"

In my peripheral vision, I catch Frazier staring. He's monitoring our conversation, ready to pounce should I reveal any more sensitive information that will make his job more difficult. "The press followed someone there," I say.

Monica clocks Frazier's attention. She moves in closer and lowers her voice. "Was there another clue?"

I lower my eyelids and flutter the lashes, the more subtle version of a headshake.

"Something had to prompt this search," Monica presses. "The cops didn't invade the New Jersey Meadowlands after the data center clue. I don't even think they went into that newspaper building."

"Well, they tracked down where the letter was sent from."

Monica nods, encouraging me to elaborate on what Lee had revealed earlier. The letter had originated from a mailbox in New York's Penn Station. It went without saying that Lee didn't want Brian and me releasing that fact to the press. But what harm was there in telling Alice's best friend?

"Came from Penn Station," I whisper.

"There must be security footage, then. Did they catch anyone on camera?"

"More than half a million people commute through there every day," I say. "Chances of finding a needle in that haystack are pretty slim."

Monica slumps in the chair and drops her head in her hands. "You guys have nothing else to go on?"

Though I can't see her face, I hear the tears strangling her voice, raising its pitch. The mother in me wants to make them go away. "There was a diary."

She rises from the seat. "Did you say a diary? From Alice?"

Excitement dials up her volume. She's not yelling, by any means, but it would be clear to an onlooker that I've told her something of interest. I tilt my head in Frazier's direction, signaling for her to take it down. "It didn't contain another clue," I say, heading off her questions. "But it suggested Alice could have escaped. She had a plan."

Monica turns to the woods. I follow her eyeline to the agents, now scattered on the hillside and headed toward the trees. "If it worked—if she escaped—she'd be here. I mean, wouldn't she? She'd hear everyone calling and come out."

Though I know she doesn't mean to be, Monica's a needle puncturing my lungs. I need this hope right now. "We don't know that."

"Was that all Alice wrote about? An escape plan?" Monica looks down and rubs a knuckle against the corner of her eye. Though I don't see tears, the gesture suggests she's holding them back.

"You know Alice loved to write," I explain. "She went into detail about what happened, why they told her they were doing this."

Monica's head returns to attention. "You have to share that with the press."

At the mention of the media, I feel Frazier's stare. A glance in his direction would undoubtedly confirm the feeling, but I don't want accidental eye contact to invite him into the conversation. "The police want us to keep things quieter than we have been. Details are one of the ways cops separate real informants from people regurgitating whatever they saw on the news and adding their own ideas in an attempt to stumble upon the reward."

Monica lowers her voice. "Leaving a diary behind, where her kidnappers might find it, would be dangerous, especially if Alice outlined escape plans. She took that risk for a reason. Alice wants people to know what happened to her—what she did to try to get away. She deserves to have her voice heard."

My daughter said as much in the diary. "She can speak for herself when she comes home."

Monica turns her chin to the sky. She blinks rapidly, crying up. "Her kidnappers didn't take the diary. Maybe they want it out there."

"The police are tired of her kidnappers guiding the investigation."

Monica stares at me again, fire in her eyes. "If they have Alice, then they're in charge, whether we like it or not. And they want press coverage. Maybe sharing the diary will give them enough. They'll finally let her go."

Part of me wants to agree with Monica. Her theory dovetails with my own. It's not only up to me, however. Brian and I need the police and FBI on our side. We've defied them enough already. "I'll try to make that case."

It's the best I can offer. Monica pulls a phone from her pocket and begins typing. Knowing her, she's searching for stats on how many kidnappings are solved by police versus being fouled up by them.

I'm in no mood for a lecture. "The boy pictured in Alice's room," I say.

My goal is to cut off the tirade before it commences, but Monica's jaw drops. "I, um, told you. I don't know of any boyfriend."

"She must have mentioned someone. I can't imagine Alice putting up a photo of a guy kissing her neck if she wasn't exclusive with him. Every boy she brought home would see it."

Monica tracks her hand pocketing her phone, avoiding eye contact. "She didn't have anyone."

"You mean she thought I wouldn't approve of him and asked you not to mention it, right? He's older than I'd like or, I don't know, aimless."

Monica pulls at one of her curls. "I really don't know of anyone."

"Monica." All mothers who've survived the teenage years have a don't-bullshit-me voice. I use mine now. "Whoever this boyfriend is might have had access to Alice's computer, which could have linked to Zelos's servers and Brian's passwords, maybe provided the information to get into the data center. Alice *did* work for her dad last summer."

"She wouldn't have had sensitive passwords on her laptop," Monica retorts.

"Maybe not. But she'd have had the ability to connect to Zelos's systems remotely. For a hacker, that might be enough."

Monica finally looks at me. "Alice wasn't dating any techie. I'd know that. As her best friend—and only friend in the computer science department—she would have introduced us to make sure he wasn't full of it."

Despite the eye contact, it's possible Monica's lying. During the last year Alice lived with Brian and me, she became particularly adept at the bold-faced untruth. How many times had she promised to be going out with her girlfriends only for us to track her cell to a boyfriend's house? Teenagers don't consider hiding information from parents the same transgression as deceiving one another. We're their version of the Russian government, and they're all dissidents trying to avoid Siberian prison.

"Did she ever mention meeting a guy at a tech company?" I press. "Perhaps a recent graduate who'd just gotten a job?"

Monica cocks her head. "A postgraduation job would have been newsworthy. None of us know what we're going to do postcollege. At this rate, computers will be programming themselves, doing all their own debugging. I worked all summer for a big data financial firm because I thought, oh, they'll hire me off an internship if I do a good job. But the only positions they're advertising for are PhD-level quants."

The bitterness in her voice reminds me of the undercurrent of resentment in Alice's diary. She'd been so sad before her kidnapping. She'd felt so abandoned—by me.

Monica suddenly blurs, her brown face blending into the wheat-toned grass and turning tree leaves. "She hated me, huh?"

"What?"

"Alice." My voice catches on her name. "She thought I betrayed her. That I was an apologist for her father. That I didn't care—"

Monica places a hand on my arm. "Hey, Ms. Ingold. Alice loves you. I know her, and I know she does. She just felt . . ."

I blink away the tears and brace myself. "What?"

Monica smiles at me. It's a close-lipped, guilty version, though not necessarily a dishonest one. Behind it are Alice's myriad complaints over the years. Monica knows my daughter's feelings for me were complicated. "She'll tell you herself when she comes home."

Before she can continue (sort of) reassuring me, I see Frazier jump into action. He storms past us, beelining for the parking lot. Monica and I both follow, wondering why he's jogging in the opposite direction of all the agents.

Brian stands at the edge of the lot. He's red-faced despite his car being right behind him. His hands are animated. "Catherine!" he yells. "Detective!"

Frazier and I approach with Monica trailing behind.

"Did you check your email?" he asks.

"A lead came in from the data center." I'm making a statement rather than asking a question. If someone had located Alice, the entire line of FBI agents would be running toward the site. Brian's excitement is about a break in the case, not its conclusion.

He holds up his phone. Alice's photo is on the screen. I've never seen this image before. She looks gaunt. Her pale skin nearly glows in phosphorescent lighting.

"The kidnappers sent another video message!" he shouts, calling the attention of journalists hovering in the wings. "It's what we thought. It's the ransom note."

LIZA RING

FIVE DAYS AFTER

Don't drink and camp. How's that for a highway PSA? I wish someone had highlighted the potential consequences of a couple of glasses of champagne on an empty stomach with only a jug of iodine-laced lake water to wash it down. My gut sounds like a parasite's party. I'm going to be sick, which I realize is not entirely a bad thing. The more wan and dehydrated I look when emerging from my bunker, the better.

I roll over in the double sleeping bag and yank down the zipper. It's the second unzip of the tent door that wakes Sean, though. He calls out my nom de guerre as I dart behind the nearest bush to retch. As I haven't eaten in over a day, nothing comes up but water, and not even much of that. I'm gearing up to try again when I feel my hair lift from the sides of my cheeks. A warm hand strokes my back.

A picture of us right now would be meme worthy. *If he won't hold your hair while you upchuck and help orchestrate your fake kidnapping, girl, he ain't the one.* Nearly laughing somehow settles my stomach. I rest back on my haunches and wipe my mouth with the sleeve of my oversize Target shirt. It's destined for a trash bin somewhere between here and Vallejo anyway.

"You okay?" Sean keeps his voice low. Four people enjoying a late-afternoon picnic doesn't arouse as much suspicion as a single guy hovering over a sickly woman. If ever a hiker were to come check things out, it would be now.

"I will be in about three hours." I press a palm into the grass for leverage to stand. Normally I'd rock onto my toes and then dig my knees into the dirt to pop up. But my legs are still scuffed from the deliberate fall in the factory parking lot a few days ago. Sean pushed me off a three-foot-high concrete barrier onto the gravel, at my request. Though I tried jumping several times, my instincts kept kicking in and saving me from a fall.

If he won't give you a push when you ask, ladies, he ain't the one.

Sean helps me up and then walks in front of me until we reach the tent, blocking the gaze of any ambitious fishermen. Fortunately, early autumn is not a busy time for the park. Kids return to school, and work picks up for parents. The only folks here are retirees and the chronically jobless residents of the RV park—not that those guys are counted in unemployment statistics anymore, as they've long stopped looking. Some do gig work, I expect, logging on to one of the task apps that allow people like my parents to pay for chores they can't—or won't—do. My mom hasn't grocery shopped in years.

For my parents' ten-million-dollar reward, any of those RV residents would carry me out of here kicking and screaming. It wouldn't matter that I'm doing this for them as much as for me. Okay, maybe not *as* much. Certainly somewhat. Automation may have already taken their jobs, but Zelos is coming for their kids' employment. And all parents want the best for their children. Even mine.

Sometimes, when I'm in a mood to imitate my mom and make excuses for my father, I tell myself that's why he spent all those hours at Zelos instead of with me. He was racing to engineer a world in which I'd never want for anything. It wouldn't matter if I didn't win any of those senior superlatives: smartest, prettiest, most likely to succeed. Zelos's AI would be the great equalizer—for people with preexisting resources. I'd have no need to enter the workforce or develop marketable skills. I could simply sit back and let the machines take charge, augmenting my already substantial net worth by allowing Zelos's AI to trade my trust fund. I could safeguard my physical health—regardless of my diet and exercise choices—by letting a Zelos-powered app scan my body for bad cells and then eliminate them with, I don't know, ingestible nanobots that would rush around my bloodstream like microscopic Roombas, sucking up all the detritus destined to make me sick someday. (The head of Zelos's medical app had a meeting about that one.) Thanks to my dad's tech, I'd never grow ill. Maybe never age—at least not visibly. And if the world outside my castle walls went to shit, I could hole up inside my fortress and let Zelos entertain me, teaching me tennis on virtual courts, producing films tailored to my tastes, generating literature from self-selected keywords, enabling me to feel whatever I wanted and ignore whatever I didn't wish to think about. I'd be safe no matter what. A girl in a snow globe that could never be shaken.

But I'd still be trapped.

I duck into the tent first, and Sean zips it behind him. We're in a proper camping version, a beige dome with a green rain shield tied down over the top. The glamping styles with their Bedouin-inspired desert canvas or hexagonal glass windows would have attracted too much attention. This tent once belonged to Sean's grandfather. It's straight from the 1970s, when the point of a tent, aside from serving as temporary shelter, was to provide a private place to smoke weed, consume mushrooms, and have sex.

I wish the last activity was on my day's agenda. But Sean's been treating me like a born-again virgin. We want to avoid any abrasions begging the question of whether I've recently had intercourse. Poor Hugh's earnest, save-the-world schtick would hardly be believable if I had to accuse him of rape.

My mouth feels like morning breath. I reach for a travel-sized Scope, gargle the last of the contents, and then spit. Of all the things to bring, travel mouthwash might seem silly, but I don't know how to live without toiletries. My mom's true religion is cleanliness, and her sensitive nose finds teenage body odor a sacrilege. The thought of me not washing for days would have added unnecessary insult to the regrettable mental injury I'm already inflicting on her. Hence, my captors going out of their way to help me shower in my diary. I knew it would offer a little consolation.

"That has alcohol in it." Sean indicates the mouthwash as he fishes in our travel bag. "You can't have any in your bloodstream when the doctors are running tests."

"Hugh might have given me Scope, no?"

Sean hands me a toothbrush and travel Crest. "He's a kidnapper, Liza, not a butler."

"True." I accept the items. The toothbrush's lack of battery renders it a primitive relic, some artifact of a prelithium society that required people to manually vibrate bristles against their gums to remove plaque and tartar.

I apply toothpaste to the head. "When I think of him, I think of you sometimes," I say. "He becomes very gallant."

Sean takes the tube. "Gallant? You think I do this for all women?"

His green eyes glint, and I'm dying that I can't skip the hygiene routine and have him right now—that we can't make love outdoors, rolling around in the grass beneath a bluebird sky. We've yet to do it en plein air, though we have checked the Mile High Club off the list.

Private planes make that one easier. I met Sean over the summer while he was working as first officer on my dad's jet, ferrying me from SFO to New York along with my dad and Zelos's CTO. The supposed point of the trip was to help the firm's second-in-command with top-secret, due-diligence inspections. Really, I think my dad hoped to show me another area of the company that I might be interested in, since I sorely lacked the programming skills for technical work. He probably thought I'd be oohing and aahing over all of Zelos's machines, how he was completely changing the high-powered world of finance from a storage closet in a New Jersey warehouse.

Obviously I was more appalled than impressed—not that I'd revealed that to my chaperone. I did as my father expected, nodding with big eyes and feigning gratitude to be let in on the ground floor. Later, however, I faked a headache and returned to the plane rather than accompanying my dad's colleague to some obscenely priced steak restaurant where bankers were already trying to woo Brian Ingold.

And that's when I saw Sean.

He'd been in the cabin reading the *Times* in one of the recliners, waiting for Zelos's executives to stumble back in, half-drunk, and order him back into the cockpit. Our attraction was immediate. At least, mine was. In my defense, Sean had the looks and the uniform. I might as well have been a new fashion model entering the club's VIP section at Mr. DiCaprio's request. What would go down had already been scripted. When he smiled at me, I felt *blessed* for the first time in a while. And my dad owned the plane.

I asked him to keep me company, complained a bit about my day. Fortunately, Sean didn't suffer from that gender-specific version of ADHD that only kicks in for men when women open their mouths. He asked me questions: what I was studying, what I *wanted* to do. Unlike everyone else, he didn't assume I'd join my father's business postgraduation or follow in my mother's footsteps: marrying well, popping out a kid, and dedicating myself to doling out enough family money to alleviate our tax burdens and smooth the rough edges of my spouse's image. Sean wanted to know my passions. What turned me on.

So I told him. And he poured us each a glass of the fancy red wine my dad had stocked on board and told me of his own dreams: how he'd grown up wanting to be *Top Gun*'s Maverick and ended up with a bit part in *Ready Player One*.

"Even piloting drones won't be a job much longer," he said, taking a long sip of Silver Oak. "AI is guilt-free. No one asks if that's a mosque over the terrorist compound. And isn't today Friday? There are only coordinates and objectives." He refreshed his glass. "You know a Russian guy stopped World War III?"

I hadn't caught the segue. "With a drone?" I guessed.

Sean leaned forward, eyes sparking. "It was 1983, and this new Soviet early-warning radar system somehow malfunctioned—delivered a false alarm about the US launching a few nuclear missiles. This guy's orders were to report so that the USSR could retaliate. Dude refused. He flat out said that this system, on which the Russians had spent God only knows how much, was wrong. It wasn't logical, he argued, for the US to launch only a few missiles if we were really starting World War III, since the key to winning would be first-strike devastation. And, you know, this guy's Russian. If he's wrong, it's a freezing cold cell somewhere or a bullet to the forehead. Plus, what does he really know about American military strategy? Still, he figured it was better to be mistaken about killing the other guy faster and end up in Polar Wolf penitentiary than be the man whose *mistake* caused nuclear winter. Thus, he saved the world."

It was quite a story. All I could say in my warm wine haze was "Wow."

"Yeah," Sean agreed, taking another sip. "He's not the only unsung hero either. Another guy refused to launch nukes from a sub in the sixties. Same deal. The computers fouled up, and he feared ending the world over a technical glitch. He wouldn't turn a key or something."

Sean settled back into his chair and raised his glass for a toast. "Human beings worry about hurting other people in error. We'd rather die an idiot than go down in infamy. Computers don't fear history books."

Looking back, the idea to do this probably started then. I was falling for a former military pilot whom I *knew* my parents would find beneath me, yet he was the guy who'd save the world while men like my father trusted their infallible software. I wanted to be *with* the hero. And I wanted to be a hero too.

But first I wanted to sleep with him.

We did later that night. The plane was on cruise control, soaring somewhere over the middle of the country with capable Captain Luke in the cockpit, monitoring the dials and assuring his first officer that he could take a break. My father and his deputy had opted to stay in New York for the weekend, so I took over the back cabin. Sometime later, Sean came to chat, finding me in full makeup and a nightie, sprawled on my parents' jet bed.

What else can I say? The earth moved beneath us.

All that's moving now, though, is my forearm and a toothbrush over my back molars. I can't imagine that the hospital's wellness check will include a dentist, but I do a cursory job just in case. Afterward, I don the ill-fitting Target sweat suit purchased by Demi but supposedly lent by my female captor. Though it's the first time I'm wearing it, I figure it will smell enough like my BO after a four-mile hike from the highway to the tip of Mare Island.

Sean's ready before me. He sits on the double sleeping bag and scrolls through his phone as I brush my hair. Leaving my tresses matted might be more believable. However, I'm sure there will be photographers snapping before I have a chance to get myself together. I don't want the first image of me to look crazy. Besides, I wrote that my female kidnapper had given me a brush.

"What the hell?" The question isn't as attention grabbing as an epithet, but Sean's tone makes up for it. He sounds like a driver cut off by an 18-wheeler. Looks like it too. The blood has drained from his face, pooling in his reddened neck.

"What's wrong?" I kneel on the nylon blanket beside him, my mind flipping through worst-case scenarios. The main one would be my father's CTO leaking that I'd previously been to the data center, thus raising the question of whether I could access my father's pod. This is the fear that's been keeping Monica up at night.

A little more digging would reveal that I lacked the required retina scan to enter the building, which I'd insisted would throw off suspicion. Though missing biometric data isn't the problem one might think when your best friend is interning for RenCap's infrastructure team and can tell you when she'll be on-site for scheduled maintenance, not to mention sneakily open the door for another apparent employee wearing a gifted RenCap puffer vest and company-issue ball cap. As for my dad's top-secret passwords, they've been the same amalgamation of his birthday and full name for years—the month, date, and year replacing the vowels.

"Whatever it is, we can figure it out," I say, more to assure myself. "We've thought this all through."

Sean turns up his phone's volume. A video player is embedded in an article titled "Ransom Demand for Kidnapped Ingold." He taps the screen.

An ad plays.

"You didn't?" he asks as we watch a truck race across a rough mountain road. "Because I thought we—"

"Abandoned the idea of a ransom," I interrupt. "Yeah. I tore up the letter."

We had written one initially—a couple of lines to my parents stating that we had their daughter and would send the GPS coordinates of her location in exchange for them funding an AI think tank. Ultimately we decided against sending it. The world didn't need more rich people paying for reports destined for the desks of clueless senators beholden to tech lobbyists. Moreover, we feared getting a think tank involved would encourage the public to forget what we'd shown them and assume *experts* were handling things.

This charade's whole purpose is to get the public involved, to clue in the average American who didn't spend a summer peering and poking around beneath Zelos's hood to my father's vision: a world controlled by and beholden to his AI. We want folks writing their senators and union reps, demanding labor protections and new regulations before Brian Ingold makes his official announcements at razzle-dazzle marketing events and has his spin doctors working on government officials. Before the technology is completely out of the box.

Practically, a ransom note also created a host of logistical problems. We needed time for my imagined kidnappers to become untraceable. If

I escaped and hid out for a few days out of fear of my captors, the trail would have plenty of time to get cold.

The ad stops playing. An anchor appears. "New developments in the kidnapping case of Alice Ingold today," she says as a smiling photo of me appears in the upper-right corner. "Her kidnappers sending a ransom note from Alice's own email."

My photo takes over the screen, only to cut to another video. "Dear Mom and Dad," a blond girl reads, her face partially blocked by a current newspaper, "the game is over, and now my kidnappers want their reward for playing."

She continues talking, but I'm too shocked for the rest of her words to process. She sounds exactly like me. And when her head rises and her blue eyes focus on the camera, I know what I'll see: a perfect replica of my face.

CATHERINE NEWHOUSE INGOLD

FIVE DAYS AFTER

My daughter is starving. Five days of scant meals are not enough to hollow Alice's cheeks or gray her complexion, but I see the hunger in her bloodshot eyes as she stares into the camera lens. The fear.

Only once do I remember her looking so afflicted. It was February 2020, those early pandemic days when government officials were downplaying the threat, calling the strange sickness a "novel coronavirus" or "Wuhan flu"—likening it to a tropical storm that had flooded foreign cities but might yet peter out over the ocean rather than touch down here as a hurricane.

Brian spent more nights home back then, though Zelos business regularly took him to foreign hotels. He'd returned from an Asia trip complaining of shortness of breath and a stuffed nose. I should have known things were bad when he ceased going to the office to quarantine in the guest bedroom. His prior travel had left me feeling more neglected than usual, however, and I was in no mood to mommy my husband. I blamed his outsize symptoms on a combination of jet lag and "man flu." Brian was rarely ill, so of course a bad cold had become the bubonic plague. He'd be fine with nasal spray and cough medicine, I thought, both of which I left outside his door along with the occasional bowl of soup and whatever he'd ordered for delivery.

Alice was kinder. She'd relished her father's house arrest, visiting with him after returning from play practice and track meets. Their time together lasted five days. After that, Brian returned to work, and Alice was left feeling "odd." She wasn't congested, as Brian had been, nor suffering from a sore throat, but her head felt clouded. Smells were fainter.

At first we assumed she'd caught a mild version of her father's rhinovirus. Within a few days, however, it became clear to us—and the nation—that something far worse was happening. Schools went remote, and Alice lost all sense of taste. The sensory malfunction sapped her appetite. Without flavor, food possessed only texture, and Alice's favorite meals had unfortunate mouthfeels. Spaghetti was writhing worms. Shrimp—slimy cockroaches. Rice pudding? Apparently, I didn't want to know. Every meal was an episode of *Fear Factor* where she was blindfolded and asked to identify the morsel by consistency alone.

For a week, she barely choked down cereal. She grew thin. Tired. Most of all, scared. As her doctor's office had shut down and hospitals were overwhelmed, I emailed a photo of her to Brian and the pediatrician along with a list of symptoms. The woman wrote back: COVID-19.

Ultimately Alice's anxiety about neurological damage became the worst symptom of all. She worried that she'd never taste or smell again, feared what else she might lose.

I now know that fear. In the video, Alice outlined her kidnappers' demand: ten million in Bitcoin sent to their digital wallet, a sequence of thirty-four random numbers interspersed with upper- and lowercase letters. In exchange, they'd send Alice's GPS coordinates.

Wiring the money is a given. No matter what Lee and Frazier say about not negotiating with terrorists, I won't risk my daughter's safety for any amount, let alone less than my family's estate pays in capital gains taxes every few years. But I know that sending the money is no guarantee that Alice's kidnappers will keep their promise.

The way I see it, the transaction could yield one of three outcomes. Number one, everything could go as the kidnappers have promised. This harrowing week will end with my daughter back home, and I will begin the work of building her back up, bringing her to therapists and doctors, doing whatever's necessary to make her feel safe and secure.

Number two, the money could lead to more gameplay. Once the kidnappers receive the cash, they could send GPS coordinates to another clue or perhaps another ransom demand. Alice's captors must be aware that Brian and I have far more than ten million liquid. This first amount may be little more than a test, a way to ensure their Bitcoin wallet is secure and the federal government won't block a transaction. Once the first wire clears, I'll be told to deliver the big bucks.

Number three, I'll give them the money, and they'll lead me to my daughter's body.

The third option is unthinkable, and the first almost too good to be true. I must assume the most likely outcome is two. This ten million is the drop preceding the deluge.

Not for the first time, I try to imagine my life after I've drained my finances to secure Alice's release. I'll be even more beholden to Brian just as I'm finally realizing how much I need my own life outside of him—maybe completely apart from him.

Leaving my husband won't be easy. If I know Brian, he will not share Zelos's wealth after I pay Alice's kidnappers—even if I did fund his company in its early days and should, by all rights, own a substantial part of it. Brian is clever. I'm certain that he and his accountants will finagle a way to move his assets into untouchable corporate accounts, enabling him to appear like a pauper on paper, barely getting by on an annual salary of a dollar per year.

Plus, there's the question of what I'll do with my life once I'm stripped of the title "wife of tech visionary." I'm a forty-three-year-old woman who has never worked a nine-to-five. Though internet memes assert that it's never too late to start over, I can't see myself beginning a new career. Who would want to hire a middle-aged mom without job experience? *Any job experience.* Sure, I have an environmental studies degree from an impressive school, but I've never done anything significant with it. I fell for Brian at Stanford and was married and pregnant within two years of graduation. I had an entry-level job at the EPA for less than a year before leaving to have Alice. By twenty-four, I was a stay-at-home mom funding an initial investment in my husband's first start-up. Zelos was born. Brian raised his favorite. I raised mine.

Now my child is locked away because the baby I never loved grew into a monster. Its father—her father too—apparently feels no guilt about his tech marvel endangering our flesh-and-blood miracle. That kills me! How can I continue living with someone the sight of whom fills me with remorse and regret?

That's a problem for the future, however. Right now, I will pay the ransom and take those GPS coordinates. Then I will do whatever it takes—pay whatever it takes—to walk through whatever door leads to my daughter.

But first I must walk through the lobby of my bank. Agent Lee holds the door for Brian and me, aware that we are now leading the way. He called off the search party as soon as it became clear that Alice was still being held by the kidnappers. The woods had been his domain. Money is my realm.

Kevin, our personal banker, meets us on the ground floor and hurries us to an elevator, away from tellers' curious stares and sympathetic smiles. We're escorted to the fourth floor and then brought into a den-style room with a computer, desk, couch, and coffee table topped with cookies and a crystal decanter glittering with Scotch. Sugar and alcohol: probably the cheapest ways to cajole a client into shifting more cash from checking to savings.

I smell the caramel as Brian and I sit on the couch. Lee, to his credit, doesn't plunk down next to us like an equal shareholder. He stands off to the side, a competing financial adviser checking out the other guy's offerings.

"I gather you've been following the news?" Brian asks.

Kevin's long poodle face turns hound dog. "I heard about the ransom."

I pull out a piece of paper with the wallet key transcribed. "We need to convert ten million into cryptocurrency and send it to this digital account."

Kevin takes the paper and then glances at Agent Lee. "You're with the police?"

"The Federal Bureau of Investigation," Lee corrects. "While we do not agree with paying ransoms, in this case we believe dispensing funds and monitoring the transaction may result in the best outcome."

It's as good a way to save face as any. Brian made calls to his friends in government. There's no way Lee will block us from buying back our daughter.

"Monitoring any Bitcoin transaction will be difficult." Kevin puffs his cheeks and exhales, emphasizing his point with a mini explosion. "These wallets are made to be anonymous. People have all sorts of ways of hiding who is collecting the money. As soon as you send it to this wallet, it'll likely be transferred to another wallet and then another."

"I'm aware," Lee groans.

I lean forward, reclaiming the attention. There may be two men in the room, but the account we're drawing from contains my inheritance. "We need this done as soon as possible. Today. Yesterday would have been better."

Brian grimaces at our banker, as if what I've said has embarrassed him. "Excuse my wife. She's upset. I'm sure that the transaction will be fast enough." He glances at me. "Wires are instantaneous."

Kevin frowns. "Not exactly. Ten million is a good portion of the amount that you have in this particular account, and we do need—"

"It's in the savings," Brian interrupts. "The money can be transferred at any time, so transfer it."

The vein pulsing in Kevin's neck betrays his internal turmoil. He's been trained not to let clients like Brian and me liquidate accounts without a fight. "Special circumstances," he mutters, turning to his computer.

Instantaneous depends on the situation. The five minutes that the wire transfer takes to go through feel like an eternity. I invent new ways to fidget, swapping finger-combing my hair for tracing my veins with an index finger, occasionally tapping them to attention, a nurse searching for a spot to stick the needle.

When it clears, Kevin turns his computer toward us so I can verify the transaction. A negative sign is in front of a one followed by seven zeroes. Just like that, ten million dollars. Gone.

I hold my breath, waiting for a pop-up window to appear with Alice's coordinates. It's an unreasonable expectation, perhaps. Her kidnappers may be hackers, but that doesn't mean they can breach my bank to send messages. Still, I'm surprised when sixty seconds pass without any response. There's no note for the bank. My phone fails to buzz with a new email or text alert.

Without thinking, I grab Brian's arm. "Did you get anything? Did they send it to you?"

Brian considers me like I'm a beggar pleading for a dollar. "It's too soon to know."

"It's coming, though. It has to be." I stand from the couch and bring my face to the computer screen, willing a message to appear. "They promised coordinates. They'll give us coordinates. Even if it's not Alice, it'll be something else to find her." I whirl back around to face Brian and Agent Lee. "We did what they wanted. We did exactly what they said. They have to—"

"Catherine, breathe," Brian orders, reaching for my arm. "Sit down."

I wrench away from his hand. "No. NO! You said they were going to give us a ransom demand and then we'd get Alice. So where is it? Where are the coordinates?"

Rather than respond, Brian looks down.

"They'll send them, right?" I look to Lee. "We've done everything they've said. Given them everything they want. They'll have to."

Lee squares his shoulders. "We will do everything in our power to trace where that money ends up and find out who collects it."

It's not enough. For all I know, the wallet is based in Panama, in Switzerland, or on the Isle of Man, some place where bankers don't ask too many questions. Alice is close. I can feel her presence, a tingling in my skin like an electrical storm on the horizon.

"We'll get her back." Brian snarls the assurance, as if it's a threat. "I promise."

Breaking promises is my husband's specialty. *I'll be home at six. I'll be there for dinner. I'll get to Allie's game this weekend.* I have no reason to believe him now.

I increase the distance between us. "No more following the kidnappers' lead. I'm Alice's mother. And I will find my daughter."

LIZA RING

FIVE DAYS AFTER

I've been betrayed by my own image. It's me on-screen, for all intents and purposes. Fear has enlarged my eyes' almond shape, and a strong light has expanded the irises, but the shade of blue is the same as in my reflection. The nose possesses the identical slope and width as the one centered on my face. The voice, though shaky, has my inflections and timbre. My digital doppelgänger shares every significant, identifiable characteristic of mine except for the most important part: my opinions.

Whoever made this copy cares nothing about Zelos's tech further concentrating wealth among the 0.01 percent or eroding our individual purposes and dignity. After all, they had no qualms about turning my entire being into bits for a quick ten million. Worse, the ransom demand makes our whole carefully orchestrated affair seem like a sideshow to the real point of the kidnapping: extracting money from my parents. It won't take long for the media to maintain that the riddles and treasure hunt were nothing more than distractions from possible leads, providing the kidnappers with more time to stow me someplace and then escape to a country without a US extradition treaty. What do people remember about the Patty Hearst kidnapping? A media heiress with an M1 carbine robbing a bank, of course. Once money becomes the matter, nothing else is worth a damn.

And clearly the kidnappers are fans of professional-grade AI art tools. This ransom video was not made with any try-for-free app. Those cheap programs still add an artificial glow to the skin and symmetry to the face, unintentionally caricaturing their source material. The result might look real at a glance, but closer examination always reveals something *off*. Whatever program created my ransom demand is good, worthy of what Zelos sells to movie studios. Not once do I look airbrushed.

"Pinch me and say this isn't happening."

Sean hands me his phone instead, as if rewatching the video while physically holding the device will help things sink in. "Must be rogue AI programmers," he says. "We caught their attention with the treasure hunt, so they deepfaked a ransom video."

I turn down the volume on his cell and hit "Replay." Again, my face appears. I pay attention to virtual me's head motions and mouth movement, the places where programs often stretch an image or glitch. There's no jerk or odd twist that I can discern, no place where my expression appears painted on rather than emanating from muscles beneath the surface.

"How did they make this? And off what? My one headshot on the news?"

"They must have a graphic designer or artist in their crew," Sean says. "Someone truly gifted at manipulating the software."

I hit "Replay" again. Not only are my features exact, but the avatar has my mannerisms. It mimics how I personally show uncertainty by pulling in the corner of my mouth—the way I flutter my eyelashes when trying not to cry. "They *had* to have more references than one photo. They'd have needed videos of me."

Sean shrugs. "Maybe they broke into your social media accounts."

"Maybe. I don't have much on there, though. No videos. My father always said that AI would clone me if I put any of that online. I'd find myself hawking hair dye in China or something."

I look up from the phone to my laptop, peeking from an open backpack. Watching this video on a larger screen might provide additional clues, though I can't risk turning it on. Having the computer in our tent all this time has felt risky enough. Neither Sean nor I are 100 percent sure that Apple corporate doesn't have some backdoor way to access devices that have ostensibly been taken offline.

We only brought it in case we needed to throw the police off the hunt for our real location. There are always private flights from Napa back to New York that require a first officer. Had the cops gotten close, Sean could have taken a shift and then discarded the laptop with the internet enabled, drawing law enforcement across the country.

Sean follows my eyeline. "We can't," he warns. "Even with the internet off, the Bluetooth might turn on and connect to my phone. All it would take is one location ping."

Resigned, I return my attention to the phone and zoom in to my face. "They even got my vein that sticks out when I'm dehydrated." I point to the offending pale-blue line leading from the end of my left eyebrow to my scalp. "And the scar below my chin."

Sean tucks my hair behind my ear to better see the real mark. He considers it a moment before turning back to the screen. When he looks at me a second time, his palms are raised. "Promise not to shoot the messenger."

"What?" I ask the question even though I've already guessed the coming accusation.

"Monica would have videos. You guys were roommates for years. She'd have pictures and clips of you in all kinds of states. Plus, she's a computer science major. She's familiar with AI and how it works. She's probably taken programming classes."

I tap Sean's phone. "No way. Monica's smart—she can code relationships between numbers and datasets—but whoever made this video is doing something much more complicated with professional software. The kind of stuff Hollywood would buy."

Sean isn't listening. He's crawling around the tent, collecting the spent champagne bottle, toiletries, and discarded clothes, shoving everything into one of two hiking packs. "Then she subscribed to Adobe or whatever and learned how to use it."

I kneel on the sleeping bag, getting down to his level. "Monica wouldn't do this. Not only is she my best friend, but she signed on to this when she thought no money was involved. Plus, she and Demi might end up with ten million for helping my parents with that clue."

Sean begins rolling up our bed, despite my knees on the nylon. "You've always had money, Allie, so you don't understand the allure of it. Plenty of people would sell out their own mothers for a chance at the good life."

"It's not *that* good a life," I mumble.

"The fact that you'd even say that . . ." Sean releases the sleeping bag. It unravels in slow motion, grasping at air before giving way to gravity. "Your college is paid for. You have a house. If you want a car, you can pick one out tomorrow."

"I don't want a car."

"That's not the point!" Sean shouts.

He's never yelled at me before. Something inside me deflates. "Dreams matter, Sean. My dreams, yours. We deserve a chance to do something with our lives. My dad and his tech shouldn't be allowed to control everything."

Sean shoots me a look that I've never seen from him before, though I recognize it from my father's face. Disappointment.

He strides over and reclaims his phone. "I'm doing this because we shouldn't let Zelos's AI drop bombs on targets with some sort of equation for acceptable collateral damage. There should be people making those decisions. People who will have to live with themselves afterward."

Being on my knees weakens me. I stand to reclaim some power. "My reasons are worthy too. I'm not doing this to punish my mom and dad."

Sean remains crouched by the sleeping bag. He looks up at me, eyebrows raised.

"I'm not." There's a whine in my tone. *Poor little rich girl.* I swallow hard to purge it from my speech. "We're waking up the world."

Sean resumes rolling the sleeping bag. "Your mom probably paid the ransom already. That means Monica's sending our coordinates. We gotta move."

He isn't asking. For the first time, I glimpse what Sean might have been like in the military—giving orders, taking orders. My protests and justifications are irrelevant. He has one task: get us to a secure location.

But there's no rush. Monica's background was not inspiration for my female captor. Her parents are in finance; her college is paid for, as well as grad school, should she want to attend. She signed up for this because she's a true believer in being the change she wants to see in the world. And she loves me—not romantically but the way one loves someone who's experienced a series of firsts with them: first loves, first breakups, first failures, first major successes. She would not sell out the cause or me.

"Monica didn't do this," I repeat.

Sean buckles our now-rolled sleeping bag to the exterior of his backpack. "You're letting emotion cloud your judgment. Monica would have access to the necessary images. If you look closely, you can tell the pictures are a little younger than you are now. You're wearing your hair different. Parted down the middle rather than on the side."

Suddenly, I know where I've seen the look on my face from the beginning of the video—the one with the big fearful eyes. My mom took that picture when I had COVID. She sent it to the doctor—and my father.

"My dad has access to all the necessary photos and videos too." I point to the phone, now poking from Sean's pants' pocket. "Guess he figured, if your daughter's a disappointment, just have Zelos make a version to do whatever you say."

Sean stops packing. He looks at me with yet another emotion I've never seen from him: pity.

I turn away. "He knows what I did. But he doesn't know where to find me."

Sean nods, an idea coming to him. "And he won't know where you'll be next."

CATHERINE NEWHOUSE INGOLD

FIVE DAYS AFTER

Alice is *not* dead.

The room's male majority disagrees. When I insist on returning to Alice's apartment, they react like I've suggested a search and rescue mission at the site of an overwater plane explosion. My banker directs his attention to the whisky decanter atop the coffee table. Lee stares at his hands. Even Brian refuses eye contact.

"There has to be a clue in that apartment!" I shout.

Agent Lee raises his chin, though he directs his attention to Brian. "Anything of possible use was bagged and tagged. Forensics dusted every inch of that place."

"And you only found Alice's prints?" I ask.

"Nothing that matched anyone in the system," Lee replies. "If we find the kidnappers, we can potentially use the unidentified prints to place them there. But without an existing record . . ." Lee trails off, letting his exhale declare how hopeless it is. "My guess is whoever took her used gloves and had never been there before," he adds. "Alice had only recently moved in, correct?"

His question hits upon my reason for going back. Alice would not have had many visitors. Even if her kidnappers did steal her address by hacking into Berkeley's system, surely they'd have scouted the place before barging in—to make certain she didn't have a roommate or live-in boyfriend, if nothing else.

"That's why someone in her building must have seen something," I argue. "Anyone asking about the new tenant or hanging around her unit would stand out."

Lee continues appealing to Brian. "Detective Frazier and his team interviewed all her neighbors. No one noticed anyone unusual."

"Who said these people would seem unusual?" I also aim my retort at Brian. "Alice's kidnappers are sophisticated. They'd be smart enough to blend in with the area's Berkeley students or other folks from the neighborhood."

Brian drops his head into his hands, grumbling into his palms. "It doesn't matter."

I'm unsure that I heard him correctly. If this doesn't matter, what on earth possibly does? "What are you saying? Of course it matters. This is our daughter."

His head springs back to attention. "That's not what I mean."

"Just because they're not attacking Zelos anymore doesn't—"

"SHUT THE FUCK UP!" Brian roars, obliterating his profanity rule. In fairness, I broke the cursing seal first, but an f-bomb deployed in anger sounds far more threatening in a male voice.

I glance at Lee and our banker. Both scrutinize the room's details. The books. The whisky.

"These people," Brian continues, regaining his composure, "they'll, uh—well, they'll need time to escape. If they were with her, waiting to see if we've paid, they'd need to create some distance before giving us her location. Otherwise they would still be in the vicinity when we arrived and would risk getting caught."

"You think they're waiting until tomorrow to send the coordinates?"

"Or the next day." Brian shrugs. "Or, who knows? Maybe they've already released her from the middle of nowhere, and she's slowly heading back to civilization."

"So you think we should search the woods again?"

Brian shoots me a look that's somehow scarier than his prior epithet. "I think," he hisses, "that we need to be patient."

Agent Lee punctuates Brian's sentence with a nod. He loves this logic. It absolves him of the need to do anything extraordinary.

"It's been five days," I counter. "Five days of Alice not knowing what these people will do to her—if she'll live or die. Five days of *torture*. You want me to patiently wait for a sixth?"

Brian raises his voice. "It's not up to you, Catherine."

I stand from the couch, full of fury and, maybe, privilege. I am sick of people telling me what is up to me and what's not. We're talking about my daughter. Everything should be up to me. "I'm heading back to that apartment. I am knocking on her neighbors' doors. I will find something."

Lee steps toward me. I glare at him, ready for him to complain that I'm compromising the investigation, ready to retort that I don't give a damn.

He pulls out his phone. "Let me call Frazier. You shouldn't go alone."

———

Alice's neighborhood is more ominous the second time around. The makeshift tenements are gone, though remnants of their materials are scattered throughout the alley, a postdemolition collage of ripped tarps, crushed cardboard, and broken tent poles. A car with two cinder blocks for tires and a duct-taped windshield has been pushed to the side of the parking lot turned encampment turned garbage heap.

As unnerving as the prior settlement was, what's left is more menacing. I'm in that zombie-movie scene where the protagonist heads down the seemingly empty street only to be ambushed by flesh eaters.

Detective Frazier's presence makes me feel better. He's large, armed, and blessed with the authority to shoot. Not that I want him to. The fight in the homeless shelter gave enough fodder to the narrative of the ultrarich trampling on the poor. And, in truth, Alice's abduction has probably caused the unhoused people in this area plenty of trouble.

The media attention likely led to the encampment's bulldozing. The thought brings a twinge of guilt, a small pinch in my neck that I shrug off. It's the kidnappers' fault, not mine. By taking my daughter to prove a political point, they hurt the very people whom they want to champion. That's the danger of zealotism. Devotion to an ideal always has unintended consequences.

I follow Frazier across the street to Alice's building. Her captors' motivations are concerns for their defense attorneys. My duty is to find someone who saw them.

Frazier pulls back the building's front door. Again, I find myself in the small vestibule with the antique push-button call box. Again, I test the interior door only to find it locked.

I turn to Frazier. "Last time I hit buttons until someone let me in."

"We want to talk to folks." Frazier considers the last name appended to each unit. "Might as well see who's home."

He starts with the first-floor residences. Though I think it makes more sense to ring the units closest to Alice's apartment, there's a logic with beginning at the bottom and working our way up. In this building, the people on the ground level would hear the front door opening, which might make them more aware of residents' comings and goings, as well as guests.

Apartment 1A doesn't respond. The neighboring unit is also a bust. It occurs to me that I've insisted on coming in the middle of a Tuesday, when most people would be at the office. Business hours isn't a concept that's ever meant much to me. Brian's always at work. I've always been home.

Brian should be here now, I think. Regardless of whether he believes patience to be the best strategy, talking to Alice's neighbors can't hurt.

He should want to ask his own questions of them, see if anything they say sparks something. Perhaps someone will describe a visitor who recalls a Zelos employee. A computer programmer who works for Brian would have a far easier time hacking into Zelos's system for its data center passwords than someone outside the company's firewall.

Apartment 2A answers the buzz. "Hello?"

The female voice vibrates with age. I almost recognize it—though it's not until the woman opens her front door that I realize who's let us into the building.

Gloria Harris is the same elderly lady who'd monopolized officers' time with the description of another girl. She's eighty if a day and likely Black, given Oakland's demographics, though the red-brown skin stretching over her prominent cheekbones makes me think Native American. Her hair is a shocking white and worn in a teased crop that recalls a dandelion seed head before a strong wind.

Her willingness to open the door deserves my gratitude, though I don't want to waste too much time with her. If she had anything useful to say, she would have shared it with the cops already. "Thank you for letting us in," I offer, after Frazier shows his badge. "I'm Alice's mother."

The sight of handsome African American Frazier brings a smile to Gloria's face. Seeing me peek from behind his broad shoulders erases the expression.

"I'm sorry," she says. "I watch the news."

"We're hoping you saw someone around Alice's apartment in the couple of weeks that she lived here," Frazier says.

She looks up at him. "As I told you, I saw that girl. The curly-haired one. Hispanic, maybe? Or light-skinned Black."

It's the second time I've heard her describe this woman. However, now that she's no longer claiming the person is Alice, I'm able to put a face to the features. "Monica? Does that sound familiar?"

The name fails to light Gloria's brown eyes. "I never heard her announce herself."

"I should have a picture." I pull my crossbody bag in front of my stomach and begin digging for my cell. Alice's photos are all tagged in my Google Cloud. If I click on her face and scroll to the first day of freshman year, I'm sure I'll have an image of her and her new roommate.

As I grab my cell and search for Alice's move-in day three years prior, I feel the intensity of Frazier's stare. He thinks I should have shared that the visitor was Monica earlier, I guess. For all I know, Oakland PD has wasted days trying to track down Gloria's mystery woman.

I pass the phone. "Is that her?"

Gloria considers the picture on the screen. It's Alice, with Monica's longer arm draped over her shoulder. Both girls are smiling, though Monica's mirth is slightly more genuine. Alice, if I remember correctly, had thought I was overstaying my welcome.

Gloria holds the cell away from her face to better focus and then pulls out glasses peeking from a shirt pocket. Donning the round bifocals makes her appear more confident. "That's the girl, yes."

"Her best friend," I explain, taking back my phone. "She helped her move in."

"That's why I thought she lived here." Gloria glances at Frazier. "I told you I thought I saw her carrying something. And she was ordering around the other guy."

The statement is a record scratch. I'd specifically asked Monica if Alice had a boyfriend or any other significant man in her life. (A casual date—unless truly desperate—wouldn't help someone move.) Monica said she didn't know of anyone.

Except she didn't *exactly* say that, I realize. She'd harped on semantics, maintaining that Alice didn't have a boyfriend.

"What did this boy look like?" I ask.

Gloria's brow scrunches, pushing out the memory. "Handsome young man. And strong. Muscular."

Frazier pipes up. "You could tell through his clothes?"

"Suppose more because he was carrying that couch."

The detective asks several follow-ups about the man's appearance, gleaning from Gloria that he was over six feet tall—guessing by how far his chest rose above the sofa when he set it down—with dark hair and green eyes. The first detail catches my attention. The boy kissing Alice's neck in that photo had dark hair.

"Why didn't you mention this man when we spoke earlier?" Frazier asks.

Gloria looks sheepish. "My memory's not what it used to be. I was trying to place who Alice even was, and then the news showed that security footage and said that the kidnapper was likely a lady. I thought it didn't matter."

Detective Frazier shoots me an apologetic look. "We'll follow up on this."

"We need to talk to Monica," I say.

"Because she met the boy," Frazier adds, trying to finish my thought.

"No." My nails dig into my palms. "Because she lied to me."

LIZA RING

FIVE DAYS AFTER

The fighter pilot insists we move. Though my father can't possibly know our location, Sean estimates we've got mere hours before Monica is grilled, reluctantly spills the plot, and every uniformed officer in the Bay Area pours into our park, alongside anyone else in the vicinity with a gun and designs on ten million dollars.

Personally, I don't think he's giving my best friend enough credit. And I think he's giving my dad far too much. For one, Monica's not so easily broken. Her Achilles' heel is sympathy, not cowardice. If my mother's tears didn't spur her to slip my location, my dad's furious demands to share whatever she knows won't make her sweat. Claiming ignorance is too easy for her, not to mention safer. After all, my father can't *prove* I'm involved in my own kidnapping. I've been far too careful. The most he has is a hunch based on my general knowledge of his passwords and the data center, as well as—possibly—a list of Fortix visitors that includes Monica's name.

Which brings me to my second point: My father doesn't even know Monica's name. In my dad's estimation, keeping up with my social circle is below his pay grade. In all the years that Monica and I were roommates, he embarrassingly referred to her as "the computer science major" or "your Black friend." The chances of her name standing out to him among thousands on Fortix's access list are slim.

I tell Sean all this as I watch him methodically dismantle our tent. "He wants me to freak and do something stupid like rush out into the open."

Sean pulls the tent's curved center pole from its nylon loops. "We *are* out in the open. Anyone can come in here."

I indicate the trees sheltering our camping spot. "We're in the middle of the woods."

"Hardly." Sean yanks out the last link of pole and adds it to an accordion fold of metal rods. The vinyl deflates, a hot-air balloon out of gas. "We're in an obvious camping location. Near water. Away from the RV park. Plus, we've been seen."

"No one's seen me."

Sean stuffs the poles into the bag. "They might not have known who you were with that trucker hat pulled low. But people saw a male/female couple head out onto a trail. Now your face has been all over the news. Someone will put two and two together if police start searching anywhere near here."

I slump onto the ground in protest. If Sean wants to pack up, I can't stop him. It's his gear. But I don't have to help. "My father isn't coming. Trust me."

Sean begins rolling the tent from the corner diagonally opposite my seat. "You're his daughter. If Monica reveals this location, he'll be here in a heartbeat."

I dig my elbows into the grass and lean back, letting the early-morning sun lap my face. As much as I dislike lake showers and a lack of temperature control, I've enjoyed feeling the earth beneath my bare feet, breathing in the scent of green. Not staring at screens. There's something grounding about going out into nature, reminding myself that I'm flesh and blood, the product of six million years of evolution from the single-celled organisms beneath my bare forearms and flattened palms—that I'm alive.

"We have to go," Sean reiterates.

"Monica won't tell my father anything," I sigh. "But even if she did, he's not going to send the cavalry here. You don't know him like I do. His brain runs on C Sharp or Python. He thinks in if-then statements. Binary choices."

Sean looks at me like I'm speaking in beep bop boops. I sit up straighter, wrapping my arms around my bent knees. "Here's what went through his head before he made that deepfake video," I explain. "*If* I reveal my daughter kidnapped herself, *then* the press will not only hate her but also wonder how awful Zelos is that it would turn my only child against me. On the other hand, *if* I don't reveal that she's involved and treat her abduction like a ransom kidnapping, *then* the press will forget about the anti-Zelos component and consider this whole thing a criminal enterprise's attempt to extort a wealthy entrepreneur. He's already optimized his outcomes. Option B won. He's not coming with the cops."

Sean finishes wrapping the tent into a tight cylinder. "Even so," he says, stuffing it into a sack, "it doesn't mean he won't try to find you."

There's nothing left for Sean to roll up or shove inside something. And there's no camping without gear.

Resigned, I move to the two stuffed backpacks crammed with our week's worth of essentials. "I guess we were planning on moving today anyway. But I really can't show up on the highway now. Everyone will assume the kidnappers let me go because my parents paid them."

Sean buckles the tent bag onto his pack. "You can still claim that you escaped and that some opportunist asked for the ransom. Not your kidnappers."

I pick up a pack. "How would I know that?"

Sean slings his far heavier bag over his shoulders. He buckles the padded belt around his waist for more support. "You have a point." He shakes his head. "Alright. We'll figure out how to salvage this. But first we head to a more secure location. The hangar."

Though I've never been, Sean's talked enough about the place that I can picture it: a small structure on a wooded lot in Middletown, California, holding his very own prop plane, a 1985 Cessna 402 with two propellers and a pair of boxy wings reaching out from the cockpit. The plane required new paint and several pricey parts, which is why he got it for less than the cost of a four-year-old BMW. The lot itself was also cheap, owing to its location outside any real town, just far enough from wine country that Realtors couldn't charge a premium for terroir.

"We should get on the road before traffic picks up," Sean continues.

I grab my trucker hat out of my backpack's front pocket and slap it on my head, tucking my hair under for good measure. "We can't hide out there forever, though."

Sean grunts affirmatively as he keeps walking. He's focused only on this mission: escape the park. What happens after that is tomorrow's problem.

"I'll call my dad with the burner." I pick up the pace so that we're abreast of each other and can speak without shouting. "I'll tell him to meet us in secret. Make sure no one follows. We can explain what we're doing. Come to an understanding."

Sean looks at me like I've suggested having a sit-down with a mafioso. "What kind of an understanding?"

"Mutually assured destruction," I say. "If my dad forces this ransom idea, I'll confess to the media that I faked the kidnapping because I was so scared about what his company is doing. But if he lets my kidnappers keep their message and agrees to publicly admit that the ransom appears to have been requested by other opportunistic criminals, I'll come out, and this will end more quickly. The story won't linger for as long as it would if I were put on trial, and he'll have a better shot at getting out his side's message without all the sensationalism. We all win something."

Sean stops walking. "There's never a way we all win."

I touch his arm, making him look at me. "We've got to believe it's possible, don't we? That's the world we're working toward, right? One in which we all win, at least a little."

Sean cracks a smile. I exasperate him, but he'd follow me into battle—if only to keep me from stepping on a grenade. "That's the dream." He resumes walking. "Oh well. Guess I had to meet your dad sometime."

CATHERINE
NEWHOUSE INGOLD

FIVE DAYS AFTER

If Alice lived here, she'd be home by now. The thought pops up like a highway road sign as Frazier drives toward a sunshine-yellow building plopped atop Berkeley's northeast hill. According to the university's website, these residences are reserved for "womenx," self-identifying female and gender-fluid students who either wish to live in a single-sex setting or simply desire a short walk to the science and engineering buildings. I assume Monica chose these dorms for the latter reason, but they come with the added benefit of making men stand out like football players in a ballet class. Alice's male kidnapper couldn't have idled unnoticed in front of these dorms, and I doubt her masked female assailant would have made it past the security guard.

A stocky woman in a flak jacket stares Frazier down through his windshield. As he pulls his unmarked cruiser into a marked spot, she shouts that he can't park there. Frazier exits the car with apologies and explanations rather than a raised badge, bestowing the courtesy of not pulling rank. I open my door carefully, to both avoid the woman turning her ire on me and keep from scraping a nearby madrone. The tree's sunburned bark peels like a scab, revealing the raw pink wood beneath. It's the time of year for shedding. In my current frame of mind, though, I see the tree as vulnerable and suffering, needing extra care from the world around it. Nicking it with the door might kill me.

By the time I join Frazier at the glass entrance, the guard has already radioed ahead to her superiors and cleared us to come inside. Through a four-story wall of windows, I see an open staircase leading to the various floors. Again, I consider how useful this setup would have been to Alice. Even if the kidnappers had somehow entered her apartment, everyone in the area would have seen her exit. Someone would have clocked her distress and called for help.

The guard presses a key card to a wall sensor. I hear a dead bolt retract. "You two know where you're headed?"

We do. Monica's address is in Berkeley's system, which the police have had access to for the past several days. She lives in unit 23, Stern Hall, 2700 Hearst Avenue.

The Hearst name gave me pause. I know tragedy encourages people to seek meaning in coincidence. We all want to believe that a higher power pays attention to our suffering, that a godly referee is counting hits from on high, judging when we've had enough and diving in to end the match. Merely skimming the local news explodes this logic. People shoulder the unbearable all the time, driving on as cars with cracked axles and duct-taped windshields, their needles below empty. Still, seeing *Hearst* seemed a sign that I was on the right track. Like my child, the Hearst family's daughter had been kidnapped. She'd survived, as my child had to.

We head to the third unit on the second floor. Though the door is closed, I hear music. It's slow and piano driven, a possible mash-up of Billie Eilish and an AI-resurrected Billie Holiday. Someone's inside.

Frazier stands closer to the doorknob. I jerk my head at the wall, encouraging him to knock. Surprisingly, he steps aside. "She knows you. We want to start this conversation friendly."

I note the word *start*. Like me, Frazier considers a lie to be a smoke signal. Something burns beneath.

"Monica?" I rap the wood three times. "Monica. It's Alice's mother. I need to speak with you."

The music lowers. I swear I hear a curse—"Oh shit" or an unabbreviated WTF. Silence follows.

"Monica. Are you in there?" I try again. "It's Catherine Ingold."

"Just a minute." Monica's voice is higher than I remember from hours ago. An internal door slams. Footsteps hurry closer.

I step back as the door opens. Monica fills the crack, her curls mussed and wilder than usual. Her tank top strap falls low on one shoulder, a result of her shirt riding up on the opposite side.

"Um. Hi. Ms. Ingold, is, uh, everything alright?" Her eyes dart to Frazier beside me. "Do you have any news? Did you, um, did you get a location?"

The questions arrive without any implied invitation to come inside. Though she holds the door ajar with one hand, her torso barricades the entrance. I notice her neck pulse with repeated swallows. She's nervous. I'd blame the presence of an armed police officer, but Monica was surrounded by cops at the search location and had no qualms about barging into an off-limits area.

Of course, she was outdoors then, not at her home. People are protective of their private spaces. "This is Detective Frazier. Perhaps you met at the search. He's with the Oakland PD."

Frazier extends a palm toward the door. "May we?"

Monica pushes the door forward, decreasing the already small entryway. "Oh, um." She touches a hand to her forehead. "The place is a mess."

"I won't judge," I say. "There are much more important things than tidiness."

She glances over her shoulder into the apartment and then back at Frazier. "Please come in, Ms. Ingold and Detective," she says, retreating into the apartment.

As I follow her inside, I expect to smell marijuana or spot a line of cocaine on the table, something to justify Monica's reluctance to let us in. Instead, I'm greeted with vanilla perfume wafting from an incense burner and an otherwise-neat single. The bed is even made, though the linens are askew, as if Monica had been lying atop the covers when she heard the knock.

She gestures to an egg chair dangling from a metal stand. "Singles don't get living rooms."

The coming conversation is better standing anyway. "I'm here because one of Alice's neighbors saw you and a young man helping Alice bring in her couch."

Monica's brown eyes go all doe in headlights. "What?"

"I asked you if my daughter had a boyfriend, and you never gave me a straight answer. Was she seeing the boy who helped her move?"

"One of the kidnappers is a man," Frazier adds.

"You think Alice knew her kidnapper?" Again, I see Monica's neck pulse, choking down a secret.

"If a young man knows where she lives, that's relevant," I say. "We need to speak with him. At a minimum, he could have told the wrong person about Alice's whereabouts."

Monica yanks a curl straight. "I don't remember any—"

"STOP LYING!" I shout. "Alice's neighbor saw you with the guy. She didn't make that up, and you're not forgetting moving a couch with someone."

"We've pulled all the security camera footage in the neighborhood from the past month." The rumble in Frazier's tone negates any need for yelling. "We'll check for any sightings of you and every guy who entered the building on that date. And if we see you together . . ." Frazier trails off, letting Monica fill in the blank with whatever frightens her most: academic suspension, jail time, accusing press headlines. All three.

"Alice's kidnappers were a man *and a woman*." I stress the last part. "She said so in her diary."

Monica's skittishness turns defiant. She stops pulling at her hair to glare at me. "I'm sure she didn't say one was me. If she thought I had anything to do with it, Alice would have written her suspicions in that diary you found."

She's right. Still, I press my luck. Monica doesn't know what Alice wrote, after all. "Maybe not. They had masks and voice changers."

Monica opens her mouth to retort and then abruptly shuts it. I'm reminded that both her parents are affluent financiers. They've no doubt given her the same talk most rich parents give their children: *If you get in trouble, be quiet and let me handle it.*

I must get her to crack before she calls them, and playing bad cop isn't working. "You're Alice's best friend, Monica." I soften my tone. "No, I don't think you'd hurt her. But I can't understand why you won't tell me about this boy. Is he your boyfriend? Do you think he did something, and you're protecting him?"

Monica pulls a phone from her pocket. She's going to dial her folks.

"Please, Monica!" Desperation saturates my voice. "Tell me what this boy did to my daughter. Tell me!"

"Nothing!" Monica yells.

She slumps onto the edge of her bed. "He didn't do anything, okay? Really." She rubs her hands over her face before looking directly at me. "He loves her."

"Does she love him back?"

It's the wrong question. Completely irrelevant to the investigation. Yet, suddenly, it's all I want to know: Is my daughter in love?

"I'm sorry," Monica says. "Alice should have told you."

The confirmation that Alice didn't trust me enough to share something so important gives me a new reason to cry. Instead, I take Monica up on her offer of the swing chair, sinking into the overstuffed cushion and dropping my purse beside me, freeing both my hands to swipe at possible tears.

"She asked you not to tell me." It's not a question.

Monica's shoulders round. "She didn't think you'd approve."

I imagine the boy: some skinny vegan philosophy major wearing daytime pajamas that stink of marijuana. Worse, a tenant in her new building—five years her senior—who never went to college, dreams of becoming an actor—no, a comedian—but is too busy waiting tables to do open mic nights. *And* stinks of marijuana.

"He's older, isn't he?"

Monica's eyes narrow like she's guessed what I'm thinking. "He was in the military. He joined to help pay for college, served for five years as an officer before he met Alice."

I redevelop my mental Polaroid, recalling what the neighbor said about the strange man being muscular and handsome, with green eyes. I add a military uniform. The emerging image isn't a bad one. Marine Corps Ken to go with Alice's blond Barbie. "Why would she think I'd have an issue with that?"

Monica cocks her head: *You know.*

And I do know. This boy signed over his mind and body to the US government for a scholarship. Clearly, he doesn't come from money.

Alice thought I'd object to any man without a pedigree—that I'd find him beneath her. She was right about my resistance, albeit for the wrong reason. I didn't want her to end up like me. Though I might not have realized it twenty-some-odd years ago, Brian married me because my money could foster his ambitions, and I ended up a work widow as a result. I wanted better for Alice: a husband who'd want to spend as much time as possible with her, who'd adore *her* regardless of her financial assets. One way to be sure of that was if the boy had enough of his own money not to care about hers.

"She wouldn't have wanted you to treat him like a suspect." Monica turns to Frazier. "Being accused of something like that by your girlfriend's parents when you're already concerned that they'll think less of you because you're working class. That's a hard thing for a relationship to recover from."

Frazier's expression is sympathetic. What he says, however, is dispassionate. "He's working class? What does he do for a living?"

Monica shakes her head, apparently disappointed in herself for letting such a detail slip. "Oh. Um. I'm not sure he—"

I glare at her.

She sighs. "He's a pilot."

After answering, she sneaks a glance at me, checking for a reaction. If I find pilot an acceptable job?

No, I realize. Monica's sure she knows my opinions and that I already don't approve. She's looking for recognition . . . I've met Alice's boyfriend before.

Again, my mental picture changes. The tall, muscular man in my imagination now wears a black pilot's uniform. Beneath his cap are striking green eyes.

And I know where I've seen him.

I wrest myself from the chair's vacuous cushion. "She met him on her dad's plane." I address Frazier, no longer seeking Monica's assistance. "He's the first officer."

Frazier continues grilling Monica with his stare. "What's the man's name?"

"Sean," she mutters. "I, uh, don't know his last name."

I'm not sure I believe her, but it doesn't matter. Zelos will have all the necessary information on its pilots or who it contracts with for crew. "I'll call Brian from the car."

Frazier doesn't take his eyes off our host. "Anything else you want to say that may be relevant to our investigation? Now's the time."

Monica resumes pulling at one of her curls, stretching the lock before letting it bounce back, bigger than before. "Don't harass him, okay? Alice would hate me for that."

I'm not making any promises. Monica's lied too much for me to owe her assurances. Part of me wants to tell her that, to admonish her for wasting valuable time trying to shield Alice's boyfriend from an uncomfortable conversation—time that could be causing irreparable damage to my daughter, her supposed best friend. *Should anything happen to Alice,* I want to scream, *it's all your fault!*

Even in my current state of constant anger and fear, however, I know blaming Monica for withholding the boyfriend's name won't accomplish anything. He might have nothing to do with all this, after all. Plus, I'll need Monica's help to build Alice back up after she comes home. *If she comes home.*

I force the doubt from my mind. "I'll be in touch." I borrow my tone from Brian so it sounds like a threat.

Frazier holds the door. I storm through, a new purpose lengthening my stride. I must find this man and determine what he knows, as well as to whom he might have bragged about dating the boss's daughter. Maybe he told an ex–military friend? A soldier might have the fortitude to pull off something like this.

I make it halfway down the hall before I register that my arm is lighter than it was coming in. In my haste to find the boy, I've forgotten my purse.

"I left my bag," I shout to Frazier. "Meet you at the car."

Before he can respond, I'm jogging back toward the dorm. As I approach, I see that Frazier did not close the door all the way. Light slips between the wood and the jamb.

I push the panel back. "Monica, I forgot my—"

She whirls around, eyes inexplicably wide. A blink later, I understand why. My purse dangles from a pale hand belonging to a person with a head of soft pink hair.

Forgetting a face might be common. A bubblegum dye job, however, is rare enough in my world to make an impression, especially when it belongs to someone whom you might owe ten million dollars. "You're the makeup artist!"

This freak occurrence is not as simple as Monica living on Hearst Avenue. The Hearst family name is plastered all over California. There is only one of this woman. Her presence here is *not* a coincidence.

Somewhere in my brain, the lock wheels pick up. I can almost hear them turning, their notches aligning as my subconscious assembles a combination still fenced off from my active mind. Then, suddenly, it all gives way. The bolt slams back, the safe door opens, and I see everything Alice has hidden in the vault: this boy, her friends, and, above all, her mountain of disappointments, a lifetime of resentment for her father's abandonment and her mother's apologies for him—my own rage multiplied by her vulnerability, youth, and expectations.

I grab the door for support. "You're in on it," I say. "You're all in on it together."

LIZA RING

FIVE DAYS AFTER

Sean's dream is bigger than I expected. The hangar I pictured was quaint: an overgrown Amish-style shed with peeling country-red paint and two sliding barn doors affixed to a rusted track. An aspiration in its DIY infancy. What's in front of me belongs in a private airport or maybe a painting. A paved runway cuts through a mile-long field of lavender bushes and waist-high grasses ending in a steel arc reminiscent of a Richard Serra sculpture.

From a distance, the structure appears hollow, an arch over a black hole. As Sean pilots his Subaru closer, I realize that what I assumed was a void is a two-story garage-style door painted matte black. It's topped by a transom window that runs the entire width of the building.

Sean catches me marveling as he pulls the car over to the asphalt's edge. "The glass lets in light."

"You built this?"

He puts the car in park, then flashes a wry grin. "Don't act so surprised."

It occurs to me that my mouth hangs open. I shut it as I step outside. Standing in front of the towering structure emphasizes its size, rendering it even more impressive. "How do you put together something like this?"

Sean rounds the car, closing the door I left ajar. "A buddy helped. You know him, actually. Captain Luke."

Another person's involvement makes the building seem possible, though still not probable. "Just the two of you?"

Sean stands beside me, hands on his hips. The commanding stance recalls my father. "The company sends a series of these metal arches. You raise them and then bolt each one to the ground and to its neighbor." He turns to me, the momentary bravado gone. "To be honest, clearing the vegetation to pour the concrete and asphalt was probably the hardest part. That and the door."

"You made the door?"

Sean laughs. "Hell no. Hangar doors are super involved. All these cables are required to lift it, and then there's a motor, plus rubber to create a seal so there's temperature control."

As Sean explains, he rounds the arch's side. A lockbox is soldered to the metal. He taps in a code, and the door rumbles awake. I watch the massive black wall crack in half and bulge outward before folding up and in on itself like giant origami. "There she is," Sean crows.

For a second, I think he's talking about me. Here I am. Found at last.

Then I see it: the long white beak of a 1985 Cessna 402. The plane looks like the love child of an egret and Edward Scissorhands, only with propeller blades appended to its extremities instead of knives. I think the comparison comes to me because the left wing is missing panels, revealing the tubes, pipes, and assorted innards that somehow power a flying machine.

I know better than to tell Sean his baby looks like a Frankenstein creation. "So this is the other woman, then?"

Sean strides over and pats the remaining fiberglass on the work-in-progress wing. "Parts take forever to find, but once she's done . . ." Sean whistles. "I'll be taking up passengers, cargo—my girl."

This time, I assume he's *not* referring to me. It's only when he wraps his arms around my waist and bends to kiss me that I realize he wasn't marveling at the plane. "No bed, though," he says. "I'm afraid the level of service to which you've become accustomed from your flight crew won't be available."

I peck his lips. "I'm not so sure about that." I kiss him again, more passionately. "Who needs a queen-size bed inside a plane? My dad's wasteful."

Sean pulls away. He smiles, though not in a naughty let-me-show-you-the-cabin way. "How long until he gets here?"

I wince at my mistake. I've unintentionally reminded him of the coming confrontation—though it's not like either of us could really forget. "Maybe a few hours."

The estimate is more of a shot in the dark than an educated guess. I called him from the burner phone during the drive. According to the internet, disposable phones don't have GPS tracking enabled, meaning the cops would have to derive the location from triangulating cell phone towers. Even so, I identified myself and then hung up in the hope that a quickly dropped connection would further complicate finding me. When I called back, I cryptically told my father that I knew what he'd done with the deepfake, and it required a *private* discussion. He replied with a single word: "Agreed."

After hanging up a second time, I texted an address about three miles from Sean's property and told him to wait there. Once we verified that he was alone, my kidnappers would deliver me to him. As soon as the text went through, I flung the phone from the open passenger-side window and into the woods. On the off chance that my father had the FBI somehow trace the number, as Sean feared, they'd find a dead cell far from our ultimate destination.

Though my father was *not* going to involve the authorities. Discrediting my message is more important to him than punishing me. He knows any jailhouse interviews on my behalf will only prolong Zelos's negative publicity cycle—and I would most certainly end up behind bars. The last woman to fake her own kidnapping in California got eighteen months in minimum security, and another got three years of house arrest. I checked.

"You think he'll like me?" Sean's question pulls me back to the present. His twisted mouth underscores the sarcasm.

"At least as much as he likes me right now."

Sean snorts, conceding the point. He separates from me and heads toward a metal panel affixed to the wall. Tools are lined up on the sheet, each cradled in a holster. "You know, if he was in San Francisco and left right away, he could conceivably arrive at the drop point in twenty minutes."

Sean speaks as he reaches for tools. His hand passes a hammer and a drill, wrenches of varied shapes and sizes. All these items could be weapons, but my boyfriend doesn't possess any of the "deadly" variety. The air force only issues guns to officers providing security on the base. Pilots get bombs.

He grabs a pair of binoculars. "I'll climb on top of the car and look to the road. If he parks where we said, I'll be able to spot him through the trees and then head on over. I'll monitor the air, too, though helicopters are noisy enough for us to hear before they become visible."

I turn toward the plane's exposed machinery, needing something else to engage my brain other than thoughts of what my father will or won't do, how our coming conversation might or might not go. "How much money do you think it will take for this to fly?" I ask.

Sean's face lights up. "Money's not the problem. It's waiting for the parts. Time to do it."

"Money is time," I counter. "It buys time. People to do what you don't want to do or can't. Engineers for the labor. Custom equipment."

Sean carries his binoculars toward the retracted wall/door. Before he exits, he whirls around to look at me with the smirk that floored me months earlier. "Oh, come on now," he laughs. "Where's the fun in that?"

CATHERINE NEWHOUSE INGOLD

FIVE DAYS AFTER

These girls are no good at gaslighting. Monica insists I'm confusing her girlfriend with another pink-haired woman—that my recent stress is forcing false assumptions. Her nervous expression undercuts her argument, however. And I know faces. If there's one skill a socialite must master, it's properly placing people she's briefly met and digging out tiny details from her memory bank to make them feel seen at the next charity function. *Your daughter, the one at Columbia. How's she liking the East Coast?* Or, *Your girlfriend, the one who tipped me off about the first clue, has she received the ransom yet?*

The only time Monica appears semicertain is when she assures me that Alice will return soon. If she isn't involved, how can she know? "Because a week was the plan?" I ask. "Take Alice for seven days—"

"No," Monica objects. "I don't know—"

"Then why are you sure she's okay? Why do you think she'll be back?"

Monica takes my purse from Princess Bubblegum and hands it to me. "You paid the kidnappers, right? That's what the news said. They must plan to let her go. You pay the ransom; she's released. I mean, that makes sense, right?"

She's asking if I believe her. I snatch my purse. "None of this makes sense."

"I'd assume if they—"

"Don't assume when you know."

Monica lowers her eyes from mine. "Ms. Ingold, I can imagine how difficult this is. But—"

"You're telling me that if I ask the police to compare the name of the makeup artist who tipped me off with the names on Berkeley's student registry, I'm not going to find punk-rock Barbie over there?" I pull out my phone. "Detective Frazier's in the car."

The pink-haired girl steps forward. "I apologize, Ms. Ingold. Monica's mistaken. She knows I do makeup for extra cash and didn't realize I was on set that day. Given how upset she's been about Alice, bringing up my job seemed irrelevant. In hindsight, I should have mentioned it. I assure you, it's only a coincidence." The woman places her hand on her heart as she says this last part, as if the pose conveys sincerity instead of practice.

I move forward, bringing my face inches from her own. "Tell me where my daughter is."

Monica grabs her girlfriend's arm, pulling her back while simultaneously taking her place. "We don't know where Alice is. We—"

"Tell me—"

"I don't know. I—"

"Can't you see this is killing me, Monica? Just tell me where my daughter is. TELL ME!" My scream breaks a dam. The emotion I've carried pours out, water from a broken amniotic sac. Contractions wrench my mouth. "Tell me! TELL me. TELL ME!"

Tears muddy Monica's brown eyes. "I don't know anymore."

Anymore.

Monica cups a hand over the lower half of her face, as if she might shove the word back into her mouth and swallow it. But it's too late. I know what I heard, same as I know that Monica's girlfriend was the makeup artist.

Alice's *supposed* best friend swats at a tear. "I didn't kidnap Alice, and Demi had nothing to do with any of this. We don't know where she is."

"But you did know."

Monica tugs on her girlfriend's arm, leading the woman to the edge of her bed. She grips Demi's hand as they sit. "Alice is a good person. She wants to change the world—or at least keep her dad from screwing it up more."

I tap my cell screen, a visual threat as clear as flicking off a gun's safety. "Where is she?"

Monica glances at her girlfriend. Demi lowers her eyelids, signaling acquiescence.

"I really don't know, Ms. Ingold." Monica places her other hand over her girlfriend's own. "Alice had been camping, but now . . ." She trails off, shaking her head.

I scroll to my contacts app. "Maybe Detective Frazier can help you remember."

Demi dives forward as if to grab the phone. She stops short of touching me, restrained by Monica's grasp. "If you bring the police into this, it won't only be bad for us. Alice will face charges. Faking a kidnapping has serious consequences, even when it's your own."

I've been standing on a cliff's edge, but Demi's words push me over. The moment I realized Alice's friend was in on the kidnapping, I suspected my daughter wasn't simply a victim. But this is the first confirmation of Alice's culpability.

"She was supposed to be back by now." Monica leans farther into Demi's side. They already sit so close. It's as if they're attempting to meld.

"I don't know what happened," she continues. "We can't reach her. Plus, this ransom? That was never part of the plan. Alice doesn't want money. None of us do."

I dart a glance at pink-haired Demi. She, at least, will have to admit that's not true.

She huddles impossibly closer to Monica. "I didn't plan on claiming the reward. I should never have left my information."

The fact that she apparently provided her real name undercuts that statement. Before I can press her on that, Monica pipes up. "The plan was always to guide you to the answers so that you'd lead the press to Zelos's less public operations. People need to know that Alice's dad's version of utopia is a dystopia for many, especially those of us starting out. I mean, Alice wants to be a writer, and her dad created software that pens its own *novels* in seconds. I'm studying computer science, and his AI fixes its own code and writes its own algorithms. And Alice has seen it do even more incredible things, taking over for doctors and lawyers. She says that her dad plans to outsource everybody with it, make it so we're all hooked on Zelos's all-powerful AI assistant like some sort of drug. Meanwhile, Zelos will keep learning from all the information people share with it, reporting back to the cloud so that its underlying technology gets more and more advanced. Ultimately, even the computer programmers won't know what the AI is doing or how it's manipulating us. We'll all be walking around in a daze saying, 'Hey, Zelos.'"

Demi nods along, a congregant listening to a firebrand preacher. "It's already changing the movie industry. Zelos can make dead celebrities star in roles that should go to up-and-coming actresses. It can change people's faces so they can play parts they should have aged out of long ago. And forget doing background work to hold on to your SAG card and health insurance. All those people can be computer generated."

I'm not really listening. As Demi talks, my vision blurs. Before me, I see my daughter through the years: a smiling toddler playing with me in the park, a happy elementary schooler hot-gluing a project under my supervision, a moody teenager always avoiding me, studying in her room. I knew Alice was furious with her dad. When did she come to hate me?

"How could she do this?" The question's a lament rather than a legitimate request for an explanation.

Even so, Monica volunteers one. "Alice is trying to call attention to the consequences of innovation without updated laws and regulations, get people to see what's coming and fight back against the rampant spread of this software before—"

"And I'm what? Collateral damage in this war against the machines? Her own mother?"

"Not everything is about you," Monica retorts. Her tone is hard because she's lying again. This isn't *only* about me.

Sure, Brian's to blame. He wasn't around, and Alice craved his presence. The cliché of girls with daddy issues is that they fulfill their desire for male parental attention with a string of meaningless relationships. Alice has never been casual about anything, however. She's her father's child: creative, logical, *relentless*. Of course she'd find an inventive way to force a reckoning.

But Alice isn't only punishing Brian. She had to realize this stunt would torture me most. I'm the one who made raising her my reason for being. On some level, my daughter believes I deserve this pain. What is it she said to me the day she left? *You need another passion project.* It was a warning: Stop meddling in her life—or else.

I pull my purse onto my shoulder. "She doesn't want my influence and control, fine. You tell her I'm not bailing her out. The police will investigate and come to whatever conclusions make sense. She'll have to deal with the consequences without my influence or money."

Demi looks up at me, her blue eyes brighter thanks to the contrasting cotton-candy hair. "You won't tell them, though? About our involvement?"

Their lies don't dignify an answer. For the second time, I storm into the hallway, leaving the door slam as my response. Let them feel what it's like to fear the following morning. Have them experience a modicum of what I've been put through these past few days.

Besides, I don't know what I'll do. Though I need to figure it out fast.

Frazier waits outside the sedan, a valet without keys. I approach, mind climbing the branches of the decision tree before me. If I reveal what Monica said, the police will either find evidence of Alice's involvement and press charges or investigate and come up empty. In the former scenario, my daughter will most certainly be made an example of to discourage any future fanatics willing to waste police resources for political grandstanding. She'll serve time. Our family will be humiliated. Pundits will wonder how I created someone who'd be so cruel to her own parents. Did I beat her with coat hangers for A-minus grades? Promise her hand in marriage to an impoverished European duke for cachet? Ignore her?

If Frazier *can't* implicate Alice, on the other hand, I'll appear to be a crazy woman who shamed her victimized child.

Saying anything is a losing proposition for both my daughter *and* me. Moreover, as much as I despise Alice right now, I don't want her pilloried in the press. I want her indiscretions to be handled the way wealthy families have always dealt with such things: in private and, perhaps, in the will.

I pull open the car door and settle into the back seat. Frazier notices my silence as he assumes the driver's position. He looks to my reflection in the rearview mirror. "Took time to retrieve your purse."

Rather than respond, I gaze out the window. The sun has ducked behind coming rain clouds, creating enough shadow to see my tearstained reflection.

Frazier starts the car. "Did you call Brian? Ask for information on this Sean person?"

"Not yet." I sound mechanical.

"I'll call the company," he offers.

My reflection's disgusted with me. It knows what I'm about to say before I do. "There's no need. The boy is probably worried enough without cops showing up at his door. Alice wouldn't want our first interaction to be an interrogation."

"But Monica lied about him," Frazier says.

"That's what teenagers do." I lean my head against the glass rather than look at myself. "Alice wanted to introduce this guy on her own terms. She told her best friend not to tell me, and Monica was determined to honor that promise. The girl swears the young man has nothing to do with Alice's disappearance. He loves her, apparently."

In the rearview mirror, I see Frazier's skeptical squint. "So you don't want to track him down?"

"Right now, I just want to go home."

Frazier's vision toggles between the road and my reflection as he pulls the car from the building. My about-face bothers him.

But what else can I say?

I direct my attention back out the window, pretending to take an interest in the zoetrope of trees and hills. I watch the greenery blur into an impressionist landscape. At some point, I fall asleep.

It's not until the car stops that I realize I've drifted off. My house gate looms through the windshield. I've lost time, Rip van Winkle realizing that half his life has passed him by. I grab the door handle. "Thank you, Detective."

Pulling the lever fails to pop the lock. I clear my throat. "Thank you—"

"You wanted to find this boy, and now you don't," Frazier says. "What changed?"

I pull the handle again, even though I know it won't work. He's engaged the cop equivalent of a child lock.

"Did Monica reveal something else? Something to change your mind?"

I fall back into the seat. "Alice was in love, Detective. And she didn't tell me." My voice cracks. "She didn't even want me to know."

He leans over the console to face me. "Locating this boy makes sense. We need to know who he might have shared Alice's new address with."

"Or we wait, like Brian suggested." I control a shudder. Agreeing with Brian makes me sound like my old self.

Frazier turns back to the windshield. The back locks unclick. "Alright. You rest. I'll call in a few hours."

I'm out the door before he's finished speaking, and I don't watch him leave. Instead, I key in the gate code and shuffle toward my home. My shoulders are hunched. My legs are stiff. It seems my body has aged ten years in the past ten hours. The only thing left to do is bury myself under comforters and fall into oblivion, to lose consciousness like Aurora's parents in the original Disney movie, not to wake until the princess's return.

What Alice is still holding out for, I don't know. Her kidnapping did what she wanted, pushing the press to expose Zelos's operations and discuss its implications. The last news program I watched had pundits comparing AI coders to caged rat snakes, trapped in their firms' on-site micro-studios, consuming themselves by designing software destined to eliminate their jobs. Monica couldn't have written the anchor's script better herself.

I key into my house, aiming for the bedroom. As I reach the stairs, I hear voices. For a moment, I fear someone has broken in—journalists desperate for a scoop, perhaps, or even Alice and the mystery boyfriend.

I don't know what I'll say to her—to either of them.

A second later, I realize the conversation is far too civil to be happening in real life. Actual discussions do not include sound bites without overlap or interruption. The TV's on.

"What do you make of this ten-million-dollar ransom?" an anchor asks.

"It's not a lot of money," a panelist responds.

"Well, for most people, it . . ."

The chatter grows louder as I enter the living room. I scan for the remote without looking at the flat-screen. The voices are recognizable. They belong to the CNBC talking heads whom Brian prefers to watch. Apparently, he left the set on when he was last here.

"We're not talking about most people, though," the anchor continues. "We're discussing two individuals in the 0.01 percent. Why not ask for more?"

I grab the remote. "That's the ten-million-dollar question," I mutter to myself. "Why ask for a ransom at all when you have multiple millions coming to you? Because you expect your mother to cut you off after discovering your lie?"

I point the remote at the sensor.

"Maybe because their real goal is political," the anchor suggests. "The kidnappers want to highlight concerns about Zelos. They chose Alice because she's Brian Ingold's heir apparent."

"Then you don't ask for a payday," the pundit retorts. "I think it's now clear they only picked her because her family's wealthy. Ten million must simply be easier to launder or—"

The flat-screen goes dark, though the last point remains in my brain, fading slowly like the center glow on an old rear-projection set. Alice had to know any ransom demand would undermine the purpose of staging her kidnapping, and she took pains in her fake diary to have her captors explain that their goal was *not* to extort money. Clearly, she'd hoped I'd share the diary with the media to clarify her viewpoint. Why confuse things now?

Monica's arguments rush back to me: *The ransom wasn't part of the plan.*

Alice wasn't kidnapped—at first. But who's to say she hasn't been now? It's possible someone close to her decided to change plans. Someone lacking parental money, perhaps, who'd needed to enlist in the military to pay for college. That someone could be holding her hostage at this very moment.

I pull out my phone, grateful that Captain Luke is in my contact list. He answers on the first ring. "Mrs. Ingold, have there been any developments?"

I appreciate him getting right to it. This is not a time for pleasantries. "The first officer who worked for you on our last flight. His name?"

"Sean?" Captain Luke sounds rightfully concerned. "Sean Whalen."

"Do you know how I can get in touch with him?"

"I'm not sure why—"

"He and Alice were dating." I try to sound as if this information is not news.

"He was seeing your daughter?" Unlike Monica's girlfriend, Captain Luke isn't in the pretending business. His bewilderment is genuine.

"I need to speak with him as soon as possible."

Captain Luke exhales, adding a bunch of white noise to the speaker. "The little I know of him, he's a good kid. I can't imagine he has anything to do with this."

"I appreciate your judgment, Captain, but I still need to talk to him."

"Right. Of course. I have his cell. Hold on a moment."

As I wait for the captain to retrieve the information, I remember something else Monica said during her teary confession: She hasn't been able to get in touch with Alice either. Surely if my child isn't answering the phone for her friend, her kidnapper boyfriend won't pick up for me.

"Do you know where he lives?" I ask.

"He moved recently, I think. An apartment in Oakland."

I close my eyes. Of course he did. "Does he have anyplace else? Something more rural, maybe?"

"A hangar outside of Sonoma." Captain Luke sounds resigned. "Though I'm guessing you knew that."

There's no reason to let on that I didn't. "Please have the plane ready. I need you to—"

"I'm afraid I can't," he interrupts. "Mr. Ingold instructed me to stay grounded until I hear from him. I'm sorry."

For the second time today, I feel the urge to scream. There's no guarantee Brian will authorize my trip. He's decided the best course of action is to wait, and once Brian's determined an optimal path, he's not easily swayed. Revealing that Alice was involved will probably only make him more determined to sit tight.

"Please." In place of a shout is a choked whisper. "Please, Luke. I need to find this boy."

Silence answers. I catch my breath, preparing my next argument. Thankfully, the captain speaks first. "Driving is faster anyway for a trip like this. Stay there. I'll pick you up."

LIZA RING

FIVE DAYS AFTER

The hangar is shut for my protection. Sean thought it best to keep a wall between me and the outside world until he returned with my father. He was picking him up from the texted location—a winery turned into a wild-horse sanctuary by some finance billionaire's first wife. As instructed, my father parked on a dirt path leading to the staff entrance of the sprawling estate. Sean's binoculars didn't reveal any other cars in the vicinity aside from a Tesla Roadster. My dad appeared to be alone.

But we couldn't be certain. Before leaving, Sean insisted that I return to the hangar, waving goodbye as he watched the door close. Even if my father had the police follow him here without us realizing it, the cops wouldn't be able to break into the hangar so easily. Once the thousand-pound door was down, it wasn't coming up without Sean unlocking it or me hitting the controls. I'd be safe inside from any cowboy FBI agents or police officers—at least until they could obtain a warrant and a blowtorch.

Nerves glue my gaze to the retractable steel wall. In some ways, the contraption recalls the plane's exposed wing. All the levers and pulleys enabling the door to fold are visible. Six cables extend from the base to the ceiling. Foot-long hinges run across the middle of the door's metal facade. Two motors are spaced out on the base, and rollers run up tracks on both sides. Thick rubber panels connect the door to the wall. I feel hermetically sealed.

Surprisingly, the hangar isn't 100 percent soundproof. Though I don't hear birds or the braying donkey rumored to roam with the stallions on the neighboring property, I do hear my boyfriend's shout as he approaches the door. "It's me, Liza."

"Who the hell is Liza?" It's the question I'd expect my father to ask. His tone also matches the emotion I've been bracing for: barely restrained anger.

Sean doesn't appear to answer. In place of a response, I hear motors churn and the crack of a separating seal. The door's prior origami fold happens in reverse, the steel sheet collapsing on itself before pulling upward. When the door is halfway to the ceiling, I see my dad. Sean's relative height renders him less physically imposing, but his presence somehow makes my boyfriend seem far younger than his twenty-six years. My father is in the middle of nowhere, on a property that isn't his—yet somehow he's in charge.

He strides in, one hand in the pocket of a fleece pullover, the other dangling by the side of his khaki pants. To the uninitiated, it might seem that he's come straight from the office on a casual Friday to assess some indulgent purchase: a plane to tool around with on weekends. But Zelos employees don't distinguish between Friday and any other day ending in *y*, and only the marketing execs ever wear suits. My dad wears whatever he happens to throw on. Dressing to impress is for people seeking to climb the corporate ladder. My father has reached wear-your-pj's-to-work rich.

Sean's camping attire does him a favor in this respect. To my dad, it will seem that my boyfriend doesn't think him worthy of donning a suit, which he'll read as a power move. If *the* Brian Ingold can show up like a Patagonia ad, then so can the guy dating his daughter.

"You've been here the whole time?" It's a strange opening, though I can't imagine what remark my father could make that wouldn't strike me as odd under the circumstances. Asking if I've been *well* would sound sarcastic.

"No. I had to come here after you made that fake video."

My dad scans the room, perhaps looking for a recording device. "Are you referring to the ransom demand?"

It's a lawyer's retort, a question that neither confirms nor denies involvement. "I'm referring to the AI deepfake that only Zelos could do."

His head wobbles. Maybe yes, maybe no. "Debatable. Makes sense your kidnappers would want money. Their goal surely couldn't be to turn public opinion against my company's AI. To destroy decades of my hard work."

I move closer to him, fighting the urge to ask for a hug. An irrational part of me still hopes my dad will pull me into his arms and confess his relief that I'm alive. He'll be thankful that there's still time to repair our relationship, and he'll finally hear out my concerns for his AI-does-everything bespoke future. Seeing the extremes to which I've gone—extrapolating the fear that drove me to do all this—he'll turn into the benevolent king that he pretends to be on business news programs. He'll promise to slow or stall his software releases so the public can weigh in on the right way forward. He'll sacrifice near-term profits in favor of safeguards.

As I approach, he shoves his hand farther into his fleece pocket. Fat chance.

I stop several feet away. "No one wants to destroy Zelos, Dad. But the public needs to understand what your software is capable of. We need it to be responsible."

His eyes narrow. "You never did understand technology, Alice. You think it's, what? A religion? Something with a moral code? It's a tool, plain and simple. A device like a telephone or a typewriter."

Behind my dad, the door descends. Gears rumble. Cables vibrate. I raise my voice to be heard over the clatter. "You don't feel *any* responsibility for people using what you've built to cheat and lie? To plagiarize papers or disseminate fabricated news articles? To copy others' ideas and art and—"

"Zelos follows prompts, solves problems." He interrupts with a shrug, hands in his pockets like he doesn't have a care. "People give it a goal, and it executes."

"What about when the goal hurts society at large?"

"Example?"

"Take what you're doing at that data center," I say, ready to show that I paid attention during my summer internship. "Zelos buys stocks based on momentum calls rather than any intelligent take on whether a company's business model is viable, or its CEO is smart, or it treats its employees well. Financial markets are supposed to reward good companies with higher stock prices, enabling them to pay their employees more and grow their businesses. Zelos is simply calling short-term upswings and downturns a fraction of a second faster than the next guy. Stealing pennies."

"That's for the market to figure out."

"What if it can't," I retort. "People don't understand Zelos's capabilities. They don't even know when they're watching a video with someone's stolen identity and voice."

My dad snorts. "All's fair in work and war, kiddo. You did the same thing with a plain old paper and pen, making people think you were kidnapped."

"Motivation matters." Sean brushes past my father to stand at my side. "We're trying to show people the truth."

My father laughs. The sound bounces against the hangar's metal walls, morphing his voice into something echoey and hollow. "The truth is, technology makes things easier. People feared computers; now everyone uses them to work faster. Productivity has skyrocketed. With Zelos's AI, people will accomplish tasks they never dreamed of in seconds. Here's an example everyone likes. Foreign languages. It requires decades for a person to learn another tongue. With Zelos, everyone can communicate in whatever language they choose via our translation apps. No hesitation. Just conversation."

The last four words sound like they came straight from Zelos's marketing department. I bar my arms across my chest. "But you're taking jobs—"

He throws up a hand. "What's this really about, huh? You're angry I wasn't around. That's it, right? Well, thanks to what I built, people will be able to spend more time with their families."

"That's not how this will work, Dad." Tears weigh on my lashes. "If Zelos achieves everything you want, it'll take over everything and—"

"So?" My father's left hand exits the pocket to land on his hip. The right remains in his fleece, as if he's posing for a *GQ* article. "Maybe it should take over everything."

Sean shoots me a surprised look. I've told him my father cares more about his work than me or anyone else. He didn't fully believe me.

"You think that's awful?" He stares down Sean from his lower vantage point. "You're an ex–military pilot, right? You must have seen things. How great is this world with people making the decisions? For all we know, human beings will be wiped out in a nuclear war in the coming years. All that will be left is radiation and the machines able to withstand it."

Sean holds my hand. "AI is more likely to blow up the planet than human beings. We've had nukes for decades, and yet we've restrained ourselves. We've contained the technology because people want the world to exist for themselves and their children."

"Their children." My dad looks me up and down, his curled lip betraying his disgust. "Artificial intelligence is the next stage in human evolution. It'll inherit the sum of all our knowledge and improve on it, be better than our progeny could ever be."

My dad's not revealing any opinion that I haven't guessed he holds. Still, hearing it aloud hurts. "Fathers are supposed to want to make things better for their kids, Dad. Not replace them."

He scoffs. "That's just speciesist."

Sean pats my shoulder. "That's human. It's human to want to leave the world better for your descendants."

My dad looks directly at me and smirks. "They do call me the father of AI."

His glibness burns through my sadness. My father will never sympathize with what I've done. He'll go to his grave claiming my kidnappers only wanted money.

I step from the protection of Sean's reach. "I'll admit to everything. I'll tell everyone how scared I became working at your company, how I realized that I needed to do something dramatic for people to see what you were doing behind the scenes, to start pushing for controls."

"They'll put you in prison," my father says. "Both of you."

"It'll be worth it! People need to know who you really are, who they're trusting to design the future."

"You stupid little brat." My father throws up both hands in frustration.

His right holds something.

"Gun!" Sean shouts.

The word clarifies the flash of metal. My dad holds the weapon like a novice, cupping the handle between both palms. "I'm through debating, Alice. You're coming with me."

Sean stands in front of me before I fully register that the barrel is pointed at my chest. He steps toward my father, hands raised in surrender. "Put that down, Mr. Ingold."

My dad keeps the gun on Sean. "Alice," he says, "you'll tell everyone that we paid the ransom."

"What are you doing?" I move abreast of my boyfriend. "You don't want to shoot—"

"Your kidnapper?"

I see the idea spark in my dad's eyes and shoot across synapses, drawing lines across his brow as his brain processes the new command. His grip tightens on the gun. He's going to kill Sean and claim to have saved me.

I throw all my weight into Sean's side, sending him toward the concrete. The gun discharges with a deafening pop as I fall alongside my boyfriend. Pain erupts in my shoulder.

Sean's torso softens the floor's blow. I hear him yell, though I can't make out the words. My heart pounds in my ears. Instinctually, I grab at my pulsing arm.

It's wet.

"Sean?" The name is all I can manage as my body absorbs the reality. I've been shot. My dad shot me.

That thought, as much as the burn in my arm, sets my nervous system ablaze. I shake, suddenly freezing despite the searing sensation radiating from above my right breast.

"Breathe. Okay. Breathe." Sean coaches me through the agony while pressing something into my hand gripping my shoulder. It's soft. Cotton? I open my eyes to see Sean's bare chest rising and falling in front of me.

"Hold that on it. Hard." He stares at me, green eyes like burning copper. "Hard, okay?" A whimper emerges from my mouth. Sean hollers over his shoulder, "Put the gun down."

From the floor, I see my father still standing with his weapon extended. It's pointed where Sean's chest had been moments before.

Sean rises. His hands are no longer palms out, but neither are they curled into fists. "I'm going for my phone." He reaches into his pants pocket. "She's bleeding badly. She needs an ambulance."

"Throw me your keys and your cell." The voice that responds to him is strange: high and frantic. It sounds nothing like my father.

"You're not taking her." Sean sounds different too. Firmer.

"Throw me your keys and phone or I'll blow your fucking head off." Whoever is speaking seems like a character in a Scorsese film. This is not happening.

Sean takes off. From the ground, I have a better view of his feet than his destination. He heads to the hangar's side. The door controls are there.

Bang!

Another shot reverberates. A ping pierces the echo, a bullet hitting a metal wall.

"Don't!" I shriek. The effort explodes my shoulder. I press Sean's shirt harder into the wound. "Don't shoot him!"

Another blast answers. This one is followed by the sharp snap of a cable.

"Stop it. Stop!"

There's a crack as the door seal breaks, followed by another ping and snap. Gears strain. A crash shakes the floor. From my squinted view, I see half the door slam into the ground. The other portion continues to rise. Steel strains and groans. A succession of snaps follows and then a slam, almost on a delay, as if someone accidentally hit a mute button.

The impact is followed by a scream—more bone chilling because it's distinctly male. Men don't sound like that, particularly not trained military men, unless they're in immense pain.

I force myself onto the elbow linked to my working shoulder and scan for the source. Sean writhes on the floor, clutching his thigh. One of the door's broken cables lies beside him. The black rubber is somehow slick. Beside it, blood stains the floor in a swirling impression, a snake that's left its skin behind.

What happened dawns on me. A cable that supported a few hundred pounds of door abruptly released its burden and whipped toward the wall. It caught my boyfriend in the process, tearing through his quad with ten times the strength of a leather whip. The femoral artery is in the thigh.

My father strides over to him. He raises his gun over Sean like my boyfriend's little more than a lame horse.

"No." I push myself onto my knees and crawl toward them. Every movement is a brand burning into my flesh, but I must reach him. I must drape my body over his own, becoming a shield of bone and sinew. My father wouldn't deliberately shoot me. I need to believe that.

Before I get more than a few feet, I hear the click. Reflexively, I close my eyes, bracing for the sound of a shot. But it doesn't come. There's only a click and then another. Then another.

"Sean," I continue to pull myself toward him. "Sean!"

A hand wraps around my good arm, pulling it from under me. My chin dives toward concrete. Before it connects, I'm yanked semiupright and dragged across the floor, away from my destination.

"No!" I wail. "No! Sean. SEAN! We need an ambulance. We've got to call—"

"I have his phone," my father growls. "And his car key. I'm taking you out of here."

I dig my heels into the floor. Though my sneakers leave skid marks on the concrete, they fail to stop me. My father's so much stronger. And I'm in so much pain. "Please. I have to help him."

"You've been shot." His tone is suddenly matter-of-fact. "We're going to the hospital. You'll tell them all about escaping your kidnappers who tried to kill you after receiving the ransom."

"I won't."

"You were able to get the guy's phone and call me. I rescued you," he continues.

"I won't. I won't say it."

"You will." He pulls me harder. "Even if you don't, no one will believe you. They'll think you have Stockholm syndrome. Your kidnappers brainwashed you into believing you were all on the same side. A few years in a mental institution should sort things out."

I continue to fight even as my father pulls me beneath the mangled door's raised section and onto the asphalt. Grit tears at my back and bottom. My diary is becoming a true story. I'm being kidnapped, dragged to a car by a furious gunman.

Only no one was dying in my tale. My boyfriend wasn't lying on concrete with his thigh ripped open, scared and alone. Exsanguinating.

In my story, only *I* got hurt.

CATHERINE
NEWHOUSE INGOLD

FIVE DAYS AFTER

Captain Luke and I aren't friendly enough for silence. As we barrel down the wide 101 in his Jeep, he tells me everything he thinks he knows about Sean Whalen, portraying him as an assiduous Boy Scout incapable of kidnapping a nineteen-year-old. All the first-date humblebrags have been shared. Sean's parents are "salt of the earth" folks, a teacher and a trucker who attend church on Sundays and volunteer to coach Little League. Sean graduated from the University of Michigan and was an officer in the air force. He was honorably discharged.

"Kid's a bleeding-heart type," Captain Luke says as we pass the exit for Napa. "Told me he left the military because he didn't approve of fighting wars remotely. Made depersonalizing the other guy too easy."

"Kidnapping is certainly personal," I quip.

Captain Luke grips the wheel a bit more tightly. "I can't see it. He's not the kind."

I murmur something noncommittal rather than engage. Who seems like a kidnapper save for a disheveled man in a white van spray-painted with the words *free candy*? Captain Luke is talking up Sean to justify giving the boy free rein to flirt with my daughter. He wants me to believe that anyone who so fooled him would have blindsided the most discerning hiring manager.

Part of me hopes he's right about *Saint Sean*, though. As much as I want Alice to be in this young man's garage, I'm ill-prepared to fight a real kidnapper. I didn't tell Detective Frazier or Agent Lee my plans for fear they'd escalate the situation, putting Alice in more danger with a trigger-happy SWAT team. If I'm honest with myself, I also didn't want to risk them hearing of her initial involvement.

Without the cops, it's possible that Sean and I can come to a private financial agreement that frees my child without prison time or public shaming for either of them. If Alice's boyfriend has turned kidnapper, she's likely suffered enough. Realizing that the man you love is primarily interested in your money is devastating. I know. I've finally accepted it after twenty years of peeling off the Band-Aid, micron by micron. Alice would have had it ripped away in one motion.

"He's industrious," Captain Luke adds. "This place we're going. He bought the land himself and built the hangar." The captain nods as he watches the road, genuinely impressed. He must see something of himself in this guy. Maybe they're both military men. Luke has the enlisted look: fit with crew cut hair and a matching gray beard, steel eyes that have *seen things*. "Nothing came up on a background check," Captain Luke continues. "No arrests."

"*That* hardly means anything."

He presses his lips together, restraining himself from sharing more résumé items about his first officer, maybe giving me space to share my own thoughts. My quip resurrected a memory, though I'm unwilling to relay it to Luke, as it wasn't Alice's finest moment. Revealing my daughter's flaws when he's been boasting about her boyfriend isn't fair. Though, now that the memory has come back to me, it's all I can think about.

Alice was arrested once. She'd turned fourteen three weeks prior to "the incident," as I refer to that terrible day. The age is notorious, especially for girls. Fresh hormones encourage them to abhor all seasoned

305

sources of estrogen and seek approval solely from developmentally deficient peers. To make matters worse, years of straining against the childhood leash have finally stretched it enough to whirl on the one who's been keeping them out of traffic. Fourteen-year-olds routinely bite the hands that feed them. They don't yet understand that those hands restrain wolves that they can't yet recognize, and don't yet know to fear.

Money exacerbated the situation, as it can. One of Alice's friends—an early bloomer with large breasts and stubborn acne that she covered with too much bronzer—convinced her chauffeur to ferry the group into the city for *shopping*. Of course, no one intended to do anything as boring as popping into stores they could easily access online. The real activity was taking selfies at an abandoned bank.

I could hardly blame Alice for being curious about the place. The structure was a neoclassical masterpiece that once housed the flagship branch of the same chain that an assault rifle–wielding Patty Hearst later robbed. Doric columns stretched several stories to a curved copper cap. Inside, a dome worthy of a Saudi Arabian mosque sheltered marble floors and graffiti-covered walls. For kids in perpetual search of cool pics to send their Snapchat friends, the bank was gold.

The cops called while I was at lunch. As soon as they said *trespassing*, I was off the phone and in my car. Frustration weighed my lead foot. I was annoyed at the police for hauling a bunch of ninth graders down to the station for a disorderly person's offense, thereby putting their future college acceptances at risk. I was irritated at Alice for acting reckless and abusing my trust, violating our inferred agreement that she'd refrain from criminal activity. I was pissed at the friend's driver for letting a bunch of puberty-impaired teens traipse around a city unsupervised.

I was *not* worried for my daughter's safety. The entire thirty-minute drive to San Francisco, I invented punishments that I'd enforce after our family attorney had reduced her misdemeanor to some form of semivoluntary community service. One of my more interesting ideas was to make her go on daily hikes, supervised by me, where she could indulge her apparent *need to explore* while absorbing lessons on adult judgment.

By the time I pulled into the police station, I was ready with mea culpas for the authorities and promised penalties for my wayward child. Only Alice wasn't there. The "friend" who'd brought everyone to the bank in the first place had decided it would be hilarious to close Alice and another girl in the vault. The little genius hadn't considered that the door would lock, or that no one would have the keys to rooms in a long-abandoned building.

"Our concern is the oxygen," a uniformed cop explained, hat in hand like a casualty notification officer on a front stoop. "Bank vaults typically pump in air conditioning. But with everything shut down for so long and in disrepair . . ."

Every punishment I'd invented dissipated in that moment. By the time Alice was rescued, I was too relieved to so much as ground her. She made it out with a bruised ego and a weeklong sore throat from the smoke generated by the industrial-strength blowtorch that had cut a kid-sized hole in the vault's door. Even the police hadn't had the heart to press charges.

The media coverage proved penalizing enough anyway. Someone leaked the story to the press and, almost immediately, the articles went viral. For two weeks, Alice's clickbait face was everywhere: the poor, pretty, gullible victim of a mean-girl prank. One headline read: "Poor Little Rich Girl Trapped in Bank Vault." Much to Alice's dismay, the title stuck with her for the remainder of high school.

Was that when this all started? Did Alice realize then how interested the media would be in whatever happened to her? That she possessed the right combination of beauty and notoriety so that the mere thought of her in peril would lead the news? Had she learned nothing at fourteen about how a harmless prank could turn life threatening? About whom—and whom not—to trust?

Like when Alice was in that vault, my fear for her safety supersedes any desire to punish her. I need my child back unharmed. Only after

I've held her in my arms—after I've checked her body for bruises and probed for psychological damage, asked the hard questions about what a guy who sees you as little more than a bargaining chip might do when he has all the power—can I consider the fallout of Alice's actions and my own feelings.

The click of the car's blinker calls my attention back to my current journey. According to Captain Luke's GPS, we're on the outskirts of Sonoma, somewhere in the surrounding hills shadowed by the mountains. Captain Luke turns onto a street that his map has pictured, albeit not named. It's one and a half lanes, big enough for a landscaping truck but not two cars side by side. The pavement's skate-park fresh. As it curves, Luke taps his horn, alerting any unseen vehicles to his presence around the bend.

"Technically, it's a private road," he says. "A woman with a horse farm or some such owns it."

The scene outside the window is less pastoral than postapocalyptic. A winery has gone to seed. Tall grasses overwhelm evenly spaced grape stalks. Dandelions, their yellow heads bleached white, lace the landscape like cobwebs. Harvest season is around the corner, yet I don't spot grapes dangling from the vines. That doesn't mean they're not there. Untamed *Vitis* leaves, as broad as hen feathers, conceal whatever ripens beneath, saving it for the field mice and other roaming rodents. I can almost smell the fruit in the air, the sweet scent of something souring, wine changing to vinegar.

I don't see the horses until we've traveled several minutes up the road. They're in the distance, far from the domain of the cars that humans made to replace them. A herd of gray, brown, black, and white coats shimmers in the orange light. The sun will set in a few hours. I want to be done talking to Sean before nightfall.

I turn from my window to Captain Luke. "Can we go a bit faster?"

The speedometer inches from thirty to forty. "It should be up ahead. Trying to be careful of other cars."

No sooner does he say it than I hear a horn. An SUV flies around the corner. Captain Luke jerks the Jeep's wheel to the left, putting half the car into the dirt. Even so, the speeding vehicle nearly clips the Jeep's right mirror. As Captain Luke slams on the brakes, I hear the skid of wheels rolling in dirt followed by the thump of a car returning to a road. By the time I turn around, it's too far for me to see the driver. "Was that Sean?"

The veins in Captain Luke's hands threaten to pop from his skin. He exhales as he pulls the car back onto the road. "It could have been his car."

There's no easy way to check. The SUV has already vanished around the bend. My daughter might be in the back seat, but she's as likely to be at Sean's place, waiting for rescue. For all I know, her kidnapper could have been tipped off about our arrival and opted to flee.

It's a best-case scenario that I can't pass up. "Let's keep going."

Luke brings his speed up from zero to forty. A moment later, I spy a glint of metal through the driver's-side window. We hang a left onto another butter-paved road, about as narrow as the first. The main difference between the two paths is the presence of trees. Whereas the winery road had patches of maples and cedars creeping toward the asphalt, nothing taller than two feet lines this stretch. Everything is a grass or untended lavender bush. An herbal, soapy scent saturates the air.

The reason for the clear-cutting soon becomes evident. A steel hangar looms at the end of the road. Its door is twisted upright like a half-open can of tuna. Peeking out from the open part is the unmistakable nose of a plane. We're on a runway.

"What happened here?" Captain Luke asks.

The question sparks my nerves. "Isn't it under construction?"

"No."

My body suddenly burns. Something has gone wrong.

I open the door while the car rolls to a stop. "ALICE!" I rush through the hangar's sneering mouth. The interior smells like metal and something else, rusted but somehow organic. "Alice, are you in here? ALICE!"

A groan responds.

It takes a moment to spot the source. I see the plane and a pool of dark red beneath its torn-open wing. The color smears outward from this center blob, as if a bloody limb has been dragged. "ALICE!"

"Help."

The word is more moan than cry. It emanates from the far side of the room. A shirtless man leans against the hangar's metal wall, his body crumpled along the curve. Both of his arms are pressed against either side of his right thigh. His face is paper pale.

"HELP!" I amplify his call and append Luke's name to it. As injured as Sean appears, he's still a young man. I don't know what he's capable of.

Footsteps sound outside. I approach Sean at half their speed, scanning for a weapon or anything else he might use against me. A cable, apparently from the door, lies beside his leg. "Where is Alice?"

Sean looks up at me. His pupils nearly consume the ring of green around them. "Her dad. Took her."

Pain can cause delirium. I wonder if he's lying or hallucinating. Surely he doesn't mean Brian was here.

Sean's head dips forward. I crouch to reestablish eye contact only to see what has immobilized him. His thigh is split like a spatchcocked chicken, the meat on either side parted in a V, revealing an open cavity of blood and bone. War wounds look like this.

I scramble backward. The sound that emerges from me belongs to a dying animal, a calf or young goat. Something being slaughtered.

Captain Luke rushes past me to Sean's side. In one motion, he rips off his cotton shirt, tears off a strip, and cinches it around Sean's open leg. The boy screams, another animal sound, though in a lower register.

"Call an ambulance!" Luke shouts.

The direction snaps me from my shock. I dig into my purse for my cell, struggling to feel it among the makeup and keys and other useless items. I pull out a smooth compact. A lipstick.

"Do you have them?" Captain Luke asks. "9-1-1. Emergency?"

I turn the bag upside down. The compact crashes on concrete, spewing flesh-toned powder in all directions. The lipstick cracks open. I catch my cell a nanosecond before it joins the broken mess. Though I pull the device toward my face, the screen remains locked. Horror has morphed my features into something even the software can't recognize.

I tap in my code and wait for the home screen. Everything is taking too long. The phone app. Dialing 9-1-1. There's silence as my cell struggles to connect. "It's not working!"

Luke whispers to Sean, coaching him to breathe as he tightens the tourniquet. "Try again!" he yells.

I'm about to end the call when a voice shoots through the speaker. "Sonoma 9-1-1. What's the address of the emergency?"

I don't know. "Luke, the address here?"

If the captain hears me, he doesn't respond. He's too busy ripping his shirt into pieces, creating ribbons with which to tie together Sean's leg, closing it up like the back of a wedding gown. The effort is so valiant that I can't help but want him to succeed, though a part of me wonders if I'm wishing for the wrong outcome. If Sean did kidnap Alice, maybe this is his punishment. A dead man can't implicate his ex-girlfriend in a federal offense.

"Ma'am, are you there?" The voice rumbles through my cell's speakers. "What's the address?"

Sean squeals. He sounds so scared. So young.

"Let me check my GPS." I call up the Find My app and click on my own device. It shows a circle over a portion of Sonoma next to Mustang Creek Ranch. I say the name of the marked location. "If you enter the property and then travel up the road, there's another paved stretch that connects, which leads to an airplane hangar. It's not marked."

As I talk, I scan for signs of an exact location, a number or street name. All I see is the plane and, rolling away from it, my lipstick. Beside that is a cylindrical piece of copper that I don't recognize from my purse. I squint to see better.

It's a bullet casing.

"What's the nature of your emergency? Fire, medical, or—"

"We need an ambulance." I know they won't send one without a cop, as much as I might want them to. "It looks like there was an accident with a door, and this boy's leg is nearly torn in two. He's bleeding. My friend is trying to cut off the circulation, but I don't know if he can."

"Okay. You stay on the line. Is he breathing?"

Sean's bare chest moves up and down, though far too fast. "Not well. He could hyperventilate."

"Okay. We don't want him passing out. Can you elevate his legs?"

I force myself to look at Sean's mangled extremity. Another bullet casing lies beside his foot. "Were you shot?" I ask.

Sean speaks through gritted teeth. "No. Alice."

I'm swept into a shock wave. Suddenly, everything is quiet. Sean mouths words I can't understand. Luke ties another band around his leg, his own lips moving. What I hear is a buzz, growing louder and louder. Finally, the sound blasts from my own mouth.

"Is Alice alive?" I've forgotten the phone in my hand. I see only Sean: my sole connection to my daughter.

He manages a wincing nod. "He took her. Minutes ago."

"Ma'am, did I hear someone was shot?"

Answering the dispatcher won't help me save my child. "Is the ambulance on its way?" I ask. "Do you know where we are?"

"Yes. We need for you to stay on the line so we can talk—"

I end the call. "Where is Brian taking her?"

Sean sucks in a breath. The answer comes out in one run-on exhalation. "He left his car on the road to the ranch."

I drop to my knees beside the captain. "Give me your keys."

LIZA RING

FIVE DAYS AFTER

If he dies, I won't live with myself. I come to the decision while buckled into the back of Sean's speeding Subaru. There's no way out for me. The child locks are engaged, and the way we're flying, I'd never survive a jump. I may not survive this drive. Moments ago, we nearly clipped another car. My dad responded to the near miss by pressing the gas.

He's in the driver's seat, literally and figuratively. Brian Ingold has already programmed our near future. First, we'll switch vehicles. He'll force me into his Tesla and then navigate to the nearest hospital, no doubt leaving the car in self-driving mode so he can concentrate on keeping me restrained. Afterward, he'll drag me through emergency room doors, doing his best impression of a frantic father. A lack of acting skills won't matter. His natural wooden affect will read as shock while my inevitable hysterics—kicking, screaming, swearing I faked my kidnapping, begging staff to send Sean an ambulance—will fit right into his planned narrative.

I'll be strapped to a gurney and pumped full of sedatives, prepped for emergency surgery. Meanwhile, my father will explain to the police how I've been brainwashed by abuse. "Her kidnapper tormented her, raped her, convinced her that she loved him and the whole thing was her idea. He turned her against her own parents."

Everyone will believe him. He's rich. He's a man. He's technically one of my legal guardians. Above all, he's Brian Ingold, celebrated tech genius. And who am I? A kidnapped heiress. It's the story I made up, and it's a good one. No one will want to believe it's a lie.

My lie will kill my love. A writerly end. What choice is there but to close out my story Shakespearean-style? Juliet with the dagger. Her feigned death led to her lover's suicide. My kidnapping resulted in my lover bleeding out on a concrete floor. Our fates should be the same.

The car swings left, pressing the seat belt into the shirt blood-pasted to my wound. Sean's shirt.

Earth and twigs crunch beneath the tires. We've reached the dirt road. The second phase of my father's plan can commence.

He pulls onto a grass embankment beside the path. The car pitches right. Again, the seat belt digs into the place where the bullet tore through my skin. I yelp despite my promises to be strong, to deny my dad the satisfaction of seeing how weak and vulnerable I really am—inferior flesh, blood, and brain.

His door opens. I unbuckle and try my door, hoping that the lock disengages automatically when the car is off. It doesn't budge. My father's face suddenly looms through the window. He taps Sean's key against the glass, his finger on the "Lock" button. It's a smug gesture. *I have all the power.*

The door beeps. I pivot to my good shoulder, push the handle, and slam my weight into the frame. With luck, the metal will swing out like a loose beam and knock my dad over, giving me a chance to run. Where to, will be a game-time decision. The highway? Back to the hangar? The horse sanctuary must have some sort of center.

My father anticipates the move. As I step out, I see that he's positioned himself opposite the door hinge, blocking my way. His hand wraps around my forearm. He yanks me into his torso and then wraps both arms around my waist, bear-carrying me toward his electric Roadster.

The Tesla senses his presence. Its cat eyes light up. A falcon-wing door rises, bending back like the hangar wall would have had my father not shot through its supports—one of which butterflied Sean's right thigh. The femoral artery inside is the main conduit of blood to the lower body. Opening it is akin to breaking one of the body's internal levees. The ensuing flood is not survivable for long. Sean has ten minutes at most to close the gap. Three have already passed.

My dad tosses me into the seat. Hard leather connects with my injured shoulder. Pain blackens my vision, so I hear the door descend before I see it. When my sight returns, it's already locked in the closed position. Through the windshield, I see my father head toward the driver's side. I lean over to the center console and wake the screen. A tap later, I see a visual rendering of the entire car. I hit the doors, locking them.

My dad's key overrides the command. As he approaches, the driver's door cracks open and begins to rise. I fling myself into his seat and swipe the touch-screen gearshift, switching from park to drive. I stretch my foot to the gas pedal.

Nothing happens.

My father shoves me back into the passenger seat. "You think Elon Musk would design a vehicle capable of going 220 miles per hour that drives with the door ajar?"

No, though he might design one with an emergency mode. "Tesla!" I shout. "Call 9-1-1."

My dad assumes his position in the driver's seat. "Not going to work. There hasn't been an accident."

He pulls Sean's phone from his pocket and rubs the screen against the sleeve of his fleece. When I grab for it, he slams his palm into my injured shoulder. The pain steals my breath. I fall backward, panting. "Why are you doing this?"

He pitches Sean's phone out the open door. "You did this." He jams his finger into the door-close button, the closest he can get to slamming an electronic version. "I got you a job, an internship other people would have worked their hides off to get, been *grateful* to get—yet I gave it to you, despite no relevant skills or knowledge. You were a pure nepotism hire, a flagrant push to help my kid rise in the world. And how do you repay me? By exploiting your access and insider knowledge to rile the public against me."

"I didn't want a handout. I want—"

"To incite a mob into lighting torches and sharpening pitchforks." The door clicks shut. He touches the screen and puts the vehicle in drive. Though we're not yet moving, there's no way the door will open now.

"*Yes!*" Shouting alleviates the burning in my arm, or at least distracts me from it. "I want people to pay attention!"

My father grabs the steering wheel. I brace for him to drive. Instead, he looks out the front window. "See those horses?"

The subject switch is so abrupt that it takes me a moment to spot them. A half-dozen shining mustangs are visible in the distance, caught at the golden hour. A brown stallion rears onto its back legs, challenging one with a white face and black feet, its gray body dyed ombré by nature. Bridled, the herd could belong to any derby grouping. But something about their gaits, the way they pitch their weight from one side to another as they race, suggests they've never had a person pulling the reins.

"Once, those horses would have been used to move people about," my father says. "They'd have spent their lives in stables, trotted out to pull the family wagon or carry the cavalry. They'd have been worked until their bodies degraded with arthritis and age or broke completely. Then, if they were lucky, they'd be put out to pasture just when they could enjoy life the least. If unlucky, they'd be . . ." He doesn't look at me, unwilling to face his metaphor made real.

"They'd be shot," I say.

He sighs. To my ears, the sound seems more annoyed than regretful. "But cars were invented," he continues. "So now these horses roam free. They're able to do what they will, thanks to technology."

I turn to my dad. For the first time, his eyes water. I wonder if any of the tears are for me.

"The ones on this sanctuary might enjoy their lives." I lower my voice, treating my dad like one of those mustangs. "Others are culled to make way for tractors and oil rigs and housing developments. Nothing obsolete is allowed to flourish. You know that better than anyone. People should not be made obsolete. I deserve a chance. And Sean. Please. Let me call—"

Tires spin on dirt. "Buckle up."

We sail down the road, a dust cloud in our wake. I secure my seat belt, resigned to the last chapter I've already outlined in my head. My father will have his way at first. I'll go the hospital, let them drug me unconscious and fix my arm. Then, when I wake up, I'll write a letter admitting to everything and apologizing. For whatever my words will be worth, I'll make it clear that Sean isn't the villain my dad will make him out to be. Afterward, I'll hug my mom one last time, hand her the letter, and swear it's the truth. Then I'll take whatever pain medication the hospital supplies postsurgery and swallow the contents of the entire bottle in one sitting.

I close my eyes and let the tears come. They fall down my face, thick and sticky, mixing with a lace veil of dirt, dust, and sweat. Sean is probably gone now. The police will eventually find him on the floor. Even with my letter, some people will always believe his death was justified. Fate doled out capital punishment for my kidnapping rather than a life sentence.

The car screeches to a stop. "What the f—"

My father doesn't finish. I open my eyes to see a Jeep parked where the path meets fresh pavement. It's been pulled sideways to block the road.

Standing in front of it is my mother.

I'm hallucinating. This must be the stage after shock. My mind is sending soothing images to dull my anguish. Though a vision of my mom fails to make me feel anything but guilty. She excused and enabled my father's behavior, but she never realized he was capable of this. Even I didn't know.

"Catherine?" my father whispers.

I rub my eyes. She stands in front of the car, dressed in jeans and a white top, dark hair billowing behind her, an unlikely action hero. I'm still not sure whether I'm seeing things. Can illusions be shared like delusions?

"Brian," she shouts, "let Alice go!"

He lowers the car window and sticks his head outside. "I'm taking her to the—"

"Mom!" I scream. Somehow she's real. She found me. "Help me. Mom!"

"She's hysterical!" my father shouts over me. "You were in that car I almost hit trying to get her out of here. You must have gone up to the place and seen the boy. I shot at him, and a bullet grazed Alice's shoulder. We—"

"I'll take her to the hospital." My mom steps toward the Tesla's headlights. "Unlock the doors. Give her to me."

"She's bleeding!" My father feigns panic to drown out my banging on the passenger-side window. "We need to get there now. There's no time to switch cars."

My mom makes eye contact with me through the windshield. It's one look, but in it I see that she knows nearly everything.

"Is Sean alive?" I lean over to be heard through my father's open window. "You saw him, right? You called an ambulance? You need to call an ambulance."

She answers while keeping my father in her sights. "The police and paramedics are already on their way."

My dad slams his palms into the steering wheel. "Move the car, Catherine! We need to get out of here. Get her help. He brainwashed her. She'd never want Zelos damaged. She worked for the company. She knows the good that we'll do."

My mom slams her palm onto the car's hood. "You realized Alice was in on this. You came here to control the narrative."

"And you didn't?" My dad's voice takes on the crazed quality it had in the hangar. "You didn't want to keep the press from tarring and feathering your family name? To stop this privileged, spoiled bitch from galivanting around the talk show circuit with that boy, justifying faking her kidnapping to show how terrible her parents are? How disastrous her father's company is? Displaying her injuries and dragging down my stock? Ruining my legacy? And after everything we've done for her. How we've set her up. Everything you gave."

My mom raises her hands in surrender. "People are not projects, Brian. She's my daughter, but she's her own person. All I want is her safe." She shifts her gaze to me. "That's all I can ask. It's her life. I only want her to live it." Her expression hardens as she looks back at my father. "Unlock the door." She storms over to the passenger side and pulls the door handle. "Let her go, Brian."

The car takes off like a roller coaster released from its highest point. Gravity tugs my hair to the headrest. My brain takes cover in the back of my skull.

We slam into the Jeep. My body pitches forward, unable to adjust to the sudden momentum change. The seat belt strains against its pulleys. Metal crunches and cracks. It's the hangar door all over again.

Only, it's not. A cloud of nylon and nitrogen catches my hurtling form. It envelops my head and shoulders, shrouding my face in white.

I push the fabric away, gasping. Beside me, my father paws at the airbag, clawing his way to the steering wheel. He still hopes to drive this thing, to turn onto the main road now that he's rammed the Jeep out of the way.

But the Tesla won't let him. A mechanical voice shoots through the speakers. "An emergency call has been triggered."

The car rendering dominates the vehicle's interior screen. I hit my door on the image. It screeches open and starts to rise. I yank off my belt and jump outside.

"MOM!" I'm shouting, but there's no need. Her arms are already around me. She leads me from the car and then lets me collapse into her chest. If my ribs aren't already cracked, the force of my sobs threatens to break them. In my ear, she tells me to breathe. In and out. One . . . two . . .

"The police are on their way," she whispers. "It'll be okay. We'll figure this out." She cups my cheek, lifting my head to look me in the eyes. "We'll figure this out. Together."

CATHERINE NEWHOUSE INGOLD

TWO MONTHS AFTER

Stockholm syndrome. That was the defense our family lawyer settled on for Alice's staged kidnapping trial. Sean Whalen, an older man radicalized by negative military experiences, sought out a teenage Alice Ingold and manipulated her into opposing her father's firm. He exploited her empathy for the less fortunate, making her feel guilty for her inherited wealth, ashamed of being born a member of the investor class and profiting from technology-driven improvements in corporate efficiency. A trained veteran, he'd engaged in psychological warfare against a far less adept opponent, taking advantage of her sexually and emotionally until Alice lost any sense of self and self-worth. His victory was decisive. Alice was a victim.

It was an argument cooked up to feed political grievances. All the key ingredients were baked in: intimations that "coddling" the less fortunate had damaged the nation's psyche and that the vilification of the rich runs counter to our country's foundations as a capitalist society, as well as an underlying assumption that women are the weaker sex and require protection, not only from male physical dominance but also from their superior intellects.

Alice would have none of it.

She pled guilty to lying to federal authorities. The judge, under pressure from prosecutors offended by the resources expended to find her, imposed a half-million-dollar fine along with a six-month prison sentence and an additional year under house arrest. I'm paying the fine, though Alice will reimburse me once she comes into her inheritance at twenty-five. We've signed paperwork to that effect.

Her time will be served at a federal women's facility in the Mojave Desert. In another time, she'd have been held closer to me in the same minimum-security institution that housed Patricia Hearst, the actresses involved in the *Varsity Blues* cheating scandal, and, back in the 1980s, a robbery accomplice who was nearly freed by her ex–military pilot boyfriend after the guy stole a helicopter and landed it in the yard. But that prison was closed due to rampant sexual assaults by the guards.

My lawyer has assured me that "Camp Victorville" is one of the safest, most sought-after women's facilities in the state. To hear him tell it, Alice will be attending the Harvard-Radcliffe of penal institutions. I don't think comparing prison to any college is apt, so I'm just praying that she'll be treated decently and that the entire California correctional system is on high alert for abuse after being forced to shutter the other facility.

There's nothing else I can do but pray. Alice wanted this consequence. She insisted that she deserved it after everything she put the authorities and me through. Provided that nothing bad happens to her inside, I agree that the punishment fits the crime. While I understand why my daughter did what she did—both her stated reasons and the underlying ones stemming from her emotionally abusive father—I can't wholly excuse her behavior. I'm done apologizing for others, including my soon-to-be ex-husband.

My daughter's boyfriend was handed a similar sentence, though Sean won't start serving until after he's finished physical therapy. Doctors say he'll walk without a cane eventually, but it'll take a year or two for his leg to be back in working order. Chances are, it won't ever feel the same.

Alice was far more physically fortunate in comparison. Though her injury seemed to be in her right shoulder, the bullet actually passed through the muscle on the upper part of her arm, blessedly missing all the important bones connecting the limb to her torso. She'll have a scar but no permanent nerve damage. The cracked rib from the car accident has caused her more pain these past two months.

I watch her head from the bedroom section of her Oakland loft to a duffel bag splayed open on her dining table. She's carrying a pack of thermal underwear. Apparently, you can't have enough warm clothing in the clink. Also in the bag: sweaters; sweatpants; two towels; a washcloth; several shirts; underwear; sports bras; and four paperback books, two of which are for class. Surprisingly, Berkeley is letting her take an academic gap year. Two of the deans on the advisory review committee were revolutionaries back in the day and sympathetic to her cause. They promised to mail her additional reading material, which is a blessing. The way Alice goes through books, she'll be finished with her stash in a week.

She bends to place the socks inside and then clasps her right side.

"Do you want me to fix the ACE bandage?" I ask.

Alice takes a breath and shoves the socks into the bag. "I'm alright. I'll need your help carrying it down to the car."

I square my shoulders, ready for the challenge. Hoisting hefty luggage is a traditional dad job, but I suppose Alice never really had one of those. She definitely doesn't now. I don't know if she and Brian will ever have a relationship after what he did: trying to institutionalize her to save his company the bad PR, and shooting at an unarmed young man who he knew hadn't posed any threat to him.

Brian, of course, tells a different tale. He's sticking to the version that makes him a hero. He saved his kidnapped, Stockholm syndrome–afflicted daughter from a sexually manipulative monster who turned her against her own father and his life-changing company. When I arrived, he claims, worry about having accidentally injured his daughter had driven him a little crazy. Hence, why he panicked and tried to drive through the Jeep to the hospital.

Public opinion has divided along generational and wealth lines. Tech investors and Zelos fans see Brian as a savior. They post on blogs about Alice's delusions and gleefully speculate about the awful things Sean did to transform her into a mind-controlled zombie who would do whatever he asked. People more wary of Brian's AI and its impact on their industries see Alice as a saint who turned against her own family to reveal the truth to the public. Many of Alice's peers fall into this category. They'll be the ones buying her memoir after she finishes writing it in prison.

The truth is somewhere in the middle, as it always is. All that Alice saw and heard during her Zelos internship frightened her. She wanted to make people aware of Zelos's hidden influence in various industries and her father's view of his AI as primarily a labor replacement tool, and get them to take to the streets, demanding rules and regulations and a different future than the one her father had planned.

And at least a small part of her also wanted to assert her independence, punish her father and me, and force her dad to pay attention to what she had to say for once. Although she may never admit it, I think Alice secretly hoped that her kidnapping might make Brian feel guilty for giving all his time to his work and missing her childhood, that having to face her absence might finally alter his priorities and even his plans for Zelos's AI. She'd thought, maybe—just maybe—he'd be so grateful to have his only child back that he'd want to create the kind of future she'd want to live in.

Alice has since accepted that Brian was never going to choose her over his work. He's determined to go down in the history books as the father of AI, not her dad. And he'd still do anything—even ruin his daughter's reputation and lock her away in a mental institution—to usher in his vision of the future, one in which Zelos runs the world.

That fact and the state's punishment have sapped my anger at her. Alice has suffered, and she's sorry. She was selfish, sure. She was also nineteen.

She'll turn twenty soon. Already, she's grown up considerably over the past few months, developing a deeper appreciation for what she put people through—me, of course, but also Frazier, Lee, and the many police officers and volunteers who looked for her and answered tip lines. She says sorry multiple times each day, often apropos of nothing. We'll make errant eye contact, and she'll start apologizing, telling me how thankful she is that I didn't stop looking for her, even after I suspected she was in on the whole scheme—how grateful she is that I saved her and Sean. The truth is, she didn't think I had that in me. Alice dismissed me as a socialite with little better to do than throw charity parties and control her life. I'm now the woman who put together the clues and saved two lives. I'm her hero.

That knowledge has given me the strength to start over without Brian and my "wife of" society title. And it's helping me now as I watch Alice pack. Because I'm not my ex-husband. I can't choose whether to love my daughter. All I can do is love her. Love her and let her go.

"What do you think of this one?" Alice holds up a photo. I expect to see a picture of her and a friend or the one of Sean kissing her neck. She's been pulling snapshots off her pushpin corkboard and slipping them into books, friendly faces for when she feels lonely. One of Monica and Demi has already been packed. Alice's insistence that the plan was hers and Sean's alone saved that pair from any charges.

I can't see the image from a distance. As I squint, she walks closer, holding it out. "I kinda like it."

She hands me the four-by-six glossy. The two of us are centered in the frame. My chin rests on Alice's head, and my arms are draped over her shoulders, forming a cowl beneath her clavicle. She's smiling, blue eyes bright with anticipation. I am, too, though my look is more tense. "This is from the day I dropped you off freshman year."

"You asked for a photo before you left. Monica took it with my phone."

"I never saw it."

"I had it framed. I can send you the file. If you like it, you can make a copy."

I hand back the picture. "You look great. I look nervous."

Alice considers the photo. "You look like you always do around me." She lowers the printout. Tears cloud her eyes.

I place my hand lightly on her healing shoulder. "I don't always look that way. Sometimes I look proud. I'm proud of you, Alice." The words have the opposite effect of my desired one, adding to her tears. "I don't know if you're right about everything," I add. "But your heart is in the right place. You want your life to have meaning and to make a difference, and you will. You'll figure it all out."

She wraps her arms around me. The hug is warm and real but not desperate. She's not afraid of where she's going. On some level, I think prison was always part of her plan. Still, the contact threatens to make me cry. I won't get to hug my child like this for some time.

We separate before the waterworks start for both of us. She slips our picture into the bag and zips it up. "Think that's everything I'm allowed."

I grab the duffel's handles and hoist it onto my shoulder, relieved that it's not nearly as heavy as it looks. "Okay, then." I pat her arm and force a smile, thinking of the cell she'll soon inhabit. "Let's get you to your new dorm."

Author's Note

As I writer, I'm loath to rely on clichés, yet there's a chestnut too apt for me to avoid: "The more things change, the more they stay the same." I wrote this story partly because of the similarities I see between what is happening in America now and what was going on in the 1970s when the country faced another technological revolution: the computer, which both expanded opportunities and upended what many young people thought they would do with their lives. As computers became standard in business, companies wanted tech-savvy labor capable of using the software, and the generation graduating into this new world didn't have the skills. At least, not right away.

Abrupt changes in the workplace often underpin more visible examples of civil unrest. They also force us, as a society, to consider what we want our future to look like and whether the old economic models and laws are up to the task of dealing with new realities. I obviously don't think AI is going away, nor should it. The potential it presents to better life for all of us is too great.

But I do think we are being called, in this moment, to reckon with the way technological advancement has consolidated wealth and consider how we handle that going forward so entire swaths of the population aren't left feeling discarded and purposeless. I don't have the answers. Like Alice, however, I'd like the conversation to be thoughtful, robust, honest, and widespread. And I do believe I'm asking some of the right questions.

About the Author

Cate Holahan is the *USA Today* bestselling author of seven standalone novels and is the coauthor of the #1 Audible bestselling title *Young Rich Widows* and its sequel, *Desperate Deadly Widows*. Her novels have been translated into multiple languages and optioned for television. She has also written two original movies for MarVista Entertainment: *Deadly Estate* and *Midnight Hustle*. In a former life, she was a journalist and TV producer. She has written for *Bloomberg Businessweek* magazine, New Jersey's *The Record* newspaper, *The Boston Globe*, MSN Money, and CNBC.

A biracial Jamaican and Irish American writer, Cate is a member of Crime Writers of Color, Sisters in Crime, and the Authors Guild. She has an MFA in dramatic writing from New York University's Tisch School of the Arts and a BA from Princeton University. She lives in Tenafly, New Jersey, with her husband, two daughters, and two dogs, and spends time in Jamaica, where she's also a citizen. For more information, visit www.cateholahan.com.